FLASH POINTS

BY DAVID HAGBERG

Twister
The Capsule
Last Come the Children
Heartland
Heroes
Without Honor*
Countdown*
Crossfire*
Critical Mass*
Desert Fire
High Flight*
Assassin*
White House*
Joshua's Hammer*
Eden's Gate
The Kill Zone*
Castro's Daughter*
By Dawn's Early Light
Soldier of God*
Allah's Scorpion*
Dance with the Dragon*
The Expediter*
The Cabal*
Abyss*
Burned
Blood Pact*
Retribution*
The Fourth Horseman*
End Game*
Tower Down*
The Shadowmen*†
24 Hours*†

WRITING AS SEAN FLANNERY

The Kremlin Conspiracy
Eagles Fly
The Trinity Factor
The Hollow Men
Broken Idols
Gulag
Moscow Crossing
The Zebra Network
Crossed Swords
Moving Targets
Winner Take All
Kilo Option
Achilles' Heel

WITH BYRON DORGAN

Blowout
Gridlock

NONFICTION WITH BORIS GINDIN

Mutiny!

*Kirk McGarvey adventures
*†Kirk McGarvey Ebook original novellas

FLASH POINTS

DAVID HAGBERG

A TOM DOHERTY ASSOCIATES BOOK

NEW YORK

FLASH POINTS

Copyright © 2018 by David Hagberg

A Forge Book
Published by Tom Doherty Associates
175 Fifth Avenue
New York, NY 10010

www.tor-forge.com

Forge® is a registered trademark of Macmillan Publishing Group, LLC.

The Library of Congress Cataloging-in-Publication Data is available upon request.

ISBN 978-0-7653-8488-1 (hardcover)
ISBN 978-0-7653-8490-4 (ebook)

Our books may be purchased in bulk for promotional, educational, or business use.
Please contact your local bookseller or the Macmillan Corporate and Premium
Sales Department at 1-800-221-7945, extension 5442, or by email at
MacmillanSpecialMarkets@macmillan.com.

First Edition: March 2018

Printed in the United States of America

0 9 8 7 6 5 4 3 2 1

AND NOW FOR MARY

PART

Coma

ONE

It was early March but summer had already arrived in southern Florida, and except for a pleasant breeze off Sarasota Bay, the afternoon would have been overly hot for Kirk McGarvey and the eight philosophy students seated in front of him on the grass.

McGarvey, Mac to his friends, had been the youngest director ever of the Central Intelligence Agency—a job he had detested because he was no administrator. Since then he'd taken on a variety of freelance assignments for the Company, all of which had been too urgent or simply impossible for the government to handle on its own.

In between times he taught philosophy for one dollar per year at Sarasota's New College, a semi-private ultra-liberal and prestigious small college. His specialty was Voltaire, the eighteenth-century intellectual and wit, who'd maintained that common sense wasn't so common after all.

Slightly under six feet with the build of a rugby player and the grace of a ballet dancer, Mac was a man around fifty, with eyes that were sometimes green, or gray, like now, when he felt something or someone was gaining on him.

"How many of you know the name O. J. Simpson?" he asked.

One of the boys said, "He's the one who killed his girlfriend and some guy."

"His ex-wife and her lover," one of the other students said.

"He was acquitted," McGarvey said. His own philosophy had always been if you throw a stick into a pack of dogs, the one that barks got hit. His students over the past three years knew that they were being manipulated, but they loved it, because of the sometimes intense discussions that usually followed.

"Yes, but he did it."

"No doubt?"

One of the girls laughed. "You've been hoisted on your own petard, Mac," she said. "Voltaire, and I quote: 'It is better to risk saving a guilty person than to condemn an innocent one.'"

"Nice try, Darlene, but it's you who've been had, unless you don't believe in the basic premise of American jurisprudence."

Someone groaned. "Presumed innocent until proven guilty. But this is a course on Voltaire. Not fair."

McGarvey chuckled. A distant buzzer sounded, which marked the end of this period. "Five hundred words by Monday on what Voltaire would have thought about the trial. Arguments for why he would believe that O. J. was guilty and for why he would believe the man was innocent."

A forty-foot sloop out on the bay was heading south, probably for New Pass and the Gulf of Mexico. She was low on her lines, her dinghy was stowed and she had a wind vane for self-steering on the stern. A small, well-provisioned ship heading for happy places.

It was the last class on Friday, and his students, who often hung around to talk, took off. All across the small campus kids and instructors alike were heading out. Everyone here worked hard but played hard too.

His phone rang. It was Pete calling from his house on Casey Key, a barrier island a few miles south. She'd come down from Washington to spend a few days with him, as she'd been doing from time to time over the past year or so.

At one time she'd been an interrogator for the Company, but she'd fallen into helping McGarvey with an assignment that had started to go bad. And since then she'd been his unofficial partner, and a damned good operator in her own right. On top of all that she was in love with him, and he with her.

"How'd your day go?" she asked. She was nearly fifteen years younger than him, and in her interrogator days when she always worked with a male partner, the agency wags had labeled her and whoever her partner might be Beauty and the Beast. She was shorter than Mac, with the voluptuous figure of a movie star and a pretty oval face, and had become a crack shot with just about any variety of pistol.

"Good," he said automatically. But something had been nagging at him for the past week or so, and for some reason especially today. In his career, mostly as a shooter for the CIA, he'd had a chance to make a lot of enemies. From time to time one of them came gunning for him.

It had happened before, and he'd been getting the feeling that someone was nearby, watching him, tracking his routines, coming up on his six.

"I can drive up and meet you someplace for an early supper."

He wanted to say no. He wanted her out of the way, for the simple reason he was afraid for her safety. Every woman in his life—including his wife and daughter—had been assassinated because of who he was and what he did. And he was in love with her—against his will—and that frightened him even more.

"Marina Jack, outside," he said. The marina and restaurant on the bay just south of the Ringling Bridge was popular with the locals as well as tourists. It was almost always busy, and just now if Pete was going to be at his side, he wanted to be surrounded with people.

"Half hour," she said.

"See you there," McGarvey said, and as he headed back to his office he phoned his old friend Otto Rencke, who was the director of special projects for the CIA and the resident computer genius on campus there. He and Mac had a long history.

"You're done teaching for the day," Otto said without preamble. "You and Pete are meeting somewhere for a drink and something to eat."

"Right and right. Have your darlings been picking up on anything interesting lately?"

Otto's darlings were actually search engines a quantum leap even above Google, which sampled just about every known intelligence source on the entire planet, looking for threats to the U.S., especially to the CIA.

"Lotsa shit going down, but no nine/elevens just now. You getting premos?"

What Otto called "premos" were McGarvey's premonitions. He and just about everyone else on campus respected Mac's premos.

"Just around the edges."

"I'll call you back in a couple of minutes."

"Good enough," McGarvey said.

His tiny book-lined office was on the second floor of the philosophy department, already all but deserted for the weekend, one small window looking out across the campus toward the bay. The sailboat was approaching the buoy in the Intracoastal Waterway, which led out to the Gulf through New Pass.

He watched it for several moments, thinking about his wife, Katy. They had taken several trips from Casey Key on their Whitby 42 center cockpit ketch, twice out to the Abacos in the Bahamas. Good times, in sharp contrast to the sometimes almost impossibly bad times in his career and life. He'd been behind the limo in which his wife and their daughter were riding in when it exploded.

It was a memory permanently etched in his brain.

He took his Walther PPK in the 7.65mm version, his spare pistol, and an old friend, out of his desk and put it in his pocket. At that moment he thought it was important, though he couldn't say why.

Downstairs he nodded to a couple of instructors, but they didn't acknowledge him. He was wealthy by most standards, teaching for free, while they were scraping by on small salaries, and to hear them talk, busting their humps. In their view he was a dilettante, whose grades were always way too high on the curve.

Pete had sounded upbeat, looking forward to the weekend. She was leaving Sunday evening to return to Langley, where she was involved with training a half-dozen senior interrogators. The only complaints about her, so far as Otto had heard, came from the suits on the seventh floor who thought her methods had become overly aggressive in the past year or so. McGarvey had rubbed off on her.

Otto had sounded good too. Much happier now than in the old days because he was married to Louise, a woman nearly as smart as he was, and for whom he had an immense respect, and because of their adopted three-year-old daughter, Audie, who was Mac's daughter's only child.

The soft top on his '56 Porsche Speedster was down, the red-leather driver and passenger seat backs moved forward because of the sun. The car was one of his only indulgences—other than the Whitby. He had bought it totally restored two years ago for around fifty times the price when it had been new.

Maybe not a dilettante, he thought, getting in and starting the engine, and certainly not a billionaire like some he knew, but well off enough so that he could afford the toy, as Pete called it.

"You have the time in grade, and you deserve it," she'd said.

Something was wrong. Desperately wrong. A smell, a noise, something.

McGarvey looked for a shooter, for the glint of a gun scope lens on the rooftops across the street.

A car with tinted windows nearby.

Someone who obviously didn't belong on the school's campus walking away with a purpose.

A drone somewhere above.

Not bothering with the ignition key, he clambered over the door and got two feet away from the car when an impossibly bright flash enveloped him.

And then nothing.

TWO

The explosion echoed off the administration building across the street. Students within a hundred yards of what was left of the furiously burning Porsche hunkered down, bits of debris, rubber, plastic and leather raining from the clear blue sky.

One of the students, who went by the name of Antonio Gomez, stepped back, placing the cell phone he'd used to detonate the bomb in the pocket of his Bermuda shorts. He was a slightly built man with a dark complexion who could have been eighteen or nineteen, but in reality was twenty-nine. He'd come from Mexico City to study American government under Professor Frank Alcock. This was his first semester, and last, because he'd accomplished what he'd been paid to accomplish.

A girl who'd been standing a few feet away was on her knees, hands raised to the sky. "My God, my God, what's happening!" she screamed.

Within seconds other students who'd dropped to the ground were looking up, fear on their faces as if they knew that the bombing was just the first blow in a terrorist attack. More was coming and for the moment they were petrified.

Gomez wanted to pull out the Russian-made PSM pistol and put a couple of rounds into the silly girl's head to shut her up. He had two sisters, who like their mother were always whining about something, never satisfied with anything in their lives. Unlike him they were going nowhere.

Students started running in all directions, some across the street, others back through the campus toward the bay and still others to the north end of the parking lot and through the arch, to get away from the flames.

Gomez hunched up his backpack and followed a half-dozen students and several faculty to the south toward the Ringling Museum as the first of the campus cops from the nearby station came on the run. Already sirens were headed this way.

At one point he looked back, but the thick black smoke rising from the destroyed hulk of McGarvey's car obscured just about everything. The man had to have been killed instantly. The charred remains of his body could burn in hell forever.

Gomez's father, Arturo, had started out as a small-time attorney who specialized in defending Mexicans or those from Central and South America who'd illegally gotten into the U.S. and who were processed and sent by bus back across the border. He was paid to fast-track their legal immigration, and to represent them in the U.S. court system, mostly in El Paso but sometimes in San Diego.

Money had been tight until someone from the Sinaloa drug cartel showed up in his office and hired him on a handsome retainer to defend mules—the runners who brought the product across the border into the U.S. He wasn't very successful, but he diverted the attention of the Mexican and U.S. drug enforcement people, making it easier for the real mules to operate.

His son, Antonio had drifted for the next few years, playing drums in a rock band, working as a towel boy at a resort in Cancún, a waiter in Cabo San Lucas, and finally as a bartender at Puerto Vallarta. He was young and handsome, so he'd made decent money as a gigolo for older women coming down from the States for a little adventure.

All of it was more or less meaningless, until the same man from the cartel who'd hired his father, hired him on a retainer to do odd jobs at the resorts in Puerto Vallarta, such as passing instructions and very often cash to start-up operators from the States. Three times over the past two years he'd been sent to the States, once to San Francisco and twice to Detroit, with messages that couldn't be trusted even to encrypted phones or computers or area managers.

Two months ago he'd been instructed to fly to Atlanta, where he was to meet with a man named Rupert Hollman at a room in the Holiday Inn near the airport. This time he carried no message. His only instruction was to do as Rupert instructed him to do, then return to Mexico City, where he would be paid one hundred thousand dollars U.S. It would be by far his largest payday ever.

"And this will be just the start," his cartel contact promised.

Rupert, wearing jeans and a long-sleeved polo shirt, had met him in a second-floor room. He was a tall man, with dirty-blond hair, blue eyes and an accent that Gomez couldn't quite place, except it sounded faintly French.

The meeting lasted less than ten minutes, during which Antonio was shown several photographs of a man Rupert identified as Kirk McGarvey.

"Do you know this man?"

"Never seen him before."

"He is a professor of philosophy at a college in Sarasota, Florida. Your job will be to leave for Sarasota this evening, where you will enroll in the school as a first-term student in American government. You have been accepted, your first year's tuition and room and board have been paid. You will be given a small stipend. Do you understand?"

"Yes."

Rupert handed him a manila envelope. "Everything is there, including your dorm assignment. You'll make friends, you'll study hard, maybe even fall in love with the right girl. You will fit in. Do you understand this as well?"

"Yes, sir; will I be meeting with a drug dealer on campus?"

"Nothing like that. Your main job, besides blending in, will be to study McGarvey. In fact you are enrolled in one of his classes. Watch his movements. Especially how he comes and goes from campus. Does he drive himself, or is he chauffeured by this woman?"

Rupert, whose real name was Kamal al-Daran, and who'd once worked as a freelancer for Saudi Arabian intelligence under the code name al Nassr, "the Eagle," handed Gomez several photographs of an attractive woman.

"Her name is not important, just finding out if she shows up will be enough."

"Yes, sir. Then what?"

"Once a week you will call a number. It will ring twice but no one will answer. You will enter a five-digit code, make your report and then hang up."

Gomez nodded uncertainly.

"Within two months, three at the most, a package will be delivered to you. Sweets and other presents from home. In fact, make sure to share the top layer with your roommate, a young man by the name of Dana Cyr."

"What else will be in the package? Drugs?"

"The instructions and the means for you to assassinate McGarvey and the woman if she happens to be with him."

Gomez sank into himself just a little. He'd known for the last year or so that his cartel contact would have other work for him someday. Real work. That of eliminating enemies of the Sinaloas. Six months ago he'd been taken to a remote private shooting range up north, where he'd spent an entire week learning how to use a variety of weapons—handguns and sniper rifles, mostly. He'd also been taught how to use a number of poisons, and explosives—almost exclusively Semtex, a substance for which he'd developed a deep respect.

Gomez walked as far as the Ringling Museum and then up to Tamiami Trail, just making the bus out to the airport.

Yesterday the package of sweets plus the one-kilo brick of Semtex, the electronic detonator and the special phone to send the signal, and the instructions to place the explosives under the driver's seat of McGarvey's Porsche and send the signal as soon as the instructor got into his car, had arrived by FedEx.

He was given the bus schedule and tickets to fly from Sarasota to Atlanta and from there back to Mexico City. His plane left one hour from now.

Sitting in the backseat of the bus for the short ride to the airport, Gomez had time to examine his feelings now that he had made what he figured was probably his first kill. But he felt nothing, other than being successful, and rich—with more to come. And with being his own man.

He was no longer a gigolo. He was an operator.

THREE

☐

Pete Boylan—Pete because her father, now dead, had wanted a boy—drove Mac's old Mercedes CLK 350 convertible, the top down, north on Tamiami Trail just coming into Sarasota, past the mall, when Otto called.

She remembered thinking later that until that point the day had been absolutely gorgeous; pale blue sky, a few puffy fair-weather cumulus clouds drifting in from the Gulf and some of the snowbirds already leaving for the north. But then the day had been shattered for her.

"Hi, Otto. Tell me that you and Louise and Audie are at the airport right now as a surprise, and I'll come to pick you up."

"Mac's been seriously hurt. His car blew up, and they took him to Sarasota Memorial."

A million horrible images flew through her brain at the speed of light, and she nearly sideswiped a pickup in the lane next to hers until she got herself under control.

"How badly?" she demanded, flooring the gas pedal.

"The docs are evaluating him now. He's alive but not conscious. Lots of damage to his back and legs. I think he wasn't inside the car when it blew, probably getting out."

"I'm just a few miles away. What else?"

"I've chartered a Lear from Dolphin Aviation there at the airport to get him up here as soon as he's stabilized. Franklin and his team will be ready at All Saints as soon as Mac arrives."

Dr. Alan Franklin was the chief medical officer at a private hospital in Georgetown, not far from the Jesuit university campus. Its only patients were wounded intelligence officers, mostly from the CIA, who were brought to the small state-of-the-art facility. Mac had been patched up there a couple of times, and Franklin, one of the very best trauma doctors anywhere in the world, had taken care of Pete.

"What else?"

"I talked to their chief of trauma and he wants to keep Mac there. Guy name of Singh. I checked and he's damned good, but he's not in Franklin's league. I want him out of there."

"I'll take care of it."

"It won't be that easy. Singh carries a lot of weight and if he says Mac's not fit to be moved, it won't happen. Not unless Mac's wife demands it."

"I can play the part," Pete said. No force on earth was going to stop her from getting Mac up to All Saints. If she had to shoot the son of a bitch she would do it. "But someone might ask for my ID."

"They can check online. You and Mac were married by a JP right there in Sarasota May third last year. Louise and I were witnesses."

The light at Palmer Ranch was red but she blew through it, angry drivers slamming on their brakes and honking their horns.

"There's another wrinkle coming your way," Otto said. "Five minutes ago the AP said that it had unconfirmed but reliable reports that the former director of the CIA had been assassinated in a car bomb attack. The media will be all over the place by the time you get there."

"My God, it's not true, is it?"

"He's in bad shape, but no," Otto said. "But obviously it was no accident."

"Someone is gunning for him, it's happened before. Maybe we should call the Bureau in Tampa for some help."

"I want to make them think that they've succeeded."

"That he's dead?"

"Yes."

"Soon as an ambulance shows up to take him to the airport, they'll know."

"I'm sending a hearse," Otto said. "It'll be up to you to convince the hospital to confirm his death. It's a matter of national emergency. Doesn't matter what you tell them, just do it!"

Pete had been so taken up with her own fear that she hadn't heard it in Otto's voice until this moment. "I'll get him out of there. But I'm not armed."

"Won't matter. Nobody is going to shoot someone delivering a corpse."

Dr. Roshan Singh was a large dark-skinned man with thick dark hair and wide, nearly pitch-black eyes. He came out of the operating room fifteen minutes after Pete had arrived and met her in the empty waiting room.

Seeing the look on his face, Pete was instantly more frightened than she'd ever been in her life.

"You are Mrs. McGarvey?" he asked, his voice deep from his chest.

"Yes. How is he?"

"May I be frank with you, Mrs. McGarvey?"

"Please."

"He seems like a tough fellow, and he should survive if he makes it through the night. He's stable, but there are complications, not the least of which are his burns, which are susceptible to infection. But there is likely brain trauma. We won't know until after he wakes up and we can evaluate him if he's suffered any serious cognitive degeneration."

"Christ," Pete said softly, and she reached for something to keep from falling.

The doctor held her arm. "We've induced a coma, and we're going to keep him there to give his body a chance to start healing itself. His leg can wait."

How much more, Pete wanted to ask. "His leg?"

"He's almost certainly going to lose it from below the knee."

She closed her eyes for a moment.

The doctor led her over to a couch and he sat down next to her. "Your husband is not going to die. He's obviously been through other traumas—gunshot wounds, I would guess. And it looks as if he has only one kidney, which itself was replaced at one point or another not too long ago."

"It was mine. We're a match."

"He was the director of the CIA and a field officer. I assume he got the wounds in the line of duty. Including this today."

"Someone tried to kill him. And they'll try again if they believe he survived."

"The hospital has a security staff."

Pete almost laughed. "Not good enough."

"The police will be notified."

"I'm taking him out of here within the next fifteen to twenty minutes. I want you to prep him to leave."

Singh was not impressed. "I'm sorry, but that is not possible."

"A jet is standing by to take him to Washington. We have a private hospital in Georgetown where he'll be treated."

"No," Singh said and he started to get up.

Pete put a hand on his arm and drew him down. He tried to pull away, but she wouldn't let him.

"A hearse will take him to the airport, for a funeral service at Arlington. The president will attend."

"He's my patient, goddamnit."

"His injuries were too grave. There was nothing you could do for him. It was unfortunate."

"I will call security and have you restrained."

Pete phoned Otto. "He's not cooperating."

"Let me talk to him."

Pete handed the phone to the doctor, who reluctantly took it.

One minute later, he handed the phone back. His expression was that of a stricken man. "You bastards," he said. "You unutterable bastards."

FOUR

□

Kamal waited in the old Ford pickup, the bed filled with paint cans and dirty tarps, at the airport arrivals gate in Atlanta, wearing dirty white coveralls but the same blond wig as before when one of the security cops came over. Several flights had come in and the place was a madhouse of private cars, limos, cabs and buses.

"You can't wait here, pal."

"I'm picking up a friend."

"Move it."

Gomez, a backpack slung over his shoulder, came out of the doors. Kamal honked and waved him over. "Sorry, but here he is, and I'm out of your hair."

With any luck the cop would remember the brief incident, and provide a decent description of him and his flat Midwestern accent in the unlikely event that someone came asking questions. But with McGarvey he'd learned to take no chances. The man was dead, but he had very well connected friends who would stop at nothing to learn the who and the why. And if they got this far Kamal was going to point them in the direction of his own choosing.

Gomez got in and Kamal headed away.

"You did a good job," Kamal said, switching to his French accent.

"Thank you, sir. It went almost like you said it would."

"Did you see the actual explosion?"

"I saw it, and felt the heat."

"And McGarvey's body?"

"I couldn't see much of anything through the smoke and flames. But he was behind the wheel when I pushed the button. The was no possibility for him to survive. Just some body parts, there couldn't have been much left."

The first glimmerings of doubt crossed Kamal's mind. "CBS reported his body was taken to Sarasota Memorial."

"I'm surprised anything was left to take to any hospital," Gomez said. "I'm telling you, Mr. Hollman, the explosion was huge, no one could have survived intact."

They got onto I-285, the ring road around the city, and headed north. Kamal was seeing visions of McGarvey in Monaco and again in New York. Just snapshots. His Saudi intel contact at the time had warned him about the former director of the CIA.

"The man is nothing short of formidable," Sa'ad al-Sakr had told him when they met in Paris and again on an encrypted satphone link. "If you come face-to-face with him, either kill him on the spot or run away. If you escape you may consider yourself a very lucky man."

"But you didn't see him," Kamal asked.

"Only when he got in his car. Then I pushed the button and walked away, just like you told me. Is there a problem?"

"No."

Gomez looked in the door mirror as a jetliner took off and headed south. "My flight leaves at eight. I don't want to miss it."

"You won't," Kamal said, something the boy had told him suddenly bothersome. "You said it went *almost* like I told you it would. What did you mean, exactly?"

"I put the bomb under the seat, walked off, and when Mr. McGarvey got behind the wheel I pushed the button."

"Those were *exactly* my instructions."

Gomez was becoming uncomfortable; he kept looking in the door mirror as if he expected someone to be following them.

"Tell me."

"It was an old Porsche convertible. A two-seater, very small."

"But you put the bomb in the car, not on the ground under it."

"In the car, yes."

"Under the driver's seat."

Gomez hesitated. "Someone was coming across the parking lot. I only had a second or two to lean over the door and shove the package under the seat."

"The driver's seat."

"Like I said, the car was very small."

"The driver's seat."

"No, the passenger seat," Gomez said. "It was the best I could do. There wasn't enough time."

There was nothing to be said. The car was small, the Semtex more than sufficient for the job. McGarvey was dead. His body had been taken from the hospital to the airport for transport back to Washington. He would be buried with full honors at Arlington.

Kamal had the errant thought that a carefully crafted attack on the graveside service would be fitting, but then he was getting ahead of himself.

"Stick to the plan," his tactics instructor had told the class at Sandhurst. "Believe in the plan, believe in yourselves as tactical geniuses."

The twelve candidates in the class had gotten a chuckle.

"But what if the plan is crap and goes south?" one of them asked.

"Then you're buggered. So make damned sure that your plan is not only a good one, but is flexible. Because, as the Frenchies say, *Merde arrive.* Shit happens."

The only time he'd ever failed was when he'd gone up against McGarvey. And above all things he hated failure the most.

But the man was dead, he kept telling himself. Trouble was, he had a hard time believing it.

Interstate 20 East took them back into the city center. Gomez didn't say a word. It was obvious to Kamal that he knew he'd screwed up. He hadn't followed his instructions to the letter. And he was afraid to make any more excuses.

Downtown, Kamal took Peachtree up to the central parking ramp just off Ellis Street NE. It was early evening and traffic was fairly light, the garage mostly empty because the downtown weekend wouldn't really start until later.

Kamal took his ticket from the dispenser and drove up to the second floor, where he parked in a slot on the west side.

"You can catch a cab back out to the airport," Kamal said. He gave the kid a hundred dollars in cash. "When you get back, call the number and stay available, do you understand?"

"There'll be something else for me?" Gomez asked hopefully.

"Life changing," Kamal said.

He took out his silenced Glock G29 Gen 4, in the 10mm version, and fired one shot into the kid's heart.

Gomez slumped over in his seat, his head coming to rest against the window frame.

Kamal put an insurance round into the side of the Mexican's head. He got out of the truck, pulled off his coveralls and blond wig, dropped them into the truck bed, and walked up the ramp to the third floor, where he'd parked his rental Impala earlier this afternoon.

Leaving the ramp he paid his ticket and drove over to the shopping mall at Underground Atlanta, where he left the car, and took a cab over to the Ritz Carlton, where he'd stayed for the past two nights.

He'd tipped well, and the doormen recognized him, as did the staff at the front desk.

"Unfortunately I have a flight to Chicago first thing in the morning," he told the girl at the front desk. He used his German accent. "I'll need a wake-up call at five."

"Of course, Herr Zimmer. Will you require limo service?"

"Yes."

"I hope that your business in Atlanta was to your satisfaction."

"Completely," Kamal said and he went up to his suite.

Dinner en suite, he thought. A good bottle of wine—probably Krug—and a decent woman afterward. But not for the entire night. Just for a few hours of entertainment.

He deserved it.

FIVE

□

The Lear touched down at Joint Base Andrews a little before nine-thirty in the evening. Pete had sat beside McGarvey holding his hand most of the way down. Her fear still roared inside her like a nearly out of control freight train, but a blinding rage had built up beside it.

Whoever had done this to him would pay, and pay dearly, if it was the last act she'd ever do on this earth.

The media were kept away and the only ones to meet them in the navy hangar that the CIA used from time to time were Otto and a pair of minders from the Company, along with the hearse driver and two paramedics from All Saints.

Otto came aboard and gave Pete a hug.

"He's breathing okay, and his pulse is strong," she said, amazed that she had a voice and could actually talk without completely breaking down.

Otto looked at his old friend, and shook his head. But his expression remained completely neutral. There was nothing in his eyes that Pete could see.

The paramedics came aboard with a backboard. As they were strapping him in, Otto went forward, Pete behind him to get out of the way.

Otto showed the pilot and co-pilot his CIA identification. "So far as you gentlemen know, you did nothing more than transport a body from Sarasota. A woman was aboard the flight, but you were never told her name. A hearse delivered the body to your aircraft and another hearse picked it up here and drove away. Are we perfectly clear on these points, gentlemen?"

The pilot looked past Otto and Pete as the paramedics took Mac out the hatch. He was clearly impressed. "Yes, sir."

"Good," Otto said, pocketing his ID.

"I was a Navy SEAL We all know about him. Will he make it?"

"Guaranteed."

"We're pulling for him."

Pete was at the hearse when Otto came out of the aircraft. "I'm riding with him," she said.

"You're coming with me. Franklin is worried about infections."

"Goddamnit."

"There's nothing we can do for him now," Otto said. "You've brought him this far, now let the docs take over."

Tears welled up in Pete's eyes as the paramedics climbed aboard, shut the doors and the hearse sped away, no sirens, the minders right behind in their armored Caddy Escalade.

A fuel truck was trundling over to service the Lear.

Pete came into Otto's arms. "Dear God, I don't know what to do now. What about Audie?"

"Louise took her down to the Farm soon as we heard. She should be getting back here within the next hour or so."

The Farm was the CIA's training facility near Colonial Williamsburg. Whenever there was any trouble Audie was hustled down there, where she'd become the unofficial mascot. The staff and students doted on her. It was the safest place other than the bunker inside the White House.

Otto had driven over in his battered old Mercedes diesel, a car he'd had forever.

"You okay to drive?" Pete asked.

"Yeah."

Mac was already upstairs in the third-floor operating room when Pete and Otto arrived at the hospital and went up to the waiting room just down the hall.

"We've been here way too many times," Pete said.

"Nature of the business," Otto replied.

"It's a sick business, and I'm getting fucking tired of it."

"Me too sometimes, but what else is there?"

"Retirement."

Otto shrugged. "They're lined up in the wings waiting for the chance to come after us. That was no random accident down there."

Marty Bambridge, the deputy director of the CIA's National Clandestine Service—unofficially known as the Directorate of Operations—got off the elevator and came down the corridor to them. He was a small man with narrow shoulders and a nearly permanent scowl etched on his face. He and Mac had never gotten along, but in the past year or so they had come to a cease-fire agreement.

"How's he doing?"

"We just got here. He's being prepped now," Otto said.

"He's in an induced coma," Pete told him. "His color and pulse seemed okay on the way up. But he looks like shit." She turned away.

Bambridge touched her shoulder. "He's tough, and right now he's in the best hospital in the world. On top of that the media is buying the fiction that he's dead. Means whoever did it has gone to ground, and won't be showing up for the foreseeable future."

Pete nodded, and Bambridge turned back to Otto.

"The Watch had nothing, how about your threat board?"

"Nada at this point, but my darlings are working the issue. My snap guess was one of his enemies came gunning for him. The Bureau sent a team down from Tampa to take a look, and their preliminaries should be showing up on the overnights."

"The guy who took down the pencil tower in Manhattan? He's still at large."

"Could be, but there's no real reason for him to come after Mac."

"Unless it's a vendetta."

"Or something else," Otto said.

"What are you thinking?"

Otto shrugged.

"Talk to me, goddamnit. If something is coming our way, and trying to kill McGarvey was the opening shot, we need to know about it."

Otto hesitated.

"What?" Pete asked.

"I don't know."

"But you have a guess. It's Mac lying in there."

"Misdirection."

"Explain," Bambridge demanded.

Otto looked down the corridor toward the operating room doors. "No real reason for someone to kill him that way."

"Revenge," Bambridge said. "Makes sense."

"Too easy."

"They want us to concentrate on Mac," Pete said. "While we're taking care of him, something else is going to happen. So it really doesn't matter if he lives or dies, mission accomplished."

"No, that's not it either. They wanted him dead. The chances of him surviving a car bomb were small. Means whatever they're trying to do, they need to get Mac out of it. He's the key."

"He's been given no assignment," Bambridge said. "He's not working on anything for us."

Otto took a couple of steps down toward the operating room doors.

Bambridge started after him, but Pete put out an arm to stop him.

After a long minute Otto turned back. "Something is going to turn up in the next day or so, maybe as long as a month. Something we'd need Mac to look into."

"We have a veritable army of operators."

"None of whom are willing to cross any political lines. It's coming and we'd damned well better be prepared because it'll be a son of a bitch."

SIX

☐

Kamal, hair salt-and-pepper in a military cut, wearing a dark blue blazer, khakis and an open collar white shirt, registered at the Grand Hyatt Hotel under the name Paul O'Neal, from San Francisco. He was given a room facing 42nd Street, and he tipped the bellman well but not extravagantly.

His fiction with the hotel clerk in Atlanta that he was flying to Chicago hadn't been necessary, but it was one extra layer of cover.

It was one in the afternoon as he stood looking down at the busy traffic; every other car, it seemed, was a yellow cab. New York had always been too frenetic for his tastes. Even frantic at times. Like London, or even more like Berlin. But after his attack on the pencil tower on East Fifty-seventh the city had gotten back to normal. After nine/eleven New Yorkers had gotten used to the disasters.

He liked the calm quiet of France. The countryside just west of Dijon suited him well. He had set up as an upscale Australian by the name of Harris Frampton who'd retired early. He had a housekeeper and a cook, but lived a completely ordinary life, even participating in church services and acting on the board of directors of a support group for Médecins Sans Frontières.

In the year he'd been in place, he'd gained the respect of just about all the locals.

Once a month he took the train to Paris, where from an apartment in the Sixteenth Arrondissement near the Bois de Boulogne he maintained an internet website under the address SpecialServices.com.

"Any undertaking of an international nature, to right wrongs committed by establishment powers, for a fee. Results guaranteed."

He'd gotten a few queries, most of which were extremely minor: a wife hinting that she wished her husband would vanish. A request for a missing persons search in Syria. Another simply wishing help blowing up shit.

Until nine months ago when he was asked to meet someone in Beijing. The request specified that the meeting was to be a private one, and that the gentlemen involved were not Chinese nor were they representatives of the Chinese government.

Assassinating McGarvey was job one, and his bank account in Guernsey had been credited with five hundred thousand euros as a down payment.

The remainder of the assignment had taken the entire nine months to this point merely to rough out the plans, and to make his preparations.

Today would be the first of his dress rehearsals.

His pistol, silencer, spare magazines, ammunition and a package containing several sets of identification, including credit cards, were concealed in the false bottom of his roll-about suitcase. Thin sheets of gold foil stamped with images of clothing and toiletries lined the compartment. Airport scanners would see only the items etched on the foil, along with the actual pieces of clothing in the rest of the bag.

This little piece of engineering he'd commissioned from an international diamond smuggler had gotten him through airports with no trouble.

Kamal changed his blazer and shirt for a light sweater, and put a pair of thick-rimmed glasses in his pocket. He took the elevator down to the mezzanine, and from there the stairs to the lobby, and then another set to the Lexington Avenue level. At the end of a short corridor he came to an unmarked glass door that led to a tunnel that came out in Grand Central Terminal in what was called the Lexington Passage, and the Grand Central Market, busy at this hour.

More than two dozen shops, selling everything from specialty foods and stationery, eyeglasses and cosmetics, and odds and ends were packed with shoppers on late lunch hours.

Putting on his glasses, he took the stairs up to the main concourse and without hesitating he walked across to the stairs leading up to the west balcony.

A lot people were coming and going from the lower levels, possibly as many as a thousand. Security officers, most of them in uniforms, patrolled the vast space. But no one paid any attention to the balconies, or the windows under the domed ceiling.

He'd never been here before but he'd studied photographs and a couple of videos. The terminal reminded him of places in Europe—the size of it, the grandness, the magnificent architecture, yet no one seemed to be paying any attention, intent on getting to wherever they were going as quickly as possible.

A man in a business suit gave him a passing glance, but then looked away.

Plainclothes security, Kamal thought. The man had the look. Scanning the people for something, anything: a touch of fear, some nervousness, furtive looks at the uniformed officers, maybe even a hint of fatalism—this was to be their last day on earth before they set off their vest explosives.

But they were so obvious it almost seemed ludicrous to him. The American expression was the same as the English one: like shooting fish in a barrel.

"We want to send a clear message," he'd been told in Beijing.

There were three of them and they met him in an absolute shithole of a hotel just off Tiananmen Square called Dong Jiao Min Xiang, which he didn't think any Westerner would have ever stayed in, unless they were totally down on their luck.

The men didn't identify themselves, but Kamal had taken them for Westerners by their English. He didn't think they were connected with ISIS. They seemed too mainstream. And yet they handed him a slip of paper with three locations where terrorist attacks were to take place: San Francisco, New Orleans and Colby, Kansas, a place he'd never heard of. A specific target and date and time—noon EST—was listed for each location.

"What you ask will be dangerous, perhaps even impossible," he'd told them. "In any event it will be very expensive."

"Name your price, Mr. al-Daran," one of them said. All three were dressed in ordinary Western business suits. But they had connections. They knew his real name. It was bothersome.

"When it's over I will have to go to ground permanently. I'll never be able to work again."

They simply looked at him.

"One million euros to kill McGarvey. One million five for each of the other three events."

"Five point five million euros total. An impressive sum."

"It will send the message you want to send, for whatever your reasons are," Kamal said. "Reasons I'm not interested in."

"How do you wish to be paid?"

"One million in full for McGarvey," Kamal said. "Half in advance, and when it is a confirmed kill I'll require the second half, and one-third of the remaining balance after each successful operation." He wrote his account number and password on a slip of paper and handed it across the table. The room stank of something disagreeable, and he wanted to be gone as quickly as possible. "How do I contact you?"

"After today you do not," the one who'd done most of the talking said.

"I'll need a source of intelligence information."

"That will be your concern."

It had been as easy as that, except for the last part.

Kamal took the stairs up to the west balcony to the Italian restaurant Cipriani Dolci. The place was mostly full with the late lunch crowd; nevertheless he managed to get a table at the railing looking down on the main concourse.

"Some bread, olive oil and a bottle of Dom Pérignon," he told the waiter. "Very cold, please."

The concourse was still busy. Dropping or throwing a package over the railing into the concourse from here would be a simple thing. Especially if it were disguised to look like something not dangerous. Something that would cause the crowd to converge rather than run away.

It would take some thought.

His bread and oil with herbs came first, followed by his wine in an ice bucket.

"Will someone be joining you, sir?" the waiter asked.

"One glass will be sufficient."

"Yes, sir," the waiter said. He opened the bottle and poured a small tasting amount.

"I'm sure it's fine," Kamal said.

The waiter filled the glass and left.

Kamal was taking his first sip when a young woman with an infant in a stroller came in and the waiter sat her.

Problem solved, he thought.

SEVEN

□

The sun was coming up when Otto, bone tired, arrived home. Louise was waiting for him at the kitchen door as he parked the car in the garage, a concerned expression on her long, narrow face.

She'd shown up at All Saints around ten in the evening, and had waited for Mac to come through his second of three surgeries.

Dr. Franklin, his mask around his neck, his gloves off, came down the corridor to the waiting room as he pulled off his surgical cap. Otto couldn't read anything from his neutral expression.

"He'll live."

"Thank God," Pete said. She was almost on the verge of collapse.

"But he's not out of the woods yet. He's going to need skin grafts on his back. I have some friends up in Toronto who're doing some cutting-edge research on three-D printing. We'll be sending some of Mac's skin cells by courier tonight."

"Any brain trauma?" Pete had asked.

"I'd say no, but we'll have to wait until he comes around to evaluate him."

"How long?"

"We're going to keep him under for at least two weeks."

Pete half turned away, and looked at Otto and Louise and Marty. "Shit," she'd said.

"Maybe you'd better try to convince him to retire," Franklin had said.

"Not him," Pete had said bleakly.

.   .   .

Otto had left Pete at the hospital and had driven back out to his darlings in his office. She was planning on spending the night. Bambridge had gone home, and so had Louise.

"Call when you're finished," she'd told her husband.

"I don't know how long I'll be," he said.

"I know."

First he had pulled up every scrap of information on every single op Mac had ever been involved with. And that included his stint as deputy director of operations, as well as his even shorter tenure as temporary director of the Company.

The number of countries that had grudges against him serious enough to order his assassination was long; Chile, North Korea, China, Japan, and Russia, plus France, Germany and Switzerland, whose intel agencies had all but officially listed him as a persona non grata.

Pakistan was at the top of the list, as were any number of organizations such as AQAP—al-Qaeda in the Arabian Peninsula—the Taliban in Afghanistan and, in the past year or so, ISIS.

But the number of individuals who would want revenge was fairly small, for the simple reason that when Mac had come up against them—one on one—he'd killed them.

Otto set his darlings to work just after midnight, and by eight, when he was sure that they had grasped the problem of what he wanted to know, he'd finally gone home. When something showed up he would be notified.

"Bed or something to eat first?" Louise asked.

"I think I'm hungry."

"Take a shower, it'll be ready when you are."

In the shower Otto kept trying to work out the timing of the thing. It'd been a year since the attack on the pencil towers, so if the assassin had been the guy behind it, who managed to escape in the end, why the delay?

His darlings had done a database search of every airline and car rental company from Atlanta to Tampa and Sarasota, looking for someone who might even remotely fit the profile, coming up with nothing.

Before he'd left he expanded the search out five hundred miles from Sarasota.

He'd also set his machines to search for cell phone calls and especially cell phone photos and videos taken on the New College campus. For that task he'd hacked into the National Security Agency's mainframe, but with the billions of calls and trillions of key phrases monitored on a daily basis, even his specially crafted algorithms would take time to come up with anything useful.

Drying off he could feel something closing in on them. One of McGarvey's premos. It had rubbed off on him.

Back what seemed like a million years ago he'd been biding his time in France, outside Paris, where he'd gone to ground. Back home he was a freak. A mess. Always unkempt with his long hair; his clothing raggedy and dirty, no laces in his sneakers.

On top of that he was a genius—an odd duck—whom most people were either disgusted with or afraid of. He had the bad habit of laughing at people who didn't "get it." He did partial differential equations, including tensor analysis, or matrix calculus—the stuff of Einstein—in his head, and couldn't fathom the person who wasn't able to do the same.

"Are you slow or just stupid?" he'd ask.

Until Mac, with his own brand of intelligence, and his sense of fair play, showed up and asked for his help. That was the day he'd realized that he didn't know everything, and it also was the first day of his life.

Louise had eggs with cream slowly scrambled in the French fashion, bacon, an English muffin and black tea waiting for him.

He sat at the kitchen counter and she watched him with love, respect for who he was and concern for his almost all-consuming worry about Mac, his only friend in the entire world except for her.

"Good," Otto said, hungrier than he'd thought he was.

"Any progress?" Louise prompted.

"They're working the problem."

"Tell me."

Otto ran through everything he'd sent his computer programs to look for, including cell phone records. "NSA's got data coming out its Fort Meade rectum. So much shit they don't know what to do with it all."

"They upgraded."

"They still don't have the processing power they need for what they're trying to do."

"Why not piggyback with them? Add your two cents."

"I'm on it," Otto said. He was frustrated. "But it's still going to take time. We need quantum algorithms, and the machines to handle them, right now."

Louise turned away and made herself a cup of tea. She used lemon in it. "Maybe you're going at it bass ackward."

Otto laughed, but it wasn't funny. "Explain."

"Someone put a bomb in Mac's car. At New College."

"Right."

"Why did it have to be our bad guy?"

"Who else?"

"I mean, why him in person? Your darlings are checking all the airline and rental car records trying to come up with someone who might fit a set of your parameters. But couldn't he, or she, have hired a local, maybe a student, to drop a package into the car?"

Otto slammed down his fork. "Fuck fuck, fuck, I'm stupid!" He started to get up.

"Don't you dare," Louise shouted him down. "I'll set your darlings to work the issue. In the meantime you're going to finish eating and then get a few hours of z's. I shit you not."

E I G H T

□

The morning was impossibly bright but chilly when Kamal left the Bellagio Hotel in the Mini Cooper he'd rented through the concierge. Vegas was billed as a 24/7 city, where whatever happened there stayed there, but mostly it was a night place.

Only a few drunks were out and about, but the bulk of the sparse weekday traffic was service workers: liquor and food vendors, janitorial and other casino employees on the overnight shift heading home, armored-truck drivers picking up overnight receipts and trundling off to the various banks in town, and hookers heading for breakfast after a long night's work.

On Friday night the college girls, and some boys, from L.A. would be showing up in town to meet with their pimps and start the long weekend gigs that earned their tuition and a lot more. They wouldn't be leaving until sometime Sunday morning.

A hearse pulled out from the rear of one of the hotels and headed south, passing Kamal, who was heading west out Sahara Avenue, where a number of used car dealers were located.

Vegas was an anonymous town. No one wanted to know anyone else's business. Everything was better that way.

Kamal had done his homework on his laptop last night after flying in from Atlanta, and by nine he pulled into a scruffy car lot under the banner BIG AL'S—PURVEYOR OF FINE IRON. Most of the vehicles on the lot were older-model SUVs and a number of smaller campers and pickups with camper caps on back.

A man dressed in jeans, a striped shirt with a string tie, cowboy boots and a Stetson came out of the sales office.

"I called last night," Kamal said, his accent neutral now, big, dark-framed glasses perched on his nose.

"Tom Edwards, you're looking for a small motor home to take you out in the desert," the man bellowed. "And today is your lucky day."

Kamal had looked through the inventory online. "You have an oh-six Lexor TS, sixty-two thousand miles, sleeps two. Forty-two thousand."

"You don't want that one. Too old and it's only a touch over twenty feet. A dog, if you ask me. You want something bigger and definitely newer."

"Does it run?"

"I'm telling you, I have a twelve in the same B class at eighty-two thousand, a steal. At least you'd be driving in luxury."

Kamal took a small leather case—one of the items he'd carried in the roll-about's false bottom—from the car. "I'll pay you forty-five thousand cash for the oh-six. You'll have it gassed up and ready for me by noon. Fresh plates, insurance, liability will be sufficient, and stocked with a week's worth of groceries, including a couple of cases of Mich Ultra."

The salesman smiled. What happened with someone's winnings was no business of his. If some sucker wanted to blow an extra five or ten grand on a piece of shit, so be it.

"Let's step into my office, shall we?"

Kamal checked out of the hotel shortly before ten, even though he'd booked the room for five days. "Unfortunately my company has called me back to New York," he explained unnecessarily to the desk clerk. "I guess they don't want me having fun."

"Yes, sir."

He had the cabbie take him to the airport, waited a few minutes and then took another cab back out to Big Al's, where the small camper van was ready on the front lot. It had been freshly washed, and the interior, though worn and a little faded, was clean. A small galley was on the right, a head and storage on the left, and just aft a dining table with seating for four. A pull-out across the back converted from a sofa during the day to a double bed at night, beneath which was more storage.

The rig was plain-looking, innocuous, something no one would ever pay any attention to. Just another camper on the road. Some blue-collar family's idea of a dream vacation getaway.

"Perfect," he told the salesman.

And a couple of minutes past noon he was on US 95, a decent highway running north that was divided for the first fifty miles. Mountains and deserts were all around him. The landscape looked like something on the moon; dry, lifeless and surreal, where no one in their right mind would want to be, unless they were on business. Some specific business.

By six Kamal pulled into the Sunrise Valley RV Park just off US 95, near the tiny town of Mina. He paid his one-night fee and parked near the back in a slot under some shade trees, away from the office. It was a weekday and not summer yet, so the park was less than half filled. In the distance the peak of some low mountain rose up out of the desert.

He didn't bother plugging in or connecting to the water, but he opened a couple of the windows for the cross breeze, which carried oddly spiced desert smells, and got a beer from the fridge.

Sitting at the tiny table, he took apart his Glock Gen4 pistol and cleaned it, just for something to do. He ejected the 10mm rounds from both magazines, cleaned the bullets and oiled the springs, then reloaded.

At eight he phoned a local number. A man answered after three rings. A baby was crying in the background and a woman was saying something.

"What?"

"Do you have the package?" Kamal asked.

"Yes, and I'm telling you, pal, it wasn't so fucking easy as I thought it would be."

"But you have the items?"

"Listen, I'm going to need more than the five thousand. I could have a lot of shit coming my way, you know what I mean?"

"I know exactly what you mean, my friend. How much more do you think would make things right?"

The woman shouted something that Kamal couldn't make out. But she sounded angry and maybe drunk. Americans never ceased to amaze him.

"Another thousand—no, make it two."

"This will not be the first shipment. There'll be others."

The sergeant first class, who worked at the Hawthorne Army Depot about forty miles away, hesitated. "Jesus."

"How about if I make it an even ten thousand? Cash. Hundred-dollar bills. One hundred of them. And to make it easy the next delivery wouldn't be for at least two months. Another ten thousand cash. Does that sound okay?"

"I gotta think about it."

"Fine, think about it. In the meantime I'll get someone else."

"Wait the fuck up. I didn't say anything like that."

"Midnight. Wildcat Brothel. A Lexor RV, white with black trim, will be parked in back. The doors will be unlocked. A package with your money will be left on the passenger seat. Put the stuff for me in the back on the floor and leave."

"There's a lot of shit. Dangerous in the wrong hands."

"Place the detonators on the floor between the driver's and passenger seats."

"Yes, sir," the sergeant said. "The Wildcat. A nice place. I could use a little R-and-R. How's about us meeting—"

"No," Kamal said. "If we ever meet face-to-face, I will kill you. Do you understand me?"

"Listen, goddamnit, I was just talking."

"Are you clear, Sergeant?"

"Yes."

"Perfectly clear?"

"Yes, sir."

NINE

It was two in the afternoon when Otto and Louise got back to All Saints, where Pete had spent the night on the couch in the waiting room. She looked like hell, but not so stressed out as she had been yesterday.

"How is he?" Louise asked.

"Better, if you can believe it. Franklin says he's seen a lot of really tough people come through here, but never anyone like Mac. He spent a good night. His blood pressure has settled down, and all his other numbers are coming back, including his cranial pressure and EKG."

"How long is Franklin going to keep him in a coma?" Otto asked.

"If he continues to improve, another five or six days," Pete said. "Beyond that he'll start to lose muscle tone. But it'll be a long haul before he's at one hundred percent. If ever."

Otto's darlings had come up with the answers that Louise had suggested they might find. It was one of the students by the name of Antonio Gomez who'd placed the bomb in Mac's car. But it was under the passenger side. If it had been under the driver's seat Mac would not have had one chance in a million of surviving.

As it was, something had apparently spooked Mac because one of the faculty who'd witnessed the explosion said that for whatever reason, Mac had climbed over the car door and had managed to get a few feet away when the thing went off.

"Like he'd known something was wrong," the teacher had told police in a follow-up interview.

Otto wanted to tell Mac about it, and get his take. Find out what he knew or suspected.

"Maybe Franklin's right, maybe he should think about retiring," Louise said.

Pete managed a slight smile. "I'd quit with him in a heartbeat, if that's what he wanted. But I don't think it's going to happen. He's only fifty, what would he do? Sit behind a desk and tell other people how to do field work? He tried that a couple of times, as DDO and DCI, and he hated every minute of it."

Otto looked away for a moment. "One of these days he won't be so lucky," he said. He didn't know what he would do without Mac. He had Louise and they had the baby, and he had his work, but nothing would ever be the same.

Pete squeezed his hand. "Don't count him out just yet. I'll backstop him for whatever it's worth and for however long he needs or wants me."

"When can you break free from here?"

Pete was surprised. "I hadn't thought about it. Why?"

"I could use your help."

"I'm listening."

"I just found out that a student by the name of Gomez was the one who put the bomb in Mac's car. I've seen the Bureau's preliminary forensics report—fifty-eight percent PETN and twenty-three percent RDX, plus trace amounts of a binder, a plasticizer, an antioxidant N-phenyl-2-napthylamine and a brown dye."

"Semtex," Pete said.

"Semtex 2P. We need to find the kid—he's disappeared—and we need to find out where he got the stuff."

"And who hired him. What about your darlings?"

"They're chewing on the big picture. Someone wanted Mac dead, and I'm trying to find out not only who wanted it, but why."

"Somebody out of his past? Just revenge?"

"Somebody out of his past, maybe. But I don't think it'll be just revenge. I don't know why, so for now don't ask. Can you help me?"

Pete looked down the corridor to the intensive care unit just off the operating theater. "I can't do anything for him right now," she said, her voice soft. She shook her head. "Christ."

Otto waited.

She turned back and nodded. "I need to go home and get cleaned up first. What do you need?"

"I'll send you what I've come up with on Gomez. I want you to go out to the school and find out who he was, and where he's gotten himself to."

"You'll be at your office?"

"I'm going there now."

"I'm going to stick it out here for a few hours," Louise said. "Keep me in the loop, okay?"

"Sure thing, sweetheart," Otto said. "You going to be okay?"

"Guaranteed. Now both of you get the hell out of here and catch some bad guys."

Bambridge showed up at Otto's office at three-thirty. He wasn't as combative as usual, and in fact he was there almost hat in hand. "Any progress?"

Otto was tweaking the work his darlings were doing, much of it displayed at nearly blinding speed on four one-hundred-inch OLED monitors on the wall, as well as a flat table monitor about the size of a door.

"I want to meet with Page and you and anyone else with half a brain on campus who isn't scared shitless of the White House. Six o'clock upstairs."

"Do I get a clue?"

"A student on campus put what was probably a kilo of Semtex in Mac's car. That stuff isn't so easy to come by, which means he got it along with instructions from someone who's connected, who has financial backing and who has a mission other than simply taking out one man."

"Do we know this student?"

"Antonio Gomez. He was one of Mac's students, but he's disappeared. Pete's working on it."

"You said a mission. What mission?"

"For starters I don't think it was revenge, otherwise the bastard, whoever he is, would have wanted to do it himself. He was—and is—busy with something else."

"Working for who? And don't tell me it's the Saudis again, blaming it all on ISIS. Or ISIS itself; they have their hands full in Syria. And no such connection was ever proven when the pencil tower in New York came down. It was a lone operator."

"I'm sure that it's a comfort to believe something like that. A nice tidy package."

"The truth is sometimes tidy."

"What was his motive and where'd he get the money?"

"The guy was insane, even Ms. Boylan testified to that much. And he's rich. His house outside of Monaco was over the top."

"Insanity doesn't have anything to do with being smart. But he needed a source of intel. Shit only available at the government level."

"Speculation."

"What government, Marty, if not Saudi Arabia?"

"You tell me."

"Them, I think. Along with Russia, China, North Korea, Chile, Pakistan."

"You're fucking certifiable."

"Maybe he has friends in French or German intel."

Bambridge waved him off, and turned to leave.

"Maybe Japan's PSI." The Public Security Intelligence Agency was Japan's counterpart to the CIA.

Bambridge stopped at the inner door. "Are you hearing yourself?"

"How about MI6?" Otto asked. "Kamal al-Daran. He went to Sandhurst. Maybe he still has pals with connections."

Bambridge had the door open and was about to step into the corridor.

"How about right here in D.C.?" Otto said.

Bambridge left, and Otto turned back to his darlings.

"Or maybe all of the above," he said to himself. An old boys' network. A consortium. But for what purpose? To what end?

T E N

Pete parked the Mercedes a couple of rows beyond where Mac had parked his Porsche. Almost all of the debris had been cleaned up, but the pavement where his car had been was scorched, the leaves on several trees were missing on one side, and there was a dark stain on the nearby sidewalk that could have been oil or blood.

Police tape was strung around a fifty-foot radius of the blast.

She stopped a few feet away, unable to approach the spot, her heart racing, her breath short. It had been close this time. She could almost feel the heat from the explosion. A kilo of Semtex was way over the top, enough to easily take down an airplane, derail a train, even take out an entire floor of a building.

Whoever had come gunning for Mac not only wanted to make sure of the kill, but also wanted to make a statement.

Kamal al-Daran. His face, and even the scent of his cologne, was etched in her mind. She could hear his cultured, upper-class British accent, see the set of his mouth when he was pleased with something, and the downturn of his lips when he was angry or vexed.

He'd kidnapped her in Monaco in an effort to lure Mac in for the kill, and he had almost succeeded.

The son of a bitch was insane, but he was brilliant, and as Otto said, he was well connected to a good source of intelligence. A source almost certainly at the government level. Saudi Arabia's GIP, or General Intelligence Presidency—in Arabic, Al Mukhabarat Al A'amah—had been Otto's best guess last year.

But the man had simply vanished. Gone to ground somewhere. Not back to Monaco; the French DGSI had kept an eye on Kamal's house as a courtesy. But totally under anyone's radar, which was in itself no mean feat in this electronically connected age.

Otto was certain this was something Kamal could have engineered. But Pete had not been completely convinced until just this moment, though she couldn't point to any single reason. She just felt it. Otto was almost never wrong.

Kamal wanted Mac dead. The question was: Why? If it wasn't simple revenge, who was the bastard working for this time?

And for what purpose? What were they preparing to do that was so important they had to take Mac out of the picture first?

She walked across the lot and across College Street to the campus police headquarters, housed in a low one-story building not much bigger than a mobile home. A woman in uniform sat behind a desk just inside the front door. Her name tag read: MOLINARI.

"May I help you?"

Pete showed the woman her CIA identification. "I'm doing a follow-up, and I could use your help."

"We've pretty well covered everything with the SPD and Bureau people from Tampa. I don't know if there's much else I can tell you."

"I'm looking for a student by the name of Antonio Gomez. If possible I'd like to see his jacket. Talk to his roommate, maybe some of his instructors."

"Two witnesses put him at the scene, but he's disappeared," Molinari said.

"Anyone know where he went?"

"No. But nothing we've come up with ties him to putting something in Mr. M's car. We think he just got scared and took off."

"I'd like to have access to his dorm room."

"Look, the kid checks out. You have to know that we had another car bomb incident last year, almost exactly on the same spot. And Mr. M was a witness. A lot of the students and faculty are still a little spooked."

"I'd still like to take a look at his room."

Molinari was hesitant. "I'll have to get authorization, and that won't be until Monday."

"We're pretty sure Gomez was hired by someone to plant the bomb. I'm looking for a clue, even something insignificant, anything at all that might tell us where he went."

"I'm sorry."

"Mr. M, as you call him, was a close personal friend. Very close. In fact he and I were talking about getting married. But he's dead, and I have a personal stake in catching the bastard who killed him."

Molinari lowered her eyes. "We weren't sure if his wounds were fatal."

"I assume that you saw his car. No one could have survived. One kilo of Semtex packs a very big punch."

Molinari brought something up on her computer screen. "Dort Residence Hall across the Trail. You can take the pedestrian bridge, easier than driving over. Two twenty-five."

A plastic key card came out of a reader.

"It's only good for twenty-four hours, so you can toss it. But just so you know, his roommate was moved, and the police put tape on the door."

Four students were seated around a table in the lobby when Pete came in. But they didn't pay any attention to her. Upstairs she found Gomez's room, pulled the yellow DO NOT CROSS tape off the door and let herself in.

The room had been tossed, probably by the Bureau guys, but it looked like a simple pass. Gomez had been at the scene, but nothing linked him to the actual bombing, so at this point he was considered to be only a possible witness.

She closed the door behind her and simply looked from where she stood.

Two single beds flanked the window. The one on the left had apparently belonged to the roommate. It had been stripped of its blankets and pillow. The desk and tiny combined closet/chest of drawers on that side were empty too.

But on the right Gomez's bed was made up. His closet and drawers were open and held a few items of clothing. Nothing outwardly indicated that he was leaving any time soon. If he had a laptop, he'd taken it with him; most students took them to class.

A large FedEx box was lying on the floor next to a trash can on the roommate's side. A cardboard box that could have been big enough to hold a pair of boots was open on the desk. Several half-empty packages of candy and cookies were scattered on the desk, the floor beside it and on the bed.

A couple of Spanish-language magazines and a Sunday edition of a news-paper called *Bionero* were lying on the chair.

Gomez had apparently gotten a care package from home.

Something, Pete didn't know exactly what, bothered her.

She went to the desk and looked at the box. The bottom was filled with Styrofoam packing peanuts. They'd been pushed aside. Whoever had searched the room wanted to see if anything was left in the box. But there was only the peanuts.

She took a handful and smelled them. Something was odd to her. Vinegar. . . . *Semtex*.

She got the FedEx box from beside the roommate's trash can. The address label had been mostly torn off, but a shipping code was partially intact.

She put the cover on the box that had held the cookies and candies—and whatever else that had been packed in the peanuts—and put it in the FedEx box. It was a perfect fit.

She called Otto as she headed out the door in a run. She knew.

He answered by the time she'd raced downstairs, the box in hand, and was heading toward where she'd parked the car.

"A FedEx shipping code," she shouted, and she read it off.

"Stand by."

Halfway down the block Otto came back. "Atlanta," he said.

"That's where Gomez went. Check the airport. I'm on my way back."

ＥＬＥＶＥＮ

☐

When Otto was a little boy, about five, Leonard, the man his mother had married the year before, was trying to repair the rocking horse that some aunt had sent as a gift. Even then it wasn't something Otto was interested in.

The four legs were suspended by two wire struts connected to the four upright posts in the frame. The screws had loosened and they'd come out of their brackets. The horse was upside down on the back porch, the wire struts in the air.

But Otto could see that the geometry was wrong. Once the struts were screwed in place and the rocking horse turned upright, the legs would not swing down into position.

"It's not going to work that way," he said.

Leonard ignored him. When he'd set the last screw, he turned the rocking horse over and the struts hung up on the uprights.

Otto had laughed. He didn't understand at that point that Leonard wasn't a bright man, but at least he had tried to fix the rocking horse.

"I told you."

Leonard turned and backhanded Otto.

It was the first of many times his stepfather had beaten him. No one liked to be thought of as stupid. And since then he'd at least learned a little diplomacy—though not much, until Louise had come into his life and cleaned up his act the best she could.

It was a quarter to six, and he stood in the back room of his suite of offices staring at one of his darlings. He knew just about everything with about an 85 percent level of confidence except for the one last detail.

But he had all but nailed the man who'd tried to kill Mac.

Pete had the key card to get her past the first barrier into Otto's office. The most important barrier was facial recognition.

"Ms. Boylan is here," his security program announced. The voice was Louise's.

He glanced at the surveillance monitor in the corridor. "Let her in, please."

Pete came back to his inner office. She looked haggard. "Anything on Atlanta?"

"Take a look at this," Otto said, and he brought up the Atlanta PD's preliminary report on the homicide of a white male whose body was found in Atlanta's central parking ramp.

"Antonio Gomez," Pete said. "Our boy."

"He took the eight o'clock Delta up to Atlanta, but he was a no-show for his flight to Mexico City.

"He was the bomber. But who hired him and who killed him?"

"Read the rest," Otto said.

After a moment or two Pete looked at him. "The kid was probably dead, shot in the heart. But he'd been shot in the side of the head."

"Postmortem."

"An insurance shot. Kamal al-Daran."

"I'm assuming it wasn't simple revenge for how Mac stopped him in New York last year," Otto said.

Kamal had been given the job to take down two skyscrapers in Manhattan's Midtown. It was supposed to look like an ISIS attack—just like the one al-Qaeda had done on nine/eleven. In this case a Saudi prince had engineered the plan in an attempt to cause the U.S. to ramp up its attacks against the Islamic terrorist organization—thus taking pressure off the Saudi border.

Mac had stopped the worst part of the operation—the part where more than two thousand children could have been killed.

"Why that assumption?"

"We've gone over that before."

"Humor me," Pete pressed.

"He'd have no need to spend the money or take the risk, unless something else was on the table."

"I'm listening."

"He's gone to ground, and has done a damned good job of it. Says to me that he wants to stay deep, maybe enjoy the rest of his life, or at least for a few years until the dust from his last op has settled. Which it hasn't."

Pete glanced at the screens. "Okay, your darlings have come up with that scenario."

"Because I pointed them that way in the first place."

"If not simple revenge, then why kill Mac?"

Otto had come up with something like this as early as last March, before the elections, and he'd flown down to Florida, making sure that no one in the Company knew that he was gone, and that Pete was still in Washington.

But Mac hadn't been very much surprised with what Otto had suggested.

"No one inside the Beltway will want to believe it," McGarvey had said.

"Not a chance."

"What's Louise's take?"

"She suggested I talk to you."

"How about Pete?"

"That'd be your call," Otto said. They were drinking a beer sitting in the gazebo on the Intracoastal Waterway behind Mac's Casey Key house. The weather was warm, only a slight breeze off the Gulf.

"I'll talk to her."

"Trouble is I don't have a concrete leg to stand on," Otto said. "Only a gut feeling."

"I know," McGarvey said. "The problem is, even if we're right—and I hope to Christ we're not—there's not a thing we can do to get ready."

"Page might listen if you were to sign off."

"Listen to what? What are you going to tell him? What can we say that would make any difference? The problem—and you and I both know it—is that something has to happen first."

The sun was setting behind them, the light on the palm trees along the waterway red and gold and pink, and even green. Soft, like the weather, but in Technicolor. Peaceful. Nothing bad happening here. For the moment.

"Even after it happens—if it does—no one will want to believe it," Otto said. "I mean, how long did it take after nine/eleven for us to nail bin Laden? And he wasn't even directly responsible. Not really. It was only his philosophy."

McGarvey went to get them another beer.

A Gulfstream G650 was waiting at Dolphin Aviation up at Sarasota to take Otto back to Andrews. The bogus flight plan was for London, with a return sometime tomorrow. Otto's name was on the manifest, but that record would get all but buried, at least for the time being. But it had given him all the time he needed to get down here and hide his movements. At this point he wanted no questions for which he had no answers.

McGarvey came back with the Heinekens. "Do you want to stay the night?"

"I have to get back."

"Louise?"

"No. Pete. She needs to know what I'm thinking. If you're called up, she'll want to be right there. Wouldn't be fair to keep her out in the cold until the last minute."

"My call."

Otto shook his head. He'd known this was coming. "Insulating her won't help. She's at the Farm training the newbies on interrogation techniques. She has to be ready if and when the shit hits the fan. Anyway, she's just an employee of the CIA. She's not your wife."

McGarvey started to say something, but then merely nodded.

Otto had a clear memory of the look on his friend's face last year. It was the first time he'd ever seen fear in Mac's eyes. Not for himself, of course, but for Pete. He didn't want any harm to come to her. He didn't even want her to worry.

Impossible wishes, of course, for someone in the business. But Mac had a track record that he didn't want to continue.

Pete sat across from Otto in his office in the Old Headquarters Building.

"Even if you were right before the election, what does Mac have to do with it? Why kill him?"

"Because he could be the key," Otto said.

"To what?" she asked with obvious bitterness.

"Let's go lay it out for Page and the others."

"They're not going to like it."

TWELVE

□

The DCI's secretary, a former analyst for the Defense Intelligence Agency, and a sharp individual, showed them to the director's private conference room next door.

Walter Page, a former CEO of IBM who had tried twice to resign as director of the CIA, but who'd been denied by two successive presidents because he was doing a good job, was waiting at the head of the small table when Otto and Pete walked in.

Carleton Patterson, the eighty-year-old general counsel for the agency, along with Bambridge and Ursula Olson, the new head of the Directorate of Analysis—which had started out as the Directorate of Intelligence—and a man in a flannel suit with leather patches at the elbows whom Otto didn't recognize looked up.

"How is Kirk doing?" Page asked.

"Better than Dr. Franklin thought he would," Pete said.

"We're all glad to hear it."

"But I need the fiction of his death to remain in place for everyone outside this room," Otto said as he and Pete took their places.

The conference room, which also served as the DCI's private dining room, was electronically and mechanically secure. It was a fairly small, windowless space with a couple of Wyeth originals on the walls, but institutional green carpet on the floor.

"The president will have to be told."

"Especially not the president."

Bambridge started to say something, but Page held him off. "You'll tell us why."

"Excuse me," Pete said. "But could you introduce us to the gentleman at the end of the table?"

"Dr. Harold Estes has come to us from Harvard to help make some sense of what we'll be facing in the next four years plus if our new president is reelected," Ursula Olson said. She was a small slender woman who in the first year with the Company had proven her intelligence and clear thinking to everyone, including Otto.

"I'm studying the new geopolitical dynamic," Estes said, his accent British.

"Oxford?" Otto asked.

"Actually, yes. How'd you guess?"

"It shows. But it's good that you're here, because you're probably the only one other than Ms. Boylan and myself who might see the sense of what I've come to warn you about."

"This will not be a lecture," Bambridge said.

"No, a discussion after I lay out my points."

"Is there a valid reason for keeping Kirk dead?" Patterson asked. "Many people in this organization are shook up. He was a rock to many of them. Someone steady."

"Yes."

"Then continue, my dear boy, we're all ears."

"A young Mexican national by the name of Antonio Gomez, who posed as a student at New College, placed the bomb in Mac's car. The Bureau estimates a full kilo of Semtex. He took an eight o'clock flight to Atlanta, where he was picked up and driven to a parking garage in the city. He was shot in the heart, which caused his immediate death, but then was shot again in the side of the head at close range."

"After he was already dead?" Ursula asked.

"Yes."

"On that one fact alone you're assuming that the shooter was the same man who took down the pencil tower in New York last year," Bambridge said.

"It's a signature move, rare these days."

"If it was the terrorist we've identified as Kamal al-Daran, then it was revenge," Page said.

"No need for it. He's gone to ground, completely off the radar. Could mean he retired and has the money to do so."

"Could mean," Bambridge said. "And I know where you're going with this."

"No, you don't."

"Continue," Page said.

"He hired Gomez to take out Mac, but not for the reason that Mac was the one who stopped him last year from taking down a second pencil tower that would have killed two thousand kids."

"Granted," Page said. "So if not for revenge, then what?"

"Kamal has been hired to take on another assignment. But job one for him was to get Mac out of the way."

"No," Bambridge said. "You're making another assumption, one that discounts every other law enforcement and intel officer, that only McGarvey can figure out what's coming our way, if anything is coming our way. My bet is still on revenge."

"No one, even the engineers, wanted to believe that someone could take down a pencil tower without using an airliner or a lot of explosives. No one wanted to listen to Mac, so he had to do it outside the established wisdom, with just Ms. Boylan's help."

"And Otto's and Louise's," Pete said. "The point is that sometimes when all else fails his unorthodox methods are the only things that work. And that scares you people, but you don't want to admit it. And I hate to tell you this, but we're there again, and you'd just better hope that Mac's being publicly dead will give the rest of us the advantage. We need it."

"Flash points," Otto said.

"What do you mean?" Bambridge asked.

"Russia, with Putin's almost pathological necessity to bring his country back to the old days of the Soviet Union. China and the issue not only of Taiwan, but the modernization of her military, and having to walk a thin line to keep us happy as a trading partner.

"North Korea and her nuclear and missile programs. She needs to keep us distracted enough with bluster and with misinformation until she's ready to confront us with a viable threat—at least to our West Coast. They've sent satellites into orbit, and they've weaponized their nukes to the degree that they can be attached to their missiles.

"Pakistan is no friend of ours, especially after Mac took down their supposed messiah and put a cap—a temporary cap—on their nuclear stockpile. If something breaks out between them and India, the entire hemisphere could be in a serious world of shit. We'd be pulled into it, of course.

"Not to mention Chile. Some hardliners remember Mac's taking out one of their generals. Maybe Saudi Arabia again. Maybe Syria, Iran, hell, just about every Arabic-speaking country—Shiite or Sunni. We've made a lot of enemies."

"Points taken," Page said. "And for a long time McGarvey has been a man with a target painted on his back. So who hired Kamal and why?"

"Let me finish. Mac had a run-in with Israel a number of years ago. He's been an on again/off again persona non grata of France, Switzerland and, of course, Germany, for operations outside of their laws. Japan over his handling of the expediter issue."

"He has enemies, that's already been established," Bambridge said, exasperated. "His own doing."

"Working for us."

"Very often, no."

"Working for our best interests, then, or do you want to argue that point as well, Marty?"

"Maybe he has enemies right here at home," Pete said.

"We all do," Page said.

"My real point is that I think Kamal has an ironclad source of intel. He's been told what's coming down the pike, and perhaps he's even been hired to take part in whatever it is. His first job was to eliminate McGarvey."

"We're back to why," Page said. "What's coming at us that would make McGarvey the key?"

"I have some ideas but I'm not sure yet."

"What would make all of those countries cooperate with each other? What's the common thread? And who's the ringleader?"

"The ringleader is some Saudi royal, who's probably insane, and is carrying a grudge for us. Maybe he thinks he can make some sort of a mark for himself," Estes said. "Only, none of this is happening at the leadership level—though it's the unspoken desire. Handpicked individuals in each of the intelligence services of those and perhaps other countries were the ones who've hatched a plot, if indeed there is a plot. A consortium, if you will, with a common goal. If it goes south because of something or someone—perhaps McGarvey—no one would take the blame."

"The common thread?" Page asked.

Otto had it. Estes, the pompous son of a bitch, was right.

"Well?" Bambridge said.

"Our new president made no foreign friends even before the election."

"Christ," Bambridge said. "Are you talking about assassinating the president?"

"Perhaps," Estes said.

"No," Otto said. "Completely discrediting him."

"How?" someone asked, but Otto was lost in himself and it didn't register who'd asked the question.

THIRTEEN

□

Kamal rolled into the San Francisco area on I-580 before noon, taking the San Rafael Bridge across the entrance to the upper part of San Francisco Bay. The morning was bright and sunny, weekday traffic heavy but steady. In his estimation California drivers were mostly crazy but were some of the best in the world on the freeways.

Once across he took the highway south that ran down into the city itself and over the Golden Gate Bridge just as a freighter was coming in from the sea. The breeze was a little heavy on the center span, but nothing difficult for the camper loaded with explosives he'd driven across the mountains to get here.

Where to hide a needle? In a haystack? Too easy, he'd always thought. The best place was to hide the needle where everyone would have the chance to spot it, but no one would actually see the thing. It was a childhood game from the West that his mother had taught him when he was growing up in London's tony Knightsbridge district.

She'd called it hide the thimble. The game was to place the thing out in plain view, on the fireplace mantel, on a windowsill, on the coffee table, and invite him to find it.

But it had been hard at first, until he'd learned the trick of not looking for it, but to take in the entire room.

That was before he'd made his first kill while he was still a young boy living at home.

Just across the bridge the highway split, Interstate 280 South toward San Bruno and US 101 straight south along the Bay to a construction site at what had been the old Candlestick Park.

Five miles later he followed the signs to San Francisco's International

Airport and then to the long-term parking garage, where he found a spot near the southwest back wall, on the third floor.

Switching off the engine he waited for a full five minutes on the off chance that his arrival had been noticed. A couple of pickups, and many SUVs and even a few station wagons were parked in the garage, but his was the only camper.

The blinds in the back windows were closed, so no one could look directly inside. And the explosives were packed out of sight in just about every storage area and cupboard.

Each twenty-kilo package was equipped with an encrypted cell phone receiver and detonator. Each receiver also contained a GPS chip that was accurate to within three or four meters.

Unless he sent the signal to detonate, all the packages would explode at the same moment when the camper reached the pre-programmed set of GPS coordinates.

Even if he was dead or incarcerated, this explosion and the next two would happen no matter what.

The only one he wanted to personally witness—the one he hadn't been paid for, the one he had planned purely for his own pleasure—was at Grand Central Terminal, for the simple reason he wanted to be right there to watch it unfold. Smelling the Semtex, the blood and bodily fluids of one hundred or more innocent people; hear the screams, the cries for help, the frantic announcements on the PA system for people to immediately evacuate the terminal. And when he got out to Lexington Avenue, the ambulances, the cops, the emergency responders and SWAT teams, the media all converging for just the first of the four greatest shows this side of the Atlantic since nine/eleven, would be nothing less than mind-blowing. He almost got an erection thinking about it.

No one had followed him this far, which was exactly what he wanted. He drove to the exit, paid his fee to the indifferent attendant, and took Highway 101 back into the city to a private garage a few blocks from St. Mary's Cathedral. He'd found the place online and had paid for one year in advance, and had been sent the key for the padlock to his accommodations address in New York City.

The small camper barely fit into the narrow space, which had been used for an apartment's off-street parking. Either the apartment had been sold separately, or the owners, needing the extra money, had rented it out.

Neither reason was important.

He got out of the camper with his roll-about bag, put his own combination lock on the door and walked up to Geary Street to find a cab.

His flight for Denver left at three, which would put him in a rental car heading to the massive First Congregational United Church of Christ Ministry Headquarters outside the tiny town of Colby in far-western Kansas in plenty of time for the evening service.

The fact that McGarvey had been born and raised on a ranch not too far from there was an irony he particularly enjoyed. He almost wished that the bastard could have survived to witness the next step in the long road to America's fall into hell.

The November meeting in Beijing nine months ago had been so casual and apparently open that Kamal had almost walked away even before he'd entered the hotel. There'd been no security precautions, so far as he'd been able to spot, nor had he been met in the shabby lobby or upstairs to be frisked.

He'd merely gone up, found the room, knocked on the door and was let in by one of the three men, all of them middle-aged, all of them dressed in plain business attire, no ties, their shirt sleeves rolled up, their jackets over the backs of their chairs.

There'd been no bodyguards, no surveillance cameras in evidence, nor were any of them armed so far as he could tell.

And they were calm, no agitation in their eyes or in their mannerisms. No hesitation in their speech—their English nearly too perfect, as if they'd studied under precise masters. They knew who he was, who he'd worked for and the jobs he'd done. Most notably, the pencil tower project for an offshoot of Saudi intelligence.

"I have no interest in learning your identities," he'd begun, but the middle one, with intensely dark hair and thin eyebrows and thin lips, motioned him to stop.

"You would not survive your inquiries."

Kamal wasn't impressed. He crossed his legs. The man had been educated in a good East Coast school; it was obvious from his cultured accent.
He would be relatively easy to track down if the need arose. "You brought
me here, what do you want?"

"Within the next four to six months, you will hit three separate targets
within the continental United States. We want the events to happen as simultaneously as possible. All of them within the same one-hour period at
noon eastern standard time. All of them on the same day."

"May I know the purpose of these attacks?" Kamal said. "I only ask so
that I can better judge their nature."

"To terrorize, of course," the same thin-lipped man had said.

Neither of the other two spoke, nor did they seem very interested, and
Kamal had thought for a moment that he was in the middle of a badly
scripted and poorly acted stage drama.

"To terrorize, with the purpose of destabilizing the normal day-to-day
routines of the population?"

"Yes."

"A tall order."

"We believe that you are currently the best in the business."

The decision had been an easy one, made not so much for the money—
he still had plenty—but for the thrill of the hunt, and for the prospect of
killing a great number of people. And even before he'd left the hotel and
had flown back to France, he'd worked out the rough methodology for each
of the three.

"I'll take the job."

"You will not try to contact us ever again."

"Nor will you try to contact me. Once I leave this room you will have
no further control over the operation, other than the timely deposits of
monies into my account."

"Your first deposit will be made within the hour," the thin-lipped man
said. "Good day."

Kamal's preparations had begun the next day.

Kamal arrived at Denver's International Airport late in the afternoon.
Within a half hour he'd collected his one roll-about, had rented a car

from Hertz, and was on Interstate 70 heading east the 175-mile drive to Colby, and his meeting with Pastor Buddy Holliday, whom he'd spoken with on the phone eight days ago.

"I've come to Christ," he'd begun, once he'd gotten through to the preacher. "And I have a pile of money to give back to the Lord's good work!"

His accent was Texan and it sounded in his ear a lot more authentic than Pastor Holliday's west Kansas drawl.

"Are we talking substantial?"

"How does a mil grab you, Buddy?" Kamal had said. "All I want in return is someplace to lay my head when I'm in the area, get to hear your sermons in person, and figure out how to strike back at the Islamic radicals who want to take over our great country."

"You got it, pal."

Pastor Buddy was the wealthiest Baptist preacher in the U.S., with his syndicated radio and television shows, a sprawling campus with biblical schools, a children's hospital, a ward for expectant mothers without husbands and even a ten-thousand-acre amusement park and entertainment complex.

Plus a massive church that seated twenty thousand people.

And yet, from what Kamal had learned, the man was little more than an ignorant hillbilly. Charismatic, but ignorant.

F O U R T E E N

□

It was after eight in the evening when the night-duty intensive care nurse came down the corridor from the ICU to the waiting room where Pete was watching some stupid movie on television, trying to get her mind off everything swirling around her.

No one but Estes had wanted to believe what Otto had tried to tell them, but Page had given him the provisional go-ahead.

"Nothing leaves this building without my approval," the DCI had warned. "Clear?"

"Yes, sir," Otto had promised, getting up.

"I wonder if we could put our heads together," Estes said.

"Why not?" Otto said, even though he'd never particularly liked academics.

"Twice-daily briefings, gentlemen," Page said. "I want to know if something is coming at us, what it might be and when it might happen."

Pete had a sandwich and glass of wine in the CIA cafeteria, and had driven directly back to All Saints.

She looked up when the nurse came to the door.

"He's awake."

Pete jumped up. "Oh my God. How is he?"

"He's asking for you and Otto."

Pete hurried down the corridor, where she had to use hand sanitizer and put on a mask before she was allowed inside.

"Thirty minutes tops," the nurse said. "If he wants something to drink there's a glass of ice chips on the stand. I'll be just down the hall. Dr. Franklin has been notified. He'll be here soon."

McGarvey was lying flat on his stomach, his back draped in damp cloths. The artificial skin grafts had been processed practically overnight, much faster than even Franklin had thought possible, and sent down by courier.

The lights in the compact, state-of-the-art unit were low, and McGarvey was hooked up to just about every conceivable piece of electronic medical equipment possible.

He turned his head when Pete came in. He was pale, bruises on his face, his eyes blackened, some of the hair on the back of his head partially singed.

Something emitted a steady low beeping sound, and the place smelled strongly of disinfectant and a number of other chemicals.

A sheet covered him from the waist down, but it was impossible not to see that his left leg had been taken off somewhere below the knee, and Pete had just a moment when she almost lost it.

"I don't think I'm looking my best," he said. His voice was harsh, as if his throat was dry.

He was no longer on oxygen, and though he looked wan, his skin color was much better than it had been last night.

She went to his side, not sure what she could touch, but he raised his right hand a couple of inches off the bed and she took it. His squeeze was weak, his fingers cool but not cold.

"You look good to me," she said. "In fact you look fabulous."

McGarvey smiled. "Liar."

She had to laugh to keep from crying. "Everybody who knows is pulling for you. Otto and Louise send their love."

"I hope the list is small," he said. "I'm supposed to be dead."

"What are you talking about?"

"I've heard most everything from just before we touched down at Andrews. I could hear the pilot talking to the tower, and the paramedics getting me ready for the ambulance."

"You were unconscious. And Franklin put you in a coma."

"I was gone for stretches, but I heard him warn someone to watch what they were saying around me, because even people on the operating table under anesthesia can sometimes be aware."

Pete didn't know what to say.

"I'm thirsty."

She got the Styrofoam cup of chips from the stand and put it to his lips. He couldn't lift his head high enough so she had to hand-feed him.

When he'd had enough he actually laughed. "I was thinking more along the lines of an ice-cold Heineken," he said.

"That'll come."

He was silent for a longish minute. "One of the students put the bomb in my car. Semtex, I could smell it. But they got it on the wrong side, only reason I got out in one piece."

Again Pete was at a loss for words, but just for the moment. "Not in one piece, darling," she said.

"My leg, I know. I heard them talking about it. Thing is, the bottom of that foot itches, but I'll get used to it."

"Goddamnit to hell," Pete said, lowering her head.

McGarvey gave her hand another squeeze. "I don't like it any more than you do. But it is what it is, and we'll deal with it. Right now I want to know what Otto's come up with. Who targeted me and why?"

"We think it was al-Daran. Antonio Gomez was the student who placed the Semtex in your car and was on a flight to Atlanta within a couple of hours. They found his body in a parking garage downtown. Shot in the heart, and again in the side of the head after he was dead."

"Insurance. No guarantee it's him."

"Otto has it at eighty-seven percent confidence."

"That's high. Revenge?"

"Everyone but Otto thinks so."

"He's right. Al-Daran has gone to ground, and from his past performance he'll be comfortable, he has the money. Only a project that interested him would make him surface. Otto have any ideas?"

"One, but it's over the top."

McGarvey smiled. "Give me the short version for now."

"More terrorist attacks, like Paris, Brussels, Tokyo and New York."

"Otto thinks he's back working for the Saudis? We never proved it."

"Possibly worse than that. He's called them flash points."

"China–Taiwan, Pakistan–India, North and South Korea, Putin and Ukraine, for starts."

"Among others."

"What's the common thread?"

"We'll talk about this tomorrow."

"Because there's no way in hell all of those countries could possibly agree to any sort of an alliance. It makes no sense, except that Otto's apparently got a bug up his ass."

Pete let him work out the next step.

"The common thread is me. He was hired to take me out of the picture because of something I know, or something I can do." McGarvey closed his eyes for a moment. "But I know all of those countries. I've been on operations in every one of them. I'm no friend."

"You know their intel people and methods."

"I know MI6, DGSE and the BND; doesn't mean Britain, France and Germany are plotting something against us."

"No, but they might want to provide some back-burner help, as long as it would never lead to anything like Paris or Brussels."

Mac raised his head to look at her. "What the hell are you talking about?"

"We had a meeting upstairs with Walt, Marty, Carleton, Ursula and some PhD from Harvard a few hours ago. But before we went upstairs Otto told me that he was worried about what he called a soft coup d'état."

"Because of our new president?" Mac said.

Before the election there had been some talk at the Pentagon that a couple of the generals might have to think twice about following the orders of a president who, in their estimation, didn't have a grasp of how the real world works. But it was just talk.

"It's possible."

"That makes no sense," Mac said softly.

"No. But it scares the shit out of me."

F I F T E E N

☐

Western Kansas near the Colorado border was nothing but vast tracts of rolling grasslands, the interstate highway cutting through them like the prow of an ocean liner through the waves. The feeling for Kamal was lonely, feral, almost to the point of a throwback to historic times; no civilization, no people, nothing but the dots of cattle grazing in the far distance.

The prairie was completely opposite of places like London and New York and Paris and even the Côte d'Azur.

Then came the big billboard showing Pastor Holliday, his hands raised in supplication, which stood in front of his vast complex, the biggest building of which was fronted by a massive white cross at least two hundred feet tall. Beyond the church were a roller coaster, a gigantic, four-tiered carousel—supposedly the largest in all of North America—and dozens of other rides and attractions, including a replica of Noah's Ark and the crucifixion site of Jesus. Vast crowds of smiling, ordinary people—moms and dads and happy children—were everywhere.

Off to the left were a series of buildings—one of them the children's hospital, others dormitories, administrative buildings, a television and communications center, and next to it a fenced-in space bristling with satellite dishes and a couple of microwave towers, and a complete village of houses and cottages and even a town square with businesses.

Kamal realized that except for the nearly full amusement park parking lot there were almost no cars or trucks, just people on foot, on bicycles or riding in horse-drawn carriages. The few motorized vehicles looked like maintenance and delivery vans, except for a pair of long black Caddy limousines parked in front of the main two-story office center.

He'd called ahead when he was ten miles out, and Pastor Buddy himself appeared at the gaudy glass and crystal front entrance, the gigantic cross looming overhead.

"Brother Watson, welcome to Paradise," the pastor boomed, his arms outstretched as Kamal got out of his rental Impala.

"This is more impressive than I thought it would be," Kamal said, accepting the embrace as best he could.

It would give him no end of pleasure to kill the bastard. Squeeze the man's carotid arteries and watch as the lights in the idiot's eyes went out. If the pastor was as good as he claimed to be he would realize that the end was near and he was finally going to the real paradise he'd always imagined.

But then Kamal never believed in that crap, nor did he think that Holliday was a believer either—just a buffoon who knew how to take money from hopefuls.

Holliday took his arm and led him inside, up an escalator to a broad, thickly carpeted corridor to his palatial office.

No one was anywhere in sight, but a lot of people were talking in nearby offices. They sounded like snake oil salesmen and -women. Ten dollars per month for salvation.

Crucifixes were everywhere, as were what appeared to be original paintings of the Madonna and baby Jesus.

Broad floor-to-ceiling windows looked toward the church and beyond it to the amusement park. A huge, intricately hand-carved desk with a leather top dominated the room. A half-dozen chairs were grouped in front of it, for supplicants to meet with him.

To the left a couch and two easy chairs faced a coffee table for more intimate meetings.

To the right an open door looked in at a conference room with a long table that had seating for ten. Presumably his board of directors.

Holliday sat them down in the easy chairs facing each other.

"I can't tell you how surprised and gratified I was when you called. But miracles happen every day. I know from personal experience. Daily personal experience."

Kamal took a check for $150,000 U.S. out of his pocket and laid it on the coffee table in front of the pastor.

Holliday picked up the check, which was drawn on a Dubai bank. "Generous," he said. "Very generous."

"Merely a down payment. More will arrive in the coming months."

"We will put this to good use."

"Of course there will be no further paper checks."

Holliday nodded. He took a business card and a golden pen from his pocket and jotted down a number. He passed the card across. "It's a secure account in the Caymans, where money goes much further than here, if you catch my meaning."

"Perfectly," Kamal said, pocketing the card. He now had an independent means of finance, and the amount he'd had to pay out was relatively small compared to the money he expected to take from the pastor's Cayman account at the end.

As a bonus it gave him an extra measure of independence from the Gang of Three, as he'd begun to think of his employees in Beijing.

"Have you had dinner?"

"Something on the road. But first I would like to see your church."

"My house of divine enlightenment."

Kamal couldn't help but chuckle.

"Yes, but they eat it up," Holliday said. A shrewd look came over his face. "My people checked on you."

"As I did you."

"And?"

"You're a good investment."

"By all accounts you're a savvy investor on the Bourse."

It was the French stock market. Thomas Watson was the British name Kamal had used over the past number of years as a licensed trader. He had a short list of clients, all of whom were in fact him.

"Yes."

"What do you hope to gain by investing in me? Other than salvation."

"At this point you're capitalized at fifty-seven million. Your ministry collections amount to five million per year, but your park's admission price at fifty dollars is too low, and you're losing money."

"We're breaking even on our Heavenly Village."

"Point of sales including restaurant and concessions are making almost nothing, as are your tourist items."

"What do you suggest?"

"Raise the park admissions in keeping with Disney, Busch and SeaWorld, raise your concessions and cut costs."

"Salaries."

"I could move a management team in here, and within a year you'll be left holding the goose that laid the golden egg."

"In return?"

"Ten percent of the gross."

"No."

"Ten percent only of the net increase."

"And what's your investment?"

"I'd pay for the management team and their on-site housing. Net cost to you will be zero."

"If you're wrong, and there's a loss, then what?"

"If you noticed, my check was written out to you, personally."

"I did," Holliday said.

"As will the remainder of the one mil. If all else fails you can walk away with whatever you can salvage along with my golden parachute."

Holliday hesitated a moment, then grinned. "Are you a Budweiser man, or do you prefer something a little more exotic?"

"Krug if you have it, or Cristal. But afterwards I want to see my quarters, and those of the people I'll be sending to you. Just a couple of them at first, seeking salvation."

"*Sinners* seeking salvation," Holliday said.

"Exactly."

"They'll be welcome."

SIXTEEN

□

It was nearing five in the afternoon, and Otto was staring at the main flat-screen monitor in his office, which showed an ongoing summary of what his darlings were homing in on. The background color had been changing all day from a pale blue to now a lavender that was deepening by the hour.

Blue was just above the radar, most of the time way behind what Otto's estimation of the current threat level was, but lavender was getting into some serious territory.

Estes, the Harvard PhD, had stopped by for fifteen minutes earlier, but he hadn't come up with anything other than what he'd suggested at the meeting with Page and the others. And yet the man was possibly on to something, but Otto's idea of a coup d'état here in the States was so monstrous it was almost beyond belief, yet Estes agreed.

Louise had called a couple hours ago and asked if he would be home in time for dinner.

"Six, honest injun," he'd promised.

"Good, then afterwards we'll go over to see Mac."

His darlings had come up with a personnel list of the foreign directorates or clandestine services of each of the top fifteen intelligence agencies in the world. Some like Russia's SVR, China's MSS, and North Korea's State Security Department were not friends of the U.S., and their lists of personnel were tightly held secrets. But others like Britain's MI6, France's DGSE and Germany's BND were well known to the CIA.

He had started with the chiefs earlier this afternoon, and had expanded the lists to the number two, three and four down the chains of command. By the time he'd hit the number three name, the color on his main screen had begun to turn lavender.

And by four, which had just come up fifteen minutes ago, the color had deepened.

"Open sesame," he said.

"Good afternoon, darling," one of his programs responded.

"Where is Dr. Estes at the moment?" he asked. "Is he still on campus?"

"Yes, he is on campus. Currently he's in a meeting with four DA personnel, including Mr. Pitken and three analysts. Do you wish their names?"

Raymond Pitken was the assistant deputy director of the Directorate of Analysis and Intelligence.

"That won't be necessary. Where is the meeting taking place?"

"Three-one-five in the NHB." The New Headquarters Building. Next door, connected via a covered walkway on the fourth floor.

"Thank you."

"Shall I announce that you are on the way?"

Otto had to smile. He'd put a lot of his wife's personality into the search program, and like Louise the machine often guessed his next move.

"Yes, please do. And, thank you."

"You're welcome."

He phoned home, and Louise answered on the first ring.

"How late will you be?" she asked.

"I don't know. Maybe an hour or two."

Otto's security pass did not work and Estes, his jacket off, tie loose, had to let him in. Whatever the office, large by campus standards, had been used for before, now it housed a circle of chairs in the middle surrounded by computer monitor stations, and three large interactive whiteboards.

"Sorry about the extra security precaution, but it was Ms. Olson's call."

Otto was impressed. Someone was actually using their brain and thinking outside of the box for a change. "Means you guys have probably come up with the same thing as I did."

"I sincerely hope not," Estes said.

They went to where Pitken and the three analysts were sitting around the circle. An extra chair had been pulled over for Otto, and he and Estes sat down. Meetings like this were called brainstorms, like cramming for a college exam. The notion was that no idea, no matter how far-fetched or impossible seeming, would be left off the table. Absolutely anything brought up would be given serious consideration.

On the other side of the coin, it was the team's duty to try its best to shoot down every idea, even the ones that made the most sense.

"Welcome to the club," Pitken said.

He didn't have to introduce Otto to the analysts—two of them older women, another just a kid in his midtwenties from Munich. Nor did they have to be introduced. They were the DA's dream team. When they had a consensus everyone, including the DCI, listened.

Estes carried some serious weight to have the team helping him.

A list of thirteen of the fifteen intelligence agencies that Otto had come up with were written on one of the whiteboards. Lines with arrows connected most of them to each other.

"You're missing MI6 and the DGSE," Otto said.

"Neither of them are making any noise, official or unofficial," Pitken said.

He was such an ordinary-looking man he could have been anything from a school bus driver to a mailman—anything but the number two in the CIA's intelligence and analytical directorate.

"You haven't dug deeply enough."

"Division chiefs and their number twos," Estes said.

"Try number threes and fours, mostly operational and logistics officers. The people directly in charge of the boots-on-the-ground personnel."

June Lowrey, one of the analysts, who looked like a grandmother with white hair and pince-nez glasses on a chain, shook her head. "They'd be spokesmen. Actual policy would have to come farther up the chain of command."

"Deniability, in case the shit goes south on them," Otto said.

Toni Jurist, the other woman on the team, smiled. "Just like us," she said. "Once we get this figured out and take it upstairs we'll be on the firing line."

"That's why we get paid the big bucks," Pitken said, and they all got a laugh. He was the highest-ranking officer here, and if things fell apart his would be the first head on the chopping block.

"So I submit the reports under my name," Estes said. "What are they going to do, take away my degrees?"

Otto all of a sudden liked him. The man had balls for an academic. "Under my name too," he said. "They try anything and I'll crash the main-frame." He waited a moment. "Not."

Pitken actually looked relieved. "Okay, Otto, what are we all talking about here? You came to us."

"Harold named it over in the DCI's office. He called it a consortium to discredit President Weaver."

"I can understand Putin and his tribe, and nut cases like Kim Jong-un, going after the president," Estes said. "He's made himself a damned easy target with his twist on foreign policy. But we've come up with nothing from the Germans or anyone else."

"We've all but given up on possible assassination attempts," Pitken said.

"It'll be worse than that," Otto said.

"Our intel ops could be hamstrung, or at least put in serious jeopardy if all of a sudden everyone stops cooperating with us. Is that what you're thinking?"

"If it were that easy they wouldn't have tried to kill Mac."

Ludwig Mueller, the boy genius from Munich, sat forward all at once. "Tried?" he asked.

"He's not dead."

The others, including Pitken, were stunned.

"Jesus," someone said.

"And that will not leave this room under any circumstances," Otto warned. "I shit you not, if one of you guys even talks in your sleep, I'll personally see to your destruction."

Pitken and everyone else held their silence for a long moment, until Otto spoke.

"Let's put our heads together to make sure that we're all thinking the same thing."

"You're talking about a coup d'état," Estes said.

"Yeah."

SEVENTEEN

It was well after nine by the time Otto finished with Estes and the dream team and made it back to his office. His stomach was rumbling but his head was in much worse shape. In his entire career he'd never been up against this kind of a wall, nor did he think Mac or anyone else he knew had either.

For the first time for as long as he could remember he was frightened.

He phoned home, and as usual Louise answered on the first ring.

"Do you want to give me the good news or the bad news?" she said. "Assuming there's good news."

"I'm leaving for All Saints now," Otto said, and his voice sounded shaky in his own ear.

Louise was suddenly concerned. "You okay?"

"I'll live."

"I'll call Pete and give the heads-up."

"Meet you there," Otto said and he hung up.

He stared at his main monitor for a long time. The lavender color had definitely deepened, now more purple than blue. And the thing is he had no idea what to do.

The hospital was quiet at this hour. McGarvey and one of the Company's deep-cover agents who'd managed to get out from North Korea and all the way to Seoul before he'd collapsed from multiple gunshot wounds were the only patients.

"Mr. M is doing well," the security officer on the first floor said. "Your wife and Ms. Boylan are already upstairs." He was dressed in scrubs to blend in, but he was a former Navy SEAL operator and very good at what he did.

Otto started for the elevator but then turned back. "The guy who got out of badland, how's he doing?"

"The doc says he'll do just fine, but he's probably never going back into the field again. His days as an NOC are done."

An NOC was an agent who lived and worked in a foreign country with No Official Cover. Those people never visited a U.S. embassy, nor did they ever have any contacts with the CIA other than with their operational officer. Once they did come in out of the cold, for whatever reason, their careers as deep-cover agents were over.

"What room is he in?"

"Next door to Mr. M."

"Name?"

"No idea what his cover name was, but his real name is Larry Kyung-won."

Louise was in the third-floor waiting room down the hall from Mac and the other man when Otto got upstairs. She had brought him a bag dinner.

"Twinkies," she said.

They had been his favorite guilty pleasure for a long time. Now Louise only let him have them when she knew that he was upset and needed a boost. Otherwise the massive amounts of sugar and chemical preservatives were almost impossible to digest.

"Later," he said and he gave her a hug. "Is Pete with Mac?"

"They're waiting for you," Louise said. She gave him a critical look. "Sure you're okay?"

"I don't know," Otto said. "Wait here for a mo, I want to talk to the NOC next door to Mac."

He didn't wait for her to ask why, but went directly down to the wounded field officer's room. The door was open, and light but no sound came from a television on the wall. He knocked on the door frame and the slight man in the bed looked up.

"Holy shit, Mr. Rencke," he said. His voice was weak, but held no hint of a Korean accent.

"May I come in?"

"Of course, even though I'm thinking you're not here on a courtesy call."

Otto went in and stopped at the foot of the bed. "I want to ask you something about North Korea."

"Why I suddenly broke cover and got the hell out?" Kyung-won asked.

"Something like that. But I want to know if you made a snap decision—someone was on your six? Or was it a long time coming before you decided to bail out?"

The man's complexion was olive, his eyes were dark and his thick hair was shaved at the sides. "It was no snap decision, and that was in my file."

"I haven't seen your file. In fact I didn't know that you were here until a couple of minutes ago."

"Then what do you want?"

"Why'd you cut and run?"

"It was getting squirrely. The SSD guys were flooding Pyongyang—wall to wall. Random stops on the street for ID checks. Hit-and-run squads rousting entire apartment blocks, tossing every square millimeter. Damned near checking your shit before you had the time to flush."

"Looking for you?" Otto asked.

"Looking for anyone."

"When did it start?"

"End of November, beginning of December. Hard to nail down an exact date. But last month it got really intense, so I got out. Almost too late. By the time I got to Mundung-ni—that's in the east on the DMZ about fifteen klicks from the Sea of Japan—half the DPRK Army was waiting."

"For you?"

"For anyone wanting to get across. And I was damned lucky."

"Thanks," Otto said. "I'll get out of your hair now."

"My turn," Kyung-won said. "What's going on in North Korea?"

"I'm not sure."

The NOC started to object, but Otto overrode him.

"I don't know for sure, but I think something pretty big is going on in a number of places," he said.

"Let me guess. Russia, China, Pakistan. The list isn't endless but it's big."

"It's possible."

"Bullshit. It's likely and you guys are scared shitless."

Otto looked at the man for a long moment or two. "Just a suggestion, Larry, but you might want to keep that sort of speculation under your cap for now."

Kyung-won glanced at the open door. He switched on the TV sound with the remote and turned the volume up. "I can be out of here in five or six days. Do I need to disappear?"

Otto hesitated. The agent had damned near nailed it—or at least as far as anyone else had dared to take it to this point. Even Estes, who for all practical purposes was fairly bulletproof behind the walls of academia, hadn't gone any further. He could always plead that he was merely engaged in a philosophical exercise and walk away reasonably clean.

But everyone else was right on the edge of the firing line.

"Maybe not."

"What are you telling me?"

"Maybe we can use your help," Otto said.

"I'm listening," Kyung-won said after a beat.

"Do you know who's in the room next to you?"

"No. But a VIP by the way everyone is pussyfooting around."

"Kirk McGarvey," Otto said.

"No shit?"

"Someone tried to kill him, and damn near succeeded. Far as the media is concerned he's dead for now."

The NOC thought it over. He nodded. "If it's what I think it is—"

"It is."

"Count me in."

EIGHTEEN

□

Franklin's order to McGarvey was simple: Mac was to remain on his stomach for seven days until the skin grafts on his back had a chance to take.

"It's already starting to itch," Mac had said irritably that afternoon.

"That's a good sign. But if you screw it up, we'll have to start from scratch and keep you totally isolated to guard against infection."

"Shit."

"I've told Pete, Otto and Louise the same thing."

"So I'm screwed."

Franklin managed a slight grin. "Totally, Mr. Director," he'd said and went to the door. "The anesthetic is gone from your system. If you behave you can have a beer—one beer—with your dinner."

A mirror had been set up at the head of Mac's bed, so that he could see what was going on without having to roll over. Pete had been with him since dinnertime, and they had mostly avoided talking about anything except for the car bomb, the body of the kid in Atlanta and who al-Daran, if that's who had directed the attack, was working for this time.

They'd only skirted around the why of it, the bigger picture.

Otto and Louise came in.

"How are you two getting along?" Otto asked.

"Franklin let him have a Heineken with his dinner," Pete said.

"Through a straw," McGarvey said.

Otto looked serious, his jaw set, his eyes squinty. "Estes and Ray Pitken have been closeted with the dream team pretty much all day and they don't like what they're coming up with."

"The same as your darlings?"

"Pretty much."

"Did you share with them?" Mac asked.

"Yeah. And I told them about you. We need them, and they promised to keep their mouths shut except when they're in one of their brainstorms."

McGarvey understood where Otto was coming from—the more heads in the mix on an issue, the more likely the outcome would be a good one— but the sessions were always recorded and could be leaked. He said as much to Otto.

"I left a bug behind. My darlings will shut down anything electronic leaving the room. Won't stop someone from the team having a chat with someone outside the group. But for now it's the best I can do."

Lying in bed, even with Pete sitting next to him, McGarvey had been unable to pull his mind away from what he thought was becoming an in- evitable conclusion. The trouble was no matter what scenario he came up with, he could see no favorable endgame.

And for the first time that he could remember he was truly afraid, and it was the same look he was seeing on Otto's face now. They were possi- bly going into something much greater than the both of them.

"If it is al-Daran again he's gotta be working for someone way high up on the food chain," Otto said, but with no conviction.

"Why?" Mac asked.

"There're just too many coincidences piling up, so many similarities leading to a common thread that even my programs are having a hard time digesting them."

"Maybe we're all wrong."

"I don't think so," Otto said. "Do you?"

McGarvey had searched his soul from the moment he'd woken up out of his coma in this bed, and the first startling bit he'd come up with was that he'd been working the issue even before he'd woken up.

Franklin had admitted that patients in a coma could not only hear things but that it was even possible their brains were in a sort of dream state in which some of the logic pathways might still work.

"If you've done a lot of reading all your life, it's possible that your brain will recall entire passages or even whole pages from some long-ago book," he'd said.

Or operational details from times past. The anomalies which for McGarvey had always seemed to point to the truth of a thing.

"No," McGarvey told them. "But I'm have trouble wrapping my head around it."

"Hang on, there's someone I want you to meet," Otto said.

He left and came back almost immediately with the NOC from the next room.

"I was just outside listening to you guys," Kyung-won said. "Bad habit of mine."

Otto introduced him. "He was shot getting out of North Korea."

"It was getting bad up there. No one was safe. Kim Jong-un is nuts, everyone in country knows it, but it got a whole lot worse in the past few months. Everybody went crazy and it happened almost overnight."

"When did it start?" McGarvey asked.

"Late fall. Early winter, maybe."

"November, sometime after the second Tuesday?"

"Could have been," Kyung-won said, but then he suddenly stopped. "You're shitting me, right?"

"I wish I were."

"So North Korea is on board, I can understand that," Otto said. "But I don't think they've got the wherewithal or the balls to go beyond their usual bombast. Certainly not to hire an assassin to take you out."

"I have a history with his father."

"But why take you out?" Otto demanded. He was frustrated. "Why now, goddamnit?"

"Not just them," Mac said. "We need to take a hard look at the others."

"I already have," Otto said, his face falling even further. He explained the lavender that had begun to seriously deepen by the time he got to the number fours in just about every intelligence agency from Britain to Japan, and from Pakistan to North Korea.

"They wanted to take Mac out, which makes him the common thread," Pete responded.

"But a common thread for what?" Louise asked the same question they were all thinking.

"Because Mr. McGarvey is the only one with the background and the balls to figure it out," Kyung-won said.

"Figure out what?" Louise demanded, but McGarvey could see that Otto and the NOC had it.

"November," Pete said. "The election of T. Wallace Weaver as our president."

McGarvey let her finish it for the rest of them.

"During the campaign he promised to nuke Pyongyang if they continued to develop missiles to reach our West Coast. Shut Iran down if they didn't cooperate with us. Stop all aid to Pakistan if they couldn't control their own nuclear weapons. Walk away from Iraq and Afghanistan if they didn't play ball. Stop all aid to Israel if they didn't solve their Palestine problem."

"Finish the Mexican wall," Louise said.

"Blow Assad out of the water if he didn't get his head out," Kyung-won said.

"Stop every Muslim at our borders," Pete said. "Ship every illegal immigrant home."

"Then we start seeing fifty-dollar-a-head lettuce," Louise griped.

"A consortium of medium-ranking intel officers from a lot of countries Weaver has pissed off," Otto said. "But not to assassinate the president, just to discredit him so badly he'd have to be impeached."

McGarvey held his silence.

"A consortium needs a comptroller," Otto said. "An expediter, whose job one was to eliminate Mac."

"We need to find him," Louise said.

"Yes," Pete said. "But what's job two?"

ΠΙΠΕΤΕΕΠ

The stewardess Pastor Buddy had sent to see to Kamal's needs on the short flight to Memphis came aft a few minutes after twelve local. She was an exotic-looking young woman, possibly Persian with sloping eyes and a wide, sensuous mouth, dressed in a sheer blouse and miniskirt.

"Skipper says we'll be touching down in fifteen minutes. Is there anything else I can get for you, sir? Or do?"

"Not for the moment, thanks, luv. But perhaps on another, longer flight?"

She smiled. "It would be my pleasure. Pastor Buddy's top priority is taking care of his honored guests every way possible."

"I'm sure," Kamal said. She went forward and strapped in.

She could have been a clone of the two women who'd come to his luxurious quarters last night. They'd brought a decent bottle of Krug with them, and some Indian *Kama Sutra* positions that even he'd never experienced.

"Pastor Buddy's top priority is taking care of his guests, in every way possible," one of the girls had told him, apparently the standard line among Holliday's people. And it was almost dawn before he'd sent them away and managed to get a few hours sleep.

A limo had taken him to the private airstrip after breakfast where the pastor's fully decked out Gulfstream G280 was waiting to take him anywhere he wanted to go.

"We'll get your rental car back to Denver for you," Buddy told him. "We aim to please our best friends."

"I'll have the first of my security teams to you within a month," Kamal said.

Buddy was startled. "You won't need anybody like that out here. We're perfectly safe."

"After Paris and Brussels and Athens and Tokyo and Orlando and Las Vegas, can you say that anywhere is safe these days?"

"Terrible times."

"I'll feel better sending my financial team in, with more cash, by the way, once their security—and yours and your peoples'—is assured."

"It's not what I expected."

Kamal clapped him on the shoulder. "Trust me, I'm not trying to take over anything of yours. I want to invest in a good bet, is all. And you're the best thing coming down the pike I've seen ever since the dot-com boom."

"You were in on that?"

"I was just a kid, but trust me, I made a killing, an absolute killing, just like I plan to do for both of us here."

Buddy had smiled and nodded and clapped Kamal on the back, for which Kamal almost broke his neck on the spot.

"I'm looking forward to working with you and your people," Buddy said. "Believe me, in Christ's name."

Kamal never bothered to get the Gulfstream crew's names, nor did he bother leaving a tip or even saying thanks or goodbye. They were nothings in his mind. Like the cows who'd come to his room last night, and Pastor Buddy and his staff—just about every one of them drooling at the prospect of fleecing another sucker.

A black Mercedes S550 was waiting for him at the Wilson Air Center across the Memphis airport from the main terminal, courtesy of Pastor Holliday. He only had to show his U.S. driver's license and sign for the car under his Watson identification.

"I may not be able to return the car here," he'd told the accommodating clerk.

"No problem, sir. Let us know where and when, and we'll send a driver."

"Houston. I'll call with the hotel."

All it took was money, something he'd never been without since his parents had moved from Saudi Arabia to Knightsbridge, the upscale area of London. He'd gone to some fine prep schools and then Sandhurst for his military training.

After he'd faked his death, changed his identity and went out on his own as an underground freelancer, it had taken less than eighteen months to make his first million. More came quickly. But not in the dot-com boom as he'd told Pastor Holliday, but by killing people.

Important people, like Bernhardt Schey, the German minister of finance who had almost singlehandedly blocked a major Autobahn rebuilding project. He died when his Audi had mysteriously exploded while he was coming back from the apartment of his mistress.

The project went ahead as planned.

Or the number two man in the DGI, Cuba's intelligence service, who was blackmailing a finance minister trying to block the lucrative U.S. tourist trade. He was shot to death walking along the Malecón with his girlfriend by someone speeding by in a van. The murder was never solved, but the tourist trade deals continued without opposition.

Or bringing down one of the pencil towers in New York, killing a couple dozen billionaires in the building and others on the ground. ISIS had taken the blame for that one, but Kamal—in his one and only failure to date—had been stopped from bringing down a second tower and killing even more people.

Kirk McGarvey, briefly a director of the CIA, but now a shooter for the Company, had been behind that debacle.

The man would not interfere again. Ever.

He made the Loews New Orleans Hotel, across the street from Harrah's Casino, in plenty of time to check in to a suite facing the river, have an early dinner of something called blackened redfish with wild rice—odd, but not bad—with a couple of bottles of extra-cold Pilsner Urquell beer, and get his car back from the valet.

He'd spent some time studying maps and engineering details of the dikes of New Orleans, especially the ones in the southeast side of the Industrial Canal. When the two between Florida and Claiborne avenues had failed during Hurricane Katrina in August 2005, most of the Lower Ninth Ward had been devastated.

The London Avenue Canal, the Seventeenth Street Canal and the Mississippi River–Gulf Outlet Canal had been breached in more than twenty places.

Pumping stations too had suffered major breakdowns, including the Duncan and Bonnabel facilities, as well as all of those in Jefferson and Orleans parishes, which caused the extensive flooding to get even worse.

The destruction of the city had been massive—and even now New Orleans was not back a hundred percent. But the Army Corps of Engineers, responsible for the building and maintenance of the dikes and pumping stations, promised that such a catastrophe would never happen again.

He drove over to the Intracoastal Waterway where State Road 39 crossed over toward St. Bernard Parish, then worked his way back along the south bank of the river on Fifth Street then Fourth and across to the north side on the Huey P. Long Bridge, and past Audubon Park, the Children's Hospital and finally, under I-10 and back into the French Quarter.

The weather was mild, the city was alive, the residents, but especially the tourists, seemed to be optimistic. Cars stopped for people crossing the street. Jazz bands played on corners, and even a funeral procession with about twenty mourners, all on foot following a hearse decorated with flowers, played music and danced and sang.

He had heard about this place, but he'd never experienced anything like it in his life. Despite everything, despite all the calamities the people had suffered—everyone was happy.

But not for long, he told himself back at his hotel. Not much longer at all.

TWENTY

☐

In Moscow it was one in the morning when the bedside telephone of SVR Major Vasili Rankov rang, breaking him out of a dream of the dacha up near Dmitrov he and his wife, Tania, were in the process of buying.

He was the fourth-ranking officer in the intelligence service's Directorate S, a descendant of the old KGB's Directorate One, which planned and directed terrorist and sabotage operations around the world. His division concentrated on North America; Canada and Mexico but especially the U.S.

Catching the phone on the third ring, just as Tania was starting to come awake, he went into the living room of their decent apartment just two blocks from the Bolshoi.

The caller ID was blocked. "*Da*," he said cautiously.

"We may have a problem," the person said in English. But the voice was electronically distorted.

"Tell me," Rankov said, going to the window and looking down at the sparse traffic on the street. There were no obvious surveillance vehicles parked at the curb.

"The primary problem we thought had been solved may still be on the table."

Rankov was a slightly built man for a Russian; his hair was blond and his eyes, which Tania had loved from the first time they'd met, were blue. "I think a Swede got in there before your father," she'd teased.

He didn't care for the joke, nor for some of the others he endured at Moscow University, where he'd studied foreign relations with an emphasis on English-speaking countries. "How do we know you won't turn out defecting to the States?" was one of the common lines.

When he'd been hired by the SVR and enrolled in the Academy of Foreign Intelligence, which was housed in the Science Directorate, everything had changed for the better. He wasn't a rising superstar, but he was on his way up, eventually to a position as an assistant director.

He was slow and steady. Balanced on his feet, on all of his directorate's positions.

"The rumor is out that the original plan didn't materialize as we had hoped."

It was the worst possible news Rankov could be told. The plan was Kirk McGarvey, and he was supposed to be dead. They had to talk in generalities because of the American National Security Agency's telephone intercept program.

"Are you sure?"

"No, goddamnit. For now it's just speculation, but you needed to be given the heads-up in case it's true, and our future shipments must either be changed or canceled."

"That may not be possible."

"Work on it. We all know what's at stake."

"Everything," Rankov said bitterly. His position, the dacha, almost certainly his life and Tania's. "But listen to me, it simply may not be possible to back away. I was given the task, and it is expected that I will succeed. That *we'll* succeed. Do you understand?"

"Don't try to throw me under the bus, you son of a bitch. My neck is out a mile."

Rankov only vaguely understood the Americanisms, but he understood fear when he heard it. His network contact in the National Security Agency was running scared. "Nothing is going to happen on vague rumors."

"Haven't you been listening to me?"

"Too much is at stake to stop now."

"You don't understand. None of you sons of bitches ever understood, except for one."

"Enough," Rankov said. "If and when you have something definitive for me, call again, otherwise we will continue as planned. Even Riyadh is still on board, and they have the most to lose."

"I'll call the others, you limp-dicked cocksucker."

"Don't call me again with speculation," Rankov said. "Only with facts." He hung up.

For a long time he stood staring out the window. It was still cold in Moscow. Spring was coming late. But nothing could be as cold as the feeling in his heart.

What they were doing was monstrous, even though it had the tacit approval of just about every government official in both hemispheres. Nothing like this had ever been done in history. Hadn't even been contemplated, to his knowledge.

He leaned his forehead against the cool window glass.

"Vasha," Tania said from the bedroom door. "Is everything okay?"

He turned and managed a smile. "I was dreaming about the future."

She shook her head. "It's only a dacha. It's not the end of the world."

Air Force Brigadier General Walter Echo changed into a civilian blazer and khaki slacks before he left his office on the Pentagon's D Ring a few minutes after five in the afternoon, and got in his car and drove over to the Watergate's Next Whisky Bar.

The word was circulating that McGarvey might not be dead after all and it was the most frightening thing he'd ever heard since Lieutenant Colonel Moses Chambeau had come to him in August last year with his just-speculating scenario.

Chambeau, who worked in the Defense Intelligence Agency as an analyst, was one of the people assessing not only strength, orders of battle and deployments of foreign military forces, but the civilian and military leaderships' willingness to commit to engagement.

He was married to Echo's sister, Jen, a certified bitch who'd always been a thorn in the family's side. And Echo had gone out of his way to give thanks to the hapless bastard who'd taken her off everyone's hands.

In addition, Chambeau was bright: Harvard-educated with a PhD in the works for the past five years.

"The problem is our new president," Chambeau had said at their August meeting.

"We have three months."

"The bastard's going to win, and everyone knows it."

Echo had spread his hands. They were in his office just before lunch. "Your point?"

"My threat board is lighting up like a fucking Christmas tree. No one wants the bastard to become our president. No one."

"A few tens of millions of Americans might disagree with them— whoever the *them* are."

"You know what I'm talking about, Walt."

"No, I don't."

"When he's elected we need to be ready for the consequences."

Echo remembered that precise moment.

He would always remember it, because it was the instant that he had become, if nothing else, a complicit traitor. He'd not had his brother-in-law arrested on the spot. "What consequences?"

"The military consequences," Chambeau said. "And we need to be prepared."

It was just the start of the cocktail hour, and the Next Whisky Bar was filling up. Susan Fischer, who was a signals intelligence supervisor with the National Security Agency, was working on her first martini when Echo showed up.

"Hi, Walt," she said. "You seen the latest?"

Echo sat next to her and ordered them both another martini. She was a friend of his brother-in-law's and probably sleeping with him. She was a lush but she was bright. "No, what?"

"Merkel has canceled her Washington trip to meet with Weaver."

"Happens."

"You don't understand. Weaver personally called Deutsche Welle and asked who the hell needs her. Called her the most weak-in-the-knees leader in Germany's history. Couldn't make up her mind on the immigration issue." Susan shook her head. "Christ, he called her a 'typical cunt.'"

"Your point is?" Echo asked, even though he knew exactly what point she was making.

"You know exactly what I'm talking about. We can't stop now, or do you have cold feet?"

"You're talking about treason."

The woman shook her head. "Not me, Walt. Us."

PART
TWO

Leak
April

□

It was drizzling when McGarvey showed up at the front gate of Camp Peary, the CIA training facility near Williamsburg, and presented his pass and ID. He was driving a battered old Toyota SUV that Pete had come up with, and was dressed in faded jeans, an old sweatshirt, a dirty black nylon jacket and a baseball cap to hide the nearly bald patch on the back of his head.

He hadn't shaved or cut his hair since the assassination attempt and he looked like a street bum, but his papers were in order.

"Just a minute, sir, I don't have you on my list," the civilian guard said. He went into the gatehouse, while another security officer, also dressed in BDUs, stood to one side, his hand on a Heckler & Koch compact submachine gun slung over his shoulder.

McGarvey's papers identified him as Damon West, an unassigned officer in the Clandestine Service, Marty Bambridge's signature forged. He was an NOC come out of the cold.

"I need to get back in shape," he'd told Pete two days ago.

She and Louise thought it was way too soon.

"The time is right," Otto said. "Everyone's gone to ground for now."

"Maybe they quit," Louise suggested.

"They're waiting for me to show up or waiting for someone to finally come up with the proof I'm dead," McGarvey had said.

He'd felt increasingly irascible in the hospital, especially in the past eight or ten days. He'd wanted out, but Franklin had held him back. And so had Pete. And more than once he had almost lashed out at them.

"Well, you're not going to show up," Pete had told him two days ago, once he was out. "At least not right now. Otto's handling everything as if it were a cyber crime."

"It won't be that easy," McGarvey had shot back.

"You're not ready."

"Nor will I ever be sitting here on my ass."

They were meeting for pizzas and beer at Otto's safe house in McLean. Larry Kyung-won and Estes had joined them.

"I'm surprised Franklin let you off the reservation," Kyung-won said.

"He didn't," McGarvey said. "What about you? I'd have thought Marty would have snagged you for something?"

"Training officer at the Farm."

"When do you start?"

"Last week," Kyung-won said. "And I know exactly what you're going to say next. But you won't be given any recognition nor will anyone cut you any slack."

"What the hell are you talking about?" Pete demanded.

"I'm going to the Farm to get my edge back," McGarvey said.

"Franklin won't approve it."

"He'll have to find me first."

"Why, goddamnit?"

"Because this won't stop unless we do something," Estes said. He'd just come from Langley after thirty-six hours straight and he looked pale, his eyes bloodshot, like he'd been cramming for a difficult final.

Pete had looked away, and McGarvey had touched her hand. "When it's over we'll take a vacation."

"No place will be safe," she said bitterly.

"Not until we make it safe," McGarvey had said, and sitting at the gate waiting for his credentials and pass to be checked, he realized again how silly he'd actually sounded.

His wife, Katy, in a frustrated moment, had called him a Don Quixote. And he supposed in a large measure she was right. But it's what he was— what he'd become in the past twenty years.

The guard came out of the gatehouse and handed McGarvey's papers back to him. "Mr. Salem is waiting for you up at Admin. Would you like an escort, or do you know the way?"

"Big building, flag in front."

"Yes, sir."

The gate opened and McGarvey drove up through the woods toward the administrative area called the Hill, where the offices, dorms, dispensary, dining hall, supply and weapons maintenance facilities, plus the classrooms and mock prisons for interrogations, including waterboarding, were clustered.

The physical training portions of the facility were sprawled throughout the mostly heavily wooded tracts along the York River. Firing ranges for a wide variety of weapons including simulated ground-to-air man-held missiles, like the U.S. Stinger, the U.K. Javelin and the Russian Grail; sniper rifles, like the Barrett; more than three dozen different handguns, long guns, submachine guns; and even compact missile throwers—such as ultra-lightweight compound bows—were scattered here and there.

Other areas were used for hand-to-hand-combat training, day-and-night infiltration and ex-filtration exercises, explosives from flash-bang grenades to the latest iterations of Semtex as well as homemade explosives, including a number using various off-the-shelf fertilizers.

A mock town was used for urban exercises.

A Boeing 747 was used for hijacking situations—both the prevention and the commission of.

A series of very small clearings were used for HALO—High Altitude Low Opening—precision parachute drops.

Sections of the river were used for surface and subsurface operations.

And the entire facility was crisscrossed with confidence trails, from those that could be completed in a leisurely half-hour walk, to others that could take an entire evening. And one, the Ball Buster, that was only ever completed by less than 10 percent of those who tried. It was so bad that failure carried no shame, while simply trying was a badge of honor.

Salem, who'd retired early to take the job running the Farm, had been a Navy SEAL captain who'd never quite been able to come in from field operations despite more than a dozen reprimands from his superior officers.

"High ranks belong behind desks," he'd been told more than once. "You're too fucking valuable to have your ass shot off."

He was the only one at the camp, other than Kyung-won, who knew Mac's real identity, and he had promised no special favors. Plus he was not aware that Kyung-won and McGarvey knew each other.

"You'll train when we train, eat when we eat, sleep when we sleep," Salem had said last night on the phone.

"And shit when we shit," McGarvey said. "I know."

"You're an NOC in from the cold, here for retraining."

"I need one week, and I'll be using a secure phone."

"Fine with me, so long as Otto sets it up."

Salem was waiting in the day room and he brought Mac back to his office without a word. He was a slightly built, mild-looking man, in his midforties. Bright blue eyes, short cropped hair, very neat; a long way from how he looked as a SEAL in the field.

"Appreciate the help, Bob," Mac said.

"Franklin know that you're here?"

"Not yet. Neither does Marty, and I want to keep it that way as long as possible."

They sat across Salem's desk from each other.

"Okay, Mac, I don't know what this is all about, and I don't want to know beyond the likelihood it has something to do with whoever tried to kill you. That and you look like shit."

"That'll be useful," Mac said. "I'm for retraining. But I'm a sanctimonious prick who needs to be brought down a peg."

Salem had to laugh. "Old enough to be a grandfather to most of these kids. And once they find out that you were an NOC they'll want to take a shot at you."

McGarvey took out the satphone Otto had set up for him, punched in a seven-character alphanumeric code, hit TALK and set it on the desk. "This is defeating any eavesdropping attempts."

"We're clean in here."

"I wanted to make sure because there's probably a leak somewhere in the Company. Possibly here."

Salem was impressed. "Do you think they'll try to hit you again?"

McGarvey nodded. "It's the real reason I'm here."

TWENTY-TWO

Pastor Buddy's Gulfstream touched down at the private airfield outside Kerr-ville, Texas, just before three in the afternoon. Kamal thanked the crew, got his single bag and walked across to the terminal.

Even before he went inside, the jet had turned around and was trun-dling toward the end of the runway for immediate takeoff to Kansas City for its annual inspection and scheduled maintenance.

The additional $150,000 Kamal had handed over to the pastor three weeks ago had given him practically free rein over the aircraft and his own expansive condo and staff—this time three Asian girls. More important, the money, with promises of much more to come, had guaranteed his anonymity.

For the last thirty days Kamal had holed up at the church, attending services, which were like crude farces to him, and occasionally going into the amusement park, which was even worse, with mindless mommies and daddies and kiddies herded from one attraction to the other like cattle. But between endless dinners and drunken orgies he had spent a lot of late eve-nings and early mornings on the computer dividing his time between a half-dozen hacker sites.

But the information he was coming up with was to this point anything but comforting. It was possible that McGarvey was not dead.

He'd let his beard and hair grow, and dressed now in jeans and a white shirt and a blazer he looked like a college professor, an academic.

"Mr. Watson." A clean-shaven, slender man dressed in shorts, a white T-shirt and baseball cap came over, his hand extended. He was smiling. "Welcome."

The waiting room was empty except for a woman behind the counter, and two men in an office behind glass.

Kamal was surprised, but he shook hands. "Mr. Shadid?"

"Friends call me Joe. I'm sure that I don't look like you thought I would."

"No."

"But then this is Texas and one of my jobs is publicity director for the center—which these days is a tough sell."

Shadid took Kamal's bag and outside they got into a white van, Shadid behind the wheel. The logo on the side read THE KERRVILLE CENTER FOR ISLAMIC STUDIES.

"Quite an advertisement."

"Nothing we could do about it. The locals don't want us here, though we've never been bothered. But we have to let them know who we are. Thank Allah we don't have to use the term madrassa, or we'd be in a serious world of shit."

Kamal thought he'd made a mistake coming here like this, even though his homework six months ago had led him to believe that he'd find what he was looking for. Out here, in the open, anyone taking a look saw no artifice. Nothing obvious. Just a school for Muslims.

"Do you like country and western?" Shadid asked as they pulled away.

"No."

Shadid turned on the CD player, music suddenly blasting from the speakers. "Random white noise in the background," he shouted. "Defeats their surveillance equipment."

"Who's watching you?"

"The FBI out of San Antonio, of course. Homeland Security. County mounties. Local cops. Just about every son of a bitch out here with a Bible and a rifle—which includes just about every white male."

For the first time in his life Kamal was at a loss for words. He was always in charge. But this wasn't what he'd expected. He had made a very large mistake. This place was a dead end, as was Pastor Buddy's operation. By tonight he would be long gone from here, and within twenty-four hours he would go deep to rethink everything that had been contaminated.

"It's not what you're thinking," Shadid said, glancing at him.

They headed out into the hill country toward the west—away from the town, and from the busy interstate highway.

"You're the fourth man with facial hair I've picked up at the airport in the past two days. The other three brought their sons, but perhaps you're here to visit yours."

"What are you talking about?"

"You're just another visitor."

Kamal didn't reply.

"Does the name Major Sa'ad al-Sakr mean anything to you?"

"No," Kamal said, hiding his shock. He'd thought of himself as a professional. It was one of the only reasons he was still alive or not behind bars somewhere. But he'd been caught now.

"He said that you or someone like you might show up one of these days. So that when you got onto our website we weren't surprised. In fact we looked forward to your coming."

"I don't know the name."

"He was your control officer. GIP. But he's dead now. Shot by a firing squad and buried that night, of course."

The General Intelligence Presidency was Saudi Arabia's CIA. And Sa'ad had been Kamal's control officer for the pencil tower operation last year in New York. One that had gone wrong in the end, so it was no surprise that the man, who'd been a distant relative of the royal family, had been executed.

Plausible deniability always came first before human life.

"The questions are, of course, what do you want and why have you come to us?"

Kamal took the Glock 29 Gen4 subcompact pistol from under his jacket and pointed it at Shadid. The pistol was small but reliable and fired a 10mm round.

"You're going to drop me off at a car rental agency, and if any of your people try to follow me, I will kill them. I'm going to disappear and you'll do nothing about it."

"Don't be stupid. If we'd sold out to the FBI your ass would have been nailed once you landed."

"I'm not a patient man."

"We were told that you were primarily a European operator. Well, this is the U.S. Different rules, a different game. Actually I'm surprised you got this far."

Kamal laid the muzzle against Shadid's side, just under the armpit.

Someone rose up in the backseat and placed the muzzle of a pistol against the back of his head.

Kamal began to squeeze the trigger.

"That won't be necessary, Karim," Shadid said. "Mr. Watson is here seeking our assistance with Allah's work."

Kamal eased up and the pistol was taken away from his head.

"You may stay with us in complete safety for as long as need be," Shadid said. "I assume that you came here searching for soldiers of God."

"I need to speak with the imam."

"I am he," Shadid said. "And believe me when I tell you that we have been waiting for a very long time for this opportunity."

The hidden tunnel from the subbasement of the sprawling madrassa led nearly one mile out into the scrub brush.

Upstairs on the main floors of the complex, students were taught the Quran as well as Sharia law versus ordinary American law. Guest groups in diversity classes from high schools as far away as San Antonio, Houston and Dallas–Fort Worth were bused in to learn the slight differences between Islam and Christianity.

To Muslims, Christ was an important prophet and Mary—Miriam— was equally important.

But in the rat warren of interconnecting dark spaces at the end of the tunnel, young boys and girls were taught realities: infiltration of buildings and airports and shipping terminals, weapons use, bomb making, detonating devices, secret codes, rendezvous points and creating an entire host of false documents.

But mostly they were taught the willingness and resolve to die.

TWENTY-THREE

The rain at seven in the morning was steady and cold. McGarvey, along with six other CIA recruits—one of them a female ex-marine—in the second half of their training evolution stood in an open field across from their hand-to-hand instructor, retired SEAL chief Leonard Kaiser.

They were dressed alike in BDUs, except for the chief, who wore the trousers and boots, but only a T-shirt and no cover for his bald head. He was built like a fireplug, and did not appear to mind the weather.

"Mr. West has recently come out of the field to join us for a bit of freshening up," the chief said. "I expect that he'll share with us all a few tricks he learned in badland. How long were you out there?"

"A few years off and on," McGarvey said.

"Russia?"

McGarvey nodded.

"And what was your exact mission?"

McGarvey said nothing.

The others were looking at him with curiosity, and a degree of cockiness now that they had got this far. He had at least twenty-five years on the oldest of them. But the woman was appraising him as if she'd seen him somewhere. Him or his type. He was an NOC, the real deal, and every one of them wanted to give him a try. It was obvious from their expressions.

"The gentleman teaches us the first rule in this business," the chief said. "Keep your mouths shut."

They were a thousand yards above the York River, and the only sounds this morning came from one of the long-gun ranges on the other side of the hill toward Admin. They could have been on another planet, certainly not so close to civilization. Williamsburg was only ten miles away.

"I understand that you were injured getting out. Are you here as an observer?"

"I'm here to get my edge back," McGarvey said.

"Okay, let's see," the chief said. He motioned for McGarvey to come forward.

Salem had taken him through the jackets of the instructors as well as support staff, but nothing had jumped out at him.

"Might help if you told me what you were looking for," Salem said. "Specifically."

"Someone who doesn't fit the profile."

"Looking for you?"

"Maybe," McGarvey had said.

"Well, it isn't Len Kaiser. I've known the man for ten years, and I'd vouch for him with my life." Salem shook his head. "If you're going to hurt someone, don't make it him. Okay?"

"I'm not here to hurt anyone. I'm here to find out who knows that I'm still alive and wants me dead."

"That include me?" Salem asked.

McGarvey had laughed. "Especially you, Bob."

And it was obvious that Salem didn't know if McGarvey was kidding or not.

McGarvey, his hands at his sides, stopped within arm's length of the chief.

"Are you prepared to defend yourself?" Kaiser asked.

"Yes."

The chief suddenly lashed out with a karate chop.

McGarvey simply batted the man's hand away, as if he were doing nothing more than swatting an insect.

The chief danced back a step and hooked a foot behind McGarvey's left ankle right at the prosthesis joint and pulled hard as he slid in the opposite direction.

Mac went down, and he remained for just an instant as if the wind had been knocked out of him, until the chief made the mistake of coming in for the disabling move.

It was almost as if they had rehearsed the dance in order to give the others a chance to learn that a man with a peg leg wouldn't have to be a liability in the field.

McGarvey rolled away as the chief's boot was coming toward his head, using his false leg as a lever to deflect the kick and upend the ex-SEAL, sending the man to the ground.

In an instant, McGarvey was on top of the chief, the muzzle of his Walther pressed against the man's forehead.

The chief relaxed, a big smile on his face. "You're not supposed to be carrying in this exercise."

"I take a shower with my gun," Mac said. "Hoorah."

"That's marines."

"Close enough," McGarvey said. He got up and held out a hand for the chief.

The recruits were looking at him, their mouths half-open. McGarvey's left pant leg was up to the knee beneath which was where the prosthesis was attached to the stump. A fair amount of blood had soaked the fabric and had run down his plastic leg.

The chief shrugged. "Make use of all of your assets all of the time," he said. "I wouldn't have been a bit surprised if Mr. West hadn't taken off his peg leg and tried to beat me to death with it."

McGarvey pulled down his pants leg and went back in line.

"People, you are here to make mistakes. Learn from them."

Salem came over to the dispensary after McGarvey's stump had been bandaged. He brought a couple of Heinekens with him.

"Kaiser's never heard of you, so naturally he thinks that you're a ringer, though he can't figure out why you're here."

"He's a good man," McGarvey said. The drapes were drawn around the cubicle, and he was the only patient there. He took a pull from the bottle. "Did you call Franklin?"

"Are you kidding me?" Salem said. "He'd have my ass and so would you. But it's worse than that."

"Pete called?"

"Yeah, I just got off the phone with her. She's a tough woman to say no to."

"Tell me about it. What'd you tell her?"

"The truth."

"She coming down here?"

"No," Salem said.

McGarvey was relieved that he wouldn't have to deal with her, and yet he had mixed feelings. "Anyway, I'm out of here first thing in the morning. Light duty for a couple of days. I might even limp a little around the Ball Buster tomorrow."

Salem took out a tablet and handed it to Mac. Several photos of the woman in the hand-to-hand class this morning were on the screen.

"Marine Lieutenant Grace Metal, and trust me, her last name pretty well fits the bill. She got out of the corps two years ago and finished up her law degree at Maryland in one year."

"When did she join the CIA?"

"She applied last year, but she was fast-tracked and accepted one month later."

"Who'd she know?"

"No idea, except that she was working on Weaver's campaign and took a bye until two weeks ago, and she was assigned to me."

McGarvey stared at her photographs for a long time, several random thoughts flitting through his head, though none of them made any sense. They were just feelings. Hunches. Vague guesstimates.

"Something standing out in your mind?" Salem asked.

McGarvey handed the tablet back. "She was the only woman in our group, and she looked like a hardass."

"And?"

"Nothing."

When Salem was gone McGarvey phoned Otto with the woman's name and what little background he'd gotten from Salem.

"She might be the one gunning for you?" Otto asked.

"Probably not, but something's there," McGarvey said. "How's Pete?"

Otto laughed. "Ready to storm the castle, but she'll hold for now."

TWENTY-FOUR

The high-desert camp was located in a valley thirty miles north of the tiny Mexican town of Ricardo Flores Magon, two hundred miles south of El Paso. ISIS-U.S. leased the five thousand acres from the Sinaloa drug cartel, in exchange for free passage rights for product to and from the poppy fields of Afghanistan.

Kamal stood inside a tent, the flap open, looking out at the apparently deserted training facility as night deepened. The two dozen shelters were hidden under camouflage netting, as were two satellite dishes—one for communications and the other to track the one U.S. satellite that passed over this spot on a random basis, spot-checking for drug-smuggling activities.

Saudi GIP Captain Ayman Baz, who was the camp commandant, came up behind Kamal. He was a short man with a paunch who was stuck out here in this deep-cover shit hole of an assignment because he couldn't claim one drop of royal blood.

"We're getting pretty good at taking shelter just before the bird comes up over the horizon in the west."

Kamal had been here three days and this was the first time they'd been alerted to a satellite passage. He was impressed. "What about the generator? It has to throw out a lot of heat."

"We have two guys whose only job is to shut it down, and toss a couple of thermal blankets over it, especially around the exhaust vent."

"How often does this happen?"

"This is the second time this month for us. And it's only overhead for less than four minutes."

Kamal turned around. The moment he'd gotten here by car from El Paso he'd known something was terribly wrong, and he had almost turned around on the spot and left. The captain was a drunk who had been sent here and ordered to remain.

"Sooner or later someone is bound to make a mistake," he'd said.

"We've been here a year," Baz responded.

"Riyadh would cut you loose. Admitting to the presence of a Saudi operation down here would damned near be a declaration of war."

"My legend, including my passport, is Syrian. I'm an expendable. Just like you." Baz lit a cigarette with unsteady hands. "Anyway, this is war, or are you here for something else?"

Kamal was struck as he had been in Texas at the training camp for ISIS sympathizers that despite his planning, his tradecraft, things were starting to spin out of control. Shadid had known about him or at least had expected him to show up sooner or later, and so had Captain Baz.

"I have three missions."

"Yes, you've told me, and I have come up with just the boys and girls to do your business." Baz looked away. "Stupid, actually, but this was the major's operation from start to finish. No way out for any of us, he told me. But then, he chose us well—there never was a way out for me."

"You could have gone to the Americans. They would have taken you in trade for your intel."

"Sa'ad warned me about that too. He assured me that the White House had always looked the other way when it came to Saudi Arabia. Even after nine/eleven. I would have been on the first flight to Riyadh. Ended up the same way the major did."

Baz made no sense to him. "Then why did you agree to come here? What were you offered?"

"You didn't know?"

"No."

"The lives of my wife and two children. They were allowed to come to the States eighteen months ago."

"Where?"

"I don't know."

"But here you stay."

Baz shook his head. "Suppose they aren't already dead. Suppose I found them somehow. Where would we go?"

"Disappear."

"That takes money," the captain said. "As long as we hold out here, they're safe. And, who knows, maybe in the end you'll find a way out for us."

Kamal wasn't about to dignify the remark, but Baz wasn't through.

"I know your face. I have your fingerprints, your saliva. I know what you're planning to do."

Kamal smiled. His face was not on record in any intel database, nor were his prints or DNA. The only man on earth he had any respect for was possibly out there somewhere. But even if he was still alive, he must have been severely injured in the car bomb. No threat.

And yet.

"If we succeed, I will arrange for you to find your family and go someplace where no one will find you."

"It's a trade, then?"

"Yes, a trade," Kamal said.

Baz started to turn away, but then turned back. "Most of these kids think they're going to paradise."

"But not all of them?" Kamal asked.

"No."

"Then why do the nonbelievers do it? Why Paris and Brussels and Tokyo?"

"They're nuts," Baz said.

Of the sixty-seven martyrs for Allah who were currently in training, three had been to San Francisco, two had been to New Orleans and just about all of them had heard of western Kansas and had a vague idea what it was like.

Which was remarkable to Kamal, because all but three of them were American born, graduates of high schools mostly throughout the Midwest, many of them from Minneapolis. Yet they knew more about the history of Islam than they did about the thirteen colonies, the Constitution and Bill of Rights, and more about the geography of the Middle East than of the U.S.

"We're not wiring explosive vests to geniuses," Baz had said.

And it was the same thing Shadid had told him: "The smart ones know better."

Kamal didn't bother with the names of the three who had been to San Francisco—two stocky girls in their late teens and one boy with thin eyebrows who the girls thought was handsome—but when they came into the conference tent he had them take a look at a highway map of the city and its surroundings.

"Can you find the Golden Gate Bridge?" he asked.

One of the girls looked up as if she thought Kamal was an idiot. She stabbed a finger on the bridge. "Do you want us to blow it up?" she demanded.

She was angry, and Kamal figured that she had no real idea why. "That's exactly what I want you to do."

The young man, probably in his late twenties, grinned. "No shit?"

Kamal powered up his cell phone and connected it with the Power-Point app to a computer that projected images on a small whiteboard just off the end of the table.

He showed the camper van and the explosives packed inside, the approaches and center span of the bridge at rush hour, and a detailed street map showing the location of a long-term private parking garage a few blocks from St. Mary's Cathedral off Gough Street.

"You will shave your beard, take off your burkas and dress as ordinary Americans," Kamal said.

"What is an ordinary American?" the girl whose name was Lamia asked.

"A Christian," Kamal said. "Take a taxi to within two blocks of the church, walk to the camper and drive directly to the bridge, where you will detonate the explosives. Do you see any difficulty in these instructions?"

"No."

The second girl had held her silence to this point. "I will do this as a Muslim!" she shouted.

"Or not at all?"

"Yes."

Kamal pulled out his pistol and shot her in the middle of the forehead. "We will strike a blow for Mohammed," he said. "A blow for justice."

Lamia and the young man looked like they had just slipped into some realm of insanity. They had become untouchable.

Baz appeared at the open tent flap.

"I have my first soldiers of God," Kamal said. "Bring me the next team."

TWENTY-FIVE

□

Major Rankov left his office a few minutes before noon and reached Yase-nevo Park on foot thirty minutes later.

He took care with his tradecraft, checking for reflections in store windows of someone behind him. Turning suddenly and crossing one of the wide boulevards in an effort to catch someone in a SUV or sedan tailing him. Entering buildings and passing straight through to a rear exit.

At twenty after the hour he entered the Yasanevsky Cemetery, where he mingled with a few people visiting the graves of loved ones, finally coming out from the west gate and across to the arched entrance to the park.

A hundred meters inside the park, GRU-Spetsnaz Lieutenant Colonel Mikhail Mazayev, dressed in civilian clothes, sat on a park bench feeding pigeons corn from a small paper bag. Like Rankov he could have passed for an American, and in fact he had taken his degree in international studies at Stanford, where he'd perfected his accent and idiomatic English.

He didn't look like a spy, and especially not a spymaster in charge of agents serving in the military attaché departments at the Russian embassy in Washington and the UN in New York.

To Rankov, who'd known him since the Academy of Foreign Intelligence, where they were students just one year apart, Mazayev looked more like a Wall Street banker than anything else, with his two-thousand-dollar Western tailored suits.

"Did you have any trouble getting away?" Mazayev asked in English.

"No. You?"

Mazayev shook his head. "But I think the situation is coming to a head. It would mean that our positions could be in jeopardy."

"We've always known that was a possibility. But what makes you think so this time?"

Mazayev didn't answer for a minute or two, concentrating on feeding the birds that were flocked at his feet. The day was cool, the sky overcast, and a sharp breeze came from the east. All the way from Siberia, the unbidden thought came into his head.

"I've been getting glimmerings of something else going on, and it's got my people running around in circles."

"What glimmerings?" Rankov asked.

"One of your Political Intelligence people thinks that there may have been some sort of a secret meeting in Beijing sometime in the past year."

"Who was it?"

"I can't tell you yet, we need to keep this thing compartmentalized if we're to have any chance of keeping our heads intact. But there may have been at least three people, possibly intel reps supposedly from Washington."

Rankov was confused. "What do you mean, *supposedly?*"

"I've talked to people I know and trust, and to a man they deny that any such meeting could ever have taken place. They were certain of it."

"But?"

"My SVR contact says that the meeting did in fact take place at a small hotel just off Tiananmen Square. But the point is, a foreigner, possibly French, possibly English or even American, showed up, stayed less than ten minutes and left."

"Who was it?"

"Unknown, but he was probably a professional. He lost his tail within one block of the hotel, and afterwards disappeared without a trace."

"Not one of ours."

"No one from the Consortium," Mazayev said. "Which makes me think that something is going on we know nothing about."

Rankov was worried now. "When you say *something,* are you implying that this meeting could have concerned us?"

"Yes. It's likely that someone else may be trying to accomplish the same thing we are."

"I'm not following you."

"Our people never left New York," Mazayev said. "They're still there."

Something terribly cold clutched at Rankov's chest. "They did make it to Florida but they failed. McGarvey may have survived."

"I've heard the same thing. But that's the point, Vasha, our people didn't do it. Someone else tried to assassinate the man, but may not know they failed."

"I was warned that we had to shut down at least for now. No more exchanges of information," Rankov said.

"I should fucking hope so. Until now this has just been an exercise in sharing on the old-boys network."

"With one goal."

"Yes. To discredit Weaver. The man's a buffoon. If he isn't reined in, he could get us into a shooting war that'd make al-Qaeda and ISIS minor pinpricks."

Rankov looked away.

The Consortium, as just about everyone involved was calling the movement, had started with an American general by the name of Echo in the Pentagon who'd called his counterpart on the German chief of staff's G2 section to chat about the upcoming election. It was before Weaver was thought to have any reasonable chance of winning the presidency.

The discussion group—completely off the record—spread to the DGSE, France's foreign intelligence service, then to Greece and Italy, and from there the Russian Federation in the person of Mazayev.

To this point nearly three dozen mid-level intelligence personnel—mostly military officers—had become involved.

They had discussed but soundly rejected the notion of assassinating the U.S. president, and therefore making a martyr of him.

Finally they had agreed that the best approach would be to share information that when made public could make Weaver look like a complete idiot in the geopolitical arena.

Like his calling Merkel the most weak-in-the-knees leader in Germany's history. Or cutting off aid to Israel—*let the Jews take care of themselves for a change!* Or claiming that Putin was a homosexual. Or cutting off all business with Mexico and freezing their U.S. accounts until a wall was built on the southern border paid for with confiscated funds.

And a dozen other real and manufactured gaffes.

Individually any of it would have made little or no difference in the international arena or especially in the States. But over the long haul, Weaver would come across as a president who had no idea what he was doing, and never had.

It was political sabotage at the crudest level.

But the one sticking point from the beginning had been Kirk McGarvey, the former director of the CIA, and for several years the chief troubleshooter for the White House. If he came down on the side of the president—which the common consensus said was likely—he could bring down the entire plot starting with one name at a time.

He had his own old-boys network—none of whom was in the Consortium. If he started contacting them with questions, everything could fall apart.

The opinion was unanimous that job one was to eliminate McGarvey.

"If not us, then who tried to kill him?" Rankov said.

"I don't know, but we'd better find out soon," Mazayev said.

"Why?"

Mazayev started to reply, but then held off.

"Let whoever it is try again."

"We don't know their agenda."

"Who cares, as long as they're doing what we want done? We'll put out some feelers. Find out who this Englishman or Frenchman is."

"And?"

"Help him, of course," Rankov said. "Send one of our people from New York."

"We don't need them this time," Mazayev said. "We have someone at the CIA's training facility."

"Why there?"

"We're told that if McGarvey actually did survive, he'd probably show up down there. He could end up as the victim of a training accident. Happens from time to time."

"Is our asset any good?"

"One of the best, I'm told."

TWENTY-SIX

□

McGarvey was strapping on his peg leg just before ten in the evening when the on-duty nurse came in.

"Going somewhere?" she asked. Her name was Meade. She was a navy medic who'd been assigned to the Farm three years ago. She was short and thin, and looked as if a light breeze would knock her over. But she was tough, and everyone here—instructors and students alike—had a great deal of respect for her.

"I'm going for a run."

"I'll make a deal with you. Get back in bed and I'll bring you a beer. I might even bring two and have one with you."

McGarvey pulled down his pants leg, stuck the Walther in the holster at the small of his back and pulled on his BDU blouse.

Meade blocked the doorway. "Doc wants you here for another twenty-four hours."

"I haven't tried the Ball Buster yet," McGarvey said. He gave her a peck on the cheek and pushed past her.

"Goddamnit," Meade said. "If I have to call the CO, I will."

"Do it."

McGarvey went out the front way and headed in an easy lope toward the start of the A course—the Ball Buster—on the crest of a wooded hill about a quarter mile away.

He'd told Salem what he was going to do tonight, and asked that word got out. But quietly. "We don't want to make this a full-page ad."

"If you think someone is going to come after you, we can put up a surveillance drone. Infrareds will be easy to sort out, as cold as it it'll be. Give you the heads-up."

"Someone would find out," McGarvey said. "That's what we train them to do. Think outside of the box. I'm doing this alone."

"Good luck," Salem had said.

"Thanks."

"No, I meant for the other guy. Try not to kill him."

"I'm the one with the peg leg. Anyway, I just want to ask a couple of questions."

"Yeah."

The A course which ran just under five miles, twisted and turned its way through the Farm. A lot of it was uphill, on narrow paths covered in deep sand or loose gravel or even layers of slate, each piece about the size of a paperback book, and slippery even when it wasn't raining.

Some of it pushed through dense undergrowth with sharp brambles; the only way through was on the belly, the same as for the swamps and other water hazards on the path, which were covered with thick logs or rusty metal culverts with sharp edges and coated with slick slime.

Two sections overlooking the river had to be fast-roped down fifty-foot drops, while in another place the trainee had to climb one hundred feet into a tree with only irregular handholds and drop, almost like a flying squirrel, to the branches of an adjacent tree and make it to the ground without breaking any important bones.

One quarter-mile section was to be run in under two minutes—usually with a full pack. An automatic timer lit up when the trainee crossed the starting point, and flashed the time at the finish line.

By that point most trainees had trouble even walking it in under five minutes.

At the top of the first cliff down to the river, McGarvey knew that he wasn't alone on the course, and he pulled up short and doubled over on his hands on his knees as if he were trying to catch his breath. His stump burned as if hot coals had been poured into the socket, and he thought that he was bleeding again.

He listened for several long seconds, but there was nothing, though he was sure that he'd heard the sound of footfalls on loose gravel, and perhaps the swish of a branch.

It had stopped raining and the breeze had died down so that sounds were not dampened.

Mac stepped to the cliff's edge, his back toward the way he'd just come, and to where whoever was following him could see a tempting target. Two ropes were rigged for the descent.

Someone was watching from the darkness. He could almost feel their presence.

He held his position as a chance breeze kicked up behind him for just a moment and then died. But he'd smelled something.

Sweet. Almost cloying. Familiar.

Gun oil.

McGarvey pushed off the edge of the cliff, swiveling one-eighty as he fell, grabbing one of the fast ropes with his right hand before he got five feet.

For just an instant the rope held but then it came loose or parted above and he started to fall again.

His left foot snagged on a small outcropping of rock, the sudden pain slamming up through his stump to his hip, but then he pushed to the left with every ounce of his strength and managed to grab the second rope, nearly dislocating his shoulder before he pulled up short.

Mindless of the pain he scrambled up to the top of the cliff, where he immediately rolled over and jumped to his feet.

Grace Metal, the former marine lieutenant, stood at the edge of the cliff, half in a crouch, her eyes wide as if she were a deer caught in headlights.

"You goddamned near bought it," she said, her voice just above a whisper.

"It was you behind me," McGarvey said, pulling out his pistol.

He was on her in two steps and she backed off, her hands outstretched.

"Wait," she said, still whispering.

"Who are you working for?"

"You don't understand. There was someone else about fifty feet behind you. I don't know who it is, but I saw him follow you from the clinic."

"I asked, who are you working for?"

She batted the pistol away, and shouldered into Mac's chest, knocking him off balance long enough for her to try to kick his bad leg out from under him.

Mac stepped out of the way, and smashed the handle of his pistol onto the bridge of her nose; blood gushed almost immediately.

She stepped back a pace, just out of his reach. "I'm telling you, Mr. Director, it's not me who wants you dead."

"Who wants me dead and why?"

"Whoever it was came down from New York. Or at least, we think that's where he came from. But we don't know who it is, only that he was sent here to kill you."

"Who's the we?"

"At this point that's something you don't need to know," the marine lieutenant said. Her mouth and chin were covered in blood but she didn't seem to notice. "Just that it's probably not the same people who tried to kill you down in Sarasota."

"I'm not going to fuck around with you much longer, unless you start making sense."

"Both ropes were cut almost all the way through. I tried to get here before you went over, but you were too goddamned fast for me. Someone knew you were coming out here tonight, and you might want to think about it. Narrow the list down."

"Who do you work for, let's start there?" McGarvey said.

"I can't tell you," the woman said, when a hole appeared in her temple, her head snapped to the left, and she went over the edge of the cliff.

McGarvey dropped to his good knee and swept his pistol left to right. The shooter had been somewhere down the path, and it had sounded to Mac like a pistol. Possibly 10mm."

Kyung-won appeared out of the darkness. "Jesus H. Christ, are you okay, Mac?" he asked.

"She warned me that someone was behind us on the trail."

□

TWENTY-SEVEN

McGarvey remained crouched where he was, his pistol trained on Kyung-won, who stood stock still, his 10mm Glock pointed down and to the left.

"I thought I was too late," Kyung-won said.

"What the hell are you doing here?" McGarvey demanded. He didn't lower his gun.

"Following you, and it's a goddamned good thing I was here or she would have killed you."

"She said that someone was on the trail behind us," McGarvey repeated.

"I'll bet she did."

"She told me that someone had cut the ropes."

"I'm not going to drop this on the ground," Kyung-won said. He bent down and carefully placed the pistol on a rock, his eyes never leaving McGarvey's. When he straightened up, he spread his hands. "Ball's in your court, Mac."

"How'd you know I was going to be here?"

"Bob gave me the heads-up."

"And you suspected someone might be coming after me?"

"It's what he told me."

"Did he also tell you that I wanted someone to pop out of the woodwork so that I could find out who they worked for?"

Kyung-won shrugged. "Didn't seem to me like there was a whole hell of a lot of time. Either you were going down the rope or she was going to shoot you."

"She wasn't pointing a gun at me," McGarvey said. Nothing was adding up. But he was tired and his leg hurt all the way down to his phantom foot. He straightened up and holstered his pistol. "The Bureau will have to be called, and we'll need to get our stories straight."

Kyung-won picked up his gun and holstered it after a brief hesitation. He was wary, but every NOC was jumpy after they'd come in from the cold. And his badland had been one of the worst, his crossing messy.

McGarvey went to the edge of the cliff and looked down. It was dark, but he could see the marine lieutenant's body on the rocks, just at the water's edge.

He looked over his shoulder. Kyung-won was right behind him.

"That's twice now someone's tried to off you."

"There'll probably be a third time."

"Then I'll just have to keep watching your six."

The camp commandant's quarters were right behind the Admin building, connected by a gravel walkway. McGarvey knocked lightly on the door. It was after midnight, and no night ops were on the schedule so the Farm was quiet.

"Come," Salem said.

"It's me." McGarvey eased the door open.

The room was in darkness, the only light spilling from the stanchion overheads in front.

"Who's with you?"

"Larry, and we have a problem."

"I expect you do," Salem said.

McGarvey had a twitchy feeling between his shoulder blades with Kyung-won at his back. But then, every NOC he'd ever dealt with gave him the same feeling. These people weren't operators in the normal sense of the word. They were cheats and liars and con men who wormed their way into people's lives with the sole purpose of turning their marks—their johns—into traitors.

It usually started easy. The mark—possibly a computer operator—was having financial troubles. The NOC was a low-level rep for an American or European company doing business in badland. He and the mark were neighbors in an apartment complex. They'd exchanged hellos, eventually had a beer or two—imported beer that the NOC supplied—swapped dirty jokes. At some point the NOC was invited over to dinner to meet the wife and children.

It was always a delicate operation at that stage. The NOC needed to get the john to accept something. A couple of steaks from the commissary, a bike for one of the kids, maybe even a video or magazine or newspaper or access to a Western website, something that was illegal.

And then the mark was his. A favor had been done, a favor was owed. Something small at first, the birth date of a minor government official. The private phone number of a low-level intelligence officer, perhaps the names of the officer's wife and children.

A favor returned, another given, and so it developed.

NOCs were to be used, but never to be trusted.

When the door was closed, Salem switched on a dim table lamp. He was holding a Wilson tactical pistol, which he laid on the table. "It's happened, then?"

"On the A course. The ropes on the river cliff had been cut through."

"I let the word out that you'd be there sometime tonight," Salem said. "Who was it?"

"Grace Metal," McGarvey said. "She was coming up behind me and Larry got the drop on her."

"She's dead?"

McGarvey nodded. "She was hiding something, I picked that up the first time I laid eyes on her. But I didn't think she'd been sent here to kill me."

"Me neither," Salem said. "She goes back a ways with some important people. When she was vetted she was given the highest marks."

"Almost too high?" Kyung-won asked.

A bleak look came into Salem's eyes, and he nodded.

"Only a bad legend is ever that lily-white," Kyung-won said. A legend was the invented background manufactured for someone going under deep cover. Driver's licenses and other documents, plus education and employment records, along with testimonials from real people who were either dead or unavailable for comment. A good legend always had a few flaws, to make it seem real, because no one was perfect.

"Why'd she apply for a job?" McGarvey asked. "Doesn't sound as if she was entry-level material."

"Said she was tired of sitting behind a desk. She was a former marine combat officer."

"The Bureau has to be notified," McGarvey said.

"I know. And they'll be crawling all over this place, including up my ass," Salem said. "I suggest that you get back to the clinic."

"I want to give Otto a call first," McGarvey said. He turned to Kyung-won. "Get rid of your gun, and go back to your quarters."

"Not my gun. I took it from the armory."

"Sanitize it first and return it. Without being seen."

Kyung-won grinned. "I think I can manage that," he said and he left.

"We can use the computer in my office," Salem said.

"I'll use my phone," McGarvey said. "She said that someone had come down from New York to kill me. But she said that *we* didn't know who it was."

"*We?*"

"Yeah. But it was something I didn't need to know, except that it wasn't the same people who tried in Sarasota."

Salem glanced at the door. "Do you suspect Larry?"

"At this point I suspect everyone," McGarvey said. Just about every time in his career—especially his early career—when he'd tended to trust the ones who seemed to be straight arrows, he'd been bitten in the ass. His lessons had been hard-won. He was a lot more cautious now.

"No chance she survived the fall?"

"Larry shot her in the head first."

"I'll call Langley to get the FBI out here," Salem said. "But stay in the clinic until they get here. You were in the same class as Grace, the Bureau people will want to talk to you."

TWENTY-EIGHT

□

Kamal was in his tent laying out his shaving things when someone knocked on the center pole. Razor in hand he turned. "Come in."

Ayman Baz pushed back the flap and stepped inside. The desert evening had been cold and it was still cool just before dawn, but by noon the temperature would be around one hundred.

"You're leaving," the camp commandant said.

"Yes. I'm finished here."

"I want to show you something before you go."

Kamal hesitated a moment. Just about everything was in place now and he intended to go to ground, maybe even back to France and allow the political situation to come closer to a head.

Last night Weaver had been on the television news channels, including CNN, with his latest executive order. Any Muslim who'd ever been in an ISIS or al-Qaeda war zone—whether as a participant in the fighting or even a victim—would be immediately subject to arrest the moment they applied for a visa to come to the States. And the arrest could take place at any U.S. embassy or consulate anywhere in the world. If they made an application they would not be allowed to leave the building or compound.

"What then, Mr. President?" an ABC reporter had asked at the White House news conference.

Weaver had almost laughed. "Then they'll get their wish. We'll bring them here. But the only things they'll ever see are the insides of a military courtroom and a supermax cell, or the sign saying: YOU ARE LEAVING THE UNITED STATES OF AMERICA."

"What about the innocent ones?" another network news reporter asked.

"There are no innocent ones."

The reporter tried to follow up, but Weaver held her off.

"All I'm saying is that I'm going to do everything within my power to stop another nine/eleven or any other attack from ever happening again. When it comes to immigrants my motto will be guilty until proven innocent."

"That's against the basic principles of our Constitution."

"Where were you, and the weak-kneed politicians you covered, the day before nine/eleven?" Weaver asked. "I'll tell you where: courting Saudi Arabia for its oil, instead of allowing exploration in the Gulf of Mexico or the Arctic. Or not allowing fracking to go ahead. Or blocking projects like the Keystone pipeline."

The White House press room erupted in pandemonium, but again Weaver cut through the noise.

"Haven't you people read your history?" he asked, not so much as an accusation but as a taunt. "Well, I have. And let me tell you; freedom has never come cheaply. The War of Independence, the Civil War, World War One and Two. Or do some of you think that we should not have dropped the atomic bomb on Japan?"

"How about Vietnam?" someone in the back asked.

"How about Vietnam?" Weaver demanded. "Who do you suppose lost that war for us? Our troops or our weakling politicians?"

"You would have called for a nuclear strike on Hanoi?"

"It would have done the job."

"What about China's reaction?"

"Do you honestly think that Beijing would have gone to war with us over Vietnam? Or earlier, even North Korea when we could have ended it with one decisive blow? What do you think war is all about?"

"What, Mr. President?"

"Winning," Weaver said. "And the majority of Americans agree with me, otherwise I wouldn't have been elected."

"But your poll numbers have been steadily dropping since the end of February," a CNBC reporter said. "Would you care to comment, sir?"

Weaver almost laughed again. "You haven't seen anything yet."

Again the room erupted, but Weaver held up a hand.

"Thank you," he said, and he left the podium.

In the admin tent Baz perched on the edge of the conference table, which was nothing more than a piece of plywood supported by sawhorses. He and Kamal were alone for the moment. Outside, a half-dozen or more Kalashnikov rifles were being fired, and in the distance two sharp explosions, what sounded like suicide vests, went off.

"I've talked to some engineers about your projects," Baz said.

"Saudis?" Kamal asked, though he was only slightly curious about what Baz wanted to tell him.

"Some Russians too."

"About time."

"Your camper filled with Semtex won't bring down the Golden Gate Bridge."

"It was meant to be a soft target."

"Kill a few people during rush hour? Terrorize the population?"

"Your point?" Kamal asked. He'd asked himself the same question since the meeting in Beijing. But he'd been given the specific targets and methods and he'd been promised a very large payday. No questions asked.

The strikes were weak, in his estimation. It was why he'd planned the separate strike on Grand Central Station and the method to carry it out.

"A couple of kids with suicide vests standing at the base of a dike in New Orleans won't do anything but superficial damage either. In fact, the only real target you've come up with is the church in Kansas, if my people aren't stopped at the border. Or you don't shoot them first."

"It was necessary for the others to see the seriousness of my intent."

"Yasmine would have done what you asked."

"Is that what you wanted to tell me?"

Baz was not happy, but he said nothing.

"I've been given specific instructions," Kamal said, and it sounded weak to his own ears. But except for Grand Central he was merely doing a job for enough money to retire. Or at least retire from everything except his own interests. Wherever they might carry him, simply for the thrill of the game.

He turned away for a moment. His life had gone from Krug on the Riviera to a relatively modest seclusion in France. From the thrill of the hunt and the kill to looking over his shoulder waiting for McGarvey to show up.

The e-advertisement he'd put out, and the assignment from the Gang of Three, had been a long way down for him. Almost to the beginning.

He was insane and he'd known it for a long time. But instead of reveling in the fact, he was starting to get tired of the game.

"The strike on the church in Kansas will work," Baz said. "Won't be a Christian anywhere in North America who'd feel safe again. I won't mind sending my kids to do something like that."

"Your kids?"

"I've begun to think of them that way."

Kamal nodded. "You said you wanted to show me something."

"The major said that you were the best. You'll appreciate this."

Kamal followed Baz from the tent a hundred meters or so out into the desert, over the top of a rocky sand dune and down the other side where a half-dozen soldiers for God and two instructors—all of them wearing camouflaged uniforms—were standing around a Toyota pickup, waiting.

"The sand dune is your dike," Baz said. He made a signal and he and Kamal moved about twenty meters off to the left.

Two of the young soldiers, both of them teenagers with scraggly beards, shouldered Stinger missiles, and fired.

The base of the sand dune blew away in two spots, the top collapsing downward.

"That will breach your dikes, and flood the city again," Baz said. "And Washington will be blamed for doing nothing."

TWENTY-NINE

McGarvey had used his encrypted phone to call Otto after leaving Salem's quarters, but Louise said he'd disappeared. And she'd said in it such a way that Mac wasn't to take it any further.

"Anyway, why are you calling so late?" she'd asked. "Are you okay?"

"I'm still laid up, but the doc says I'll live."

"Have you talked to Franklin?"

"Not yet. Has he been bothering you guys?"

"No, and it's not what Otto expected," she said. "Anyway, Audie is here with us, and you're at the Farm. Quite a switch."

"It's a good thing."

"Something going on?"

"I think so, but I don't know what yet. The place is starting to light up like Christmas, but they took my peg leg so I'm stuck. What about Pete?"

"I haven't talked to her in two days," Louise said, and it was obvious to McGarvey that she was lying. "Do you want me to call her?"

"Not necessary. I'll call her soon as I find out what's going on."

"Sleep tight," Louise said.

"You too."

It was a long night for McGarvey, though he was able to get a few hours' decent sleep. He kept going over in his head Grace Metal saying that it was someone from New York who wanted him dead. But there'd been no time to ask her who or why before Kyung-won had shot her to death.

At seven, Nurse Meade came into the room to check the bandages on the stump. She was brusque but not unfriendly. "Good thing you stayed in bed all night," she said. "Dr. Franklin called and said you aren't allowed to do anything physical for the next couple of days. And he was insistent, if you catch my drift."

"What's going on out there?"

"The FBI's here in force. Apparently there was an accident on the A course."

"What kind of an accident?"

"I don't know, but a bad one if they had to call the cops."

When she was finished, she pulled the sheet back over McGarvey's leg.

"Thanks."

"I was Franklin's chief nurse until eight months ago, when they asked me to do a one-year stint down here."

McGarvey realized that her face was familiar to him. "Do you know me?"

"Yes, I do, Mr. Director. And when Dr. Franklin called and asked me to keep my mouth shut, I was happy to agree." The clinic was quiet, but she glanced over her shoulder at the open door. "Was it you last night?"

"The less you know the better off you'll be," McGarvey said. "Do you understand?"

She nodded, but she was a little frightened. "Something's going on. Just about everybody's walking around as if they were on eggshells."

"What are they saying?"

She shook her head. "It's what they're not saying. Ever since maybe February or March it seems like the entire country has become jumpy. Like everyone is waiting for the shoe to drop. For something to happen."

"What something?" McGarvey asked.

"Breakfast should be up in a few minutes," Meade said. She picked up her tray of bandages and went to the door. She turned back. "Maybe another nine/eleven?"

Pete showed up at nine. She was wearing her efficient, determined expression, and she was armed. McGarvey felt the pistol in the holster on her hip under her jacket when she bent over and gave him a hug.

"Otto's working on some things," she whispered in his ear, before she straightened up. "Bob said you'd hurt your leg," she said out loud.

"Fell out of bed."

"A man your age oughta be more careful," Pete said.

Someone came into the clinic.

"That'll be one of the Bureau guys," Mac said.

"Franklin wants you back at All Saints. I'm here to pick you up. You'll need help getting to my car."

Nurse Meade showed up at the door with a man wearing a dark blue FBI jacket and baseball cap. He couldn't have been much over twenty-five, with a round baby face, wide eyes and a stern manner.

"Thank you," he said to the nurse and he came in. "Damon West?"

"Yes, and what the hell is going on here?" Mac demanded.

"And you are?" the FBI agent asked Pete.

Pete showed her CIA identification. "I'm here to take Mr. West back to All Saints. He was injured in a training accident yesterday. Let me see your ID."

"Morton Gold," the agent said and he showed Pete his ID. "Now, if you'll excuse us I have a couple of questions for Mr. West."

"Don't be long, the man is in pain," Pete said, and she left with Nurse Meade.

"I understand that you're a field agent," Morton said.

"Yes," McGarvey said. "Do you mind telling me what the hell is going on?"

"Just back from an assignment?"

"Yes."

"From where?"

"I couldn't say. And you haven't answered my question."

The FBI agent pursed his lips. "There was a fatality," he said. "Did you leave your bed during the night?"

"To use the bathroom and I screwed up my stump," McGarvey said. He pulled his blanket back to reveal the bandages.

"You get that in the field?"

"I couldn't say. Who was it got killed and how?"

"Did you hear anything unusual during the night? Anything at all?"

"Like what?"

"Like a gunshot."

"This is a training base, Mr. Morton. Gunshots and explosions occur just about twenty-four/seven."

"Last night?"

"I'm a sound sleeper."

Morton nodded curtly. "Thanks for your cooperation, sir."

He stopped at the door and gave McGarvey an odd look, but then he left.

When he was gone Pete came back in. "Let's get your leg on and get you the hell out of here," she said. She bent over him, cheek to cheek. "Did he recognize you?"

"If he did he didn't say so."

Pete got his peg leg as McGarvey pulled back the sheet and swung up so that he was sitting on the edge of the bed.

She stopped, her mouth tightening.

"Not an appealing sight," he said.

She forced a smile. "I'm seeing a warm body—a live body. Good enough for me."

THIRTY

□

It was dark, the sky transparent as only it can be in the desert, as Kamal walked a few hundred meters directly away from the cluster of tents. He had elected to stay another day at the camp; he had one more thing to do before he left for France.

Everyone seemed intent on learning how to kill a lot of people. And no one, not even the ones planning to martyr themselves as suicide bombers, seemed to be the least bit concerned that the missions they were training for were almost certainly one-way.

The seventy-one young soldiers—four more had shown up in camp earlier in the day—had finished their prayers and were having their evening meal in the mess tent with Baz, who was not only the camp commandant but the imam—the spiritual leader.

"Yes, they're all crazy," the Saudi had told Kamal after the demonstration. "But then so are you, I suspect."

Kamal had not taken offense. "And you," he said.

Baz had laughed. They were just to the west of the sand dune where Stinger missiles had been fired. "The craziest of all. But then, I have my reasons."

"As we all do."

"What about you? An unhappy childhood? A jilted love? A wrong done to you by the Americans?"

"All of the above, none of the above," Kamal said. "Most men have their reasons."

"You're a Saudi, like me. But educated elsewhere. Probably England."

Kamal considered where, but more important, if he would kill the camp commandant. The man was a loose end—he knew too much and he was a drunk.

The kids who had volunteered for the three missions wouldn't be coming back, but even if they were somehow intercepted before they blew themselves up and taken into custody they would only be able to provide Kamal's description as he looked now.

The only direct link back to him was the Gang of Three in Beijing, but Baz could cause trouble.

"It's better not to ask questions," he said.

Baz shrugged. "All soldiers die sooner or later. That includes us."

Kamal laughed "Later is better, wouldn't you agree?"

Baz offered him a smoke but Kamal declined. "You have your targets and your soldiers but you have not mentioned a timetable."

"Soon."

"It's important for our planning. I'll need at least five days, perhaps six or seven, to get my people and the weapons across the border and into position, especially because you want the three strikes to take place simultaneously," Baz said.

"How will your people get to the targets?" Kamal asked.

"They will drive in pairs. Three separate cars."

"Will they have papers to cross the border with the cars?"

"They'll take separate buses across," Baz said. "The weapons will be put in place separately. We have safe houses in Los Angeles where they'll pick up the cars and the Stingers."

"I've decided against the missiles," Kamal said.

"Why?"

"It's not important that the targets be completely destroyed, only that they are hit."

"That makes no sense."

Neither had it made much sense to Kamal when he had been given his instructions in Beijing. But his first payment had been prompt, and to satisfy his own bloodlust he had planned to hit Grand Central Station. The four attacks would be linked. And the message would come across loud and clear. The American president was an incompetent.

"Unless you're worried that my people will survive and lead the authorities back here and to you."

"That's exactly what I want to prevent. The van in San Francisco will blow up in the middle of the bridge. Your two people will die. As will the four wearing vests on the dikes, and the two in Kansas. There will be plenty of casualties."

"To what end, for what cause?" Baz asked.

"That's no concern of yours. You provide the soldiers and I provide the targets."

"You son of a bitch!" Baz shouted. "You may think of them merely as cannon fodder, but they are real people who believe in the cause."

"You've come to care for them, is that it?"

"Yes."

"More than your wife and two children?"

Baz stepped back a pace. He shook his head, sadness all over his face, in his eyes. "You bastard," he said, and he'd walked away.

Kamal stopped and looked back at the camp. Only a few lights were visible from ground level, but absolutely none from above. The next satellite overpass wasn't due for thirteen days; nevertheless he looked skyward, but nothing moved. Only the stars, unblinking in the clear, dry air, and a gibbous moon, blood orange, very low on the horizon.

This place at this exact time brought back an image of himself as a young boy with his grandfather, who'd always fancied himself a descendant of the desert Bedouin people. They were on the way from Riyadh to Jeddah on the coast, and in was night like now when his grandfather stopped the car at the side of the highway.

"Learn to appreciate this," the old man had said.

They got out and walked a few meters into the desert.

"Smell it, feel it, listen to your ancestors. Your heritage is important, never let it go from your soul."

Kamal was six or seven and he remembered thinking that the old man had been silly.

But now he understood the poetry of belonging. Only it was too late for him.

He made a call on his satphone to a number in Washington that the major had given him. It had been for his intelligence source, either in the

American Defense Intelligence Agency or possibly in the National Security Agency.

The number rang twice before a woman answered. She sounded drunk. "What?"

Kamal hesitated for a moment. "Do you know who this is?" he asked.

The phone was silent and he thought the woman had hung up.

"I thought that you had gone to ground."

"I thought this number had been taken down."

"Evidently we're both wrong. What do you want?'

"Information I can trust."

"About what?"

"Kirk McGarvey."

Again the woman remained silent for the longest time, and Kamal almost hung up before she answered.

"Son of a bitch, are you involved again?"

"Yes."

"Who is your controller?"

"I can't say, except that there are three of them and we met in Beijing. What about Kirk McGarvey?"

"He's still very much alive, and if he finds out that you've shown up he'll stop at nothing to kill you."

"It's why I called. I need your help."

"I'll find out what I can. It seems as if we're fighting the same enemy again."

THIRTY-ONE

Otto was no spy. But he'd played the part for the past twenty-four hours and he thought that he was doing a pretty good job of it.

He sat in a dark green Chevy Impala that he'd rented yesterday afternoon from Hertz at Dulles. He was parked across from the Next Whisky Bar entrance in the Watergate complex, where General Walter Echo, in civilian clothes, had shown up five minutes ago.

Two days ago his darlings had begun picking up hints of someone here in the States involved in what Otto was thinking of as a consortium. There had been some traffic among several of the key names from the French, German and British intelligence services to an office in the Pentagon.

Routine stuff, mostly, troop and equipment inventories on the ISIS battlefields in Syria and Iraq. Logistics, with only a confidential classification.

He'd almost ignored the connection. His programs were giving it only a 10 percent probability of a match with the main search parameters he'd set up, that of nailing every player in the possible consortium—whose real purpose to this point was unknown.

But then an NSA intercept of an encrypted call to the same Pentagon number from someone in Riyadh piqued his darlings' interest, upping the probability to more than 25 percent.

From that point it had taken less than ten minutes to identify the officer as Walter Echo, who was deputy chief of air force logistics, and when Otto fed that information into the program, the probability that the general was involved with the consortium rose to 78 percent.

It was then that he has kissed Louise good night, and told her not to worry. Mac was at the Farm, and this was something easy.

"Why you?" she'd asked.

"Because I'm not sure that my darlings aren't barking up a wrong tree."

"Goddamnit, you're not a field officer, and you hate dogs."

"Twenty-four hours, and I'm not going much farther than the Beltway. Honest injun."

"Take a gun," she'd told him.

"Won't need it."

A half-dozen people including two couples had shown up in the time since Echo had gone inside. From where Otto had parked he'd managed to get good head shots of all of them, which he'd sent back to the main face-recognition program that he'd designed and installed on the Company's mainframe two years ago.

Nothing had come back yet. None of the faces were in the program.

A man of medium height, wearing an obviously expensive suit, showed up in a Maserati Quattroporte, which he handed over to the valet, and went inside.

Otto snapped a couple of pictures and sent them to the program, which came back in less than thirty seconds with a hit. Lieutenant Colonel Moses Chambeau worked as an analyst in the Defense Intelligence Agency. His office handled deployments of allied troops in the ISIS battle.

But the man was a Harvard puke, who had written a position paper on the willingness of the civilian leaders in a dozen countries to send boots on the ground to the war. And one of the customers was General Echo's office, and another was Ronald F. Hatchett, the deputy adviser on national security affairs to the president.

Sending all of the new information to his darlings, they picked up the fact that Chambeau was married to Echo's sister, Jennifer.

The only curiosity about Hatchett—in Otto's mind—was that the man had spent two days in Beijing last month, meeting with what were called "top Chinese officials."

He had his darlings do a quick media search, but nothing showed up on Hatchett's visit. Nor was there anything on the websites of either the state or defense departments.

It had the earmarks of an important trip, but no other details were available.

Otto got out of his car and walked across to the Next Whisky Bar entrance. He was dressed in boat shoes, starched and crisply pressed jeans, a white dress shirt, his ponytail tucked into the collar in the back, and a blue blazer. Louise had picked it out for him last year, and it was the same outfit that Mac sometimes wore.

The bar was three-quarters full, and the minute he walked in he spotted Echo and Chambeau seated at a table across the room from where they could watch the entrance, their backs facing the wall.

Otto took a seat at the bar from where he could see the reflection of the two men in the mirror. He ordered a Heineken. When his beer came he took out his cell phone, pointed it at the mirror, and pretended that he was talking to someone.

He only had to adjust the direction he was pointing the phone when their images came up on the screen, and their voices became audible.

". . . this is getting totally out of hand just like I warned you and the others it would," one of them said. The voice, bounced off the mirror, was distorted, but Otto's program cleaned it up so it was understandable.

Otto thought it was Chambeau's.

"He's still alive?"

"Yes, but Grace is dead and the Bureau was all over the place until about two hours ago."

Echo turned away and apparently said something though Otto's phone didn't catch it.

"She was a goddamned dyke," Chambeau said. "In over her head."

"Was it McGarvey?"

"No. Someone else was apparently out on the course and figured it out. And before you ask, we don't know if his being there was coincidental, or if he's working for someone, who the hell it is. I have someone looking into it. But quietly."

"Well, you'd better fucking well find out because this is the second time McGarvey has come up clean. Sarasota wasn't ours. And whoever gunned down Grace wasn't ours either."

"Maybe—" Chambeau said, but he was cut off.

The bartender was there, blocking the line of sight to the mirror. "Would you like to see a bar menu, sir?" she asked.

For a moment the words didn't compute and Otto shook his head.

"Something to eat, sir?"

"No."

The bartender moved away.

"I don't even want to think about it," Echo was saying.

"We'd better start. McGarvey is job one; we've all agreed on at least that much. But until that happens the flash point probes will have to wait."

Both men were silent for several long beats. And Otto wasn't sure if something was wrong with his program. But then Echo was back.

"Maybe we should take advantage of the situation. Step back and let whoever else is gunning for the bastard finish the job. Maybe even help them along."

Chambeau said nothing for a long time. "You might be right. I don't think any of us ever had a true measure of the man."

"We were warned."

"I know," Chambeau said. "But we can afford to wait."

"I hope that you're right," Echo said. He finished his drink, got up and walked past Otto on his way out of the bar.

Chambeau waited for the bill to come, paid it with a credit card and followed Echo out the door.

Otto phoned Louise. "Where are you?" he asked when she answered.

"All Saints."

"How's Mac?"

"Franklin's springing him in the morning. But we all want to know where you are and what's going on."

"I'll be there in fifteen minutes," Otto said.

THIRTY-TWO

□

Pete and Louise were in McGarvey's room when Otto showed up all out of breath, as he usually was when he had a bone in his teeth. Louise went to him immediately and gave him a hug.

"We were worried sick about you," she said. "And the next time you try to run off on your own I'm going to sit on you until you come to your senses. What were you thinking?"

"No one's gunning for me. I was a fly in the corner. All but invisible."

McGarvey was sitting up in bed. They had taken his leg to make some adjustments, but Franklin had promised he would have it back in the morning, and he could discharge himself from the hospital if that's what he wanted. "Louise is right."

"Otto explained to them about the hypothetical consortium. It's bigger than just a few mid-level intel officers," he said.

"Go on."

"It's homegrown. And their job one is getting rid of you."

"What else have you got?"

"Plenty, and you're not going to like it," Otto said. He quickly went over the theory that if there was a consortium, a sort of old-boys network, it had to include someone in the States. He'd monitored incoming calls from the mid-level intel officers his darlings had already identified first to the CIA—which was a bust to this point—and next to the Pentagon, where he'd come up with General Echo's name.

"Why the Pentagon?" Pete asked.

"If this has something to do with the war on ISIS, someone in military planning could be involved," McGarvey said, and he was glad to this point it didn't seem as if anyone in the Company was a part of it. "Continue."

"One of the calls to Echo's office came from an officer in the SVR—one of the names my darlings had picked up along with the others. I plugged Echo's name into the main search engine and *bingo*, there were connections between him and just about every other officer on my list, including the Saudis."

"Enough to bring him in for questioning?" Pete asked.

"Depends on what Echo's Pentagon job is," McGarvey said.

"Deputy chief of air force logistics," Otto said.

"Then on the surface he's just doing his job coordinating equipment movements with the battlefield requirements in Syria and Iraq. There's been at least low-level communications between us and the Russians almost from the beginning. It's safer for all of us in the long run if we can talk to each other. Keep out of each other's way."

"I began to wonder if he was alone here in the States or if he was working with someone. But not by email or phone; in person, face-to-face."

"So you decided to follow him," Louise said.

Otto grinned and nodded.

"Dear God, he could have killed you."

"It's Mac they want, not me," Otto said. "Anyway, there's a lot more."

From the beginning McGarvey had gotten the feeling that whatever was going on wouldn't turn out to be so simple as someone with a grudge gunning for him.

"He left work, got some gas at a Shell station, stopped at a 7-Eleven, and from there went straight home to Fairfax around eight. I parked down the street from where I could watch the house, and monitor anything electronic coming in or leaving. His wife got a couple of calls from friends—no connections with our business that I could find. They watched TV—a movie, *We Were Soldiers*—and settled down for the night. No kids, no one staying at the house with them."

"Did you spend the night there?" Louise asked.

"I brought something to eat," Otto said. "Anyway, he left the house at seven, drove straight to the Pentagon and stayed there until six-thirty, when he drove to the Watergate."

"Where did you park all day?" Louise asked.

"Mostly in Arlington Cemetery, but I moved around. He was busy on his phone and computer pretty much most of the day. But when he left work he took the Roosevelt Bridge across the river instead of heading home."

"How did you know when he left or where he was going?" Louise asked.

"He put a bug on Echo's car," McGarvey said. "The gas station or the 7-Eleven?"

"7-Eleven," Otto said. "He went to the bar and a few minutes later a DIA light colonel by the name of Moses Chambeau showed up. I figured the coincidence had to be too great for two guys like that to show up at the same place in civvies within a few minutes of each other so I went inside and sat at the bar where I could eavesdrop."

"There's more," McGarvey said. He could see that Otto was holding something back, something that he thought was over the top.

"Before I went in I took a picture of Chambeau and sent it to the new facial-recognition program, and then to my darlings, and all sorts of cool shit came back. Like his job as an analyst in the DIA. Like the fact he's married to Echo's sister. And the fact his position papers—especially one three months ago on how willing our allies were to send troops to Syria and Iraq—ended up not only on Echo's desk, but on the desk of Ron Hatchett, the deputy NSA in the White House."

It was an unexpected turn, and yet McGarvey wasn't really surprised by the connection, though he didn't know why. Something just outside his ken was niggling at the back of his head.

"Brothers-in-law out together for an after-work drink?" Louise suggested.

"What else?" McGarvey asked.

"They talked about you not being dead. Grace Metal was evidently working for Echo, but whoever put the bomb in your car wasn't in the consortium. Someone else is coming after you and it's freaking them out."

"Not Kamal?"

"His name never came up," Otto said. "And that's not all. Chambeau said you were their number one target. But until you were eliminated the 'flash point probes'—his words—would have to wait."

Again something just outside of the box was bothersome, whispering something to McGarvey so softly he couldn't quite make out the words. But the hairs at the nape of his neck bristled. "Is there more?"

"They have a great deal of respect for you. In fact, Echo said that they had been warned—but he didn't say by who. And he suggested that they just bide their time and let whoever else was gunning for you do their thing."

"We'll need a list of everyone who knows I'm alive," McGarvey said. "And by now it's bigger than I'd like."

"Could be anyone," Otto said.

"The nurse in the clinic at the Farm knew who I was."

"And Kyung-won, and Grace Metal, and General Echo and Colonel Chambeau. Probably the entire Consortium."

"Cat's out of the bag," Louise said. "Time to go deep?"

"They found me at New College and they found me at the Farm," McGarvey said. "Let them find me at my apartment and on campus. Maybe even the Next undergrad."

"Maybe the White House," Otto said.

"Hatchett?"

"He spent two days in Beijing last month, supposedly meeting with someone in the government. But absolutely nothing showed up in the media, nor was his flight included in any logs that I had access to."

"Is someone in the MSS on your list?" McGarvey asked. The Ministry of State Security was China's main intelligence service.

"No," Otto said. "The question is, what was he doing in China?"

"Something for the president," Louise suggested. "Back-burner diplomacy, happens all the time."

"Xi Jinping can't stand Weaver," Otto said. "He's gone on record publicly that he will not work with the White House no matter the circumstances, not until—in his words—the American people come to their senses."

THIRTY-THREE

□

Kamal parked the RAV4 SUV he'd rented in Ciudad Juarez in the long-term parking garage at Chihuahua City's R. F. Villalobos International Airport, one hundred miles south of the desert training camp, just before noon. The morning was already hot.

Taking his bag he tossed the car keys in a trash can as he headed into the main terminal, reasonably busy for the size of the airport, and went down to the arrivals level and outside to the waiting cabs.

He'd booked a suite yesterday at the Sheraton Soberano, the only decent hotel in the city, for just one night under his Paul O'Neal identity, the same one he'd used in New York what seemed like an eternity ago.

The edges were beginning to unravel for him. In just about every other operation he'd been involved with, including the staging of his own death at sea, he had been the one in charge. He'd been the one who'd called the shots. Until McGarvey. On the French Riviera last year and then in Manhattan where he'd barely made it out with his life.

Two failed attempts taking out McGarvey—the first in Sarasota, the second at the Farm he knew nothing about—were disappointing. The woman on the phone admitted that she was as much in the dark as he was.

"I'm not involved this time," she'd said. "I'm just an observer on the sidelines, but since you're part of whatever's going on I have to warn you to be extremely careful around that bastard. The man has got nine lives."

"What word are you getting?"

"About what?"

"About what's going on."

The woman was silent for several beats. "I don't know what to tell you because I had no idea you'd become involved. Who are you working for, what have you been hired to do?"

"Kill Kirk McGarvey."

"And?"

"Just that."

Again the woman was silent for a beat. When she was back she sounded cautious. "Okay, whoever the hell hired you, it looks like we're on the same page. McGarvey is job one."

"Who are you working for?"

The woman laughed. "As long as McGarvey is your target, I'll continue to give you whatever information you need. But once he's out of the picture this number will be disconnected. And if you try to reach me after that . . ." She paused. "The consequences will not be to your liking."

Sitting in the cab he thought how satisfying it would be to put his hands around her neck and strangle her to death. Perhaps he would do it while he was fucking her.

But then, there was more than simple pleasure to his business this time. And even more than the money.

His reward would come when he was up close and personal with McGarvey, watching the life go out of the man's eyes; seeing the expression on the man's face when he realized that he was dying, and that there was nothing or no one to save him.

The hotel was barely tolerable by Kamal's standards, but his suite looked toward some mountains in the distance, and the sitting room had expansive floor-to-ceiling windows and a complimentary bottle of Veuve Clicuot, at the very bottom of his drinkable champagne list.

At two he called his Washington contact again. It was picked up after one ring, but no one answered.

"I'll phone this evening," he said and he hung up. She was almost certainly at work, and in a place where she was not able to answer the phone.

Downstairs in the reasonably laid out and decorated Restaurant Candiles, he ordered a filet mignon rare and a Caesar salad. Surprisingly a Dom Pérignon '06 was on the list, and he ordered a bottle, very cold.

The restaurant was less than one-third full, and the food and service were excellent.

His contact called when he was having his coffee and cognac.

"McGarvey has been discharged again from the hospital. He's at his apartment in Georgetown." She gave him the address just across from Rock Creek Park.

"What shape is he in?"

"I don't have the entire story, but evidently his back was severely burned and he lost his left leg at or below the knee in the explosion. And he was injured again in the incident at Camp Peary."

"The man is a cripple."

"Don't count him out just yet." According to a source at the Farm he managed to take down one of the hand-to-hand instructors."

"Does he have minders? Someone from the CIA watching over him?"

"Unknown at this point. But I'd doubt it. The man has the reputation as a loner, except for three people."

"I'd guess a woman by the name of Pete Boylan."

"Yes, and a computer genius friend named Otto Rencke, plus the man's wife, Louise Horn, who was an NSA satellite expert. In fact, she still has strong connections with the Agency."

"Weaknesses?"

"His granddaughter. She's four. Her mother—McGarvey's daughter—and her husband were killed in an operation, and the Renckes took over as her adopted parents."

Kamal had never had any compunctions about killing, and the thought of holding a child as hostage, and even killing it, didn't bother him in the least. "A cripple, two geeks and a woman."

"You're a macho son of a bitch. All you bastards are the same. But McGarvey's girlfriend has a rep. I've never met her, but by all accounts she's one tough broad. You might want to keep it in mind."

"I will," Kamal said. "What else do you have for me?"

"That's it. But I wish you luck, and I sincerely mean it. A lot is riding on this."

"Like what?"

But the woman was gone.

Back in his suite, Kamal made reservations for the early morning American Eagle flight to Dallas–Fort Worth, where he'd stayed at the Fairmont Hotel before heading down to Mexico. He'd used his O'Neal identification there as well, and had left a locked bag with a spare Glock pistol, three sets of IDs and three platinum Amex cards in storage at the hotel.

It had made crossing the border into Mexico marginally easier, and would make coming back into the States much safer in case some over-zealous customs agent decided to do a physical bag check. Extra security layers had been put in place over the past year or so because of all the bombings, mass shootings and airliner disasters worldwide.

He stayed awake staring out the window at the distant mountains, their dark shapes just beyond the city lights, almost ominous. A bulwark, of sorts, between him and what was left to do in Georgetown and then San Francisco, New Orleans, Colby and Grand Central.

And yet he couldn't stop worrying about something that he might be missing. Something important, something vital not only to the mission but to his personal survival.

It was well past midnight before he managed to get some sleep and in the morning he put his concerns to the back of his mind.

Clearing customs at Dallas–Fort Worth had been anticlimatic. Men in obviously expensive suits and close-shaved, carrying Louis Vuitton bags, were rarely singled out. They didn't fit the profile of the Middle Eastern terrorist.

He checked into the Fairmont, was given his suite from before, and his bag left in storage had been brought up. He gave the bellman a fifty dollar bill, and inspected the bag's telltale—a tiny piece of grit in the lock—still in place.

He ordered a bottle of Krug, his favorite wine, and when it came he took out his two Glock pistols, both of them subcompact Gen 4s, and took his time cleaning them.

The clock was ticking, and whether or not he was on a downhill slide, he forced himself to enjoy the moment.

No matter the lingering questions, this was the shit that made life bearable.

THIRTY-FOUR

☐

It was around five in the afternoon when McGarvey ran along the path in Rock Creek Park across from his apartment. The water was low this time of the year. He'd been here like this in just about every season, in every weather—sun, rain, fog even snow—and just about every time of the day—even nights sometimes—and usually he loved it. Loved the aloneness, the physicality, his thoughts.

More than Casey Key in Florida, which he'd shared for all too brief a time with Katy, this place felt like home to him. In part because of the Company, of course, but in large part because of Pete, for which he felt a certain amount of guilt. He shared the CIA with her, and Otto and Louise had all but adopted her as one of the family.

Even his granddaughter, Audie, who had no memory of her mother, Elizabeth, or grandmother, had warmed to Pete.

It had been hard trying not to fall in love with Pete. And he'd felt like a traitor to his dead wife and daughter for doing so.

"You have to move on with your life, Mac," Louise had told him one evening about eight months ago.

"I don't know if I can, or even if I should."

"It wasn't your fault that Katy and Elizabeth were assassinated."

"Yes, it was," he'd shot back, the vision of the exact moment of their deaths rising up in his head.

They'd been in Arlington Cemetery, riding in a limo coming back from the funeral of Liz's husband—himself a victim of an assassination—when the Cadillac suddenly exploded. McGarvey had been in the car directly behind them and he'd witnessed the entire thing. Nothing had been left, only small pieces of their bodies, a charred shoe, Katy's purse, the pistol Liz had been carrying in a shoulder holster under her blazer.

He'd gone nearly insane that day, and as he pushed himself on the path along the creek the same blackness came up, threatening again to block out his sanity. Making him want to strike back at something, anything.

Louise had been wrong; it was his fault that Katy and Liz had been killed. They'd died because of who he was, what he'd done. In fact, the bomb in the limo had been meant for him. Someone out of his past had surfaced.

Just like now. Only this time he didn't know why, exactly. He still had no handle on what was going on. Even more disturbing, Otto had no real idea either, except that whatever was happening had something to do with a consortium of mid-level intelligence officers in most of the developed countries around the world. And that once again McGarvey was in the crosshairs of an assassin. Very likely a name out of his recent past.

His left foot and ankle began to ache, so he picked up the pace, his body drenched in sweat.

"Phantom pains, in a part of your body you no longer have, but real pains nevertheless," Franklin had told him.

"For how long?"

Franklin was walking out the door of Mac's hospital room. He turned back. "Until something else of yours gets blown off."

Rush-hour traffic on the parkway to his left through the trees was picking up. But most of the other joggers who used the path every day had thinned out, only the occasional person walking, one man sitting on a park bench down by the water's edge.

The hair at the back of McGarvey's neck bristled. Someone was behind him, and closing.

He suddenly sprinted to the right, into a line of trees and brush, pulling the Walther from the holster at the small of his back under his sweatshirt.

Pete pulled up short on the path and looked at him, his pistol pointed directly at her. She was grinning.

McGarvey lowered his gun and reholstered it as he walked up to her, hiding his limp as best he could.

But she'd noticed and her eyes narrowed. "You okay?" she asked.

"I'll live."

"That's good to hear," she said. "Let's go back to your place. I could use a drink and you definitely could use a shower."

"I was about to turn around."

"Yeah, I noticed. But thank God you haven't lost your reflexes."

"Did Otto come up with anything solid for me?"

"For starts, Jennifer Echo is on the verge of bankruptcy. The girl likes to spend money at the better stores, but especially online."

"Could she and Chambeau be open for financial blackmail?"

"That's what Otto thinks. The DIA takes a dim view of their own analysts getting in over their heads."

"How about Echo?"

"He was the general who mouthed off about maybe not following the commander-in-chief's orders if it was Weaver sitting in the Oval Office."

McGarvey was scanning the rooftops of the buildings on 27th Street NW across the parkway for something, anything: the glint of binocular lenses, maybe a chance reflection off a small parabolic antenna pointed their way, even the gleam off a rifle scope. The shot would be an easy one.

"What else?" he asked. With Otto there was always something else.

"Looks as if Chambeau is having an affair with a coworker. A woman by the name of Susan Fischer who's a signals intelligence supervisor at Fort Meade."

"Not so uncommon."

"Except that the woman could be a drunk."

"So?"

"A drunk who talks to people on a cell phone equipped with a fairly sophisticated encryption algorithm."

"She's a SIGINT super."

"Otto designed the program. He calls it a shape-shifter. Soon as someone tries to break the algorithm, the program changes. It's theoretically unbreakable."

"Did he give it to the NSA?"

"No."

"Then how the hell did the woman get it?"

"Otto asked me to ask you," Pete said. "And he suggested that we do everything in person for the time being."

They crossed to the other side of the busy parkway. Pete took out a small device about the size of a cell phone and keyed it. The tiny screen remained blank.

"It's a spectrum analyzer. Checks to see if someone is watching us electronically. To this point we're clean. And so are both of our apartments, as well as Otto's McLean house."

"But job one is still me."

"Yeah," Pete said.

"That's a good thing. If someone gets close enough to take a shot at me, it'll mean that I'm close enough to fire back."

On the third floor of his building, McGarvey took out his pistol, unlocked the door and shoved it open with the toe of his peg leg.

Nothing had changed since he'd left forty-five minutes ago. Especially there were no new smells; cologne—men's or women's—gun oil, dry cleaning residue on someone's jacket or the distinctive residue of body soap, lotion or shampoo. Only his own smells: Irish Spring with aloe, bay rum aftershave and Dove shampoo with menthol.

Pete was on his six, her pistol drawn. "Clear?" she asked softly.

"Clear," he said, lowering his gun. "Red or white this time?"

"A merlot."

THIRTY-FIVE

☐

Otto was about to pull the pin for the day, when someone buzzed his door. Louise had called earlier and insisted that he be home for dinner for a change. Audie was asking if he was going to leave them forever, and it almost broke his heart thinking about their adopted daughter.

"Dr. Estes is here to see you," his program announced.

"Is he alone?"

"Yes."

"Let him in," Otto said.

He shut down the images on all of his screens, especially the main one that showed the ongoing results of the search his darlings were chewing on, and went to the front office of his suite as the door buzzed open and Estes walked in, a paper bag in his hand.

"I'd hoped that I would catch you before you left for the day. The front gate said you hadn't left yet."

"I was just on my way out," Otto said. "What have you got on your mind?"

"Plenty," Estes said. He took a bottle of cheap Chianti with a screw top out of the bag. "Do you have a couple of glasses?"

"No."

"Never found the need when I was in grad school." He took the top off, tossed it in a wastebasket and perched on the edge of one of the desks, piled high with newspapers and magazines. "I think I got it figured out, or at least some of it." He took a deep drink of the wine and held the bottle out. "Alcohol kills the germs."

Otto took a drink. The wine was terrible—not much more than vinegar—but he wasn't a connoisseur. He straddled one of the chairs, took another deep draft and handed the bottle back. "I never found the need for grad school."

"So I've been told. Makes you and McGarvey quite the pair. The geek and the shooter."

"I've always preferred nerd."

"Okay, so I think we have two things going at the same time. Neither of them works with the other, except for the fact they want McGarvey out of the picture for whatever reason."

"Because in the end he's the one who'll figure it out and run the bad guys down."

"Makes you a target too—'cause you're the one who'll actually unravel the thing and set your friend in the right direction," Estes said. He drank more wine and passed the bottle back to Otto, who was already feeling a slight buzz.

"If you're here coming with something new, you'd better start checking your own six," Otto said. He took another drink. Louise was going to kill him.

"Six?"

"Like the hands on a clock. Your six—it's your back."

"You're right, maybe I should start watching my six."

"Either that or have housekeeping assign you some muscle."

"A bodyguard?"

"Yes."

Estes laughed. He'd been drinking earlier and was already half-drunk. "Maybe I'll need two—one for my six and the other for my twelve. You see, the problem is one team of bad guys is coming from your mid-level spooks, and those people are sincerely motivated."

"To do what?"

"To discredit Weaver, what else?"

"Okay, we already figured that part out. But discredit him how? This guy is like an angry duck—water slides right off his back. Has from the start."

"I don't know that part yet. But I can think of a couple of scenarios that could work."

"Like?"

"Like North Korea putting up a decent-sized satellite in low orbit."

"It's already happened."

"Yeah, but then telling us they've finally weaponized one of the nukes, and have mated it to an ICBM," Estes said. "No matter what Weaver does it'll be wrong. Hell, no one in the Pentagon likes the guy. He'd come out looking like a jerk."

"Especially when we find out that the Koreans were lying."

"Disinformation."

"What else?" Otto asked.

Estes took another drink and passed the bottle to Otto. "It leaks that Israeli forces are going to take Tehran completely out of the picture, because of our nuclear agreement."

"It'd have to be credible."

"Not as long as it was made public to the American people. The Jewish voters would applaud the plan, while the doves would hate it."

"And the indifferents wouldn't give a damn. Another no-win situation for Weaver."

"China and Taiwan," Estes said.

"Pakistan and India."

"Russia and Syria, or Poland or Afghanistan again."

"Or maybe back to Cuba or even Mexico," Otto said. He took another drink, and this time he was really feeling the buzz.

"We'd have to react to something like that," Estes said. "And something like that—especially so close to our border—could easily spin totally out of control."

"Only to the position where Weaver was discredited," Otto said. "Point made, case closed. Except someone somewhere could make a mistake, leaving Weaver with his finger on the actual trigger."

"I didn't much like the notion when I came up with it," Estes said. "But that's only half of the equation."

"You said one team of mid-level spooks. What about a second team?"

Estes took a drink and handed the bottle back to Otto. "It finally came to me when I started to think in terms of Nixon and Watergate."

"He was afraid of the Democrats. They were the enemy, so he had to spy on them, find out what they were doing."

"Even Nixon had his loyalists—the true believers—who were willing to do anything for the boss," Estes said. "Just like Weaver does. Anything."

The monitors were blank, but Otto's darlings were picking up on everything, including Estes's facial gestures and body language and even the stress levels in his voice. It was a unique situation, and Otto was curious to see how well his programs did separating the beginnings of inebriation from sober stress.

"Just the opposite of what the people on Weaver's team in the White House want to do," Estes said. "They're trying to build the reputation of their president. Do something—or somethings—to make him the hero."

"Like Obama giving the order to take out bin Laden," Otto said. "But he never really got full credit for the decision."

"It was too late for him. The die in his case had already been cast. He had a reputation—deserved or not—and ordering the takedown of UBL was too little, too late to have the full effect."

"But Weaver is brand-new. The problem is, what does his team want him to do?"

"Act presidential, of course," said Estes.

"An act of terrorism, designed by them, that Weaver will quash, making him a hero," Otto said. "Like what?" he asked, though already several scenarios were running through his head.

"Doesn't matter, except that it'd have to be pretty big, and Weaver's people would have to let law enforcement know what was about to go down in time to stop it," Estes said. "Something like: 'The White House has it from usually reliable sources that an attack is going to be made on such-and-such a place at such-and-such a time.'"

"The Company would be in the loop, and it wouldn't take us long to figure out it was another Watergate dirty trick, and blow the whistle."

"It'd be too late by then, so it wouldn't matter. Weaver would come out the hero. The savior of his beloved people."

"Lots could go wrong."

"You're telling me," Estes said. "So what do we do about it?"

"What's your confidence level?"

Estes laughed. "Are you kidding me? I'm just as big a nerd as you. I come up with this shit as an exercise in what-ifs. It's up to you guys to figure out the possibilities."

"Dr. Estes may be right," the computer told Otto after the Harvard doc was gone.

"Confidence level?"

"Indeterminate with my present information."

"But?"

"If LE is notified too late, or if they are slow to respond to the proposed attack, the event could occur."

"But?" Otto asked again.

"It would depend on the abilities and determination of the person or persons hired to carry out the attack," the computer said. "Or attacks."

☐

THIRTY-SIX

McGarvey sat behind the wheel of a BMW 5-series parked in front of the Watergate complex in a spot from where he could watch the entrances to the Next Whisky Bar as well as the building where Susan Fischer lived.

For the moment, using the clutch in a car with a standard transmission was a little awkward for him, but relearning that skill was high on his list. Franklin had warned him about irritating the stump again, allowing it to completely heal first.

Pete had taken the initiative and gotten him the Bimmer with an automatic, to replace the old Toyota SUV he'd driven earlier, and Otto had outfitted it with a homing beacon, an advanced GPS system that could not be back-traced and a voice-operated computer/phone system that was connected through Otto to the CIA's mainframe.

It was almost like the cars James Bond drove in the movies of the sixties and seventies.

"You might as well take advantage of the technology," Pete had told him when she'd picked him up from the hospital with the car.

McGarvey had seen the utility of it, and the humor. "No machine guns or ejection seats?"

Pete had seemed nervous, but she'd smiled at that question. "Otto's working on it."

A smoked-silver XJS Jaguar passed where McGarvey was waiting, and drove to the entrance into the underground parking garage. The woman behind the wheel was Fischer. He recognized her from the photographs Otto had sent him.

The barrier rose as she approached and she disappeared inside.

McGarvey waited until she was just out of sight, and the barrier starting to come down, before he drove to the entrance.

"Fischer just entered the parking garage at the Watergate," he said. "I need access."

Even before the barrier was fully in place it rose again, and he drove down the ramp into the garage, his headlights out.

Fischer turned left at the second level. McGarvey hung back until she pulled in to a slot almost directly across from two elevators, and he parked a half-dozen places away.

She remained in her car, and for a minute McGarvey thought that she had spotted him.

His phone chimed softly. It was Otto.

"She's talking on her encrypted phone."

"Any idea to whom?" McGarvey asked,.

"No, dammit, and I can't even tell you if it's a local call. Could be she's talking to someone in Bangladesh."

"Or the Pentagon."

Otto was frustrated. "My darlings are working on it, but I designed the system too damned well," he said. "Is she alone?"

"Yes."

"Okay, watch yourself. Whatever team she's on, if Estes is right, taking you out is still priority one."

Otto had phoned Mac with the bare bones of Estes's take on the situation. One group wanted to discredit the president while another wanted to make a hero out of him. But both were playing a dangerous game that could spin totally out of control. And the fact that both wanted to assassinate a former director of the Central Intelligence Agency spoke volumes about their willingness to act.

Fischer got out of her car and went to the elevators. She was of medium height, slight build, with short dark hair. She was dressed in jeans and a yellow top, the long sleeves pushed above her elbows. When she reached the elevators and pushed the button for her floor, she glanced over her shoulder, the way she had driven in.

Her face was narrow and angular, but at this distance it was impossible for McGarvey to tell much else about her, except that she almost certainly was the woman in the photos Otto had given him.

"She's at the north elevator."

"I see it," Otto said. "Soon as she starts up, take the south elevator. I'll stop her between the fifth and sixth floors long enough for you to reach the eighth. Her place is eight-oh-two facing the river. How long will it take for you to crack the lock?"

"Thirty seconds," McGarvey said. "Unless she has it rigged."

"I'm seeing nothing in her apartment other than a normal intruder alarm system, which I've shut off."

"She's aboard," McGarvey said. He got out of the car and hurried to the elevators. "Can you shut down the phones in her apartment?"

"Already done, but there's nothing I can do about her cell phone. She's a bright girl."

"And cautious."

McGarvey boarded the elevator and went up to the eighth floor. "I'm there," he told Otto as he went across the corridor to 802.

The lock was a standard Yale mortise body, no telltales that McGarvey could detect. He had it open in fifteen seconds flat with an old standby SouthOrd pocket pen pick set he hadn't used in years.

"I'm going in," he told Otto. He pocketed the phone without shutting it off, and took out his pistol.

"She's on her way up," Otto said, his voice muffled.

Easing the door open he swept his pistol left to right, covering the short vestibule, expansive living room with tall windows, a corridor at the middle leading back probably to the bedroom or bedrooms, and to an open dining room and kitchen to the left.

He closed the door behind him, letting it relock itself, and went across the room and into the kitchen, where he sat on a stool at the counter from where he had a clear sight line to the entry vestibule.

"She's on the eighth floor," Otto said.

McGarvey laid the pistol on the counter within easy reach.

Moments later the door swung open and Susan Fischer entered her apartment. She didn't spot McGarvey at the kitchen counter until she'd closed the door and come in from the vestibule.

She stopped in midstride, a mixture of surprise and shock on her face that slowly turned to a look almost of resignation, her mouth downturned, her eyes narrowed.

"What the hell are you doing here?" she demanded, not much authority in her voice.

"The question is, why do your buddies General Echo and Colonel Chambeau want me dead?"

The woman said nothing, and her face fell farther.

"The fact that I'm here has to tell you something," McGarvey said. "At the very least you people—including the Saudis and a bunch of other mid-level intel and military officers—are playing a stupid game that could end up getting more people than just me killed."

"You don't understand."

"Enlighten me."

The woman stepped back. "This is bigger, more important, than you can possibly imagine."

"I don't give a shit who you voted for, but trying to discredit a president of the United States is treason no matter how you slice it," McGarvey said. "You don't like the guy, run for the office yourself, or back someone you think will do a better job."

"He doesn't belong in the White House. He's a fool. A buffoon. Dangerous."

"And you and your pals know better than a few tens of millions of voters?"

"He can't be allowed to continue."

"Then assassinate him."

Fischer stepped back closer to the door. She shook her head. "What do you take us for?" she demanded, her voice suddenly stronger, surer, indignant.

"You tried to kill me."

"It wasn't us."

"Who, then?"

"We don't know," Fischer said. She turned and fled the apartment.

McGarvey got out into the corridor as the woman disappeared into the stairwell.

But even before the door was fully shut, he heard the distinctive sound of a fired silenced automatic weapon.

□

THIRTY-SEVEN

McGarvey pulled out the phone as he raced down the corridor. "She's in the stairwell and someone's shooting."

"Do you want the cops?" Otto asked.

"Not yet. But get on the building's surveillance system."

McGarvey held up at the stairwell door and peered through the glass window. Fischer was sprawled facedown just below the landing. Blood from a head wound was already pooling on the concrete steps.

Shadows appeared to the right and above, and McGarvey ducked aside as a half-dozen shots starred the window.

"At least two men at the switchback just above you. Looks like they're armed with suppressed room brooms," Otto said. The room broom was the German-made Heckler & Koch MP5K compact submachine gun.

"Shut down the lights on this floor, then shut off the lights in the stairwell, wait one second, turn the stairwell lights back on and then off again. Now!"

More bullets slammed into the glass, finally breaking through and smacking into the corridor wall several feet beyond where McGarvey stood.

The lights in the corridor went off. A moment later they went off in the stairwell.

McGarvey laid the phone on the floor then ducked below the window, his left hand on the door handle.

The stairwell lights came on for one second then went out.

McGarvey slammed the door open, reached around the corner with his pistol and fired seven shots up the stairs, the unsilenced rounds impossibly loud.

Ejecting the spent magazine, he seated his only spare in the handle and charged the weapon as he waited for returning fire. But none came.

McGarvey picked up the phone. "Stairwell lights."

The lights came back on.

"They're gone," Otto said.

"Find them."

"The system's been shut down. I'll restart it, but it'll take a few seconds, so hold where you are. No telling where these bastards got themselves to."

"My six," McGarvey said.

He jumped up and raced toward the other end of the corridor as one of the apartment doors opened and a barefoot man, in jeans, no shirt, stuck his head out.

McGarvey stopped and pointed his gun at the man, who held up a hand, his face white.

"Get back inside."

The man immediately stepped back and closed the door.

McGarvey ran the rest of the way to the opposite stairwell door. "Otto?"

Otto was excited. "They're in the north stairwell, right behind you!" he shouted.

"I'm there."

"Do you want help?"

"No. But delay the cops if you can."

"I'm on it."

McGarvey pocketed the phone and ducked to one side so that he would be behind the door when it opened.

Someone was there. The handle came down slowly, and all of a sudden the steel door swung open and a man came halfway through.

McGarvey shouldered the door back, catching the man in the chest and wedging him against the doorframe.

A second man was right there, and shoved his partner forward.

McGarvey put two shots into the side of the first man's head. Immediately he stepped aside so that the door could fully open, and the dead man fell forward on his face.

The other one still inside the stairwell started down. McGarvey could hear the man's footfalls. He yanked the phone out of his pocket.

"The second guy is heading down the north stairwell. See where he goes."

"I've got him."

McGarvey turned the first man over on his back. His haircut looked military, and he appeared to be in very good shape, except for the fact he was dead. He carried no identification, and only three spare fifteen-round magazines of 9×19 Parabellum cartridges, plus a cell phone.

Pocketing the man's phone, he hurried to the south stairwell, where he went down to Fischer. She was dead. Two rounds had hit her in the neck just above her right shoulder and she'd taken a third to the back of her head.

McGarvey took the phone from her shoulder bag.

They must have known that McGarvey had come here to see her, and she'd been killed because of it. The question was which side she worked for—providing Estes was correct and there were two factions.

Otto was back. "Get the hell out of there right now. Nine-one-one has lit up like a Christmas tree. Two rapid-response teams are already en route along with just about every cop in D.C."

"What about the guy in the north stairwell?"

"A dark blue Toyota Corolla just pulled up. But I shit you not, Mac, move your ass."

McGarvey got one floor down, when Otto was back.

"The second shooter just came out the stairwell door."

"If the cops are going to be in time they have to be warned this is an active scene."

"Holy shit! Someone in the backseat of the Corolla just opened fire! They killed their own man and hauled ass."

"What about the cops?"

"Too late, they're still a block out."

"I'm not going to have time to get clear," McGarvey said. "Is there another way out of here?"

"Did you get any blood on you?"

"I don't think so."

"The mezzanine is one level down from the second floor. Get out there and walk over to the Next Whisky Bar. Pete will meet you there in ten."

"She was supposed to stay behind."

"Good luck with that in the future."

It was nearly a half hour by the time she walked through the doors and came over to where McGarvey was sitting at the bar having a Heineken.

She gave him a peck on the cheek and sat next to him. "Sorry I'm late, dear, but there's gotta be a thousand cops out there, and I had to run the gauntlet."

She ordered a glass of merlot and when the bartender had served her and went to the other end of the bar, she smiled. "From what Otto told me you ran into the middle of a firestorm. You okay?"

He briefly went over what had happened. "The point is Fischer told me that it wasn't her group who tried to kill me in Sarasota."

"You believed her?"

"Yes, I did."

"But then her own people killed her, and one of the shooters who tried to take you out," Pete said. She shook her head. "Killing their own people. That doesn't make sense. Unless the shooters belonged to the other faction Estes told Otto about."

"It makes sense to someone," McGarvey said.

"You say that the guy you took out wasn't carrying any ID," Pete said. "Puts us back to square one."

"I have his cell phone along with the woman's."

Pete lit up. "Otto should be able to pull something from them. Could give us a clue."

"More than that," McGarvey said. "If the guy ever used the phone, we'll have his DNA from the mouthpiece. And Otto should be able to crack Fischer's phone to see who she talked to."

THIRTY-EIGHT

□

Kamal had booked a seventh-floor suite at the Hay-Adams Hotel across from the White House, and had sent his weapons and spare identity documents, secured in gold foil, ahead via FedEx. Scanners would only detect what appeared to be a half-dozen neatly folded dress shirts and ties.

Wearing an Armani suit and Hermès tie, dressed down a little for this trip, he strode into the mahogany and gilded lobby to the registration desk, the bellman trailing with his single bag. It was two in the afternoon.

He'd stayed here briefly last year, and the manager remembered him.

"Welcome back, Mr. O'Neal," the man said. "A bottle of Krug has been sent to your suite, and our concierge Ms. Hanson will personally see to your needs while you're staying with us."

Kamal held out his platinum Amex card, but the manager declined it.

"We have it on file, sir."

"Good. My stay here is to be completely anonymous. No visitors, no phone calls, no emails, no messages. Am I clear?"

"Perfectly."

"I sent a parcel by FedEx. Has it arrived?"

"Yes, sir. It's in your suite."

"Very well."

"Enjoy your stay, sir."

"I will," Kamal said, and the bellman led him to the elevators and up to the suite, which looked out toward the White House, the Washington Monument in the near distance behind it.

Upstairs he gave the bellman a hundred-dollar bill and as the man was leaving, a well-put-together and faintly attractive woman in a blue blazer and gray skirt came in. Her gold name tag read HANSON.

"Welcome to the Hay-Adams, Mr. O'Neal, I'll be your personal concierge for your stay. If there's anything I can help you with at the moment . . . ?"

"Yes, my privacy."

"Pardon me, sir," the woman said and she turned and left, softly closing the door.

When she was gone, Kamal took off his jacket and loosened his tie. He opened the champagne, poured a glass, then turned on the television, the volume up a little, and went to the windows.

He could have killed the woman and thrown her body out in the corridor. But that would have been beyond stupid. Just an irrational impulse. But this close to McGarvey his bloodlust had risen. Had been rising since he'd left Mexico.

The bastard was unfinished business.

He phoned his Washington contact using the encrypted phone he'd gotten from his old Saudi contractor what seemed like years ago, but before the call went through he hit the END button

The channel on the television was CNN, and a photograph of a slender, not particularly good-looking woman was up on the screen. The announcer was saying something about Susan Fischer working for the National Security Agency.

On instinct alone, Kamal took the battery and SIM card out of the phone, and sat down on the end of the bed as the announcer recapped the breaking story. The woman had apparently been gunned down by at least two men, both of whom had been in turn shot to death by an unknown assailant or assailants.

The woman's body was found in a stairwell of the Watergate apartments just below the floor of her apartment. One of the suspected gunmen's bodies was found in the opposite stairwell, while a second, still unidentified man was found shot to death on the second level of the parking garage. Each man was armed with what were described as automatic weapons of a law-enforcement or military type.

"Fischer was believed to be employed by the NSA as an analyst in what was said to be a highly sensitive position.

"So far there are no suspects in the killings, though it was possible that a third armed man may have been seen by a witness on the eighth floor.

"Lieutenant Colonel Moses Chambeau, a spokesman for the agency, de-clined to comment or confirm that Ms. Fischer was an employee. How-ever, an informed source with the FBI, who declined to be cited, said that the method of Ms. Fischer's death appeared to be the work of professional assassins. In other news . . ."

The coincidence was too great for Kamal. As before, he was getting the distinct feeling that something else was going on. Something the Gang of Three in Beijing had not warned him about.

He phoned the concierge desk and Ms. Hanson answered.

"On second thought, you can be of service."

"Yes, sir."

"I want a decent laptop, as quickly as it can be sent up."

"Immediately, Mr. O'Neal. I'll bring it up personally."

Kamal poured another glass of champagne and went to the windows again as he waited. McGarvey was going to die within the next twenty-four hours, if not sooner, but first he needed to have more information. He felt as if he were being manipulated, backed into a corner. And he didn't like it, and needed to find out enough to tip the situation back in his favor.

The woman was at his door within ten minutes with an Apple laptop and a portable printer, which she set up on the desk.

"Would you like me to go through the basics?"

"No," Kamal said, and he handed her five hundred dollars, which she placed in her pocket with a nod.

At the door she turned back. "You would like your privacy. So let me suggest that you use HayAdams.com, and my password, 23PPQXR9."

"Generous."

"Shall I write it down for you?"

"No. But my business is of a confidential nature. It would be unfortu-nate if someone else were to read my emails."

"The password is mine alone, Mr. O'Neal. And when you are finished it will be changed. Let me assure you that no one will be reading your mail, least of all me. This is the Hay-Adams."

Pouring his third glass of wine, Kamal sat down at the computer and when it had booted up he got onto the concierge's personal account, and from there pulled up Runet, the Russian internet.

When he was on, he entered the search engine called EDWARD SNOWDEN, which was run by the SVR, and not the American himself, but had been built upon Snowden's original database of U.S. surveillance secrets and methodologies.

He had used the site before but always from a computer untraceable to him. This time, even if the NSA picked up on it, the track would lead back to the Hay-Adams's concierge. But by then he would be long gone.

He entered Susan Fischer's name and her position with the NSA.

Almost immediately her biography came up. She was born in Colorado Springs, her father a U.S. Air Force instructor at the academy, her mother a writer who'd published several nonfiction books on mathematics. Both were deceased. Yesterday's death of their forty-three-year-old daughter hadn't been entered yet.

The brief article identified her as a mid-level analyst with the National Security Agency; her boss was Lieutenant Colonel Moses Chambeau. An SVR sidebar indicated that Ms. Fischer was a possible resource, as was her boss, who it turned out was her lover.

Her current medical history, financial information and her Social Security number, along with her D.C. driving license and passport photos and numbers, plus the address of her Watergate apartment, were also listed.

Under Chambeau he got the same information, including an address in Alexandria, and the fact that he was married to Jennifer Echo, the sister of Brigadier General Walter Echo, who was a deputy chief of logistics at the Pentagon.

Echo's page contained the same personal information, including an address in Fairfax.

The largest surprise was that like Fischer, the SVR had evaluated the two men as possible resources.

But McGarvey's page was password protected.

Kamal sat back, the glimmer of an idea that had come to him watching the CNN newscast about the murder of the Fischer woman emerging about the so far unidentified armed man whom a witness had seen on the eighth floor of the Watergate apartment building.

He went back to Fischer's page. Her Watergate address was an apartment on the eighth floor.

McGarvey.

The bastard had been there in the middle of it. Fischer was a clue he was running down, until she was shot to death by someone with military-style weapons, then her assassins shot to death by someone else, also using military weapons.

Covering up what?

THIRTY-NINE

☐

A little before three, McGarvey, driving the BMW, Pete beside him, was passed through the main gate at the CIA's campus, and took the curving driveway up to the Old Headquarters Building.

Otto had called all out of breath forty-five minutes earlier. "Come," he'd said.

"I'm starting to get a little sick of this place," Pete said. "Every time we show up, a ton of trouble drops out of the sky right on top of us."

"Do you want to quit?" McGarvey asked. He'd been feeling the same thing lately. But each time he'd resolved to back away, something did seem to fall out of the sky for him. For both of them now.

"Can we?"

"Not until this thing is done. I take exceptions to people trying to kill me."

"Me too. But what about afterwards?"

McGarvey had been thinking about just that lately. He didn't feel too old for the business, nor did he think that having a peg leg slowed him down. Yet he wondered if all that was just some sort of a defense mechanism. Maybe he was too old; maybe hobbling around on a prosthetic leg took away whatever physical edge he once had.

"At least a long vacation."

"That'd be nice," Pete said, but it was obvious she didn't really believe it.

McGarvey still had VIP parking privileges but no security badges, so Otto came down on the elevator to escort them up to his third-floor suite of offices. He looked worn out, as if he'd worked overnight, but he also seemed excited. Once again he had a bone in his teeth, something he couldn't walk away from if he'd wanted to.

They held their silence until they were safely inside Otto's special security bubble. All the screens were deeply lavender.

"You're not going to believe the shit I came up with from the two
phones," Otto said.

"Did you get DNA back from the shooter I took down in the stairwell
already?" McGarvey asked.

"Not yet. But I finally cracked the security codes, and they're the same
algorithm I came up with last year. Fischer and the guy were using the
same encryption protocol, with the identification signature I put in before I farmed it out of this office."

"I don't understand," Pete said.

"I gave the program to five separate entities: our Clandestine Services
and our Directorate of Intel, along with the National Security Agency
and the DIA. Each had a different marker code. Just like nuclear bomb
materials—plutonium and U235. Each manufacturing facility leaves a signature code in the stuff. If a nuke is exploded the residue it leaves behind
contains the manufacturer's stamp."

"You said five users—who's the fifth?"

"The White House."

"Jesus," Pete said.

"Secure comms between the president and his staff and his Secret Service detail."

"Let's start with Fischer's phone," McGarvey said.

"It has the NSA's marker, of course. But the odd part is that she very sel-
dom used it. I'm assuming that she made most of her calls from another
phone. You just got lucky picking the right one from her purse."

"It's the first one I found."

"Her calls go back a whole year. Her received calls. The earliest are from
some place in Monaco."

"Did you retrieve a number?"

"Someone modified the program, so I'm only picking up the country
and city codes," Otto said. "But that's a fairly easy modification that some
decent techie could figure out. Just blocking the caller ID."

"Is this leading where I think it is?"

"The timing is right for your last op. Just before those calls, one came
from Riyadh, and then there was nothing for almost eight months."

"Let me guess, sometime just after the second Tuesday in November?"

"Yeah. Several here in the D.C. area. I think I can crack the ID block later today or maybe by tomorrow. My darlings are working on it. But there are a few trillion lines of code to process."

"The Monaco calls could have been from Kamal, and the one from Riyadh, his GIP control officer," McGarvey said.

"If it is the same guy who took down the pencil tower AtEighth in New York, and tried for the one up the block from the UN, he might be back in business. Three days ago someone called Fischer from a spot in Mexico out in the middle of nowhere, about a hundred miles south of El Paso."

"What's there?"

"We have a satellite that makes an occasional pass over the area. Looking for cartel operations. But nothing has shown up in the past year."

"No one's paying much attention," McGarvey said. "Could be anything or nothing. What about the Mexican army, have they shown any interest?"

Otto was hesitant. "Nothing they're talking about. But it'd be prime real estate for just about anything. Maybe a training camp."

"Are you talking about ISIS?" Pete asked.

"Or the Saudis. Al-Daran was working for them, if it was him again."

"Fischer was his intel source," McGarvey said.

"Yes. And her pals want you dead. Could be they hired al-Daran to try to take you out again."

"If it's him—and that's a big if at this point—could be he's heading back to wherever he went to ground after Monaco," Pete said.

"He's on his way here," Otto told them. "He knows his first attempt to kill Mac in Sarasota failed, so my guess is that he wants to finish the job."

"But that's not all, is it?" McGarvey said.

"Fischer used the same phone to make several other calls in D.C., and several just across the river to a seven-oh-three area code. I'm betting the Pentagon. To General Echo."

"Who else would she use that phone to call?"

"Two-oh-two? My guess would be the White House," Otto said. "Hatchett. She and Echo and Chambeau are conspirators."

"Conspirators in what?" Pete said. "None of this makes any sense. Especially not if you're telling me that Hatchett—the White House—wants Mac dead."

"Echo was one of the Pentagon people who mouthed off about not following any orders that Weaver would issue as president," Pete said. "A soft
coup."

"That's a far cry from hiring an assassin to kill the former director of
the CIA," Otto said. He looked and sounded as if he were on the verge of
a meltdown. "The problem as I see it is that Estes could be right, there are
two groups with at least one common goal—killing Mac. One could be
somehow connected with the DIA, NSA and the White House—as far-
fetched as that sounds."

"But why?" Pete asked.

"I don't know. But the second group involves fourth- and fifth-ranking
officers from at least ten or fifteen intelligence agencies."

"Including the CIA?"

"I don't know that either. But I'm working on it."

"Both with the same two common threads. Me first and then the president."

"Insanity," Pete said softly.

"I'll start with the White House," McGarvey said.

FORTY

□

It was four when McGarvey went up to the director's office on the seventh floor. He'd asked Pete to stick with Otto, and escort him home when he was ready to leave for the day.

"You could be marching straight into the lion's den," Otto had warned.

"Could be someone on the president's staff pushed and I'm going to push back."

"Jesus," Pete said.

Walt Page came down the hall from the Watch just as McGarvey was getting off the elevator. He looked like the image of a Wall Street banker, well dressed, serious in an East Coast manner and normally unflappable. But just now he did not look happy.

"Were you the unknown gunman at the Watergate the cops are looking for?"

"Yes, and we need to talk because this situation is starting to spiral out of control."

"Usually happens when you're involved."

They went straight through past his secretary to his office, which looked over the woods behind the Old Headquarters Building. It was a tranquil view that very often did not match the situation inside the various buildings on the campus. In many ways this place was more of a crisis center than either the Pentagon's War Room or the White House Situation Room.

"Coffee?" Page asked, directing Mac to have a seat.

"I need to see the president this afternoon," McGarvey said.

Page was in the act of sitting down, but he stopped, his left hand on the desk. "Okay, Mac, you have my attention, if that's what you wanted."

"I've come up with some pretty strong evidence that two groups of people want me dead. One of them has hired the terrorist who took down AtEighth last year, and the other may involve a consortium of mid-level intelligence officers from perhaps as many as a dozen agencies around the world. Including the DIA."

"They've already tried and missed. But why have you been targeted?"

"Otto says that I'm a rogue operator."

"You both are, but it doesn't answer my question."

"We're in the middle of a soft coup, directed by a few people in the Pentagon and the intel officers we've already identified."

"A soft coup, if you're right, to do what? Depose Weaver?"

"Make him look like a fool. Maybe force his hand into doing something so completely irresponsible that he'd have to be impeached."

"Irresponsible how?"

"Maybe getting us on the brink of another war that nobody could win."

"A war with who?"

"With any number of countries, along the flash point divides."

"You're talking about Pakistan and India, Israel and North Korea and just about everyone else on their borders."

"And others."

"You said there were two groups. Who is the second?"

"Someone inside the White House."

Page sat down and called his secretary in the outer office. "We're not to be disturbed for any reason." He hung up, his mood unreadable. "Are you accusing the president of trying to kill you?"

"I don't think he's involved, at least not directly."

"The intel group—and I'm assuming you believe that could involve someone inside the Company—wants to push the president into making a blunder, make him look bad, and they believe that you have to be eliminated before you expose them. Your soft coup."

"Yes," McGarvey said. "The problem is the blunder could get out of hand and a shooting war could actually start."

"But the White House group, the one you think the president has no knowledge of, wants you dead for what reason? It'd have to be a very good one."

"The intel people want him to look bad, but his own people want the opposite, of course."

"Of course."

"The real problem is, who hired al-Daran—al Nassr, 'the Eagle'—to kill me?"

"Providing that you're on the right track, I'd have to guess it was your flash points people. Providing anything you've come up with is even close to reality. Or perhaps your Eagle came after you purely out of revenge for stopping him from taking down the second pencil tower in New York."

"Someone tried to kill me at the Farm, and the woman gunned down at the Watergate was killed by guys I'm pretty sure were military or ex-military, sent because she was meeting with me."

"She was one of your flash point people?"

"Yes, and she was possibly in contact at some point with al-Daran in Monaco and with the Saudi intelligence agency."

"Lets the White House off the hook."

"I shot one of them in the stairwell outside of Fischer's apartment, but the second shooter was gunned down in the parking garage by someone else."

"Someone from the White House group?"

"It's a possibility, Walt. And if they're willing to go that far, whatever they've got planned to make their boss look good could backfire just as easily."

Page swiveled in his chair and looked out the window. "You can see the seasons changing from here. Sometimes after it snows all night, the scene out there is beautiful. Peaceful, serene. Nothing bad creeping up on us."

He turned back. "As of a half hour ago Hezbollah had fired six rockets into the heart of Tel Aviv. Lots of casualties. We've got reasonable intel that Iran may have reneged on their nuclear treaty. Their diplomatic envoy has been called to Camp David, where the president has gone for a long weekend.

"North Korea announced that it will fire a series of ICBM's that could rain down on us. And you've told me that you think someone working on behalf of the president may have tried to assassinate the former director of this agency. Does any of that sound totally nuts to you?"

"Insanity run amok," McGarvey said. He felt sorry for Page, and for every other hapless son of a bitch who'd ever taken the job as director of the CIA. The world was a scary place and the person who sat behind this desk, and who answered not only to Congress but to the director of national security and the president, was never in an easy spot.

If he brought bad news, he was blamed. If he brought good news, he was suspected of having his head buried in the sand.

The new national director of intelligence, who was chartered to oversee all fourteen separate U.S. intelligence agencies, and supposed to shoulder all the responsibilities for reporting and analysis—the same job the CIA had been created to do—was not much more than a showpiece: a purely political appointment with little or no intelligence gathering or analysis capabilities.

McGarvey had sat in Page's seat for a very short time, and he'd hated every minute of it. At heart he was a field officer, not an administrator.

"Okay, you and I will chopper up to Camp David. To this point this president has been accessible. But once we get there, what are you going to tell him? And remember, if it doesn't make any sense to me, it surely won't to him."

"I'll tell him what I suspect is happening. What the unintended consequences might be."

"You're going to warn the president?"

"What other choice do we have?"

"Quit right now, and walk away from it."

"I've already tried that, Walt. But they came to me in Sarasota."

"Your Eagle did. Go after him, not the president," Page said. "Not this president. He'll just laugh in your face."

"I'll mention Nixon."

FORTY-ONE

Camp David, officially known as the Naval Support Facility Thurmont, was located on five thousand mostly wooded acres about sixty miles northwest of the White House. Staffed by navy and Marine Corps personnel, the place was not open to the public and even the airspace above the facility was strictly off-limits.

Except to the DCI's helicopter flying up from Langley, and squawking the proper transponder codes.

Page had phoned Martha Draper, the president's chief of staff, to ask for the meeting. As it turned out, Amir Saleh, the Iranian envoy, had already left, and the president was in a very good mood.

"Something new since your morning brief?" she'd asked.

"Yes. But we shouldn't take up too much of his weekend."

"We?"

"I'm bringing Kirk McGarvey with me. He'd like a word."

McGarvey, sitting across from Page's desk, the phone in speaker mode, had heard Draper's hesitation.

"Anything I need to brief the boss on before you get up here?"

McGarvey shook his head.

"No."

"I'll tell him you're coming."

An F-15 fighter/interceptor jet appeared off their starboard side, and flying dirty and slow kept station until the DCI's Airbus AS365 Dauphin VIP helicopter was cleared for landing, and touched down on the pad a hundred yards south of the Laurel Lodge conference room.

Three specially equipped golf carts were waiting as Page and McGarvey got out. Two of them carried Secret Service officers, while Draper and President Weaver were in the third.

Two of the Secret Service agents hustled over.

"Are you armed, Mr. McGarvey?" one them asked.

"No."

"The president has a few minutes for you, sir," the agent said. He spoke briefly into his lapel mic.

Weaver got out of his golf cart and waited until the agent escorted McGarvey and Page to him. He was a tall man, well above six feet, with a husky, but in no way overweight, build. His face, expressive eyes and square jaw had probably been seen on more television news and broadcasts and internet sites over the past two years than any other person's in history.

One of his famous lines during the run-up to the election was: "Face it, people, I'm more popular than Santa Claus."

He and Page shook hands. "Good to see you, Mr. Director."

"I don't think you've ever met Kirk McGarvey."

"Never had the pleasure," Weaver said. He and McGarvey shook hands, the president's grip dry and firm. "But your reputation precedes you, and like just about everyone else, I was happy to learn that you survived the terrorist attack. You were lucky."

"Luckier than most, Mr. President."

Weaver smiled.

"Kirk wanted to have a word with you, Mr. President," Page said.

"Let's go for a walk," Weaver said, taking McGarvey's arm. "We won't be long," he told Page.

They took a path directly away from the helicopter, down the hill through the woods. Both Secret Service carts followed at a discreet distance.

McGarvey had briefed several presidents over his career, and Weaver was the same as all of them, in that an electric aura surrounded him, like a halo, or the northern lights. The power was palpable and very real.

Away from Page and Draper his smile went away, but he said nothing until they were around a bend in the path and out of sight of everyone except his Secret Service minders. He stopped.

"I understand that you were involved in the shooting at the Watergate last night," he said.

It was a mistake. No one was supposed to know that McGarvey had been there. The man's arrogance was the first thing in McGarvey's mind, but he didn't change his neutral expression.

"Yes, sir. I was running down what I thought was an important lead that led me to Ms. Fischer—she was an analyst with the National Security Agency."

"I was briefed on her position. What lead?"

"There may be a conspiracy to bring you down."

Weaver laughed. "Every president has faced that sort of thing. And if you guys kept running after the bogeymen hiding in the woods, you'd be missing the Islamic extremist bastards lined up on our borders. This is all-out war, McGarvey, don't kid yourself. And the final outcome is just about as perilous for America as it was the day after Pearl Harbor."

"I agree with you."

Weaver smiled briefly. "That's good," he said. "Very good. Now are you telling me that you were targeted in Sarasota by these conspirators?"

"It's very likely they thought I might create a problem for them."

Again Weaver laughed, but it seemed forced. "From what I've been told you have a habit of getting into people's faces. Enemies of America. And you've damned near lost your life on more than one occasion. And you've lost your wife and daughter and son-in-law. Maybe it's time to retire."

"I've tried that, Mr. President. It never seems to stick."

"Your past catching up with you?"

"Yes, sir, just like yours."

Weaver's smile disappeared. He glanced back at his Secret Service detail, but they were far enough away to be out of earshot. McGarvey had not spotted any parabolic audio pickups on either cart, nor any other obvious surveillance devices in the trees, or beside the path.

"Your job is to catch the bad guys coming our way. You did a good job in New York, and I expect if you keep your eye on the ball this time, you'll do the same."

"Yes, sir. But that doesn't change the likelihood that you've become a target. One that could very well spiral out of control."

"The CIA has no charter to spy within our borders. I suggest that you stick to that directive."

"Wouldn't have worked in New York, Mr. President."

Weaver stepped close. "Look, you son of a bitch, I'm not going to listen to your shit. Back away, or I'll have your ass down in Guantánamo."

"I signed on to defend the Constitution of the United States against all enemies, foreign and domestic."

"Guantánamo along with your girlfriend and your geek friend."

It was a second mistake.

"Someone on your staff may have hired the same Saudi-directed terrorist who took down the pencil tower in New York to kill me."

"You're out of your fucking mind."

"One of them may be Ron Hatchett."

"Bullshit."

"You sent him to Beijing. To do what?"

"None of your fucking business."

"The thing is, he isn't your enemy. In fact, he and the others believe that they're your friends. They want to protect you. Save your presidency. Just like Haldeman and the others wanted to save Nixon's."

"Get the hell back to Washington."

"Only this time, Mr. President, more than just a few people could get killed. Could lead at least to a regional war. Maybe something worse."

Weaver stalked directly back to his Secret Service detail, who had moved up a little closer because they'd realized that a possible threat was unfolding.

"I want this son of a bitch back on the helicopter, now. If he refuses to leave, shoot him."

PART
THREE

The Consortium

Two days later

FORTY-TWO

☐

Yaser Abboud, dressed in an ordinary Western business suit, waited in the large anteroom outside of Prince Awadi bin Abdulaziz's office at a compound outside of Riyadh. He had been summoned from his office at GIP headquarters to drop everything and come immediately. He'd been expecting the call for several days now, and he had done his homework.

Although the prince was only one of at least a thousand Abdulaziz grandsons, and only held the position of deputy minister of foreign finance and communications, he was still of royal blood. And his power was nearly absolute.

It was the prince who'd directed Sa'ad al-Sakr to hire al Nassr to strike the U.S. last year, and even though the operation had been at least a partial success, it was Prince Awadi who had ordered al-Sakr's death.

Just about everyone inside the intelligence agency knew about the execution, but they had only a few glimmerings of why it had been ordered. Al-Sakr, himself a minor prince, had been a major in special projects, but in this case his royal blood had not saved him.

Prince Awadi was making a reputation for himself over the dead bodies of officers who failed him. Abboud had a feeling his own head was getting close to the chopping block. And for nothing other than obeying orders.

The ornately carved double doors opened, and Prince Awadi's personal secretary beckoned. "The prince will receive you now, Captain."

Awadi was short for an Abdulaziz, but his nose was typically prominent, his eyes hooded and his complexion dark. He was dressed in Gucci loafers, no socks, designer jeans and a white silk shirt, the sleeves rolled up above his elbows. He did a lot of traveling in the West, and he'd taken to dressing the part. No explanations for why he didn't dress traditionally, but then princes had no need to explain themselves.

He was standing looking out the sliding glass doors at the lush green of the par-three nine-hole golf course he'd built a couple of years ago. Just the cost of maintaining the fairways and greens, especially the water features, was astronomical.

But again, royalty was never questioned, even with the plunge in oil revenues.

"Good afternoon, sir," Abboud said, stopping a respectful distance away.

"What progress, Captain?" Awadi asked without turning.

"I have the complete cooperation of the others. When the moment arrives the disinformation campaign will begin. U.S. military intelligence will believe that the threats of nuclear attacks at the six key flash points are on the verge of developing."

Awadi said nothing, waiting for Abboud to continue.

"Our analysts believe, as you do, that President Weaver, faced with so many multiple problems, will be forced into making a series of missteps. The confidence of the American public will be deeply shaken."

"Deeply enough for impeachment proceedings?"

"I cannot say that with one hundred percent confidence, but the consensus within the other agencies, especially the German BND, French DGSE and Iran's MOIS, is that Congress will vote for impeachment."

"The Republican-controlled Congress?" The prince asked.

"Yes, sir. His own party has never supported him."

Prince Awadi finally turned. "And what of McGarvey?"

"He still lives."

"Yes, I know. But why have you failed me?"

Abboud had never felt closer to death in his life. "Al Nassr failed."

Awadi said nothing.

"But there is another development. A second party, we don't know who yet, may want the same thing we want. McGarvey was severely wounded; nevertheless, he showed up at the CIA's training camp south of Washington, where another attempt was made on his life. But it wasn't our operators from New York. It happened before they left their offices at the UN."

"Find out who they are, and what they wish to ultimately accomplish. Perhaps we can help them."

"Yes, sir."

"What else?"

"One of our Falcon Eye surveillance satellites that we share with the United Arab Emirates has reliable imagery that shows Mr. McGarvey arriving at Camp David two days ago."

"The resolution is not that good."

"No, sir. But one of our on-the-ground observers at Langley witnessed Mr. McGarvey along with the DCI Walter Page boarding the director's Dauphin helicopter, which landed at Camp David forty-one minutes after takeoff."

"Was Weaver in residence?"

"We believe so."

"Assuming McGarvey met with him, what was the subject of their conversation?"

"Unknown at this point. But we think that it may have had something to do with the death of a National Security Agency analyst by the name of Susan Fischer. She was one of ours."

"It was on the news. Who killed her?"

"We don't know yet, but her assassins—there were two of them—were killed. One of them we believe was killed by McGarvey. But the other we don't know yet. We have two other sources in D.C. who we're approaching."

"Will her death hamper the plan?"

"Not significantly, sir."

Awadi nodded, a small smile playing at the corner of his mouth. "And what contact have we had with al Nassr?"

"None."

"Stop his payments."

"That has been done, sir. But there may be still another issue."

Awadi's mouth tightened. "What are you telling me now, Captain? More bad news?"

"He may have another employer. We have reasonably reliable intelligence that he was spotted in Beijing last month, meeting with someone still unknown at an undistinguished hotel."

"His only mission for us was to kill McGarvey. He failed."

"Yes, sir."

The double doors opened as the Prince's secretary appeared. "Your pardon, Prince, but the king has called."

"Leave!" Awadi screamed at the top of his lungs.

The secretary withdrew and closed the doors.

Abboud didn't move a muscle. "I've changed my mind. I want you to regain contact with al Nassr. Offer the man any money he wants. You have my personal authorization; all other considerations or orders are rescinded. McGarvey must die. And soon."

"Yes, sir. I'll try."

"You'll *do*!"

"Yes, sir."

"Find out who the second group is. Offer our help. Discreetly."

"Yes, sir."

Awadi went to his desk and sat down. He opened a drawer and took out a WWII German Luger, and handled it for a moment or two, almost lovingly, like an old friend or a precious objet d'art, before he laid it down.

"Did you know Major al-Sakr?"

"Not well, but yes, sir," Abboud said. He was having a little trouble with his legs.

"He was al Nassr's control officer. He failed me. Don't you follow in his footsteps. Resolve this issue, Captain. Am I clear?"

"Perfectly."

"Get out of my sight."

Abboud saluted, did an about-face and went to the double doors, which opened before him. Back in the anteroom with the secretary, as the doors closed, he heard Prince Awadi laughing like a madman, and he was sincerely happy he had survived the encounter.

FORTY-THREE

Dinner was at the Renckes' house in McLean. Louise had made small pizza crusts and a good tomato sauce, and had laid out all the toppings, from mushrooms and anchovies to cheeses, pepperoni, hamburger and even ham and bacon. Four small pizza stones were ready in the dual ovens.

"Each man for himself," she'd said. "Beer's in the fridge."

Otto had not been himself for the past two days, ever since McGarvey had returned from meeting with the president, and he'd been working around the clock in his office and even at home.

"I've lost him," he said when they sat down at the kitchen counter while they waited for their pizzas to bake. His face was long.

"He's here in Washington," McGarvey said. He'd known that the man was coming, and he could almost feel the assassin's presence. Just the same as he'd felt it in New York.

"You're probably right, but I can't find him. He's done with his business in Mexico and he's here to finish what the kid at New College botched and whoever it was at the Farm."

"How about Grace Metal?" Pete asked.

"She came up clean on every one of my search engines," Otto said. He shook his head. "Doesn't say much for me and my darlings."

"Paper records, verbal orders," McGarvey said.

It was the one weakness in Otto's search engines, or any system that trolled the expanse of the computer-driven world. If it wasn't on some digital file somewhere it was inaccessible except the old-fashioned way: HUMINT—human intelligence gathering. Someone had to get into a file cabinet somewhere, or a daybook or calendar, to read what was written by hand. Or eavesdrop on a conversation, as Otto had done with Echo and Colonel Chambeau at the Watergate bar.

"Ball's in your park again, Kemo Sabe," Otto said. "Sorry."

"Let's take it one name at a time," McGarvey replied. "We're pretty sure he was in Atlanta and in Mexico, and assuming I'm right and he's here in D.C., he'll be living large under a cover name."

"The guy's a pro. His cover names last time were bulletproof."

"I understand. But he can't have an unlimited supply of legends— passports, credit cards, driver's licenses—which would have to lead back to histories, including Social Security numbers here in the States or national identity numbers in France and most other countries."

"It could mean that he's used whatever IDs he has more than once," Pete said. "Luxury hotels in Chihuahua, maybe Dallas or Houston or some other port of entry to the U.S. from Mexico. Atlanta. New York. And here in Washington. And we have at least three pictures of him that you could use to match passport photos."

Otto brightened and he started to get up. "I'm on it."

"After dinner," Louise said. "In the meantime I've been thinking about what our guy was doing in Mexico. I talked to a pal of mine over at the NSA who's willing to let me have a couple of very brief unscheduled looks at that slice of Mexican desert. I'd have to redirect the bird's cameras, and the look-downs would be at pretty extreme angles. But if there is some sort of an installation down there not managed by complete idiots, they'd have the ephemeris of our satellite, and would cover up when they knew it was overhead. Might catch them with their pants down."

"You'd have to burn an asset," Pete said.

"He's a good friend," Louise said. "Anyway, we're talking about more important things here."

"In the meantime we have General Echo and Colonel Chambeau, who both had contact with Fischer," McGarvey said. "I think it's time I paid them a visit."

"I'll back you up," Pete said.

McGarvey wanted to tell her no, but he thought that would be useless, and in any event, considering what had gone down at the Watergate, she was right. He could use her on his six.

He nodded. "In the meantime I want a complete list of all the intel officers your program identified as co-conspirators in your Consortium. Depending on whatever I can get from Echo and Chambeau, we might be able to pick out a couple of them that I personally worked with sometime in the past."

"In the meantime you have a big target on your back that two separate groups are aiming at," Louise said. "Walk with care, Kirk."

"I've been completely transparent for the past two days. Running in the park, walking around Georgetown. I even went to the Lincoln Memorial yesterday and sat on the steps. Waiting for someone to show up."

Pete was a little angry. "While you sent me to the campus to help Otto."

"No one was following me. No one on the rooftops. Never the same car or van circling the block. The same guy stopping to look in the window of a store across the street. Or sitting on a picnic bench in the park, or leaning against a parked car on a direct sight line to me."

"It's not the operator you see, it's the one you miss," Pete argued. "These people are pros."

"I think you're wrong. At least up to this point. The kid who put the Semtex in my car was an amateur."

"He damned near killed you."

"He would have, had he put the bomb under my seat and not on the passenger's side. Or if he'd sealed the thing in plastic so I wouldn't smell it, or attached it to the undercarriage. And cutting the ropes on the Ball Buster left too much to chance. I grabbed the second rope to stop my fall and I was lucky it didn't break."

"So they sent amateurs. If al-Daran is really here in town, he's come to finish the job. And that guy is damned good."

"You're right. But first I want to know what he was doing in Mexico."

"Whatever it was, it won't make much difference if he lays low somewhere with a decent sniper rifle," Louise said. "You walk out the front door of your apartment building, or out this front door, and he takes his shot. One shot."

"He won't play it that way," McGarvey disagreed.

"What are you talking about? He wants you dead."

"He wants more than that. He wants to look into my eyes when he's in the act of killing me. He wants to see fear, or resignation or some other crazy thing. He needs for this to be personal."

"Same difference, Mac. Dead is dead, no matter how you slice it."

"I want him face-to-face. I want to ask him who he's working for, and what they want."

"The Saudis, probably," Pete said.

"Then I'll want the name of his control officer," McGarvey told her. "But I don't think it'll be that simple."

"What, stopping him from killing you?"

"To find out who he's working for," Otto said. "There're two groups here, remember? Both of them wanting to take Mac down. But why? To make a fool of Weaver? To force him out of office?"

"Maybe we ought to take a look at Heaney," Pete suggested. Edward Heaney was the vice president.

"The man's a dolt," Louise said. "He couldn't even get out of his own way."

"Maybe it's an act."

"I don't think so," McGarvey said.

"That said, what's the plan?" Louise asked. She was the mother hen, and forever was wanting to know the details so that she could fit everything together to protect her people.

"I've already confronted Weaver—and so far there's been no retaliation. Now I'm going after the Consortium—the intel people Otto's programs have identified."

"You went after Fischer and she was assassinated," Pete said.

"I'm going to try Echo next, then Chambeau, but you're going to back-stop me," McGarvey said. "Then depending on what I turn up or don't, I'll work my way down the list. And if someone in the Company is a part of this, we need to find out who it is."

"I've come up with blanks so far," Otto said. "But I'd bet just about anything it wasn't Grace Metal."

FORTY-FOUR

☐

Kamal, dressed in a pair of jeans, a dark T-shirt and sneakers, sat on the open tailgate of an older Ford F-150 pickup that he'd bought for a few thousand dollars from a car lot across the river in Annandale the day before yesterday.

He'd used cash from the supply brought with him from France, plus what he'd gotten from Baz in Mexico.

It was after seven in the evening and he'd been parked in the trees across from a baseball diamond two blocks behind the Renckes' McLean house for the past half hour, concentrating on the control panel of the high-end civilian drone he'd bought and had delivered to an accommodations address in Manassas two days before he'd bought truck.

McGarvey had been easy, too easy, to follow from his Georgetown apartment, across to the park, in a cab to the Lincoln Memorial, where the bastard had sat eating a sandwich on the steps. He'd been alone.

The DJI Inspire Special Edition drone equipped with a fairly low lux video camera hovered several hundred feet above the two-story colonial, its four electric motors almost completely silent and undetectable from that distance.

He'd followed McGarvey and his girlfriend from Georgetown, where the Rencke woman had let them in almost two hours ago. Since then there'd been no activity, except for the occasional car on the street passing the entry to the cul-de-sac where the Renckes lived.

He took a chance and hit the HOME button on the controller and the drone immediately peeled off station and made a direct line back to Kamal's position.

It came in for a landing just a few minutes later, and Kamal quickly replaced the batteries for the third and final time, and sent it back to the cul-de-sac just as McGarvey came out of the house and got into the Toyota SUV.

At that same moment the garage door opened, and an older BMW convertible backed out and stopped next to McGarvey. The woman behind the wheel was Pete Boylan, her face clearly recognizable as she looked up into the sky directly to where the drone was hovering.

Kamal zoomed in on her face.

She turned away for a moment, evidently to say something to McGarvey, then looked back up toward the drone, and winked.

Kamal reared back from the screen. She'd been looking directly at him, the same smirk on her lips as she had when he'd briefly held her hostage last year in Monaco. She was an arrogant bitch, and once McGarvey was finally dead, no power on heaven or earth would stop him from attending to her. In detail.

McGarvey left first, the woman right behind him, and they headed directly to the Beltway, where they went south. A few minutes later McGarvey took I-66 to the west toward Fairfax while Pete Boylan took the interstate to the east, back toward town.

It suddenly occurred to him that he knew where they were going: McGarvey to see General Echo, and the woman back to her apartment in Georgetown.

The bastard knew that he was being followed and he'd sent his girlfriend out of harm's way. Touching, and Kamal toyed with the idea of letting McGarvey continue his investigations tonight, while he followed the woman and killed her.

But that would come later. Job one for the Gang of Three and even more important for himself, was McGarvey, and tonight the bastard was going to die. It was something he'd been looking forward to for a long time. Too long.

He set the drone on self-pilot and headed it southeast toward Reagan National Airport. With any luck it would get sucked into an engine of an aircraft either taking off or landing. In any event, its flying into a controlled airspace would keep the FAA and the police busy tonight.

Tossing the controller aside, he got behind the wheel of the truck at the same moment his cell phone chimed. He'd put the SIM card and battery back in but he hadn't expected a call. Very few people knew this number.

His first thought was Otto Rencke, and he was about to remove the battery, but decided against it. If it was McGarvey's friend, perhaps he and his wife would die tonight as well.

Kamal answered on the third chine. "Yes."

"Al Nassr, do you know who this is?"

The man spoke English but with an Arabic accent. Almost certainly a Saudi, and almost as certainly someone from the GIP.

"No."

"Do you know the name Sa'ad al-Sakr?"

"He's dead."

"Yes, and I've taken over his desk. I am Captain Yaser Abboud. And the fact that I know the major's name and I know yours and I know this number must mean something."

"Continue."

"I have been authorized to place you back on the payroll. You would have only the one operation for us."

"I'm listening."

"You are to kill Kirk McGarvey. And we understand that you already tried and failed to do so within the last month. Why?"

"He was lucky."

"I mean, we want to know who you are working for. Who else has hired you to kill McGarvey?"

Kamal sat back. What he was being asked made no sense. Unless the GIP was not involved with the Gang of Three he'd met in Beijing. "Susan Fischer," he said on impulse.

"She was stupid."

"And so are Echo and Chambeau?"

"Did you kill her?"

"Someone did."

"Was it you?"

"No. But I was going to her for information. She was one of my sources on my last mission."

"If not you, who, then?" Abboud demanded.

"It shouldn't be too hard to figure out, or are you people complete idiots? It was McGarvey, of course. He knows about you and the others. And he's coming after you. She was first. And at this very minute he's on his way to see the general."

"Do you mean Echo?"

"What other general are we talking about?"

"Just Echo."

"And then Chambeau. Does his name ring any bells with you bastards?"

Abboud was silent for a long time and Kamal had thought he had lost the man.

"How much money do you want for McGarvey?"

The Beijing Gang of Three was paying him a lot of money for McGarvey, and the GIP wanted to pay him even more. The fact of the matter was, now that he was on the hunt, he was willing to do the job for no money. Revenge, if for nothing else. The pure pleasure of watching the lights go out in the bastard's eyes.

"Name your price," Abboud prompted.

"Five million."

"Dollars?"

"Or euros. Doesn't matter which. But I want the payment in diamonds."

Again Abboud fell silent.

"Half to be sent immediately to my bank in London." Kamal gave the name of the bank and a safety deposit box number. "When they arrive I'll proceed."

"You're not in London now?"

"I'm near Washington."

"It will be done."

"Then consider McGarvey as good as dead."

"Do not fail this time, or you will become our next target."

"Don't threaten me, you little fucking pufta. You want me to do your dirty work, I'll do it. But fuck with me and I will find out who you are and I will kill you and your entire family. Am I clear?"

"You're clear," Abboud said. "Good hunting."

FORTY-FIVE

One exit away from Fairfax, McGarvey phoned Otto. "Is the drone following me?"

"It's headed southeast, toward Reagan."

"Not behind Pete?"

"No. I think whoever is piloting the thing wants to interfere with air traffic down there. I called the FAA and gave them the heads-up. But it doesn't look like Hatchett and whoever's working with him. They wouldn't try anything that stupid, or dangerous."

"It's al-Daran trying to keep the Bureau busy."

"Won't last for long," Otto said.

"If it was him watching your house, then he must have followed us, and he has to know that we went different ways. Could it be someone else watching your place?"

"Anything's possible, but I doubt it. The timing was too coincidental. Has to be someone trying to take you out. The sixty-four-dollar question is, why didn't he send the drone after you?"

"He has to know that Pete is heading back to Georgetown, and he might guess that I'm heading to Fairfax."

"You haven't picked up a tail?"

McGarvey glanced in his rearview mirror. So far as he could tell nothing had followed him from McLean. "Not unless he's double- or triple-teaming me."

"If it is al-Daran, and he's involved with the Consortium, he might guess that you were going after Echo. And it could have been him at the Watergate to take out Fischer."

"There were at least two shooters in the stairwells. And to this point he's worked alone."

"Then maybe he took out the shooter who made it to the garage."

"Something I'm going to ask him when we finally meet face-to-face. He shot Pete in New York and damned near killed her. I'm going to ask him about that too."

"Okay. My surveillance program got lucky picking the drone out from the clutter, but at this point we have no concrete evidence that it was al-Daran, or that he knows where you're heading. But we also don't know the opposite. Could be he's sent a second drone, or could be he's got help. You might be running into a buzz saw."

"I sincerely hope so," McGarvey said.

"Watch yourself."

"Have you brought Pete up to date?"

"She's turned around and is on her way."

McGarvey got off the interstate on Old Chain Bridge Road and phoned Echo's house. A woman answered.

"Hello?"

"Good evening. Is General Echo at home?"

"Who's calling?"

"Kirk McGarvey. He'll know the name."

The phone was silent long enough for McGarvey to think about breaking the connection, but then Echo came on.

"Mr. Director, your call has come as a surprise."

"So did my chat with the president at Camp David."

"I'm sorry, but I'm not following you."

"We talked about Ron Hatchett and the plot."

"I'm still not following you."

"Okay, General, follow this. Someone tried to kill me. And whoever it was killed Susan Fischer. You could be next. So could Colonel Chambeau and the others in your intelligence agency consortium. The problem is, I don't know who is behind it, only that you're trying to bring down the president. And how you're doing it could get a lot of people killed. By the

North Koreans, or the Chinese, or Russians or just about every military involved in any of a dozen flash points."

Echo said nothing.

"Are you following me now, General? I know about it, but I also may know something that you don't."

"You haven't proved a fucking thing."

"There's a second group out there, one we believe wants the opposite of what you want. And they've become just as willing as you to kill for it."

Again Echo was silent for a long time. "You mentioned Ron Hatchett."

"Let's talk."

"Christ, not here. Where are you?"

"Not far."

"There's a McDonald's on Old Lee Highway. Do you know where that is?"

"I'll find it."

"Okay, I'll be wearing a dark blue sweater."

"I know what you look like, General."

McGarvey phoned Pete. "I'm just a few minutes out."

"I'm on sixty-six just passing Arlington about fifteen minutes behind you. How'd he take it?"

"Said I had no proof, but I think Hatchett came as a surprise."

"I'll bet it did."

"It was probably al-Daran who was piloting the drone. So keep a sharp eye. Anything seems out of place, get the hell out."

"Doesn't make any sense, him following us to Otto's and then simply sending a drone to watch us," Pete said. "He could have taken us down when we came out."

"Unless he wants something."

"What?"

"I'll ask him."

"He knows this car," Pete said. "I'll park a block away, and come in on foot. So keep frosty until then."

"You know what this guy is capable of, so walk lightly. I don't want to lose you."

McGarvey parked in plain sight in front of the McDonald's. Inside, he got a cup of coffee and sat down at a table from where he could watch the parking lot, but where his back was to the wall, separating the dining area from the kitchen to the left and the bathrooms down a short corridor.

Only a few customers were inside at this hour, and one car at the drive-through.

A dark gray Humvee pulled up, but it took two full minutes for Echo to get out, and even then he stood with the door open as he looked around. He wasn't a very large man, far less imposing than in his dress uniform with the two stars, and ribbons and badges. Just another guy, no one special.

Echo finally closed the Humvee's door and came into the restaurant. He stopped again; his gaze passed McGarvey but then came back.

He nodded, then went to the counter, where he got a cup of coffee before he came back and sat down.

"I didn't recognize you at first," he said.

"Surviving a car bomb leaves a mark."

Echo nodded again. "What do you want?"

"The names of all your conspirators and where you got the money."

"What money?"

"To hire Kamal al-Daran to kill me, so that you could go on with your coup d'état."

FORTY-SIX

Echo remained silent for a long time, sipping his coffee and occasionally looking toward the front doors as if he thought someone was coming. It was obvious that the general knew he was in a bad position, but he had been under fire in Iraq as a light colonel and again in Afghanistan as a one-star until he took the Pentagon desk job. He knew how to keep his composure.

"Whatever you think you know, you're wrong," he said at length. "I did not order your assassination, and I've never heard the name al-Daran."

"He's a Saudi contractor. The same guy who took down the pencil tower in New York last year."

"I'm surprised he's not dead or in custody."

"He's a professional. His job was to take down a second tower, but he failed. And because of it his control officer, a major in the Saudi GIP, was executed. The royal family does not take failure lightly."

"And you believe he's come after you," Echo said. "Because you stopped him from taking down the second tower. Revenge, then?"

"I expect that he'll be coming after me again. Soon. Maybe even tonight, right here."

Echo sipped his coffee. "If that's the case, I hope that you're ready for him. I assume that you're working with the CIA again, and you have a backup team out there somewhere. Maybe surrounding this place?"

"If he shows up here, General, it'll mean that he knows about you. He'll have to wonder what you're doing talking to me."

"Okay, Mr. McGarvey, I'm here and I'm talking to you. About what? What the fuck do you want from me? Exactly what the fuck do you think I'm involved with?"

"A soft coup to discredit the president of the United States."

"You're out of your mind," Echo said. He started to get up.

"You're part of a consortium of mid-level intelligence officers from at least a dozen or more countries—some of them friends of ours—plus, of course, Susan Fischer and your brother-in-law, Colonel Chambeau."

Echo did not reply.

"We have records of your encrypted telephone calls to and from these people, starting just after the election."

"If you know that much, then you'll know that I deal with a great number of people in foreign intelligence and military organizations. Back-burner conversations in what we call the old-boys network. It's something that's totally above politics and actually works. I'm sure that you must be familiar with the principle of the thing. We prevent accidents that way. Incidents that crop up out of the blue, that could lead to an escalation of arms. Without us, Mr. McGarvey, people could get killed. Americans could get killed."

"It's not working that way now."

"I assure you that it is," Echo said. "This conversation is over." He started to rise again.

"The thing is, I agree with you. Weaver is an idiot. Like some presidents before him. But he is the president, and I'll do whatever it takes to defend the man."

"He'll be impeached," Echo said with passion. "The son of a bitch is more than an idiot, he's dangerous. He, not the conspiracy you think exists, could get us into a shooting war that once begun might not be able to be stopped. You do understand that much, I hope."

"A president cannot be impeached for poor judgment."

"Do you actually understand what you're saying? You've served your country for most of your life. You've lost more than your share. You've had more than anyone's quota of heartache and grief. And yet you can tell me that Weaver isn't unfit to lead us."

"Susan Fischer was murdered because of what you're doing."

Something occurred to Echo. "You were the unidentified armed man there. You talked to her."

"I was there, but she and I never had a chance to talk. She ran to the stairwell where someone was waiting for her. She was gunned down with an automatic weapon. A military style weapon."

Echo almost laughed. "First you accuse me of a plot to bring down Weaver and now you think I ordered Susan's death."

"We think that al-Daran has an intel contact somewhere here in Washington."

"Susan. And you think he killed her?"

"I think that she was killed not by him, but because of him. There were two gunmen. I took out one, but the other one was killed in the parking garage by someone else."

"My people again."

"On your orders, or on the White House's."

Echo toyed with his Styrofoam coffee cup, his eyes down. "It wasn't me, nor, as bad as I believe Weaver to be—not just as a president but as a human being—was it ordered by him." He looked up. "Susan was basically a decent person, but she was a lush. I think she was having an affair with my brother-in-law Moses. Colonel Chambeau. And if you want my best, by-God guess, it could have been my sister Jen who had her killed."

"She has access to people like that? They were professionals."

"Do your homework, Mr. Director. My father was General Thomas Echo, who in the last two years of his career represented the army on the Joint Chiefs. Both Jen and I were service brats. I went to VMI and then the academy, but my sister became a town pump. A slut who spread her legs for lieutenants, then captains and majors, and even a couple of generals.

"She began to drink when she was in her late twenties, so her looks started to go and with Moses, who she'd been fucking for at least a year, she figured she'd better jump off the merry-go-round and settle for a light colonel."

McGarvey was certain that at least with part of this story, Echo was telling the truth. Or at least his version of it.

"Did she have the connections?" Echo asked. "Of course she did. Not so much with active-duty guys, but with the few who went into private contracting after they got out. The pay is good, and the rush from killing people is satisfied. It's why lots of them go over to Iraq and Afghanistan and a number of other hot spots, to act as muscle for anyone from State

Department types to the odd lot of entrepreneurs who made bags of money in war zones."

"Fischer was a drunk."

"She worked for the NSA and the pressure gets to a lot of them. Same in the Pentagon, and the same, I suspect, out at Langley, and just about everywhere inside and outside the Beltway."

"Shooters are not cheap."

"Our mother was wealthy, and when she died Dad got the estate. And when he died the money came to me and Jen. She could afford it. And she's a class-A vindictive bitch. Always has been."

"Nice family," McGarvey said.

"You have no idea."

"Have you talked to her or your brother-in-law?"

"No."

"Brought it to the police?"

Echo shook his head. "She's my sister."

McGarvey almost laughed. "You and your sister are cut from the same cloth."

"Fuck you," Echo said, but without rancor.

McGarvey's phone rang. It was Pete. "He's here. Driving an old yellow pickup truck. He just pulled up in the Mickey D's parking lot."

"Where are you?"

"At the gas station down the street."

"Do you see him?"

"Through the driver's window."

"Stay put," McGarvey said.

Echo was looking at him.

"Al-Daran is here to kill me. I suggest you keep your head down, because we're not finished."

FORTY-SEVEN

Keeping below the level of the pickup truck's windows, Kamal slipped out the passenger side and hurried around to the rear from where he could see the front door of the McDonald's and the woman's Bimmer in the Shell station.

Only a few cars were in the parking lot, including the beat-up SUV McGarvey was driving, an old Chevy Camaro and a newish-looking Humvee.

McGarvey was inside the restaurant meeting with someone, which made for an interesting situation, and his woman was covering his six.

Still keeping low, Kamal darted across to the Camaro, from where he had an even better sight line to the restaurant's front door and the drive-up window, and where he couldn't be seen from anyone at the gas station.

Traffic was light, and he could hear no sirens in the distance. The woman had followed McGarvey this far, but it was likely that she had no idea who had driven up in the pickup truck and she hadn't alerted the local police.

The question was, who was inside with McGarvey? Kamal had a good hunch that it was a military type, who'd driven the Humvee. To his way of thinking most Americans were beyond stupid, driving on civilian roads in combat vehicles just to make a macho statement of some kind.

His estimation of McGarvey dropped a notch. The man had been lucky in New York last year, and again last month in Sarasota. And so had the woman. But that was about to end tonight.

McGarvey, pistol in hand, was about to open the rear door in the kitchen when Echo came up behind him. The general had what looked like a Beretta semiauto in his left hand.

The restaurant's manager, a tall skinny Hispanic man possibly in his mid-twenties, came around the corner from the end of the prep line, but pulled up short when he saw both men with guns.

"Have your people get down out of sight," McGarvey said.

Echo pulled out what looked like a badge. "We're the police. Now do what he says. We don't want anyone to get hurt."

The kid backed off.

"How do you want to play this?" Echo asked.

"Al-Daran is in the yellow pickup out front. You have two choices: either stay here and keep your head down, or walk out the front door, get in your Humvee and drive away."

"I'm a good shot, I can defend myself if need be."

"No doubt," McGarvey said. "But unless you get away from me, I'll shoot you myself."

"I did not hire whoever this guy is. I swear to Christ."

McGarvey suddenly looked over Echo's shoulder as if someone were coming. The general half turned and McGarvey snatched the Beretta out of his hand.

"Goddamnit!" Echo said.

"Get out of here."

"You're going to kill him."

"Probably, but first I want to ask him who he works for," McGarvey said. "And he's not going to wait forever, which makes you either part of the problem or part of the solution."

"Then give me my gun, and I'll walk out the front door. I'll be a distraction."

McGarvey hesitated, but then handed Echo the Beretta. He held his Walther low and to the right, his finger on the trigger. "Go."

Echo held his pistol low and to the left, away from his leg. He was a professional soldier. He knew what he was doing.

"Fact is, I'm on your side." Echo said. He turned and went back the way they had come.

McGarvey got on the phone to Pete. ""What's the situation?"

"I lost sight of him. He could be anywhere."

"I'm coming out the back, Echo will be coming out the front. He's armed."

"Jesus."

"Yeah."

Pocketing the phone, McGarvey eased open the door and stepped outside onto the driveway. The take-out window was to his left, two Dumpsters straight ahead and just beyond that the rear of the gas station.

Kamal was crouched behind the Camaro when a man in khaki slacks and a blue sweater came out of the restaurant. It was not McGarvey. His hair was cropped short, and the way he held himself, he looked military.

The man walked toward the Humvee but then stopped ten feet short. He brought his left hand away from his leg, and in the overhead lights Kamal could see that he was holding a pistol.

None of this made any sense, except that Kamal was sure that the man with the pistol was the one McGarvey had come here to meet.

Kamal raised up just far enough so that he was visible.

Echo stepped back half a pace, but then he hid his pistol behind his leg again, and gestured toward the right.

McGarvey had set a trap.

Kamal nodded.

Echo stuffed the pistol in a belt holster under his sweater, then went the rest of the way to the Humvee, climbed up behind the wheel, started the engine and drove slowly away.

McGarvey ducked out from behind the protection of the building, and keeping the Humvee between himself and the Camaro behind which Kamal had been hiding, skipped the twenty feet where the driveway turned to the street.

A car came by, and Echo held up until it passed, before he pulled out and drove away.

Kamal was nowhere in sight.

Keeping low, McGarvey zigzagged in a dead run across the parking lot to a position in the shadows where he had a good sight line on the rear and passenger sides of the Camaro, more than forty feet away, and the yellow pickup truck, ten feet farther. A nearly impossible range for a pistol shot.

The Camaro's dome light came on.

McGarvey raced toward the car, firing measured shots low at the front passenger window.

The young manager came out of the restaurant, shouting something.

The Camaro's engine came to life, and the car accelerated forward, slamming into the manager, tossing his body back into one of the plate-glass windows, which shattered.

McGarvey, still running, changed out his empty magazine, cycled a round into the chamber, and fired again into the front seat on the driver's side as the car raced past him.

But then it was out of the parking lot and screaming up the street, well out of pistol range, toward the Shell station.

McGarvey ran after it, as fast as he could pump his peg leg, changing to his third and final mag.

He recharged the pistol as the Camaro swerved to the right into the gas station directly toward Pete's car in front of one of the pumps.

FORTY-EIGHT

□

Pete drew her pistol and got away from her car as she realized what was happening. It was Kamal and the bastard meant to run her down.

She began firing directly at the driver's side when the Camaro suddenly swerved sharply to the left, missing her car, and then slammed into the next two gas pumps in a row, knocking them completely off their bases.

McGarvey was still one hundred feet away, when the Camaro tipped over on its side and skidded fifty feet, trailing a line of sparks until it came to a stop.

Only a small amount of gasoline had spewed from the destroyed pumps before the emergency shutdown activated, but the several gallons plus the rising fumes went off with an impressive crump.

Almost immediately flames spread to Pete's car and she ran behind the pumps away from the heat toward the overturned Camaro.

A woman came out of the station. "My God, my God!" she screamed.

"Get back!" Pete shouted.

The woman just looked at the fire, until the front of her white T-shirt spouted blood and she collapsed onto the tarmac.

Kamal, dressed in jeans and a dark, untucked long-sleeve shirt, had climbed out of the car and was walking directly toward where Pete stood, although it didn't seem as if he had spotted her, his attention on the gas station's front door.

She raised her pistol and as she headed directly toward him began firing, one measured shot after the other. Kamal turned toward her and fired, her hand shook. He was the bastard who had held her at his house overlooking the sea in Monaco last year. He was going to rape her then kill her, and all she'd been able to do was run.

But not this time.

Pete took a round in the fleshy part of her right arm, and she dropped her gun.

Kamal glanced toward the McDonald's, then turned back as Pete took a knee and grabbed the pistol with her left hand.

"Put it down and you might live until your boyfriend makes it this far," he said.

She started to bring up the gun, when he pointed his pistol directly at her head.

"I'll kill you now or later."

"Now," Pete said at the same moment she ducked to the right and fired, but missed.

Kamal followed her move, but then turned again toward the road.

Pete rolled onto her right side, the pain sharp from her wounded arm, and fired two more shots, as Kamal raced around the east end of the building.

McGarvey came around the edge of the still furiously burning gasoline just as Pete fell back on her left side. Blood soaked the right sleeve of her shirt. But she was conscious.

"He went around the other side!" she shouted

McGarvey dropped down next to her, put his pistol on the ground, took hers and had her clamp her left hand over the wound.

"I'll be back," he told her, a rage building inside of him. Al-Daran had hurt her once in Monaco, and had left her for dead after shooting her in the pencil tower in New York.

He reached for his pistol, when an engine roared to life at the rear of the station. He jumped up and headed that way in a dead run.

A tow truck came around the corner, accelerating, its engine screaming, belching black diesel smoke.

McGarvey got off only one shot before the truck suddenly turned sharply left and headed directly toward him and Pete lying on the tarmac.

He spun on his heel, scooped Pete off the ground, and dove toward the front wall of the building, just making it out of the way as the truck passed, missing them by inches.

McGarvey dropped her, turned and managed to hook his left arm on the edge of the truck's retracted ramp.

. . .

Kamal swerved out onto the road, sideswiping a car, sending it skidding into an oncoming delivery van.

Someone would have reported the fire and shootings, and it wouldn't be long before the police started showing up in force. Considering everything that had gone on in the past year or so, law enforcement people just about everywhere were on high alert.

McGarvey had been right there, and he'd almost had the bastard trying to save his girlfriend. The rage that Kamal had been scarcely able to control during his sabbatical in France had risen in his head to such a point that he was nearly out of his mind. It was the main reason he'd agreed to take on the assignment that the Gang of Three in Beijing had given him. He didn't care about anything else on their agenda; just killing McGarvey had been more than enough.

Even now it was a wonder to him that he hadn't acted before.

And this time around he'd already failed twice. It was almost more than he could bear.

He came to a red light but barreled through it directly into the side of an SUV coming from a residential neighborhood on the left. He got a brief impression of a woman in the passenger seat, a man driving, when he hit, blood exploding from the car along with shattered window glass.

Downshifting, Kamal pushed the destroyed SUV away and continued north, the entrance to the Army and Navy Club in the woods to the right.

He glanced in the rearview mirror in time to see McGarvey right there at the back window, just a couple of feet away, blood and glass all over his face from where he must have been thrown forward in the crash.

But it was impossible.

Kamal swerved sharply to the right, then left, traffic frantically scattering out of his way.

He pulled out his pistol and half turned in his seat, but the son of a bitch was gone.

Checking the big door-mounted rearview mirrors he looked to see if the bastard had been thrown off the truck, but he wasn't on the side of the road.

As he turned back the passenger door was flung open and McGarvey swung into the cab, feet first, his peg leg catching Kamal in the chest, making him drop the pistol and nearly run off the road.

Kamal slammed on the brakes, sending McGarvey forward into the dashboard, his head slamming into the windshield, starring the glass.

Now. Kill the bastard here and now. Finally get it over with, and leave the field of action while there was still a chance.

Fuck the Gang of Three and their political insanity, or whatever their motive was.

He hauled the truck off to the side, blocking all lanes of traffic, but McGarvey came at him with both fists, and he could do nothing else except shove open his door and bail out, even while the truck was slowing to a crawl.

McGarvey, blood streaming down his cut-up face, at least a couple of ribs on his left side broken from when he'd swung up into the bed of the truck, recovered almost instantly.

Scrambling out the driver's-side door, he was in time to see Kamal thirty feet away, hauling a driver out of a dark green car, jumping in behind the wheel and speeding away.

He bent over, his hands on his knees, blood splashing on the pavement. A dark rage blotted out nearly everything, except the thought that he had missed again, and that Pete was wounded, lying on the ground in front of the gas station.

It was a mess. A fucking mess, and it was all his fault because he had lost his edge.

☐

FORTY-NINE

Kamal, keeping to the speed limit, was back on I-66 in less than five minutes, and two miles later merging with the traffic on the Beltway heading north. It wouldn't take the police long to start their search for this specific car.

Driving away he'd seen McGarvey get to his feet and raise something to his ear, no doubt a cell phone.

On top of that the bitch had gotten lucky with one shot, grazing him in the left leg just below his buttock. The wound had bled just a little, but it felt as if his entire side from the waist down was on fire.

He had to get off the highway and under cover very soon before the cops put up a helicopter and began expanding their search from where he'd hijacked the car.

The solution came to him almost immediately as he passed a sign for Dulles International Airport exit in two miles.

McGarvey had finished on the phone with Pete to make sure that she was okay, and had just reached Otto when the first police cruiser, its siren blaring, lights flashing, showed up.

A cop, his pistol out, came forward. "Put it down, put your hands up and turn toward me!"

"I'm on it," Otto said.

McGarvey put up his hands and turned around. "The perp is driving a green Chevy, later model, I'm guessing an Impala, heading north. I didn't catch the plate, but he'll go to ground unless you call for air support right now."

The cop said something into his lapel mic, but never took his eyes or his pistol off McGarvey.

"He's a white male, about six feet tall, dark hair and eyes, muscular build. He's a professional assassin and very good at it, so warn your people to approach him with extreme caution."

A lot more sirens were coming in, mostly from the east, but at least one or two from in town.

"Drop the phone!" the cop shouted. He was an older man with buzz-cut gray hair.

"I'm on with someone at the CIA."

"I said, drop the phone!" the cop shouted again, then stopped. "Say again?" he spoke into his lapel mic.

McGarvey lowered the phone.

All traffic had come to a complete standstill. Several people had abandoned their cars and were scattering on foot either into the woods toward the Army and Navy Club or across the street into the neighborhoods.

"Who were you talking to?" the cop demanded.

"Otto Rencke. My name is Kirk McGarvey."

The cop lowered his pistol. "Do you need an ambulance, sir?"

"No. But two women have been shot at the Shell station about a mile back."

"We're on that one, sir. And we'll have at least one chopper in the air within the next few minutes."

McGarvey turned in the direction Kamal had gone. They were going to be too late.

Otto was back. "You okay?"

Kamal got a ticket from the automatic dispenser at the Dulles Airport long-term parking garage and drove up to the first floor, where he slowly cruised each lane as if he were looking for a parking spot.

Not finding what he wanted, he took the ramp up to the next floor.

He was under cover now, but he didn't think it would take McGarvey long to figure out that he might try to use the airport as a gateway either out of the area, or back into the city by taxi or shuttle bus. The bastard had gotten a decent look at the Chevy, and the driver would give them the tag number. He had maybe a ten-minute window before airport security began looking for the car.

On the third level he found exactly what he was looking for. A man, nearly his own height and build, dressed in a business suit, carrying a leather bag slung over his shoulder and wheeling a suitcase, got off the elevator and headed down the C row.

For the moment he was the only one in sight.

Kamal found a parking spot one row over, and checking to make sure that no one else was around, reached the man just as he stopped at a C-class Mercedes and popped the trunk.

He looked up at the last moment, uncertain what was happening.

Kamal was on him, twisting his head sharply to the left, the man's neck breaking with a crunch.

Still no one was coming, and as the man's legs began to give out beneath him, Kamal rolled the poor bastard into the trunk. Bad timing, was all. The unfortunate luck of the draw. It was something that had been drummed into their heads at Sandhurst.

"Be constantly on alert for the unexpected opportunity to arise," one of the instructors had told them. "Some to your advantage, some to your disadvantage. *Recognize* each one, create a *plan*, and *execute* without a moment's hesitation."

RPE; one of the students had come up with the abbreviation.

"Yes," the instructor had said. "Recognize, Plan, Execute and repeat as needed."

Kamal put the suitcase into the trunk, took the key from the dying man's hand and closed the lid as a man and woman got off the elevator and started down an adjacent row.

He got behind the wheel, just as the couple walked past, neither of them even glancing toward him.

When they had driven off, Kamal went back to the trunk and took a pair of slacks and a shirt from the suitcase The man was dead, his face almost purple, his eyes bulging.

Kamal rolled him over and took the wallet from his back pocket, closed the trunk and at the open driver's-side door, again making sure that no one was coming, removed the things from his pockets, took off his slacks and then his shirt, which he wadded up and held against the flesh wound in his right thigh, before he put on the dead man's slacks and shirt.

The fit was a little snug, but not bad.

At the trunk again he tossed in his bloody clothes, wrestled the suit coat from the man's body and put it on.

Making sure that he'd gotten no blood on himself, he took the suitcase and the leather bag from the man's shoulder, closed the trunk, locked up the car and headed to the elevators as three men got off and headed to their cars.

None of them noticed him as he got aboard and pressed the button for Baggage and Ground Transportation.

The first EMT on the scene taped up McGarvey's ribs and put several butterfly bandages on his facial cuts.

"You need a couple of stitches, sir. But I'd have your doctor take a couple of X-rays of your left side. I don't think your ribs are broken but they're probably bruised. You might want to make sure."

They were less than ten miles by air from Langley, and Otto had sent a Company helicopter out.

"Pete'll be okay," Otto said. "She's en route to All Saints right now."

"What about the other woman at the gas station?"

"She's dead."

"Damn," McGarvey said, his dark mood worsening. "Any word on the green Chevy?"

"It hasn't been spotted, but LE has three birds up looking."

"Try Dulles. I think he probably went there."

"I'm searching for last-minute ticket purchases, but nothing's come up so far."

"He's not leaving town," McGarvey said. "Not until he's finished here."

FIFTY

The helicopter that Otto sent dropped McGarvey off near the river in Georgetown, and a waiting car and two minders from the Company drove him up to All Saints.

"I hope the other guy is in worse shape," one of the men said.

"He got away," McGarvey said, his morose mood riding heavy.

They went the rest of the way in silence, and inside the hospital the nurse wanted to take him to one of the treatment rooms immediately so that she could clean up his facial lacerations and stitch whatever needed stitching.

"I need to see Ms. Boylan first."

"Franklin's finished with her, and she came out just fine. It wasn't a serious wound, but she's resting."

"Where is she?"

"Two-oh-four," the nurse said.

McGarvey recognized the nurse because of her flaming red hair, but in his present state he couldn't dredge up her name.

"You could use a few hours' sleep yourself, Mr. Director," she said. "Soon as you check on Pete, come back down here and let me take care of you, otherwise the doctor will have both of our butts in a sling."

The EMT on scene had given McGarvey a towel and an ice pack for his face. He tossed them in a waste can and took the stairs up two at a time.

Pete was propped up in bed, her arm in a sling. Her face brightened when he appeared at the door, but then fell when she realized that his face had been cut up.

The relief of having her here in one piece was immense. "I'm glad to see you."

"Just a flesh wound," she said. "But I think one of my left-handers might have hit him in the ass."

"Could be he's on his way back into town. Did they let you keep your gun?"

Pete flipped her blanket aside. Her Glock29 Gen4 was lying at her left hip. "He shows up, I won't be able to miss. Anyway, they put on some extra muscle downstairs. So take a deep breath and go get yourself cleaned up."

"You heard the girl," the nurse said at the doorway.

"I'll be back," McGarvey said.

The facial wounds were minor for the most part, and only two required stitches. The nurse replaced the butterfly bandages on the others. "You're not going to win any beauty contests for the next week or so, but unless you run into another window you'll be okay."

At the door he turned back. "Molly Harrington."

She grinned. "Thanks for remembering. Of course just about every time you've been here you've not been at your best."

"That's why I show up."

"Don't let it continue to be a habit, Mr. Director."

Otto and Louise were upstairs with Pete when McGarvey returned. Louise looked stricken.

"My God, are you okay?" she demanded.

"It looks worse than it is," McGarvey assured her. "What about al-Daran?" he asked Otto.

"We found the Chevy parked in long-term at Dulles. Some blood on the front seat. Forensics took samples and I've put a rush on the DNA analysis. It'll probably match what the DGSI picked up at Monaco last year which will nail his ID."

"Same guy, I'm a hundred percent," Pete said.

"So am I," McGarvey agreed.

"And one of his personas could be Paul O'Neal, a businessman who supposedly owns a small high-tech company called IFA in San Francisco.

Innovative Financial Applications," Otto said. "I asked the local Bureau office to check it out."

"What's the connection?"

"I managed to get a three-minute retask of the NROL-52—that's the National Reconnaissance's newest spy bird over northern Mexico—and we found what looks like a training camp on the high desert north of Chihuahua," Louise said.

She brought up some images on her tablet and showed them to McGarvey.

"Firing-range practice," he said. "Looks like ten shooters plus what could be two instructors. Has the FA set up anything like that?" The FA was the Fuerzas Especiales, the Mexican army's special forces.

"No," Otto said, "and I haven't alerted them yet. Looks like ISIS to me. But the point is, Paul O'Neal was a guest at the Grand Hyatt in New York for three days, checking out the day after the pencil tower on Fifty-seventh came down."

"And?"

"If it's the same Paul O'Neal, and I'm betting he is, he stayed one night at the Sheraton Soberano in Chihuahua four days ago. From there he flew to Dallas Fort–Worth, where he stayed at the Fairmont. I think he came to Washington, but there are a half-dozen hotels that won't give out registration details on American citizens unless they're served with a court order."

"If it's him, and he follows his same pattern, it'd be the Hay-Adams," McGarvey said.

"My guess too. Anyway, I'm checking on it. But I don't think that it'd be a good idea either to storm the castle, or send a couple of our people or the Bureau's over to snoop around. They could be running into a buzz saw."

"It stays with us," McGarvey said after the briefest of pauses.

Pete was the first to catch it. "Not a chance in hell," she said, half rising from her bed.

"He'd spot you a mile off," Otto said. "I'll crack their system. Could be some blowback, for which I'll take some shit. Justice will probably come after Page, but fuck 'em."

"I'll go," Louise said.

Everyone looked at her.

"I'm a neutral. He wouldn't be expecting me to show up."

"Jesus," Otto said. "You'll go room to room and knock on doors?"

"I'll rent a room and sit in the lobby sipping tea. If he's registered he'll have to show up sooner or later. And I'm very good at sipping tea."

"If he spots you he'll kill you," McGarvey said.

"It's you he wants, not me."

"You're right, which is why it has to be me."

"I can get past Justice with no sweat," Otto said.

Pete was looking at McGarvey, and she shook her head. "Mac is the last person he'd expect to see. Especially so soon."

McGarvey nodded.

"I'll get dressed."

Louise looked at both of them. "Both of you are nuts. Do you guys have a death wish?"

"He knows he only wounded me," Pete said, never taking her eyes off Mac. "And he knows that Kirk is still alive."

"He'll shoot first and ask questions later," Louise said.

"Not in such a public place," Pete said. "He'll do just about anything to avoid a confrontation unless it's in a time and place of his own choosing."

"You're saying he'll run?"

"Yup," Pete said. "Once he spots me I'm betting he'll run, and Kirk will be waiting."

FIFTY-ONE

On the way back into the city from Dulles, Kamal took out the dead man's wallet. His name was Richard Tepping. He had a valid Indiana driver's license, which showed a home address in Indianapolis. But the Mercedes plate was for D.C. and the car was not a rental.

Tepping had a couple of credit cards including an Amex Platinum, so whoever he had been he'd been well-to-do.

A couple of photographs showed the man embracing another at what looked like a ceremony of some sort. Possibly even a wedding.

Kamal had been raised in England, but he was born an Egyptian and he had no opinion whatsoever about homosexuality—or at least not the same opinion as most Westerners did.

The main thing that bothered him was that sooner or later someone would miss Mr. Tepping and call the police. The search would begin at Dulles, where they would find the green Impala, and eventually Tepping's body in the Mercedes. But that would take a couple of hours, perhaps longer, which gave Kamal time to go a little deeper. Unless the green Impala and Tepping's murder were linked.

Just before the Teddy Roosevelt Bridge he decided that he would have to act sooner than later. McGarvey was still alive and it was possible that he would make the connection.

He drove down to Reagan International, where he parked the car in long-term. With the suitcase in tow and the leather bag over his shoulder he went into the terminal and directly down to the baggage claim and ground transportation level, where he rented a car from Hertz using his O'Neal identity.

Within a half hour he was in a Toyota Camry heading back into the city, working out his next moves as he drove.

Killing McGarvey was a given, as far as Kamal was concerned. In fact, nothing else really mattered. Not the rest of the money—though the attacks on the New Orleans dikes, the Golden Gate Bridge and Pastor Buddy's church were set in motion now—and he would get paid for those acts.

But McGarvey had become personal after Monaco and New York.

He needed to go to ground for the short-term, right here in the area, but first he needed his things from the Hay-Adams.

Something occurred to him all at once, and he nearly ran off the road.

His Paul O'Neal identity. He had used it too often.

McGarvey had been director of the CIA for a brief stint. He still had friends inside the Agency, including Rencke—and his wife Louise Horn, who had worked at the National Reconnaissance Office. Satellites.

He was back at the training camp on the northern Mexican desert. Ayman Baz, the ISIS commander, had explained how they were able to defeat the American spy satellite because they knew when it would be overhead.

Unless the timing had been changed by someone who had an inside track with the NRO.

But it meant nothing except that he had used his Paul O'Neal papers at the hotel in Chihuahua and again in Dallas, and once again at the Hay-Adams. And the airport just now.

He'd been sloppy.

"It's not always the best man who wins, or the luckiest," the Sandhurst tactical instructor had told them. "But it's the man who never for a moment allows himself to feel safe, to become besotted with his own abilities."

Kamal remembered the lecture.

"Overconfidence could jump up and bite you on the arse."

Across the river back in the city, he took 14th Street SW up across Pennsylvania Avenue to K Street NW and around the block to 16th Street and, keeping up with traffic, passed the Hay-Adams.

A limousine under the porte cochere was discharging a man and woman in evening dress. But there were no other cars parked in front of the hotel

either in the driveway or on the street, and especially there were no police cars.

Which actually meant nothing. If McGarvey and his woman had staked
out the hotel they wouldn't be in plain sight.

Just past the hotel's front entrance he waited for a break in traffic and
turned into the service driveway, which dipped down, and left to a loading
dock. The delivery service door was closed, and only a Ford Taurus and
Honda Accord were parked next to a pair of Dumpsters.

Kamal backed the Toyota to the raised loading platform, shut off the
engine, took the keys and went up the stairs to the access door, which as
he suspected was unlocked.

Just inside he waited for a full minute to make sure that no one was
around, before he went across to the service elevators.

Two men were watching something on TV in an office blocked off by
a wire mesh wall. Down a broad corridor to the right was what appeared to
be a storage area of shelves filled with boxes and cans along one wall, and
a heavy refrigerator and cold-storage doors to the left. Beyond them, down
another corridor, he could make out what appeared to be big washing
machines and dryers.

No one noticed him until he reached the elevators, when one of the
men behind the mesh looked over.

Kamal waved as the elevator door opened and he got aboard. The man
waved back.

The elevator opened to a fifth-floor service room, shelves filled with everything from bath towels to soaps and shampoos, toilet paper and ice buckets.
It was early evening and except for emergencies almost all the maids were
off duty until morning.

He cracked the door to the empty corridor then stepped out and went
down to his suite, where he listened at the door.

He was unarmed, which wouldn't make any difference except if he had
to face McGarvey. And even then he figured that he could handle just about
any situation except at a position beyond his lunging distance of five or
ten feet.

Using his key card he unlocked the door, then easing it open with the toe of his shoe he moved to one side and held his head back slightly so that he could sniff the air.

But there were no smells other than the neutral hotel-room odors. No colognes, no perfumes, no cigarettes.

"Bellman, Mr. O'Neal," he called.

There was no answer, nor could he hear any movement from within.

Pushing the door the rest of the way open, he darted into the suite's living room, pivoting on his heel, and swung left moving fast and silently on the balls of his feet.

But the suite was empty.

In the bedroom he retrieved one of his Glock pistols from his suitcase, made sure that it hadn't been tampered with and was ready to fire, then made a quick search of the suite.

But he was alone.

Within five minutes he'd repacked his things and left with the one roll-about and Tepping's carry-on bag.

Downstairs on the service floor he went back to the loading dock door and let himself out, the two men in the office never taking their eyes off the television.

In another two minutes he was pulling out of the service driveway and heading away on 16th Street, the White House in his rearview mirror.

FIFTY-TWO

McGarvey was parked in the BMW just down from the Hay-Adams, from where he had a good sight line to the front doors, and down 16th all the way to Lafayette Square, beyond which was the White House.

A dark blue Camry came out from the hotel's delivery entrance and passed McGarvey. At the end of the block it turned left on H Street and was gone.

The windows were tinted and he'd not gotten a clear view of the driver, but the plate was D.C. Something didn't register in McGarvey's head. He phoned Pete, who was sitting in the hotel's lobby. "Any sign of him?"

"No."

"Stay where you are and keep your eyes open. I'm going to check on something. Shouldn't take more than a couple of minutes."

"Check on what?" Pete demanded.

McGarvey pulled away from the curb and headed toward the delivery ramp. "A blue Toyota just came from the back of the hotel. It was a D.C. plate but I didn't catch a number."

"Al-Daran?"

"Could have been an end run, which means he knew or suspected that we were here."

McGarvey went down the ramp and parked at the loading dock. He entered the hotel and went over to the office behind the steel mesh wall. Two hotel employees looked up, and one of them got to his feet.

"Can I help you?"

"I think I just saw a friend of mine drive off in a Camry? Did you see him?"

The man, who was dressed in blue coveralls, shook his head. "I didn't see anyone leaving, unless it was the guy who showed up about fifteen minutes ago."

"Was he making a delivery?"

"Probably something for upstairs."

"How was he dressed?"

"I don't know. An ordinary business suit, I think."

"Not jeans and a long-sleeved shirt?"

"No."

McGarvey got back on his phone and called Pete as he hurried out to his car. "If it was him, he came and went through the service entry."

"He knew we were here," Pete said. "But how?"

"I don't know, but I'll be right with you."

Pete was on her feet in the lobby when McGarvey parked at the front entrance and came in. Someone was playing a piano for a dozen people in evening dress having cocktails just up the half flight of stairs to the left.

"Was it him? she asked, as they headed directly to the front desk.

"I think so."

The man behind the desk looked up, a somber expression on his long face.

"You have a guest registered under the name Paul O'Neal," McGarvey said.

"I couldn't say, sir."

"I'm sure he booked a suite, we need to see it."

"That's not possible," the man replied.

McGarvey pulled out his pistol. "If I have to shoot you I will try not to kill you, but when I'm nervous like now, I sometimes miss what I've aimed at. Paul O'Neal is wanted internationally for multiple counts of murder. He is a dangerous man who you don't want as a guest."

"Good Lord," the man whispered.

"Give us his suite number, a universal key card, and we'll be gone in less than ten minutes."

"I will inform the police, sir."

"Please do," McGarvey said. "In the meantime the suite number and key." He raised his pistol. His back was to the pair of uniformed doormen and no one else was in sight to see the gun.

"Five-oh-four," the desk man said. He produced a key card and laid it on the desk. "I will alert security for the safety of our guests, of course."

"Be sure to mention that my name is Kirk McGarvey," Mac said, snatching up the key.

Concealing the pistol at his side, he and Pete took one of the elevators up to the fourth floor.

"He was on the phone even before we started up," Pete said.

"The cops won't be a problem, but Security could be," McGarvey said.

They raced down the empty corridor to the emergency exit, and took the stairs two at a time up to five.

Kamal had probably left in the Camry; nevertheless, McGarvey eased the fifth-floor door open an inch or so and checked the corridor before they went down to 504.

"Get ready for company," McGarvey said. "But keep your gun out of sight."

"What if Kamal is inside?"

"Then it'll get real interesting real fast," McGarvey said.

He unlocked the door and pushed it open, waited a moment, and then leading with his Walther stepped into the living room and slid immediately to the left, his aim traveling right to left as he moved.

The suite was empty. Kamal had come and gone.

Keeping his pistol at the ready McGarvey went into the bedroom. The closet door was open, and the bedcovers were mussed as if someone had placed a suitcase there.

The bathroom was empty of anything personal.

"We have company," Pete called from the corridor.

McGarvey went to the door and stepped into the corridor as two younger men in Hay-Adams's blazers, white shirts and ties came from the elevators. Their weapons were drawn but held at their sides away from their legs.

"The situation is at an end," McGarvey said. He made a deliberate show of holstering his pistol at the small of his back. "The perp we're looking for has already left the hotel."

Pete had already holstered hers.

One of them raised his pistol and pointed it at McGarvey. "Both of you need to place your weapons on the floor."

"I assume that the police have been notified."

"Now," the security officer said. He was stern but not nervous.

"Navy SEALS, Army Special Forces?" McGarvey asked.

"I will fire."

"The guy we're after took down the pencil tower in New York last year."

"Goddamnit."

McGarvey's phone chirped. "Phone," he said and keeping his movements slow and easy took the phone from his shirt pocket. It was Otto.

"What's your situation?"

"Hotel security has stopped us on the fifth floor. Weapons drawn."

"Cops are less than a minute away. And I've notified the Bureau. Help is incoming. Can you defuse the situation?"

"We're trying."

The second officer raised his weapon directly at Pete. "Your guns on the floor, or I will open fire," he said. He was younger than the other one, and seemed nervous.

"Do as he says," McGarvey said.

He and Pete both drew their weapons from their holsters and very carefully bent over and laid them on the floor.

"Now the phone."

The first officer said something into his lapel mic, and a moment later the expression on his face changed, and he lowered his weapon.

☐

FIFTY-THREE

"I'm sorry, sir, we weren't sure who you were except that you threatened the night manager with a gun," the security officer with the lapel mic said.

"You guys were just doing your jobs and no one got hurt," McGarvey said, he and Pete picking up their pistols and holstering them.

"Yes, sir."

McGarvey got back on the phone with Otto. "The situation here has been defused. You can have the district cops stand down, but get a Bureau forensics team over here. I want O'Neal's room tossed. They might come up with something we can use."

"What made him bail out?" Otto asked.

"He might have realized he'd used his O'Neal identity once too often. He sent a drone to your house, so he knows who you are and what you're capable of. And I'm pretty sure that he has to know that Louise used to work for the NRO and might still have some connections over there."

"You're talking about the Mexican training camp."

"Yes. He used the O'Neal identity in Mexico and Texas, and he may have realized I had figured it all out by now."

"That's a pretty big stretch."

"We've underestimated the man all along. He's damned good, but his own connections are feeding him real-time intel."

"Particularly the GIP?"

"The Saudis have their UN office in New York. Maybe someone should pay their head of security an unofficial visit."

"It'll have to go through Marty, but I think I can convince him that we need his help. He'll love that."

"If you have to, go to Page," McGarvey said.

"What about you and Pete?"

"We're going to pay another visit to General Echo and then his brother-in-law, Colonel Chambeau."

"You won't get anything from either of them."

"I think I will," McGarvey said.

McGarvey and Pete drove back to Fairfax to General Echo's nice home on a block with a lot of trees. It was nearing midnight, but many of the houses, including Echo's, were still lit up.

"How are you feeling?" McGarvey asked.

"A lot better than you look," Pete said. "What do you expect to get out of him that you didn't get at the McDonald's?"

"He knows al-Daran."

"What are you talking about?"

"I was watching from inside when he walked out. He nodded to someone across the parking lot before he got in his car and drove off. Could be the only reason I survived."

"Jesus. You can't kill him."

"I guess not," McGarvey said. His stump hurt and he was feeling irascible. "But this will end soon. I'm getting tired of chasing al-Daran and always watching over my shoulder to see if he's taken a bead on me."

"It's become personal," Pete said.

"You're damned right."

Pete touched his arm. "Whatever you do, make sure that it's for the right reasons. Not just revenge for what he's done to you."

"And you."

She managed a slight smile. "We're going on a long vacation when this is over and done with."

"It won't be easy," McGarvey said, half to himself. He was still missing something. They all were and it bothered the hell out of him.

"Nothing is," Pete said, picking up on his mood.

.   .   .   .

McGarvey got out in front of the Echos' house, and with the headlights off, Pete drove halfway down the block, made a U-turn and parked, the Glock beside her on the seat.

Echo opened the door before McGarvey had a chance to ring the bell. He was wearing an olive drab army T-shirt, sweats and no shoes. He was angry.

"If need be I'll call my security people and let them deal with you," he said.

"We'll wait for them together, either inside or out here."

The general started to close the door, but McGarvey stopped him. "We're pretty sure that al-Daran has worked as a freelance for Saudi intelligence."

"What does this have to do with me?"

"You've had contact recently with at least one mid-level officer in the GIP."

"Part of my job, as I've already explained to you."

"I watched when you left McDonald's. He was out there behind a Camaro, waiting for me."

"So?"

"You nodded to him."

"I nod to a lot of people I see in public. It's a matter of old-fashioned respect, like tipping your hat."

"You were warning him about me."

"No."

"He shot a friend of mine and he killed a woman at the gas station just down the street."

"I'm sorry, but it's no concern of mine." Echo started to back up.

McGarvey pulled out his pistol and jammed it into the bridge of the general's nose. "I'm getting real tired of being lied to."

"You're fucking certifiable. No wonder they kicked your ass off the seventh floor at Langley. You and Weaver make the perfect couple."

"We think that al-Daran paid a visit to what is most likely an ISIS training camp in Mexico about a hundred miles south of El Paso. If we're right it means that he's planning another terrorist attack somewhere here in the States. And whatever it is will be big."

"I don't know what you're talking about."

"If it happens you and your contacts will be complicit. Accessories after the fact. It'd be tough to get to your contacts in Saudi Arabia, or Russia or Pakistan, but you'd be easy."

"Who is it, Walt?" a woman called from inside.

"A messenger from my office," Echo said. "He's just leaving."

"A lot of people could die because of you trying to discredit Weaver. That's called treason. Hell of a way to end your career," McGarvey said. He looked past Echo into the vestibule. He stepped back and lowered his gun. "And lose all this. For what? Because you were pissed off that Weaver was elected?"

"The man is dangerous."

"Has he killed anyone?"

"Not yet. But neither did Hitler kill anyone at first."

"Jesus, do you actually hear what's coming out of your mouth?"

"I don't know Mr. al-Daran. He doesn't work for me, nor do I think he's working for the GIP. But what I'm telling my counterparts is not illegal. Nor am I or anyone else I know, for that matter, planning a military coup d'état or any other act of violence inside this country." Echo shook his head. "Weaver will be impeached and it will be of his own doing, not mine."

FIFTY-FOUR

Kamal drove directly back to Reagan International, where he left the Camry along with his roll-about in long-term parking. He kept Tepping's shoulder bag, which contained a laptop.

Downstairs he caught a cab back into the city, ordering the driver to take him to the Hyatt Regency, which was within walking distance of Union Station.

For the moment he thought that it would be a good idea to have a back door. Someplace like the cavernous, almost always busy train depot, where he could get lost in a hurry.

It had been McGarvey in the BMW parked in front of the Hay-Adams, and passing him Kamal had almost stopped, powered down his window and shot the man at nearly point-blank range. Instead, he'd turned his head slightly away and continued driving.

The time had not been right. It was possible that he would have missed, and McGarvey could have returned fire.

In any event he'd been right to get out of the hotel. Somehow the bastard's geek friend had traced his O'Neal identity here. It was even possible that they knew about the training base in Mexico.

On the way into the city, he dug out his Rupert Hollman papers, which he hadn't used since Atlanta, and when they reached the Hyatt he tipped the driver well, but not extravagantly, and checked into an ordinary-size room.

He unpacked Tepping's laptop and looked at it for a long time. Once he went online it would be as if he had shined a spotlight on himself. Especially after the man's body was found in the trunk of his car. But that could be days from now, or hours if his friend from the photographs reported him missing.

Yet he thought the laptop could serve a purpose later. Depending on who the man was.

Kamal got out of the man's clothes and took a shower. The wound in his leg was still oozing a small amount of blood, which he stanched with some wadded-up toilet paper.

Dressed in his own clothes, a decent pair of gray slacks, a white shirt and a blue blazer, he went down to the restaurant and took a seat with his back to the kitchen and from where he had a decent sight line on the entrance. He didn't think they could have traced him this far this fast, but he had learned not to underestimate McGarvey. It was a mistake he'd made too many times.

He had a light salad and a decent planked trout, along with seasoned french fries and a reasonable bottle of cold Pinot Grigio. Not the French cuisine he'd gotten used to, but certainly much better in his mind than British food and certainly better than most Saudi meals he could remember as a kid.

The dining room was half-filled, mostly with families probably here on vacation, and only a few men and women dressed in business attire. He was the only person seated alone, but no one paid him any attention and his waiter was distant but reasonably efficient.

After coffee, Kamal signed for the bill, then went across the lobby to the business center, where a half-dozen computers were lined up on a long counter. A young man was using a computer at the far end, but no one else was around, nor was anyone looking his way.

For the moment he was anonymous.

Using the password he'd been given when he checked in, he got online and brought up a couple local news channels, searching for any articles on the shooting in Fairfax, and especially anything about a man missing from Dulles.

Too soon for the media to have picked up on the stories, he wondered, or were McGarvey's friends at the CIA or someone from the FBI suppressing the stories for now because of an ongoing investigation, and a manhunt for the shooter?

Next he opened Google and searched for Richard S. Tepping. Almost immediately more than ten thousand hits came up, chief among them the Richard Tepping, born in Indianapolis and educated at Notre Dame with a bachelor's and master's in political science and a minor in media communications.

Several photographs of him came up, and it was the same man from Dulles.

Most astounding, though, was that Tepping worked in the White House as an assistant press secretary. His father owned a big construction company in New Jersey that had been involved with three of Weaver's projects a number of years ago. The son's position on the White House staff was most certainly a thank-you.

Kamal scrolled through more than a dozen media releases that were at least in part credited to Tepping, but two that stuck out involved position statements that Weaver had briefly used during the campaign outlining his plan for dealing with Muslim extremist lone wolves and terrorist cells in the U.S.

"Guantánamo is waiting for those who survive U.S. law enforcement," had been one of Weaver's talking points.

Kamal walked over to Union Station to a kiosk inside the main terminal and bought three throwaway cell phones, each loaded with thirty minutes of airtime.

He went to the Pret a Manger fast-food place on the west side of the concourse, where he got a coffee and took a stool at the long counter. Not many people were in the station at this hour.

It was four in the morning in Riyadh when Abboud finally answered on the sixth ring. "Who is this?" he demanded in Arabic.

"Al Nassr," Kamal replied. "I need information."

"Just a minute," Abboud said.

A woman in the background said something, but a few moments later Abboud was back. "What do you want?"

"I want to know about a man named Richard Tepping. He's an assistant press secretary at the White House."

"What the hell are you into? Your target is McGarvey. Is he dead?"

"I need to know if Tepping was in Beijing in the past several months."

"Are you going to explain this to me?"

"Not yet. Just get me the information."

"What else?" Abboud demanded.

"Was he alone?" Kamal asked, but he hung up before Abboud could answer.

On the way out Kamal took the SIM card and battery out of the phone, and tossed everything into a trash can.

He got across Columbus Circle, traffic light but steady, and walked a couple of blocks to a small park on D Street and Louisiana Avenue, where he sat down on a bench. He was alone here.

Using the second throwaway phone he called the CIA's main working number—the 703, not the 800, area code.

"You have reached the United States Central Intelligence Agency."

Kamal pressed zero.

A woman came on. "May I help you?"

"I am called al Nassr. I wish to talk to Mr. Kirk McGarvey about his granddaughter, Audrey. I will call this number again at one A.M. local. Have him standing by, please."

"I'm sorry, sir, but I don't know the name."

"Thank you, darling. Just pass the message along."

FIFTY-FIVE

□

Pete unlocked the door of her third-floor apartment in Georgetown, and then stepped back. She and McGarvey both had their pistols out, hers in an awkward left-hand grip because of the wound to her right arm.

They waited a full ten seconds, before McGarvey eased the door open.

Soft classical music came from inside, and a light was on down the short corridor to the bedroom and bathroom.

It was an old trick. An intruder might turn off the music so that he could hear someone coming to the door, and then the light so that he would have the advantage of darkness.

Nevertheless, McGarvey darted inside, swinging his pistol left to right.

Pete was right behind him, and in less than ten seconds they had completely cleared the apartment, and she had locked up.

McGarvey went to the window and parted the curtain slightly so that he could look down on N Street NW. A cab passed and a few seconds later a red SUV went to the end of the block and turned right.

"How do you want to play this?" Pete asked.

"He knows my place, and it's a safe bet he knows this place as well so we'll stay together for the night and get some rest. We can take turns keeping watch."

McGarvey didn't miss her little smile.

"Want something to eat?"

"Sure."

"A grilled ham and cheese and a beer?"

"Sounds good. I'll take the first watch."

McGarvey took off his jacket, sat down on the chair facing the door and laid the pistol within easy reach on the end table as Pete went into the tiny kitchen.

He was weary but not sleepy. It wasn't what Echo had said to him—he thought that the man had been telling the truth—but it was his attitude. He'd made no bones about hating Weaver and wanting the man impeached. Nor had he denied communicating on a regular basis with the same mid-level intelligence officers that Otto's search program had identified.

But the general had not ordered McGarvey's assassination. Nor had he admitted to knowing about the training camp in the Mexican desert or al-Daran's connection to it, or anything else about the contract killer.

His nodding at al-Daran could have meant nothing more than Echo had explained it meant, as lame as that seemed, but McGarvey did not believe it.

Which left him at the beginning. Al-Daran was gunning for him, and the man did not work without a stiff price tag. Echo would have a hard time coming up with that kind of cash and then hiding it. Unless someone else in the Consortium had been the money man. Maybe someone in the Saudi GIP.

Al-Daran had almost certainly visited the training base in Mexico.

But the attack at the Farm wasn't al-Daran's style, which meant a second party wanted him dead for whatever reason.

The only common thread was President Weaver. But McGarvey could not bring himself to believe that the president of the United States had hired al-Daran to make the hit.

Or someone on his staff? Ron Hatchett, the President's deputy adviser on national security affairs, had gone to Beijing for a secret meeting of some sort. But a meeting with whom?

Weaver had lost his temper when McGarvey had brought it up, which could have meant nothing other than he'd acted presidential. Many of his predecessors had gone ballistic when they were questioned.

"A penny," Pete asked, coming out with the sandwiches and cold beers.

"We're at square one, because I don't have a clue what the hell is going on except that al-Daran wants to kill me and I don't think it's for revenge."

"You believe Echo?"

"I think that he and his contacts have come up with some scheme to discredit Weaver. But I can't make myself believe that these guys want me dead."

"You know some of them, I'll bet."

"A few of the names on Otto's list rang a bell."

"Then talk to them," Pete said. "One-on-one. Unofficially, as a part of the old-boys network."

"I know some of the names, but it doesn't mean we're friends."

"Maybe not, but I'm betting that just about everyone in the business has a great deal of respect for you."

"You're prejudiced."

"Damned right I am."

McGarvey's phone chirped. It was Otto.

"Are you at Pete's?"

"Yes. I met again with Echo, and he denies knowing anything about al-Daran."

"What about Colonel Chambeau?"

"No one home."

"Echo may not know al-Daran, but I'd bet good money that he warned his brother-in-law that you were on the way over."

"Put a trace on him."

"Already in the works," Otto said. "But listen. Tony Flynn, the OD in Housekeeping, is going to phone you in a minute or two. He called me and I asked him to give me time to talk to you first."

McGarvey's gut tightened. Otto almost never talked this way. "I'm listening."

"This is a recording of a call that came in a little while ago."

May I help you? a woman asked on the recording.

"She's the night operator at our seven-oh-three number," Otto said.

I am called al Nassr. I wish to talk to Mr. Kirk McGarvey about his granddaughter, Audrey. I will call this number again at one A.M. local. Have him standing by, please.

I'm sorry, sir, but I don't know the name.

Thank you, darling. Just pass the message along.

"Audie is okay," Otto broke in. "Louise has taken her to stay with a friend. Under the circumstances the Farm didn't seem like such a hot idea."

"What friend?"

"I don't know who it is, and I don't want to know. Just an extra layer of safety."

McGarvey glanced at his watch. It was just a few minutes before one.

"It was al-Daran, my voice program pegs it at eighty-seven percent plus. British accent, especially in his use of the word *darling*."

"He's not hiding his identity."

"No."

"Audie's safe?"

"There's no one other than you who I'd trust my life with as much as I trust my wife."

"Agreed," McGarvey said, the rage boiling inside of him almost impossible to control. He wanted the son of a bitch right here, right now, in front of him. Mano a mano.

Pete was looking at him with sympathy and understanding and love in her eyes. She reached out to touch him, but he pulled his arm away.

"Did they get a trace on the call?"

"Throwaway cell phone somewhere a couple of blocks south of Union Station," Otto said. "And before you ask I didn't roll any assets; he's long gone by now."

"He's set up a back door for himself. Means he's worried."

"Soon as we get a trace we'll roll," Otto said. "It's his first mistake."

"His second," McGarvey said. "Threatening my granddaughter was his first."

FIFTY-SIX

Kamal stood in the shadow of a doorway just across O Street NW from McGarvey's apartment building on the third floor of a brownstone, Tepping's computer bag over his shoulder. From there McGarvey would have a nice view of Rock Creek Park, where, it was said, he often took morning runs.

He glanced at his watch. It lacked one minute of one, and except for the bars and restaurants down along M Street NW and the block or two toward the river before Whitehurst Freeway, which were still busy, this part of Georgetown was quiet.

No lights showed in McGarvey's windows, which really didn't mean much. The CIA would have contacted him by now—him and his friend Otto Rencke—and he could be standing up there in the darkness watching from a window.

Kamal resisted the urge to step out of the shadows and wave. Instead he used the last throwaway phone to make the call.

McGarvey answered on the fourth ring—just a little show of willpower. "Yes."

"You know who this is?" Kamal asked.

"What do you want?"

"You, of course. Same as it has been since Monaco, and then New York, where you interfered with my plans. I won't allow it to happen again."

"We know about the training camp in Mexico. Whoever you've hired will be stopped if they try to cross the border."

"The same as your immigration coppers stop all the other illegal immigrants coming to work on your farms and in your orchards? Or just to have their babies born on U.S. soil?

"What are you sending them to do?"

"Oh, you know. A little mayhem."

"Is that why you met with Ron Hatchett in Beijing?"

Kamal was rattled, but he recovered his composure as quickly as he had lost it. "I'm sorry, but I don't know that name, nor have I been in Beijing for a number of years."

"I'll ask again, what do you want?"

"You've not asked about your granddaughter."

"No need. She's safe."

"I'm sure you didn't send her back to the Farm, not after what happened to you there. Which means she's with Otto Rencke or perhaps his wife, Louise, the satellite expert. Bunkered down somewhere. But of course the kid wasn't the point, was she? It's you and me, something we both want."

"You're using another throwaway phone, which you probably bought at Union Station. Otto will have your present location by now."

"No need for that. I'm standing in the doorway of the building just across the street from your apartment. I can step into view and you can take a shot from your window, if that's your style."

Kamal moved out of the shadows.

"Or?"

"Or we can meet across the street in the park. On the path along the creek where you run whenever you're in town."

"If I see you I'll kill you."

"Please, without due process? Not very sporting for a former DCI."

"I'm not a law-abiding man," McGarvey said. "I'll even give you a head start. Ten minutes. The cops are on the way right now, but I really don't want them to arrest you."

"You mean try," Kamal said.

He shut off the phone, and at the corner he tossed it down a storm drain and hurried up to P Street NW and from there down the pathway into the park.

"I've lost contact with his phone on the corner at Twenty-sixth," Otto said. "He probably tossed it in a Dumpster."

"Or took the battery and SIM card out," McGarvey said as he hurried down the stairs and to the front door. Nothing moved on the street for the moment.

Pete was right behind him, also connected with Otto. "Or wrapped it in aluminum foil," she said.

"The signal wasn't cut off, it faded."

"He's already ahead of me," McGarvey said.

"Do you want backup?" Otto asked.

"No. He'll just run, and take out a couple of cops on the way."

"We're on our way," Pete said as McGarvey opened the front door.

"You're staying here," he said.

"Not a chance in hell."

"If he knows that you're close, he'll figure that we'll come after him together. He could just as well double back and wait upstairs in your apartment or someplace with a good sight line for us to come back."

Pete started to protest, but Otto cut her off.

"Mac is right."

Pete looked down the street toward the park. "Christ," she said. She turned back and gave McGarvey a peck on the cheek. "Get yourself killed and I'll never speak to you again."

"Deal," McGarvey said and he took off running toward the park.

Kamal crossed to the other side of the parkway and made his way back along the creek until it made a double bend just at 26th Street. He perched on the edge of a picnic table in plain view of anyone coming into the park.

It was far too long of a distance for any accuracy with a pistol. But once McGarvey came across the road he would almost certainly try for the shot.

He pulled the ultra-compact ArmaLite AR-7 out of the shoulder bag and took out the parts from inside the camouflaged stock. The receiver attached to the stock, the barrel went in next and was screwed down, along with a laser sight, and finally a fifteen-round magazine of 40-grain round-nosed .22 long-rifle ammunition.

As he worked he kept looking up to watch for McGarvey.

The survival rifle issued by the U.S. Air Force for pilots who were shot down inside enemy-held territory was small and lightweight, but even though it fired only the .22-caliber bullet, a head shot would easily take down a man.

McGarvey would spot him from across the creek, but he would not survive the encounter.

McGarvey crossed 27th Street and went directly into the park, keeping low and moving fast. His best guess was that al-Daran had crossed to the other side of the creek, possibly up across P Street, where there was a pathway.

The man would have come back down somewhere across from the end of O Street or even Dumbarton and would be waiting.

Washington had been drier than normal for the past several months and the creek was low and slow enough for McGarvey to wade across.

Away from the streetlights and stanchions along the parkway, the opposite side of the creek was in relative darkness.

McGarvey pulled out his pistol, and still keeping low, but moving with more caution now that he felt he was close to al-Daran, he worked his way through the trees and occasional opening back upriver, toward Dumbarton.

Fifty yards later he pulled up short.

A man was seated on top of a picnic table, something cradled in his lap.

It was Kamal, and he was holding what looked like a small rifle of some sort.

McGarvey raised his gun, when someone fired a pistol from behind him, the round smacking into the tree beside which he'd been standing.

FIFTY-SEVEN

☐

Kamal rolled over the edge of the picnic table, the rifle pointing downriver. It had been an unsilenced pistol shot. At first he thought that McGarvey had somehow managed to get behind him.

Something or someone moved to the left not more than ten or fifteen meters out.

Kamal brought the rifle up but whoever it was had pulled up short.

Someone else moved a bit farther away, and Kamal brought the rifle around.

It had to be McGarvey out ahead and his woman coming up from behind. But the former DCI favored a Walther PPK while his girlfriend used a Glock 29 Gen4. The pistol shot he'd heard had been fired from a much larger weapon.

They could have switched to different pistols, but somehow he didn't think that was the case. Whoever it was who'd fired the shot was not the woman, and definitely not McGarvey. He didn't think that either of them would have missed.

Taking care with his movements so as to make as little noise as possible, Kamal laid the rifle on the table then took his pistol out of its holster as he moved off to the right, and made his way downriver to a spot he figured would be just behind the nearest shooter.

Thirty yards to the west McGarvey pulled up and hunched down, watching for a movement through the trees and undergrowth back the way he'd come. A taxi came up N Street NW and made the corner onto 24th Street NW, its headlights flashing through the woods.

Before it was dark again, McGarvey got the strobe-like image of a figure about twenty yards away moving toward him.

Not al-Daran; the terrorist had been off to the right. This was the shooter who'd come up from behind. From the left in the direction of the parkway.

McGarvey's phone buzzed in his pocket. It was Otto.

"Pete just got to me. She's on Twenty-seventh, said she spotted two guys getting out of a car in front of her place and heading on foot toward the park."

"Is she behind them?" McGarvey asked, keeping his voice to a whisper.

"Yes. She thought she heard a shot. Was it you?"

"No. Tell her to stay put, but if anyone comes out of the park other than me, take them down."

"What about you?"

"I'm on one of them right now."

"I can get you backup."

"I'd rather have answers than dead bodies. There're three of them including al-Daran. I want one of them alive."

The man Kamal approached was looking toward the left, downriver, his complete attention on something in that direction. He was dressed in dark slacks and a dark shirt.

From two meters out Kamal could make out the large pistol in the man's hands. The single round had been a 10 mm, and the pistol had the unmistakable lines of a SIG Sauer. Almost certainly the fairly new P220.

Somewhere farther to the left someone else moved, then stopped.

McGarvey had come here to the park, but so had at least one other man, the one holding the SIG.

The man didn't realize that someone was on his six until Kamal was within arm's length, and he started to turn.

"I will shoot you unless you decock your weapon and let it fall to the ground," Kamal said softly.

The man was slightly built, a half-head shorter than Kamal. He stiffened, then slowly turned his head to look over his shoulder directly into the muzzle of Kamal's pistol, and into Kamal's eyes.

"Al Nassr," the man said. He wasn't afraid.

It was a shock. "How do you know my name?"

"We've come from New York to help you."

"We?"

"I'm Ahmad, my partner is Hamza. But McGarvey is here. We were just in time to see him cross the parkway."

"Who in New York sent you and exactly why?"

"The chief of station, and as I've already said we're here to help you."

"With what?"

"I've already told you that too."

"I'm losing my patience."

"We're here to make sure that Mr. McGarvey doesn't survive the night, so that your plans may go ahead."

"I don't need your help," Kamal said and as the Saudi intel officer began to raise his pistol Kamal shot him in the forehead at point-blank range.

The sound of the pistol shot cracked through the woods like a bullwhip.

McGarvey took two steps to the right in time to see a dark figure dart out of the shadows about thirty feet away and duck behind a tree, keeping it between him and the direction of the pistol shot.

The figure was smaller than Kamal and McGarvey was certain that it wasn't Pete.

He phoned Otto. "Where's Pete?"

"She's in the park just opposite N Street, just like you wanted."

"Are you sure?"

"I have her GPS position."

"Tell her to look sharp. The next one out of the park could be Kamal."

A siren sounded somewhere in the distance to the southwest. Otto heard it over the phone at the same time McGarvey did.

"Someone reported the gunfire," Otto said. "I'll give the cops the heads-up."

McGarvey pocketed the phone, and keeping his pistol aimed center mass at the back of the figure hiding behind the tree, started forward.

Nothing else moved out ahead, in the direction of the single pistol shot. But Kamal was out there; McGarvey could feel him.

Five feet out, McGarvey stopped. "Toss your gun aside and I will not shoot you."

The man stiffened and then started to turn, his gun hand coming around first.

"Stop now."

The man did.

"No reason for you to die. If you're here to help al Nassr you're too late. I suspect he's already killed your partner, not the other way around."

"Tell me who you are, and we can make a deal," the man said. His English was good but his accent was Arabic.

The siren was much closer now, and a second came from the northwest, but farther away.

"I'm Kirk McGarvey and I want some answers."

The man suddenly turned, bringing his pistol around.

McGarvey dodged left as the Saudi fired once, the shot going wide. Mac fired twice, one shot hitting the man in the side just behind his left shoulder, and the second plowing into his head just behind his ear.

FIFTY-EIGHT

Kamal stood in place beside the GIP housekeeper's body, considering his options.

The first of the police were very close now, just across the creek on the parkway. More sirens were inbound, some on the other side of the park, probably on 26th Street. They were responding to sounds of gunfire and were trying to contain the situation.

McGarvey was somewhere close, just downriver, and he'd almost certainly killed the other GIP operative.

If the New York muscle had stayed out of it, McGarvey would almost certainly be dead by now. And possibly his girlfriend too.

He didn't want it to end this way, with McGarvey. He wanted to finish the business once and for all. But he wasn't going to spend the rest of his life in some jail—possibly in Guantánamo.

None of the other actions he'd set in place really mattered to him. He could just walk away now and return to his life in France.

All that passed through his head in one piece, and the solution came to him as it always did in these sorts of circumstances.

He knew how he was going to finish the job he'd been hired to do, plus the one for his own amusement, and in the end he would kill McGarvey, who would have no other recourse than to help try to save innocent lives.

McGarvey was coming through the woods. Kamal couldn't hear him, but he knew he wouldn't remain in place and allow the police to do the job for him.

Kamal turned, and running lightly on the balls of his feet through the woods upriver with as little noise as possible, made his way the two hundred meters or so where the parkway crossed the creek and just beyond where P Street also crossed it.

Holstering his pistol, and making sure that no one was on his six, he scrambled up the embankment to the street, just as a white Lexus was approaching from Georgetown.

He pulled out his wallet, held it up, as if it were a police identification, and jumped out into the middle of the street.

A middle-aged man in a business suit, his collar undone, his tie loose, was behind the wheel. He powered the window down.

Kamal stuffed his wallet back in his pocket and pulled out his pistol as he came around to the driver's side.

"What the fuck?" the man blurted.

Kamal shot him once in the head. He reached inside the car, unlocked the door and opened it, then dragged his body out into the street, got behind the wheel and drove off.

Taillights turned north on 22nd Street NW heading toward Florida Avenue and Embassy Row, as McGarvey reached P Street from the creek.

A man in a dark business suit with thinning gray hair lay on his back gasping for breath in the middle of the street. Blood filled his left eye socket and dribbled down his cheek from a close-range bullet wound to his head.

Holstering his pistol, McGarvey bent down over the man but there wasn't much he could do.

He phoned Otto. "Got a man down on P Street just east of the creek, bullet wound in his head, but he's still alive."

"Wait one," Otto said.

McGarvey leaned closer. "Can you hear me?"

"Yes," the man whispered.

"Help is on the way."

"Ambulance is just around the corner," Otto said. "Be there in less than five."

"Am I going to die?" the man asked.

"No."

"I thought he was a cop. But he shot me."

"What'd he look like?"

"English," the man said, and his chest heaved, and suddenly he was still. His eyes were open, but he was dead.

"It was al-Daran," McGarvey told Otto. "Shot this guy and took his car. But tell the EMTs there's no hurry, he didn't make it. And embed Pete with the cops for now. He missed me but he might try for her."

"Already done," Otto said. "Give me an ID and I'll find out what he was driving."

McGarvey took the dead man's wallet out of his back pocket, the job distasteful in the extreme. If he had been a little faster he could have reached al-Daran before this happened. There was no good reason for the guy to have been killed, except that he had been in the wrong place at the wrong time.

"Charles Conrad," McGarvey read from the driver's license. The address was in Chevy Chase.

Otto was back at the same moment the ambulance arrived. "A seventeen Lexus LS Sport. White."

McGarvey backed away from the body as a pair of EMTs came from the ambulance.

"Put out an APB, but give them the heads-up that this guy is a well-motivated professional."

"Doing it," Otto replied.

One of the EMTs used a respirator bag on the man while the other listened to his chest with a stethoscope.

"What about Pete?"

"She's still on the east side of the parkway opposite O Street, but she wants to know if you're okay."

"Fine. Tell the cops there're two bodies on the opposite side of the creek between N and O. The field is clear, so far as I know, but tell them to tread with care."

"The APB has been issued."

"Probably won't do any good, he'll ditch the car as soon as possible."

Kamal parked the Lexus down the block from Union Station. Making sure that there were no cops around, and that he wasn't being observed, he locked the door and walked away.

It was just after two when he reached the Hyatt Regency and took the elevator up to his room, which looked toward the Capitol building, all lit up.

They had traced him to the Hay-Adams because he had used his O'Neal documents too many times. It was possible, though unlikely, that they might connect his Hollman documents, from when he had stayed in Atlanta, here to this hotel.

There were only a few days left until the attacks would begin, and he would have to be back in New York. By now Ayman Baz's teams from Mexico would be getting ready to cross the border for San Francisco, New Orleans and Pastor Buddy's operation in western Kansas.

Baz had agreed to send them out at the very last moment, to minimize the risk of their being detected.

"Do any of them have friends or family living anywhere near those three targets?" Kamal had asked.

"No. It was one of the first things I checked. They're clean. Means they shouldn't be on any FBI or INS directory."

"Have any of them ever been in the States?"

"As students on clean visas. None of them ever got so much as a traffic ticket."

Kamal had been satisfied at the time, but now he wasn't sure about Baz, or the GIP, or the Saudi UN mission in New York.

He went downstairs to the biz center and brought up an area map showing the locations of a half-dozen business airports within a twenty-five-kilometer radius of the Hyatt. The Washington Executive Airport at Hyde Field, not too far from Joint Base Andrews was adequate.

At the desk he told the clerk that unfortunately he had to leave early. He wanted a cab to take him to Dulles.

He was packed and in the cab in under fifteen minutes.

At Dulles he would call Pastor Buddy to send the Gulfstream for him, then rent a car and drive over to Hyde Field and wait for as long as it took.

It was time to go to ground.

□

FIFTY-NINE

A uniformed cop drove McGarvey to the other side of the river and down to the end of Dumbarton Street, where Pete was waiting with a massive police presence and several ambulances. A crowd of onlookers had gathered from the apartments and brownstones, all of it being shot live by several television stations.

"Like a three-ring circus," McGarvey said.

"You okay?" Pete asked.

"Al-Daran had help. I'm guessing GIP from New York. I shot one of them and I suspect that he took out the other."

"Here to kill you, I can understand. But you said he took out the other one. I don't understand."

"Someone's getting cold feet."

A Caddy Escalade with government plates came around the barricades. The man riding shotgun got out and came over toward where McGarvey and Pete were waiting to be released by the Bureau's SAC from the situation. It was Larry Kyung-won, dressed this time in jeans, a light polo shirt and a dark blue jacket with CIA stenciled on the back.

He showed his ID to one of plainclothes cops, who let him through.

"You're a hard man to kill, Mr. Director," he said.

"And when you come in out of the cold you do it all the way," Pete said.

McGarvey wasn't really surprised that Kyung-won was here, and yet he was.

"Marty wants you guys back on the reservation for the time being. Sent me and some muscle to fetch you."

"In the morning," McGarvey said.

"He wants you two now."

"We're going back to Pete's apartment to clean up, get something to eat and maybe a few hours of sleep. It's been a long day."

Kyung-won started to object, but then he grinned and nodded. "Yes, sir. We'll drive you back and then circle the wagons in case the son of a bitch wants to try again."

"He's gone," McGarvey said. "And we'll walk."

"We'll be outside if you need us," Kyung-won said, and he backed off.

McGarvey and Pete were cleared by the Bureau SAC who'd shown up and taken charge. They headed down N Street toward Pete's apartment two blocks away, but at the first corner Mac turned and headed to his place on O Street.

"You have the willies?" she asked.

"Just a bit."

"Is it Larry?"

"I'm not sure."

"They're right behind us, you know."

"I know. But I have a couple of things I want to get at my place."

"Tired of getting shot at?"

McGarvey had to smile. "You could say that."

"Then we're definitely going on a long vacation when this is over."

"Sounds good."

Upstairs McGarvey checked the telltale bit of clear grease on his door lock before he and Pete went inside.

"Hold off on the lights for a minute," he said and went to the front window, where he stayed to the left, out of sight from anyone on the street, and parted the edge of the blinds just enough to see the street.

The Caddy was parked across the street a few cars away. He had a clear view through the windscreen, but no one was inside.

A shadow moved half a block away, then darted across the street. It was impossible to identify who it was.

Pete was at his shoulder. "Trouble?"

The Caddy's out there, but no one's inside, and just now I saw someone cross to our side of the street."

"They're out there to watch out for us. You can't miss the car, but you might not spot someone standing in a doorway."

"Al-Daran is not coming back tonight and they know it."

"Bet your life on it?"

"Yeah," McGarvey said.

He went back to his bedroom and took a silencer and two spare magazines of ammunition from a dresser drawer. He reloaded his pistol and attached the silencer, then pocketed the magazines.

Pete was at the bedroom door, her pistol out and pointing down and away from her left leg. "If al-Daran is not coming back, what's your thinking? Larry?"

"I'm not sure. But I want you to stay here at the window. I'm going down the rear fire escape. My phone'll be on vibrate. I want you to keep an eye on the street and let me know if you see anything."

"I don't want to believe it," Pete said. "But there've been a lot of coincidences."

"Too many."

McGarvey went down the short corridor to the fire escape door, took the stairs two at a time to the roof and outside carefully looked over the edge to what had at one time been a mews. Across the alley old horse stables had been converted to apartments. No lights shone from any of the windows.

He went down the three flights of stairs to the alley, and keeping close to the wall of the building, hurried to 28th Street NW a half a block away. Nothing moved and he went to the corner of O Street just as a taxi came from the direction of the park.

From where he stood he was a half a block behind where the Caddy was parked.

He phoned Pete. "Anything?"

"Nothing, Where are you?"

"Corner of Twenty-eighth and O. I'm going to cross the street and take a look inside the Caddy."

The taxi passed and a moment later he heard it in Pete's phone.

"Where the hell are you?" he demanded.

"In the front doorway. You said someone came across the street. Make a noise and I'm going to scoot to the other side, maybe draw their fire, if that's what's going on here. Could be Larry and the other guy are just doing their jobs."

"Goddamnit," McGarvey said. He couldn't believe her and yet he did.

"Now," she said.

McGarvey stepped into view. "Here!" he shouted.

Moving low and fast, Pete raced across the street and directly down the block to the passenger side of the Caddy.

McGarvey waited at the corner for a shot to come.

Pete was back on the phone. "The driver was shot in the head. He's slumped down across the center console."

The muzzle of a pistol pressed against the back of McGarvey's head.

"Steady now, Mr. Director," Kyung-won said.

SIXTY

□

"I didn't hear you come up from behind," McGarvey said.

"Shut down your phone and drop it and your gun to the ground."

McGarvey eased down, laid the pistol on the sidewalk and straightened up.

"Now your phone."

"I don't think so. But at least you're one part of one question answered," McGarvey said. "I know the GIP hired Kamal—although I suspect he met with the president's deputy adviser for national security affairs in Beijing awhile back. And we've verified that you were an NOC in North Korea. So tell me who you're working for now?"

"I said, drop the fucking phone."

"Even if he did, the on/off function won't work," Otto's voice came over the speaker.

"Your friend is a dead man."

"A GPS chip was implanted in your body before you went up to Pyong-yang," Otto said.

"Why didn't you see me sneaking up behind Mac?"

"It was shut down, by who I haven't figured out, but I'll get it working again. So, basically, Larry, as of now you're officially fucked. We'll find you wherever you run."

"Put the gun down, and we'll talk," McGarvey said. "Tell us what you know and we'll cut you a deal."

"Too late for that."

"It wasn't Grace Metal who tried to kill me at the Farm."

"No, but she suspected someone was going to make the try, so she shadowed you."

"And you killed her."

"I needed your trust for just a little longer."

"For what?"

"To save your life."

"But it was you who cut the rope on the Ball Buster."

"Change of orders," Kyung-won said.

"Whose orders?"

"Doesn't matter."

"So here we are," McGarvey said. "Another change of plans? First you were ordered to kill me, and then you were ordered to back off and now you're back to square one. Shit or get off the pot."

"I have a lot of admiration for you. Just about every NOC I've ever met does. I don't want to kill you, I never did."

"You tried at the Farm."

"I knew that either you or one of your minders—and Grace wasn't the only one—would discover that the rope had been tampered with. I reported that I had tried."

"Reported to whom?"

"You'll never know. But I'll make a deal with you. And it'll have to include Pete and Otto, who're listening in."

"I've never been good at making deals with someone pointing a gun at me."

"For the moment I don't have any choice," Kyung-won said. "Just promise at least to hear me out."

"You turned off your GPS locator."

"Every NOC figures out that little trick almost from the get-go."

"You want to go deep, but whoever hired you to kill me will want their money back."

"They can always try."

"I'll come after you."

"But that's the deal. I won't shoot you, and you won't come looking for me."

"But you killed Grace and the housekeeper who came with you."

"They were expendable."

"Like you?"

"Like all the other guys and three women whose stars—no names, just stars—are on the wall in the lobby of the OHB. You've seen them a thou-sand times. And so has every other son of a bitch who comes through the doors. The trouble is, after a while they lose their meaning. They're just a decoration."

"No star for a traitor," McGarvey said.

Kyung-won remained silent.

"Or a coward."

"I'd prefer to be thought of as another Aldrich Ames. Only I'll be the one who got away."

McGarvey tossed the phone to the left. For just an instant Kyung-won's attention was diverted, and McGarvey swiveled on his heel as he ducked his head to the right.

Kyung-won fired one shot, which went wide, and Mac grabbed for the pistol but the other man moved away too fast, and Mac only got his wrist.

For just a second Kyung-won struggled, trying to pull free.

McGarvey doubled up his fist and hit the man in his chest—on the left side—with every ounce of his strength.

Kyung-won was staggered. Still he tried desperately to free his gun hand.

McGarvey hit him in the chest again. And again. The fourth time, the man's legs gave out from under him and he crumpled to the sidewalk.

As he went down, Mac snatched the pistol out of his hand.

"He's down."

"Help is on its way," Otto said.

Pete came running up the street, her pistol drawn, her features rigid, her complexion white. She skidded to a stop, looking from McGarvey to Kyung-won and back, and lowered her pistol. "You sure know how to show a girl an interesting time."

McGarvey released the magazine from Kyung-won's pistol and tossed it aside, then ejected the round from the firing chamber before he tossed the gun aside and picked up his Walther.

"I didn't hear it all," Pete said. "What'd he give you?"

Kyung-won sat up, rubbing his chest. "I gave him nothing," he said. "In fact, I should have shot him in the back of the head when I had the chance."

"Housekeeping is on the way," McGarvey said. "Cooperate and you might not get the death penalty. It's my only deal."

Kyung-won shook his head and smiled a little. "Do you think I give a shit about dying?" He got to one knee and then stood. "Just about every sad sack who signs up to become an NOC understands the odds."

"Back to square one," McGarvey said. "Who hired you to take me out?"

"You think you can handle it?"

"The truth, yes. But not bullshit."

"The Guoanbu."

McGarvey was surprised. "Beijing?" Guoanbu was the Ministry of State Security, the Chinese intelligence agency. Hatchett had been sent by the White House to go to Beijing, which could very well mean that the White House wanted him dead.

Everything inside him, everything he'd ever stood for, nearly an entire lifetime, seemed to be on the edge of some precipice. He shook his head.

"Makes you think, doesn't it? My control officer got me out of badland, so I owe him at least something. You know how it is."

"What's his name?"

"I forget."

McGarvey lowered his gun.

"I didn't kill you when I had the chance—more than one chance—so now you owe me a least a head start. I have enough money put away that I can go to ground permanently. And I'm pretty good at shit like that," Kyung-won said.

"Where were you recruited?"

"Pyongyang. At Outstanding Leader's compound."

"I was there a few years ago when his dad was Dear Leader. It's a wonder you got away with your head."

"The Chinese can be persuasive," Kyung-won said. "And now I'm getting out of here before the muscle Otto sent shows up. All I need is fifteen minutes." He nodded to Pete, then turned and started to walk away, still rubbing his chest with his right hand.

"You're not going to let him go, are you?"

"No," McGarvey said.

Kyung-won, suddenly turned around as if he had had a change of heart. In his hand was a Wilson X-TAC Elite Compact pistol.

McGarvey turned sideways and fired three evenly spaced shots, one hitting the man in the upper chest, one in the throat and the third in his face just to the left of his nose.

PART
FOUR

Flash Points

The next afternoon

McGarvey and Pete didn't leave his apartment until well before noon, somewhat rested, though neither of them had gotten much sleep. Twice before dawn she had awakened to find Mac standing at the front window looking down at the street where the Caddy Escalade with two minders who'd been sent out from Langley were parked.

"Larry is dead and I thought you said that al-Daran had gone to ground and the GIP wouldn't be sending anyone else from New York," she said.

"Old habits die hard," he'd told her. "Go back to bed, I'll be in shortly."

She'd gone to him and put an arm around his shoulders. "We're both light sleepers. And I can't get much these days without a warm body beside me. Give a girl a break?"

"I haven't got it figured out yet. There's something just around the edges that doesn't make sense."

"You thought that two tracks were in play. One out of the White House, and one involving the old-boys list that Otto came up with."

"That's the sticking point. The old-boys thing—which includes Echo—wants to discredit Weaver. Get him impeached."

"For what? He hasn't done anything wrong that would rise to that level. At least nothing we know about."

"It's a soft coup."

"Well, whatever it is, it'll have to be dangerous," Pete said. "Another WikiLeaks? Maybe Weaver's been sharing classified emails with his staff that Hillary Clinton was accused of doing. If something like that were to get out it could hurt him."

"I don't think it's going to be that easy," McGarvey replied, almost distantly. Something just at the edge, he thought again. Softly scratching at the door of his understanding. Not getting it was maddening.

"What then?"

"I think it's going to be worse," McGarvey said. "Larry killed Grace at the Farm and the housekeeper who'd come with him from campus. And was willing to kill me if we couldn't come to a deal, presumably on orders from his control officer who worked for Chinese intel."

"Do you think he was part of Echo's deal? We can see if one of the names on Otto's list works for the Guoanbu. I assume that we have people in Pyongyang who might know if that guy—whoever it is—showed up anytime in the past few months. Wouldn't be any sort of proof but it might shed some light."

"That's only half of it," McGarvey said.

"Yeah, al-Daran. If it was the GIP that hired him to take you out, what else are they planning?"

"And who's directing them?" McGarvey said.

The minders followed them out to Langley, where at the security gate McGarvey's VIP visitor's badge was given to him.

"Good afternoon, Mr. Director," the guard said. "Good to see you back in one piece."

"A few stitches and a little glue holding things together," McGarvey said.

They parked in the underground garage and took the elevator up to Otto's suite of offices on the third floor, where they were buzzed in.

"How's Audie?" McGarvey asked soon as they walked in.

"I talked to Louise last night, they're fine," Otto said. He'd only been on his own for a little more than twenty-four hours, but he hadn't gone home in that time, and he had reverted to his usual mess: coffee or some other stains on his CCCP sweatshirt, his jeans rumpled and his sneakers unlaced. But he was on the hunt; he had that faraway look in his eyes.

"Where are they?"

"She didn't say and I didn't ask, or trace the call."

"It's coming to a head."

"I think so too," Otto agreed and he led them into his inner sanctum.

All of his big-screen high-def monitors were showing violet and lavender backgrounds, as was his horizontal table-size interactive monitor on which were displayed photographs of fifteen men and three women.

"These are the people Echo's been talking to?" McGarvey asked.

"All mid-level intel."

Several of the photos were of Asian-looking men.

"Any Guoanbu officer in the mix?"

Otto pulled one of the photographs closer, and with a thumb and forefinger increased its size. "Recognize him?"

"No."

"Li Zhang Wei. A mid-level financial planner who's been on the team trying to help North Korea out of its monetary mess. His specialty is finding ways to come up with trade goods that can be sent out of the country. In itself not such an easy job. His main directive, of course, is to find and recruit Westerners in country to go home and spy for the Guoanbu."

"Larry," McGarvey said.

"Almost certainly."

"Okay, so the Chinese are involved," Pete said. "Why recruit someone to come home and assassinate Mac?"

"For the same reason as always. Someone figures that Mac is willing to work extrajudicially."

"That would imply that someone like Echo is working out of the Pentagon, and that someone like Hatchett is working out of the White House," Pete said. "Neither of those guys is above the law, but they're pretty much untouchable because of their positions."

"Unless you caught them with their flies unzipped," Otto said.

McGarvey had been thinking about both possibilities. If Otto was right, the two men would have to be pushed into making a mistake.

"I have something else, though it'll probably not help much," Otto said. "I've got the DNA analysis back from the phone you picked up in the Watergate after the Fischer woman was shot to death, and her killers taken out. No identification, of course, but the guy in the stairwell was definitely Middle Eastern. Sixty-seven-percent probability he was Saudi. Some Syrian, some Pakistani and eight percent Brit."

"GIP," Pete said.

"Still leaves us with who killed Fischer and why?"

McGarvey had that part. It was the only thing at this point that made any sense to him. "Jen Chambeau."

"Echo's sister?" Pete asked. "But why?"

"Her husband was fucking Fischer."

"I'll check their phone logs and the Watergate security cameras for the past year," Otto said. "But what you're saying is that the Fischer woman was killed out of simple jealousy?"

"I think that she got herself in the middle of something other than just her affair with Chambeau. She was killed for her affair, but her killers' killers were taken out because they were at the wrong place at the wrong time."

They were standing around the tabletop monitor and Pete put out a hand to steady herself. Her eyes were puffy, her complexion wan. She looked all in. "What a mess."

None of them said anything for a long moment, until Otto broke the silence.

"So what's next, Kemo Sabe?"

"I'll go upstairs and talk to Walt," McGarvey said.

"And Marty and Carleton," Otto said. "If you're going to tell them what I think you're going to tell them."

"What am I missing?" Pete asked.

"This one you're going to stay out of," McGarvey told her.

"Like hell!"

"Mac's going to challenge the president of the United States again."

SIXTY-TWO

□

Kamal came instantly awake with the late-morning Kansas sun shining directly in his second-floor window. Someone was at his door and he reached for the Glock under his pillow as one of Pastor Buddy's girls came in with a tray.

"I brought coffee, some fruit and a few rolls," the girl said.

She was the Asian, named Mio, and she wore only a very short kimono. She was bright, and she was good in bed. Pastor Buddy had called her his right arm.

She set the tray on the coffee table in front of the couch, and as she bent over, her bare ass was exposed.

"Not this morning, darling," Kamal told her.

She turned, inclined her head and came over to the side of the bed. "The pastor wanted to personally thank you not only for your latest, most generous financial contribution, but for the two very hard workers you sent us. Jacks-of-all-trades, apparently, because they weren't here more than two hours before they unloaded their tools and began work in the chapel."

"I'm glad to hear it," Kamal said.

He and Baz had discussed which people would be sent to the three targets. A white, middle-class-American-looking boy and girl to fetch the van in San Francisco and drive it to the bridge. Two redneck men who were originally from a small town in southwestern Oklahoma, and who were proficient with explosives, to mine the dikes in New Orleans. And these two guys who had been born and raised in Aleppo but whose Spanish was good enough so that they could pose as Venezuelans.

They had been the hardest talents to come up with, according to the camp commandant. "But you can't imagine the sorts of people who join the online chat rooms," Baz had said. "From schoolteachers to schizophrenic out-of-work truck drivers, to kids next door and everyone in between."

"I hope they're behaving themselves," Kamal told the girl.

"They're actually sweet," she said. "And quiet. Juan actually said he was looking forward to Sunday."

It suddenly struck Kamal that the bitch was toying with him, most likely on Pastor Buddy's orders. She was working too hard at playing the dumb broad. Which meant that the pastor was shrewder than he let on, and suspected that something was going on he needed to know about. But quietly. Without disrupting the money flow.

"Actually, I'm not very hungry," Kamal said.

Mio took off her kimono as Kamal threw back the covers and she slipped into bed beside him.

She lay on her side, one leg over his, and brushed her fingertips across his cheek, then his lips.

"I'm glad that the boys are working out here," he said. "They needed a safe haven, and I suggested that this would be a good place for them. At least for now. And they jumped at it."

"Venezuelans?"

"They went up to Maracaibo a few years ago to lay low, working as roustabouts on the oil rigs in the lake. That's where I came across them."

"I had no idea that you were involved in the oil business."

"Just around the edges. Actually, I was down there gathering information for an old friend, and I hired them to do some inside work for him."

"I'm not following you."

"Doesn't matter. Let's just say that they came to the attention of the local SEBIN office—the oil business belongs to the government—and I had to get them out of town as quickly and as quietly as possible."

"SEBIN?"

"Venezuela's intelligence agency."

"They're fugitives?"

"No one outside of Venezuela is looking for them. And while they're here they'll do just about anything Buddy wants them to do."

She smiled. "Anything?"

He rolled over and kissed the nipple of her right breast. "Anything." he said.

After the girl left, Kamal took a shower and got dressed in a pair of off-white linen slacks, a yellow guayabera shirt and brown loafers, the last of his civilian clothes he hadn't worn recently.

His time in the States, on this operation, was coming to an end. And he found that he was looking forward to his country life in France, providing that he could get back to it intact. If not, he had a number of other possibilities in mind, one of them near Bangkok, where his money and anonymity would go much further than in France.

The three operations he'd been hired for in Beijing would take place on Sunday at noon. The one he'd planned for himself at Grand Central Station would happen at exactly the same time.

Originally Grand Central had been little more for him than frosting on a sweet. But in the past weeks it had become something more. Something that McGarvey would have to react to.

He'd come to think of it as a final confrontation between the two of them.

An end cap to his career—to his career and McGarvey's life.

He studied his image in the bathroom mirror. Not handsome in any Western movie star sort of way. Not Saudi. No trace of his Arabic genes. A well-put-together American, perhaps. Certainly a Westerner. British, if he wanted. Or French, German, even Swiss.

Drying his hands, he holstered his pistol beneath his shirt at the small of his back and went downstairs and outside to a cool, sunny morning.

It was a Friday and the amusement park wasn't due to open for another hour, at ten, but the huge church was open. He walked down the flower-lined path to the rear service entrance and up onto the loading dock where workmen were unloading a couple dozen wheelchairs and three times as many walkers, which would be brought out during the service.

Some of Pastor Buddy's people were out and about—a few in business suits, but most of them in jeans and polo shirts. A few of them nodded, but most of them had no idea who he was. Just another believer who'd shown up in their midst.

Inside, he walked past the dressing rooms, the control centers for the television and radio operations, and at the far end of the broad corridor a suite of big rooms where printed materials were manufactured—the weekly newspapers, the pamphlets and brochures such as "Nine Steps To Salvation," "Let God Into Your Life," "He's Waiting," "Heaven Is Not Just a Word."

Pastor Buddy had admitted that he was looking to expand his operation to include the manufacture and distribution of books, not only his, but other religious tomes, under the imprint of God's Workshop.

Obedh and Juan Castillo were touching up the paint at the back of the stage in the main hall when Kamal walked out through the double doors.

For a minute they were not aware he'd come onstage.

The auditorium was vast, rows of seats going back so far that recognizing anyone even halfway to the main doors would be completely impossible. Four tiers of balconies rose from the floor. And dropping from the ceiling were vast crystal chandeliers, along with television cameras and microphones on moveable booms. Huge flat-screen monitors the size of Jumbotrons hung from above the main stage as well as along the walls. Every move, every word and every facial gesture that Pastor Buddy made was broadcast on the screens and speakers, here in the auditorium as well as over his television network, broadcast by satellite all over the world.

The buffoon had built an empire potentially touching one-third of the entire planet's population.

The end, when it came on Sunday, would be nothing short of spectacular.

Kamal headed over to where the two ISIS suicide bombers were painting, to reassure them that Allah was watching them even in this den of evil, and was waiting to reward them.

□

SIXTY-THREE

Page was not very happy when McGarvey showed up. The DCI was behind his desk, Marty Bambridge and Carleton Patterson seated across from him.

It almost looked to McGarvey like a pretrial hearing, which in effect he supposed it was. No one, not even Carleton, who had a long, warm history with Mac, was going to like what he was going to tell them.

"Pete and I had a spot of trouble last night," McGarvey said, sitting down.

"We read your report and listened to Otto's recording of your conversation." Page said.

"Larry was one of our best operatives," Marty said. "Took a lot of chances, but he always managed to pull through. Especially getting out of badland."

"He had help," McGarvey said.

"Apparently all along," Marty replied. "We're working on backtracking his missions."

"How about Grace Metal?"

"She was clean. A casualty of war."

"But that's not why you came to see us, my dear boy," Patterson said. He was an old man but still one of the sharpest general counsels the CIA ever had.

"I only have a few things to work out yet, but I've already pretty well pieced everything together. Should have it wrapped up later today or by morning at the latest."

"What few things?" Marty asked.

"I'm going to call some of my old contacts from when this was my office, and then I'm going to have a chat with a general and lieutenant colonel who work at the Pentagon."

"And then what?" Carleton asked.

"And then I'll know for sure what I've already figured out."

Marty was impatient. "We're listening."

"Two things are going on, both of them having to do with the president."

Marty started to object, but Page held him off with a gesture.

"A consortium of mid-level intelligence officers from around the world have been in contact with one of our generals who said that if Weaver were elected he would have trouble following any order from the White House."

"We've been over that ground already," Page said.

"Yes, but it came to me that the intel officers Echo talked to were ones whose agencies were directly, or at least heavily indirectly, involved in a number of trouble spots around the world. Places where if the wrong responses were made by Weaver it could result in fighting, possibly even the threat of nuclear strikes. Flash points. India–Pakistan, Israel and most of its neighbors, China–Taiwan, especially North and South Korea."

"We know what's at stake," Marty said. "That's what we do here, remember?"

It was Carleton's turn to interject. "That's not what Kirk is saying."

"Most of the people on Otto's Consortium list are responsible for intercommunications with each other, and in some circumstances with us," McGarvey said. "But none of them have communicated in the past several months."

"You set that up during our tenure as DCI," Page said. "Talk before shooting. Good system."

"What if the Consortium started raising false flags? Maybe the guy on Otto's list who works for India's Defence Intelligence Agency warns that he has reliable intel that Pakistan is rattling its sabers. Its nuclear sabers, and the Indian government would like some help from our government."

"A problem for the president," Page said, understanding coming into his eyes, his bad mood deepening.

"The president would be forced into telephoning Pakistan's PM, who of course would claim that nothing was going on. Weaver would come out looking like a fool, especially when his call to Shahid Abbasi was made public."

"Abbasi would have to act on Weaver's call, in case it was India want-ing to cause trouble," Page said. "Tensions would be bumped up a notch."

"Let's add China and Taiwan on the same day, and one by one a half-dozen other spots would flash. Maybe Putin would be dragged into the mix. Situ-ations beyond Weaver's ability to handle would pop up all over the place."

"Impossible for any president," Page said. "But Weaver is the one sitting in the Oval Office."

"Once the ball got rolling, trouble could very easily follow," Carleton said. "A tense situation could spiral out of control."

"The Consortium wants to make Weaver look so bad Congress would have no other choice but to impeach him."

"If we didn't get into a shooting war first," Bambridge said.

"What are you suggesting we do about it?" Page asked.

"There's more," McGarvey said. "On top of all that, someone else wants to make sure that Weaver succeeds. They're going to do something drastic to make the president look very good. Turn him into a hero."

No one said anything for a longish moment until Page spoke up.

"Someone on his staff, or directed by his staff, has put something in motion, is that what you're saying? Like Nixon's people at the Watergate break-in?"

"Watergate was just a spy mission to get intel on what the Democrats were doing. Tame stuff."

"But now?"

"Ron Hatchett, the president's deputy adviser on national security af-fairs, took an under-the-radar trip to Beijing a month ago. Something, I suspect, that even Weaver doesn't know about."

"You're guessing," Bambridge said.

"Otto is working on some secure email trails, but I think that Hatchett hired someone to do a job of work."

"Dirty tricks?" Carleton suggested.

"I think that the Saudi-born operative called al Nassr, Kamal al-Daran, was the one who met with Hatchett."

Marty and the others were startled.

"The same guy that took down the pencil tower in New York and damned near took down a second one?" he asked.

"Yes."

"To do what, specifically?"

"I think that he's been hired to direct one or more teams of ISIS recruits to attack us here in the States."

Marty came half off his chair. "Where the fucking hell did you come up with something like that?" he demanded.

"We think that he visited a training base in northern Mexico. We redirected a satellite to take a closer look at what we expected had been used by one of the drug cartels as a staging point for shipments across our border."

"Did you see his face? Did you make a positive ID?"

"No. But a man using one of Kamal's false IDs stayed a night in Chihuahua not far from the base. The next morning he took a flight to Dallas–Fort Worth."

"And?" Page asked, his voice soft. He knew what was coming.

"The base hadn't been abandoned. Looked like a dozen or more people were training with weapons. On one pass we even detected two explosions."

"Did you give the Mexican authorities a heads-up?"

"By the second day activities at the camp appeared to be winding down."

"And you think what? Page asked.

"The ISIS team or teams are already here."

"You want to go back to the president and confront him with this," Page said, not as a question but as a statement.

"Exactly that," McGarvey said. "And I also want to tell him that Hatchett or whoever hired al-Daran also hired the man to do another job."

"To assassinate you?" Carleton asked.

"Something he's already tried to do more than once."

SIXTY-FOUR

☐

Pastor Buddy's Gulfstream G280 touched down at San Francisco International Airport a little after eight in the morning local, and the pilot taxied over to the Signature private jet terminal, where a Maybach limo and driver were waiting.

No girl had accompanied Kamal, at his request.

"I'm meeting with three sets of donors, and I'm not going to have much time for pleasure," he'd told the pastor.

"Money does take precedence after all, brother," Buddy had agreed.

All told to this point, Kamal had transferred three-quarters of a million dollars to the pastor's private account, with promises of much more to come.

"My salvation," Kamal had told him piously.

Buddy had sketched the sign of the cross in the air in front of Kamal's face. "And my eternal gratitude."

The image of breaking the idiot's neck and watching his face turn blue as he died stayed with Kamal the entire journey west.

"I'll be about an hour, perhaps a little longer," he told the Gulfstream pilot.

"Shall we refuel?"

"File for New Orleans next."

"Yes, sir."

Kamal left his two bags in the aircraft's cargo hold. He'd fixed simple ultraviolet telltales on the locks that would show up only under the UV flashlight on his satphone. If they were tampered with he would know, and the faint glow would show up on the fingers of whoever had opened the locks. It would be an automatic death sentence.

"Where shall I take you, sir?" the limo driver asked when a Signature attendant had closed the rear door.

"St. Mary's Cathedral," Kamal said. "It's on Gough Street."

"Yes, sir. I know it."

It was a Friday and the middle of rush-hour traffic, so it took the better part of a half hour to get downtown and double-park in front of the church. Kamal got the driver's cell phone number.

"I should be only fifteen or twenty minutes. I'll call and let you know when you can pick me up."

Kamal got out of the car and went inside the church, where from the door he waited until the Maybach was gone. He went outside and headed to the parking garage, where he'd left the RV.

Baz hadn't said where the two people he'd sent would be staying, but he'd vouched for their reliability. "It's a matter of doing something for their eternal souls. Nothing will stop them."

Kamal walked past the garage, making sure that the place wasn't being watched. So far as he could tell the block was clean, and he went back.

The padlock on the door was gone. For a long moment he stared at the hasp, his rage threatening to block out his reason.

He tried the door, but it had been locked from inside. The only windows were above the service door, which opened and shut as a single unit. There were no cracks through which he could look inside.

Traffic on the street was light, and a man and a woman had come out of an apartment building down the block and walked away.

Kamal took his pistol put of its holster, and holding it out of sight from any passersby, knocked on the door with his free hand.

"Yes, just a moment, please," a man said from inside. His accent was Middle Eastern.

The door rattled open and one of Baz's men stepped back. Kamal didn't know his name, nor did he care, but he recognized him from the training base.

A woman he also recognized from the camp, in jeans and a yellow T-shirt, was crouched on the roof of the RV from where she could look out the windows above the door. She had seen him coming.

Kamal stepped inside and pulled the door shut. "You're two days early, what are you doing here?"

"The hotel wasn't safe. We thought we would be better off staying here," the girl said.

"What are you talking about?"

"The man at the desk looked at us like we were some kind of idiots."

Kamal almost laughed despite himself. "What about food and water?"

"The vehicle is well stocked and very comfortable," the girl said. "We will be ready on Sunday. We have made a promise."

The passenger-side door was open.

"What about the explosives?"

"We've attached the detonators, and we've already programmed the number into both of our cell phones. All but the last digit."

Kamal resisted the urge to step back. The two of them didn't look crazy, but they were only the number 9 away from taking out not only this garage, but a fair portion of the entire block.

"As we promised, al Nassr, we will not fail you," the girl said.

Kamal nodded. "Then may Allah bless and keep you."

"So as his will goes," the girl replied from the roof of the RV. "There is no one coming. If you wish to leave now, it is safe."

Kamal holstered his pistol before he left the garage. He walked back to the cathedral where he phoned the driver, who showed up a couple of minutes later.

"Back to the airport, please."

"Yes, sir."

On the way he had second thoughts about going to New Orleans. Baz's people had shown up at Buddy's church, and the pastor had taken them in with open arms. A couple of workers looking for a place to bunk, three meals a day and salvation, for which they were willing to work for no pay, was an extra bonus from his new benefactor. No questions needed to be asked.

Kamal had no doubt that they would don their explosive vests and walk down the aisles at noon in the middle of the sermon and kill a great number of Christians. Praise Allah.

Nor did he have any doubt that the couple sleeping in the RV would drive it onto the Golden Gate Bridge and set off the explosives at noon on Sunday.

New Orleans would be no different. Even more people would die.

Which left a woman with a baby at Grand Central Station and Kirk McGarvey.

Kamal gave the driver a hundred-dollar bill and went inside the terminal, where he found the pilot and co-pilot in the crew lounge.

"Ready to go, sir?" the pilot asked.

"Change of plans. Do we have enough fuel to make New York City, or do we need to top off first?"

"Plenty, with a reserve. Will we be spending the night, sir?"

"I'll be staying for a few days, but I won't be needing you for at least a week, perhaps longer."

"We'll check the en route weather and file a flight plan," the captain was saying, but Kamal had turned and walked away.

Back on board, he helped himself to a bottle of Krug from the galley, opened it, and was strapped in and starting on his second glass when the crew came aboard.

The captain hesitated a moment. "Pastor Buddy wishes you a safe flight, and looks forward to your return. He's just sorry that you'll miss Sunday's sermon."

"Not as sorry as I will be," Kamal said.

SIXTY-FIVE

McGarvey emerged from the VH-60S executive helicopter at the Pentagon's heliport at four in the afternoon. An army first lieutenant was waiting to escort him.

"Good afternoon, sir. If you'll follow me, I'll take you to the conference room."

"Thanks," McGarvey said.

Otto had arranged for the helicopter and for a CIA photo ID showing McGarvey as a special assistant deputy director to the DCI. Page's secretary had phoned to set up an appointment with General Echo and Lieutenant Colonel Chambeau, without mentioning Mac's name, for an exploratory meeting on the shooting incident at the Watergate.

McGarvey had to show his ID in order to pass through security and the lieutenant took him to the D ring and then up to the fourth floor. The building was surprisingly quiet, but operations in Iraq and Afghanistan had mostly wound down, leaving Syria as the only major hot spot for now.

They followed the ring just past corridor three to an office marked 321. "I'll be standing by to take you back to your ride, sir."

McGarvey knocked once and went in.

Echo and Chambeau, seated at a small conference table, looked up.

"Jesus H. Christ," Echo said, and he started to rise, but McGarvey waved him back.

"We can either do this the easy way here and now, or turn it over to your boss and the FBI. Your choice, gentlemen."

Echo and Chambeau exchanged a look, but the general sat back down.

"I'm only going to take a couple minutes of your time," McGarvey said.

He perched on the edge of the table across from the two men. "Cooperate and you'll probably walk free. Fuck with me, and I'll have the Bureau here within minutes. We already have enough on both of you to make charges of conspiracy to commit treason, conspiracy to commit mass murder, and conspiracy—or at least complicity—in the death of Susan Fischer."

"I wasn't involved," Chambeau blurted.

"Your wife had her killed because you were fucking her. You knew it was going to happen and you did nothing."

"Prove it," Echo said.

"You contacted your peers in a dozen intelligence services around the world, including Pakistan's ISI, and Russia's SVR, to have them help you bring down Weaver. Treason, Echo."

"Like I said, prove it."

"I want you to call it off. Tell your friends to back away. Now. This afternoon. This evening."

Echo got to his feet. "Go fuck yourself, McGarvey."

McGarvey pushed away from the table. "People could get killed, you arrogant bastard."

"We've already had this discussion," Echo said. "We won't have it again."

He headed for the door, but McGarvey put a hand on the man's chest and pushed him back.

Echo wasn't a large man, but he was reasonably fit. He threw a roundhouse. McGarvey ducked the punch and rapped the knuckles of his right fist on the bridge of the man's nose, staggering him badly enough that he almost went down. Blood gushed from both nostrils.

"Enough!" Chambeau shouted. "We'll call it off, I promise."

"You're a fucking dead man, McGarvey," Echo snarled.

Otto was already on the line when McGarvey pulled out his cell phone. "A security detail is on its way to you."

"Call the Bureau's Washington SAC to get a team over here. We'll give them what we already have."

"I'm on it. Are you carrying?"

"I left it on the chopper."

"Good. I'll let Page know what's happening. Just stand by, help is on the way."

"I have friends on the inside!" Echo shouted.

The door was flung open, and two civilian security guards, their pistols drawn, were right there.

One of them came in, while the other stayed in the corridor.

"Arrest this son of a bitch," Echo told the guards. "But watch him, he's got a gun."

McGarvey spread his arms and legs. "My name is Kirk McGarvey. I work for the CIA. I am not armed."

The first guard holstered his pistol, and while the one in the corridor covered him, he searched McGarvey. "He's clean."

"My identification is inside my jacket on the left side."

The guard got it, leaving himself wide open to be disarmed. He stepped back and checked the ID. "He's a deputy director."

"The FBI is on the way to arrest these two men on charges of treason," McGarvey said. "Keep an eye on them."

"This man's an imposter," Echo told the security officers.

The officer didn't know what to do.

Echo pulled out a Beretta semiauto pistol from beneath his uniform blouse.

Before he could point it, McGarvey stepped aside, snatched the gun from the general's hand and pushed him back against the conference table.

"You had your chance, you dumb bastard."

"He's going to get us in a war!" Echo screamed. "He's going to launch nuclear weapons. The man is unhinged. He's not qualified. He's not fit to sit in the White House. He has to be stopped, goddamnit!"

"The general needs a medic," McGarvey said.

Chambeau had remained seated through all of it. "Susan was a part of it, I think," he said. "But I never thought it would go this far, this fast. I thought it was just talk."

"What about your wife?"

Echo had fallen silent.

"She and her brother were close," Chambeau said, and then he looked away.

. . .

McGarvey was sitting back in his chair in Otto's office, taking a break, when Pete came up from the cafeteria with coffee and sandwiches. It was midnight.

"What'd I miss?" she asked.

"Sir Edmund Hanson, MI6," McGarvey said. "He's been chief liaison officer with us since I was DCI. Good man. We gave him a quick précis of what's going on, and the name of the service's military logistics planner from Otto's list."

"How'd he take it?"

"Skeptical, like the others, but he said he'd do a follow-up."

Pete glanced at the clock. "It's five in the morning in London. He couldn't have been very happy to get your call."

"He was already at his desk."

"Who's next?" Pete asked.

"We've saved the best two for last," Otto said. "Ready?"

McGarvey nodded, and Otto put through a call to the private number of North Korea's Kim Jong-un. It was two in the afternoon in Pyongyang. Like the other calls it was on speakerphone; the conversations fed into several voice-analysis programs that confirmed the identity of the person as well as their level of stress.

After two rings the man answered in Korean, "Ye." Yes.

"Good afternoon, Supreme Leader. My name is Kirk McGarvey and I'm calling from Washington, D.C."

If Kim was flustered it wasn't apparent. "My father spoke kindly of you," he said in reasonable English. "Tell me the reason for your unexpected call."

"It concerns our new president and one of your intelligence officers, Choe Jang-yop."

"I don't know this name."

"He is part of a consortium of mid-level intelligence officers around the globe who mean to discredit our president by reporting false preparations for military action to force him into making mistakes. Including orders you supposedly gave to invade the South very soon."

"Although the thought continues to cross our mind, I gave no such order."

"We didn't think so."

"This consortium has American officers involved?"

"Yes, sir. At this moment they are in custody."

"You are speaking about treason."

"Yes, sir."

"And the other governments?"

"All have been informed except for Russia."

"They have agreed to cooperate?"

"Yes, sir."

"Then so shall I," Kim said. "The war may very well be forced upon us, but not soon and not in this manner."

"Thank you, sir," McGarvey said, but Kim had already broken the connection.

It was just past eight in the morning in Moscow when General Leonid Zotov, deputy chairman of the SVR, answered his telephone. He too was already at his office on the Ring Road outside the city.

During McGarvey's tenure as deputy director of operations, and as the DCI, Zotov had been a rising star, and he and McGarvey had become, if not friends, at least amicable enemies. On a trip to Moscow he and Mac had met face-to-face for the first and only time, and had struck up an agreement that if everything was going to hell, they would talk and try to defuse the situation.

"We are the fail-safes," Zotov had toasted at dinner.

"Let's hope we never have to act," McGarvey had said.

"I was expecting your call, Mr. Director," Zotov said. "And before you ask, we have placed Major Rankov and one of his co-conspirators in the Spetsnaz under arrest. And we are definitely not going to attack Hungary, as you may have heard. It was ludicrous from the start."

"How did you know about it?"

"From an associate, but there is a complication, my friend. Rankov and the others he worked with were planning on having you assassinated. But it was not them who planted a bomb in your car in Florida. It was another group who wants you dead. And presumably still does."

"That's also my understanding," McGarvey said.

"Then good hunting."

SIXTY-SIX

□

The limo driver dropped Kamal off in front of an expensive apartment building on Lexington just above East 47th Street. Pastor Buddy's jet had landed at Teterboro Airport across the river in New Jersey just after midnight, forty-five minutes ago, and the limo had been waiting for him.

The driver took Kamal's roll-about and laptop bag from the trunk. "I hope you have a key, sir, no doorman here this late."

"I have friends expecting me," Kamal said and he handed the man a hundred-dollar bill.

"Thank you, sir. Will you be needing my services over the weekend?"

"Perhaps."

The driver gave him a business card. "I'm available twenty-four/seven."

"I'll keep you in mind."

Kamal shouldered Tepping's laptop case and took his bag to the front door, where he looked directly into the security camera and rang the buzzer for the condominiums 15 A and B.

The madam, whose only name was Kiko, answered on the first ring. "Good evening, Mr. O'Neal, welcome back."

"Can you accommodate me for a couple days?"

"Certainly. And Sushi is here now. She'll be very happy to see you, if she is your desire?"

"She'll do fine."

The door lock buzzed and Kamal went inside and took the elevator up to the fifteenth floor, where an attractive Japanese woman in her midforties was waiting at a door, dressed in a brightly patterned silk kimono.

She stepped aside to let him into a large, plushly decorated suite of rooms that included a sauna, several Jacuzzis, a couple of small but comfortable lounges and a half-dozen bedrooms where the clients were serviced by Kiko's staff of four girls, all of them in their twenties, all of them beautiful, even exotic, and all of them extremely well trained in all of the sexual arts. Next to Pastor Buddy's girls, Kiko's women were from a completely different planet.

"I received your generous fee along with the package sent for you," Kiko said.

Kamal had wired $10,000 U.S. into her account. "I'll expect complete discretion, as before," he said.

"Anything else would be impossible."

"First I'll need a bath, then a massage. Afterwards I'll want a bottle of Krug—very cold—some Beluga, and perhaps pickles and a good dark bread."

"Do you wish to be alone for your meal?"

"No. I'd like Sushi to stay with me for the rest of this evening and tomorrow. But I'll be going out sometime during the day, for how long I don't know. When I return I would like something very nice for an early dinner. Something French, I think. But I'll let you decide."

The bath was hot, the champagne was cold, the caviar outstanding and Sushi outdid herself. He sent her away sometime before three, took a shower, then got a few hours of sleep.

He was up by seven, when he got dressed in a pair of light gray slacks, and a shoulder holster over a white shirt. He inspected his Glock subcompact pistol, but before he holstered it he had the thought that if he got into a gunfight his Grand Central op would have to be canceled.

But without a means of self-defense he could be subject to arrest. It was something he simply would not allow, even if it meant he had to give up his life to avoid it.

He holstered the pistol, then opened the package that had been sent to him from the madrassa in west Texas. Besides the two kilos of Semtex and a detonator, the imam Shadid had acquired and included a set of New York City credentials that Kamal inspected and then pocketed.

He put on a black blazer, let himself out and walked over to Park Avenue, where he got a cab to take him out to JFK.

"What airline, sir?" the cabby asked.

"Air France, arrivals. I'm meeting someone. I have to be there by ten."

The morning was brightening, and traffic leaving the city was light.

Both Air France and Delta had flights coming in from Paris at a quarter after ten, which would be perfect for his operation. He had a decent chance of getting back to the city by noon, if he got lucky with his dry run this morning. And he hoped for the same luck tomorrow morning.

The driver let him off at Terminal 1 at five after ten, and Kamal tipped him well but not extravagantly. Big tippers and cheap tippers were always remembered the most accurately.

Air France flight 22 had landed almost fifteen minutes early, and Delta 1022 was due on time at ten-sixteen.

The first-class Air France passengers began to straggle in after clearing customs. Most of them were businessmen, but there were several couples and two lone women. But not who he wanted.

The business class were next, with the same results, but a few minutes later a woman pushing a baby carriage came through the doors, and eight passengers later a man and a woman pushing a baby carriage showed up.

It was enough for him.

He went down to where the Delta passengers would show up for ground transportation, but this time there was no one pushing a baby carriage.

By eleven he was in a cab heading back into the city.

Both aircraft would be serviced and would turn around for their flights back to Paris at seven in the evening, and then return Sunday morning after ten. It was a never-ending cycle that was only interrupted by weather or by an act of terrorism.

The cabby dropped him off at the New York Public Library, where he used a computer to check on the weather over the Atlantic for the next twenty-four hours. There were some high cirrus clouds and some precipitation at a lower altitude around thirty degrees east longitude—halfway between Paris and New York—and some intermittent weather just south of Labrador. But nothing was predicted that would interfere with transatlantic flights.

He walked the four blocks to Grand Central Station, where he had a light lunch of raw oysters, toast points and a half bottle of inexpensive but fairly decent Joseph Drouhin Vaudon Chablis in the Oyster Bar.

One of the two policewomen sitting at the kiosk just down the corridor from the 42nd Street entrance had smiled and winked at him as he passed. "Have a good day now," she said.

"You too, hon," Kamal had replied, returning her wink. Gross pig, he'd thought.

Had he not been dressed well, had he not shaved in the past several days, had he looked down or away and had not smiled and returned the cop's greeting, he might have been stopped. American cops profiled every person they saw, day or night, anywhere, anytime. It was a fact of law enforcement procedure, because it worked.

By the same token, it was ridiculously easy to defeat. Shave, dress decently, smile, make eye contact. Even make a joke or a pleasantry from time to time.

Kamal was an assassin here to walk through the murder not only of an innocent child in a stroller, but if his luck held, perhaps as many as fifty or one hundred travelers going to or coming from their trains.

After lunch he walked out into the main hall, then upstairs to the Lexington Avenue exit. He took his time strolling around the corner and down the block to the Grand Hyatt, where he had a drink at the lounge two levels above the street.

He'd stayed at this hotel a number of times over the past couple of years, and it amused him to return—for the last time—on the chance someone might recognize him. Someone on the staff he'd tipped well. Maybe someone at the front desk, or maybe even McGarvey himself.

He was tempting fate, of course. Perhaps he would have to kill one of them. Just for the pleasure of it.

He would never come back to the States. He would either retire in France or somewhere else, maybe Thailand.

Or he would be dead within twenty-four hours.

The thing of it—which surprised him—was that he really didn't give a damn one way or the other.

□

SIXTY-SEVEN

McGarvey and Pete spent the morning in Otto's office searching for any loose ends, but everything seemed to be in order. All of the possible flash point problems had been taken care of, even the one between the DPRK and South Korea. But they were still missing something, and Mac said so.

"Zotov told me that someone else was gunning for me," he said.

"We know that," Otto replied. "Which is why you and Page are going to see the president at one."

"Hatchett wasn't in Beijing to stir up trouble between China and Taiwan," McGarvey said. "Chunwang would have mentioned him." Xu Chungwang was a deputy chief of Guoanbu's Military Intelligence Directorate.

During McGarvey's brief tenure as DCI, the man had been number three in the Chinese agency's North American Directorate. They'd never been friends, but they sometimes shared carefully scripted intel that could have an impact on both countries.

They'd often been in the position of having to withhold information, but they'd never lied to each other.

"We never thought that he was," Pete said. "Your guess that he was trying to stir up some other sort of trouble here in the States, that Weaver would take care of, making him look presidential, still holds."

"And it's a good bet he hired al-Daran to arrange whatever," Otto said.

"And to assassinate Mac."

"It's the *whatever* that bothers me," McGarvey said.

· · ·

Page's secretary called to have McGarvey meet for lunch at eleven in the small conference room next to the DCI's office. Otto and Pete had not been invited, but Carleton Patterson was there.

"Weaver is bound to have some heavy guns with him; so will you," Page said when McGarvey came in and sat down.

"I'm going to push him, so maybe you and Carleton should let me go it alone."

"Presidents have a habit of being touchy when pushed," Carleton said. "But they tend to behave themselves if there are enough witnesses at hand."

Page was looking at McGarvey. "You tried to warn him at Camp David and according to you he practically went ballistic. The famous Weaver temper. And if I've got this correct, you plan on hitting him with the same charge. What do you think will be any different this time? Do you have anything new?"

McGarvey shook his head. "Just a hunch that whatever is going to happen will go down very soon."

"But according to you, my dear boy, whoever planned these—let's call them dirty tricks for the sake of argument—have plans to stop them and give the credit to the president's sharp thinking."

And that was the one thing that had bothered McGarvey almost from the beginning. Only now he had it. He slapped his palm on the table. "Son of a bitch."

The server bringing lunch stopped at the door, and Page waved him away.

"What?"

"They hired al Nassr to kill me so that I wouldn't figure out what Hatchett and whoever is with him were planning to do. But they also hired the man to set up whatever dirty tricks they had cooked up."

"It'd give them some plausible deniability," Page said. "They could claim that al-Daran was working alone to get his revenge against you because of what happened in New York. And if what you're saying is true, they gave him a strict timetable. It was the only way that they would have enough control over the operation to stop it."

"And he knows it," McGarvey said. "He won't stick with their timetable."

. . .

The meeting was in the Oval Office. The president, his jacket off, tie loose, stood perched against the front of his desk, his expression unreadable.

With him, seated on one of the Queen Anne couches facing the coffee table, were his chief of staff Martha Draper, a stern-looking woman in a three-piece suit, and his personal lawyer, Leonard Berliner, a tall slender man with white hair, also dressed in a three-piece suit. Seated on the other couch across from them were the president's adviser on national security affairs, Chester Watts, in a jacket, no tie, and his deputy, Ron Hatchett, a husky man with the look of old money and the Ivy League: boat shoes, jeans and a blazer with some crest on the breast pocket.

There were no places for McGarvey, Page and Patterson to sit.

"Good afternoon, Leonard," Patterson said.

"Afternoon, Carleton, I thought you'd be retired by now."

"Me too."

"We'll make this meeting very brief," the president said. "When we're done here I'll expect your resignation, Walt."

"You can have it now, Mr. President," Page said.

"And charges of interfering with the duties of the president of the United States and his staff will be filed against you, Mr. McGarvey."

"Fine," McGarvey said. "In the meantime, Mr. President, let's try to save some lives."

"Proceed," Weaver said tightly

"Two officers in the Pentagon have been in contact since November with middle-ranking officers from more than a dozen intelligence agencies around the world. Many of them our allies, but some, like the Russians and North Koreans, no friends of ours. The plan they developed was to create a series of disinformation operations that would give credence to serious problems at various flash points around the world. Between China and Taiwan. Pakistan and India. Israel and most of her Arab neighbors. North and South Korea. Major ISIS attacks in Germany, France, England and Turkey."

Hatchett was clearly uncomfortable, but the president was unmoved.

"The point of the exercise was to blindside you with so many problems, most likely all of them coming within a twenty-four- to thirty-six-hour window, that there would be nothing you could do that would turn out to be the right thing."

Still Weaver said nothing.

"They wanted to make you look so incompetent that Congress would have no other recourse than to start impeachment proceedings."

"Who are these fucking . . . these bastards?" Weaver demanded.

"The two officers were arrested by the FBI," McGarvey said. "They'll be charged with treason. That situation has been defused."

"We'll need what evidence you've gathered," Berliner said.

"It's being sent via courier to your office as we speak," Patterson said. "The AG has copies as well."

"Then we're finished?" the president's chief of staff asked.

"No, sir," McGarvey said. He turned to Hatchett. "You recently took a secret trip to Beijing, but it was not under the president's orders, nor did you meet with any Chinese government official."

"That's a lie," Hatchett blurted.

"We have your flight records, and we know the name of the hotel you stayed at. And we think that you were not alone. Someone else went with you. But the point is that you met with a Saudi-born assassin for hire. His name is Kamal al-Daran, but his code name is al Nassr. You paid him money to do something for you. What was it?"

"You don't have to answer any questions," Berliner said, and he turned to Patterson. "This meeting is over."

"No," Weaver said. "What's going on?"

"We're working for you, sir," Hatchett said.

"I never ordered any meeting in Beijing."

"No, sir. It was me and Tom Harrigan and Dick Tepping. Tom took a leave of absence—left two days ago, and Dick is missing. No one's heard from him in the last two days."

"You hired an assassin?" Weaver demanded. "I can't fucking believe this. To do what? Kill me?"

"No, sir. No, Mr. President, nothing like that. I swear to God. We hired him to set up three terrorist attacks here in the United States. But we're going to notify the Bureau and the Secret Service so they can be ready to intercept before anything happens. It'll look even better for you than taking out bin Laden looked like for Obama."

"Where?" McGarvey demanded.

"San Francisco, New Orleans and west Kansas."

"When?"

Hatchett looked away. "Tomorrow. Noon our time. All of them at once."

"Jesus," McGarvey said. "He's going to change the time."

"I'm on it," Weaver said. "Walt, I'm not going to accept your resignation. We have too much work to do." He turned to McGarvey. "And that includes you, Mr. Director. Stop this bastard. Permanently."

SIXTY-EIGHT

Page and Carleton Patterson took the DCI's limo back to Langley while McGarvey walked down to the Situation Room with a stressed-out Hatchett and the NSA, Chester Watts. The Bureau's SAC Sam Cohen and Secret Service Special Projects Director Jim Kernin had been called and were on their way.

"It was never supposed to get this far out of hand," Hatchett said.

"You son of a bitch, do you realize the harm you've already done even if this shit goes no further?" Watts demanded. He was clearly holding his temper in check, but just by a thread.

"He's been under so many attacks since the election we had to do something. You heard what the Pentagon was planning."

"How much?" McGarvey asked.

"A mil five in euros for each attack."

"I meant to have me killed. That was job one, wasn't it?"

Hatchett looked away for a moment. "A million," he said.

Watts was flabbergasted. "Where in the hell did you get that kind of money?"

"PAC contributions we set aside during the campaign."

"You started planning this shit from the beginning?"

"In case he won."

"Conspiracy to commit acts of terrorism. Conspiracy to commit murder," Watts said. "It was a fucking uphill battle to just get this far, and you might have screwed the pooch for him. Christ, I could shoot you myself."

"I need a ride back to Langley," McGarvey said. "Right now."

"How will it go down?"

"He's using ISIS fighters trained at a camp in northern Mexico, and they're already in place."

"You don't think he's going to stick with the timetable?"

"He's going to tell his people to pull the trigger as soon as possible, and in the meantime he'll come after me again. He's tried and failed twice, he won't be able to let it go."

"I'll have a car for you by the time you get to the East Portico," Watts said. "I can also get you a Secret Service detail."

"I won't need it," McGarvey said at the door. He turned back. "You said that one of your staffers was missing?"

"Dick Tepping. No one knows where he is. He was supposed to come into Dulles on a flight from Indianapolis, but he never showed up here or at his apartment."

"Who is he? What does he do here?"

"He's an assistant press secretary."

"Does he carry a laptop?"

"Of course," Hatchett said.

"It's a possibility that al-Daran killed him and took it," McGarvey said. "It's why he knows just about everything that's going on here."

The black Cadillac Escalades the Secret Service presidential detail used were the same make CIA housekeepers used, except that the CIA's were light gray for whatever reason. But the drivers were exactly the same; serious, accurate and very fast.

McGarvey called Otto and gave him Tepping's name and White House position. "He's missing, and so presumably is his laptop. Find out if anyone has been online with the thing."

"You thinking al-Daran?" Otto asked.

"It's possible."

"I'm on it. Where are you?"

"I'll be there in fifteen minutes. Have Estes come over, and I'll need Louise on the phone. I need to know what else if anything the satellite picked up from the Mexican site."

"Pete's here too," Otto said.

"Good. This shit is about to go down sooner than we thought, and we're going to need all our ducks in a row."

Estes was with Pete in Otto's office when McGarvey arrived. It was a little after three in the afternoon.

"We're running out of time," he told them.

"I'll get Louise," Otto said. He had her on one of the monitors—no video, just audio for security's sake—in under a minute.

"I'm afraid that I've got bad news for you, Mac," she said. "I just got off the line with Charlie Hays over at Surveillance Interp. He took an infrared pass over the training base last night just before midnight. The place was dark. He retasked the bird for another four-minute pass about two hours ago, and got the same results."

"Someone must have gotten to them," Estes said.

"Either that or their mission has been accomplished," McGarvey said. "How's Audie?"

"Wanting to come home."

"Keep your head down, sweetheart," Otto said.

"You too."

"The attacks were all supposed to happen at noon our time tomorrow," McGarvey told them. "One in San Francisco against the Golden Gate Bridge, the second against a big church in Colby, Kansas—not too far from where I grew up. And the third against one or more dikes and lift stations in New Orleans."

"One or two shooters in San Francisco and Colby, but probably more in New Orleans if they were planning on hitting more than one target," Pete said. "Did Hatchett give you anything else? Any other details?"

"Except for the precise time and places, he said they left it up to al-Daran."

"So why noon tomorrow?" Pete asked.

Estes answered, "Because Weaver holds a news conference in the East Room at one every Sunday afternoon. Like FDR's fireside chats, to keep the nation informed about what's going on. He would have his headlines: 'three terrorist attacks thwarted.' "

"The Bureau would want to know how he came up with the times and locations," Pete said.

"That'd come later," Estes answered again. "For the moment he would be America's hero—something he predicted during the campaign. The savior of the nation."

"Cynical."

"Isn't all politics, almost all the time?"

"If al-Daran pushed the timetable ahead for more than a couple of hours—let's say sometime this afternoon or evening—the Bureau and Secret Service might not have the time to move into place," Pete said.

"Won't happen before eleven tomorrow," Otto said. He was looking at images on a monitor.

"Are you sure?"

"The Colby target is Pastor Buddy Holliday's Baptist Ministry. Twenty thousand or more people attend his Sunday services, which don't start until eleven sharp. His people won't hit before then."

McGarvey had been listening to all of it, and he managed a slight smile that Estes caught.

"You're going to challenge the bastard," the Harvard doc said. "Mano a mano. But how are you going to reach him?"

"Tepping's laptop."

"Jesus," Pete said. "You want to meet him, but where?"

Otto saw it too. "In the only city that would make any sense to him. New York."

"Is he there?"

"He's somewhere he doesn't want us to know about. He turned off the GPS function in Tepping's laptop."

"How do you know?

"It's up and running," Otto said. "I think the bastard is waiting for Mac's email."

"Manhattan's a big place," Pete said.

"He'll tell me where," McGarvey told them.

SIXTY-NINE

□

It was dawn now, and Kamal had spent the evening with Sushi at the Lexington Avenue bordello. If there were any other clients in house Kiko and her girls were discreet; the place could have been his alone.

"I think that you will not be coming back to us again for a very long time," the girl in bed with him said. She sounded sad, but she was a good enough actor that Kamal couldn't tell.

"I might be back in the fall. Maybe I'll buy your services for an extended time and take you on a vacation."

She smiled. "That would be nice."

Again Kamal couldn't be sure if she was acting. He decided that she had the makings of a very good partner in the field. It would be something to look into if he ever came back.

"I want you to leave now. But I'd like a toasted English muffin with cream cheese, black tea with lemon, a bottle of still water and a dish of fruit."

"Then goodbye again, Paul."

She put on a kimono and left the suite. After she was gone, Kamal powered up Tepping's laptop, and ran through the seventy-five emails waiting to be read.

He stopped at one that had been sent at 4:15 P.M. EST yesterday.

I would like to get together. Just you and me before noon tomorrow. Name the time and place. Kirk McGarvey

He stared at the message for a very long time not at all surprised that the man and his geek friend had figured out he had the White House staffer's laptop, and had offered up the challenge.

Manhattan, any time this morning, any place. I'll give you one clue.
Paul O'Neal

As soon as he hit the SEND button, he shut the laptop down, then showered, shaved and got dressed in his jeans and white shirt. When he was finished, his breakfast was waiting for him along with the Sunday New York Times. He took his time, eating and skimming the paper. The food was indifferent and nothing in the news leapt out at him.

For now, it was a quiet Sunday morning.

He disassembled his Glock and gave it a thorough once-over before he holstered it, and pocketed two spare magazines.

Next he unwrapped two bricks of Semtex, bundled them along with the cell phone receiver plugged into the plastique with a two-inch probe using surgical tape from his Dopp kit. He sealed the entire thing in a plastic baggy so that if there happened to be bomb-sniffing dogs they might not detect the explosive, unless they were right on top of it.

He stuffed the flat bundle in Tepping's computer bag then put on his black blazer.

Before he left, he turned on his phone, entered an eighteen-digit code, leaving out only the last figure, which was the pound key, and shut it down. One key stroke and the Semtex would explode.

He opened the lining of his roll-about and took out his last passport, driver's license and Health Care Card that identified him as Wilson McBride, an Australian who lived in Sydney, and pocketed them along with a couple of family photos of a wife and two children and a Barclays platinum credit card with only a twenty-five-thousand-dollar limit. He would no longer travel as a rich man. And when he flew back to Europe it would be in business, not first class.

He also pocketed the badge and ID card that identified him as Peter Jones, an inspector with the New York City Taxi and Limousine Commission. At the last moment he stuffed Tepping's laptop in the bag with the Semtex. It was possible that McGarvey might have another message for him.

Kiko met him in the front vestibule. "Sushi tells me that you are going away again, and may not return until fall."

"Yes. And once again I will be leaving light."

"I will dispose of your things."

"How much did you get for them last year?"

"Unfortunately, only five hundred dollars."

Kamal handed her one thousand. "This time I want you to destroy everything I've left behind. Without looking at anything. May I trust you?"

"Of course."

Kamal looked her in the eye. "Do not disappoint me, madam."

"I value your business too much to ever let such a thing happen."

Kamal walked the opposite direction down Lexington than he'd taken yesterday, and caught a taxi to take him to the Delta arrivals gate at JFK. He was depending on the same luck he'd had yesterday. It was a state of affairs that he didn't much care for, but simply walking off with a baby in a carriage without raising immediate alarms was a delicate thing.

Later today, while the entire country was in a state of shock that another series of attacks like those of nine/eleven, but this time not by air, had struck, he would be in a rental car heading back to Atlanta, where he would hang out for a couple of days before—depending on who, if anyone, was on his trail—flying to Paris. And a well-deserved retirement.

He got out to the airport a little after nine. In the arrivals/baggage-pickup area he studied one of the overhead monitors. He needed to get out of here and back into the city as soon before ten-thirty as possible, if he was going to have enough time to be at Cipriani in Grand Central no later than eleven-thirty, tops. By then the three attacks would have taken place, and the nation's attention would be focused toward the west.

The first international flight arrived at nine-thirty from Santiago. It was ten minutes early, and Kamal stood aside as the passengers began to show up for their baggage. None of them was carrying a baby or pushing a baby carriage.

The next, Delta 7601 from Buenos Aires, came in on time at 9:55; this time a woman carrying an infant got off with two women—one of them obviously her mother, the other perhaps her sister, and they were met by two men and left as soon as their mountain of luggage was off-loaded from the carousel.

Almost immediately Delta 3833 from Montreal, almost fifteen minutes late, off-loaded its passengers. Among the last was a woman carrying a baby. She was alone and no one was there to meet her.

She was also carrying a backpack, and she picked up one roll-about suitcase and a baby carriage from the carousel.

She was a young woman, Kamal figured possibly even a teenager. She rolled her bag and the baby carriage awkwardly out to the taxi queue, and when it was her turn, Kamal approached.

"You have your hands full, let me help out," he told her.

The driver got out and Kamal showed him his commission badge. Between the two of them they got the girl's things loaded in the trunk and they were on their way to an address in Brooklyn, Kamal riding shotgun. The driver kept looking nervously at him.

"Is there trouble with my cab, sir?" the man asked. He sounded Russian or Ukrainian.

"Absolutely not," Kamal assured him.

The address was off Flatbush Avenue and the driver took I-678 from the airport. Traffic was brisk for a Sunday morning but not terrible.

Just before the exit, Kamal pulled out his pistol and pointed it at the driver, who nearly jumped out of his skin. The girl was occupied with her baby, who'd begun to fuss from the moment they'd left the airport, and she had no idea what was going on in front.

"We're going left here, to Rockaway Beach," Kamal told the driver. He kept his voice low, and the girl still had no idea that anything was wrong.

The driver hesitated. Kamal jammed the muzzle of the pistol into the man's side and he got off the highway.

An old road that Kamal had pinpointed on a street map yesterday went left again toward Dead Horse Bay.

The girl suddenly looked up. "This isn't the way," she said.

"Be just a minute, sweetheart," Kamal said.

He had the driver pull over in a deserted grassy area, and when they were stopped he shot the man in the side of the head, and when he slumped over he shot him again in the head. Insurance.

The girl was screaming.

She clutched her baby in one arm while she frantically tried to open the rear door.

Kamal turned around and shot her in the forehead. She fell back in the seat, the screaming baby slipping out of her arms. He shot her again in the head, then holstered his pistol.

It only took a minute or two to stuff the bodies of the driver and the woman into the trunk, and put the carriage in the backseat, and with the driver's shirt clean off the blood that would be visible to people passing in cars.

The baby was only crying fitfully now, its eyes half-closed with sleepiness. Kamal placed the infant on the floor, so it would be out of sight from anyone in passing cars, especially when he got into the heavier traffic in Midtown Manhattan.

SEVENTY

□

It was a few minutes after eleven when McGarvey and Pete went up to the Grand Hyatt's lounge overlooking busy 42nd Street. The place wasn't open until two, but some prep staff were already in place.

McGarvey and Pete had flown up to KLGA, which was the general aviation side of LaGuardia's main airport, last night and had taken a taxi to the Grand Hyatt, where Otto had booked them a suite overlooking 42nd Street.

"He signed his email Paul O'Neal, the name he used last year at the Grand Hyatt," McGarvey had said before they'd left for the flight.

"You think he told you where he could be found?" Otto asked.

"It's a starting point."

"Well, he's not there under that name now."

"Start your search in a one-block radius around the Hyatt," McGarvey said. "Hotel reservations, security cameras, credit cards under the identities he's used before. Anything you can think of."

A man in his midforties wearing dark slacks and a white shirt with the hotel's logo was working behind the bar and he caught their reflection in the mirror. He turned around. "Sorry, folks, we're not open till two."

"We're looking for someone, maybe you've seen him," McGarvey said. He showed his temporary CIA ID.

Pete brought up several photos of Kamal on her cell phone. "We think he might have stopped by in the last day or two."

"I can't say anything about one of our guests," the man said.

"But he's not a guest here," said Pete.

"He works with us, but he's dropped out of sight," McGarvey said. "We're here to warn him that he could be in some danger. It's ISIS."

The barman was alarmed. "Here in New York?"

"We think so. The name he's going under is Paul O'Neal."

The barman lowered his voice. "He was here yesterday, but just for a couple of drinks. You think we have another nine/eleven coming our way?"

McGarvey and Pete exchanged a glance. "Did you talk to him?" Pete asked.

"Just welcomed him back. Nice man."

"Did he tip well?"

"He did the last time he was here," the barman said, but his expression suddenly changed. "My God, he was here when AtEighth was brought down. He was working for you guys trying to stop it?"

"Something like that," Pete said. She handed him a business card with her cell number. "If you see him again have him give us a call."

"I hope he has better luck this time," the barman said.

"We're here to make sure that his luck changes," Pete said.

They walked back down to the lobby, when Otto called, linked to both of their phones so they wouldn't have to put one of them in speaker mode.

"The Bureau has the Golden Gate Bridge staked out, and they have a bunch of Louisiana National Guardsmen in Army Corps of Engineers uniforms all over the most vulnerable spots in the New Orleans dike system."

"Don't forget the lift stations."

"They're on them. But we caught a break. Two workmen were arrested at the church in Colby. They'd already wired enough C3 throughout the main hall to reduce it to rubble. Would have been a miracle if anyone survived. But Pastor Buddy, who won't talk until his lawyers show up, did admit that the photographs of al-Daran he was shown was the man he knew as Brother Watson. Had him flown up to Teterboro Airport aboard the ministry's Gulfstream."

"Did the crew wait?"

"No, they just dropped him off. A limo service picked him up and took him to an address on Lexington a half a block up from Forty-seventh. Not too far from where you are now."

"Is it a hotel?"

"A high-end bordello," Otto said. "It's probably where he went to ground last year. Are you going over to check it out, or do you want me to give the Bureau the heads-up?"

"The Bureau can interview the madam and see if he left anything behind," McGarvey said. "But there's no need for us to go over there, he's already gone by now."

"If he's going to strike something in New York, something he wants you to figure out, it'll be close to the hotel and the bordello."

"Anything going on at the UN?" Pete asked.

"Just a mo," Otto said. He was back in ten seconds. "Business as usual. But you guys have to be right on top of him."

Kamal got lucky with a parking spot on Lexington just a few steps from the corner of 44th Street. Grand Central Station was less than two blocks away.

He took the carriage out of the backseat and set it up on the sidewalk, then got the baby and strapped it in on top of the Semtex bundle.

Only a couple passersby paid any attention, but one woman who'd smiled at the child frowned when she looked up at Kamal. She'd sensed something wasn't right, but wasn't quite sure what it could be.

Kamal smiled and nodded, then headed away.

By now he was reasonably certain that McGarvey and his friends, especially Rencke, had figured out that he would be somewhere in the vicinity of the Grand Hyatt. Signing his email with the O'Neal name would have led them there.

The only real sticking point was if they'd somehow managed to find out when whatever he was going to do, was going to happen.

It was well after eleven, and by now, if Baz had gotten the message to strike earlier than planned, and if nothing had gone wrong, the three attacks would already be in progress.

He stopped at the light at the corner of 43rd Street and used his cell phone to go to a news app. When it came up, there was nothing, except for a rare spring storm that dumped seven inches of rain and hail on downtown Phoenix, causing widespread flooding, and a gang shooting spree in Chicago that left sixteen young black men dead or seriously wounded. It was the worst violence in the city in several years.

But nothing about San Francisco, New Orleans or Colby, and he was having his first glimmerings of doubt. He'd never worked with a group. He had come to learn early in his freelance career that the only person he could trust was himself. And if something was worth doing, it was worth doing right the first time, because very often there were no second chances.

He'd originally planned on using the entrance into Grand Central just off Lexington Avenue. From there he would go into Cipriani, where he would get a seat at the railing that looked down on the main concourse.

He didn't think he'd have any trouble finding the right table this early.

But he wanted McGarvey to be there. And maybe the woman with him. He could kill them both.

It would have to be foxes and hounds. With him the fox. Dangerous, but if all the other attacks had failed, he especially didn't want this one to go bad.

More than anything on earth he wanted a shot at McGarvey.

He continued down Lexington to 42nd Street where he turned right toward the Grand Hyatt's main entrance.

If McGarvey had figured out that the hotel was Kamal's center of operations, he would be there now. Waiting.

"The fox is coming," Kamal muttered, and the baby woke up and looked at him.

□

SEVENTY-ONE

McGarvey tried to calm down, but it wasn't helping. He and Pete had taken the escalator up to the mezzanine level from where they could watch the comings and goings below in the busy lobby.

"He's here, goddamnit," McGarvey said.

Otto called. "Looks like two kids in an RV with enough explosives to do some real damage to the Golden Gate, and three teams on the dikes in New Orleans. Stopped them all."

"Any casualties?" Pete asked.

"The SF cops and the Bureau set up roadblocks at the bridge welcome center. The van blew about thirty yards out, a couple of cops were seriously hurt, but no one was killed. Traffic was backed up, but whoever was in the RV took the empty oncoming lane and tried to bull their way through."

"We got lucky," McGarvey said.

"So far."

"Jesus, Mac," Pete said. "There." She pointed at a man down in the lobby in jeans and a dark coat, pushing a baby carriage, as he disappeared to the left.

Kamal went down the same corridor he'd used the last time, through an unmarked glass door and down a tunnel to the Grand Central Market, many of the thirty-plus shops busy at this hour. Some people came to the train terminal not to take a trip, but to visit the shops, or eat at one of the restaurants such as the Oyster Bar in the lower level, and Cipriani Dolci on the level above the main concourse.

He went straight through into the main concourse, traffic picking up, though the busiest times were when the morning commuters came into the city and the afternoon when they headed home.

He'd gotten a few looks in the market because the many women shopping there noticed the baby, but in the concourse people were mostly intent on getting somewhere, and another child in a carriage was nothing out of the ordinary.

For now.

Halfway across he stopped just beyond the information booth and looked behind him. He'd half hoped to see McGarvey coming his way. But the man wasn't there. Yet.

He went directly across to the west elevator, which he took up to the balcony level. The maître d' at Cipriani looked up. "Good morning, sir."

It was before noon and the restaurant was less than half-full.

"Could I have a table at the railing?"

"Of course. Will it be just you and your child, or will someone be joining you?"

"My wife should be here any minute, but then, she's always late."

The maître d' smiled. "Yes, sir." He led Kamal to a table at the balcony, and laid out two menus.

Kamal parked the baby carriage right at the rail. To this point the child hadn't seemed to miss its mother, nor was it fussing. It seemed more curious about what was going on than frightened.

A waiter came and Kamal ordered a glass of merlot.

"Something for your child? Perhaps milk?"

"It's not his feeding time."

The waiter's eyes narrowed slightly, and Kamal realized the stupid mistake. The baby's clothes were pink, which was almost universal as a girl's color.

But that didn't matter.

McGarvey and his woman appeared from the market.

McGarvey and Pete stopped just past the Hudson News shop, the information booth ahead of them in the middle of the concourse, and the ticket windows off to the left just beyond the broad corridor from Vanderbilt Hall, which led up to the 42nd Street entrance.

A fair amount of people were coming and going, many of them carrying bags or pulling suitcases.

But Kamal was nowhere in sight. It was possible he'd gone down trackside to take a train, or perhaps he'd doubled back to 42nd Street.

"If it was him, what the hell was he doing pushing a baby carriage?" Pete asked.

Something was just at the edge of Mac's ken. He was missing something.

It came to him at the same moment he glanced up and caught Kamal standing by a railing above and to the right.

"A bomb in the baby carriage," McGarvey said. He headed in a dead run directly across the concourse.

"My God," Pete shouted, right behind him. "Get down! Everybody get down, now! It's a bomb!"

It was almost exactly the scenario Kamal had envisioned. McGarvey had shown up as he knew the son of a bitch would. Sir Lancelot come on a mission of rescue.

There weren't as many passengers and shoppers crossing the concourse as he'd hoped for, maybe a hundred at the most. But despite what the Boylan bitch was screaming, most people were slow to react, even though these sorts of events had become commonplace around the world over the past few years.

The waiter had just brought the wine and was leaving when Kamal stood up, lifted the baby in its carriage and tossed it over the railing.

His timing was perfect.

McGarvey reached the carriage in time to break its fall, and roll over on his back to cushion the blow as he fell to the floor.

Kamal took out his cell phone.

The baby was screaming, and so were a lot of people in the concourse, who were finally starting to run.

Pete was twenty feet away, still shouting her warning.

No time now.

McGarvey got on his knees and felt at the baby's back and then it's bottom finding a package wrapped in plastic.

Shoving the child to the side, he yanked the heavy package out.

It was two blocks of Semtex, at least four kilos, enough to wipe out just about every living thing in the concourse. A cell phone was wired to the detonators in both bricks.

McGarvey ripped open the package and pulled out both detonators.

He tossed them as far away as he could at the same instant the cell phone chirped.

Nothing mattered to Kamal now, except McGarvey.

Tossing down the phone, he pulled out his pistol and shoved the waiter aside as he raced out of the restaurant to the Vanderbilt Avenue exit.

But then he stopped just at the doors and half turned back so he could watch the stairs from the concourse level.

People were scattering but a cop, speaking on his lapel mic, came in from the street.

Kamal turned and almost casually shot the cop in the face just above the mouth, and then the top of man's head as he crumpled.

Two other cops were now at the glass doors.

Kamal pulled off four shots in rapid succession, and the gun went dry. All of a sudden he realized that in his haste he had forgotten to count down the rounds he'd fired. Four in the cab at the driver and woman. Two at the cop talking into his mic. And four at the cops outside.

He ejected the empty magazine but before he could take a spare out of his pocket and charge the weapon, McGarvey appeared at the head of the stairs and fired one shot, catching him in the left arm just above his wrist.

"It's over," McGarvey said. Kamal's pistol was dry; he hadn't reloaded it.

"Haven't you learned by now that for people like us nothing is ever really final," Kamal said.

"Death."

Kamal shrugged, and it was clear from his expression that he didn't seem to care. "Do you mean to shoot an unarmed man?"

"No."

"I didn't think so. The American sense of fair play."

"You'll be questioned, of course, and fair play or not, it won't be pleasant. Afterwards I'll do my best to see that you don't get the death penalty. I think a lifetime in one of our supermax prisons might suit you, especially when word gets out to the prisoners and staff just who you are."

"Not one chance in hell," Kamal said.

He started to turn toward the door when Pete came up the stairs, her pistol in hand.

Kamal turned back and pointed his gun at her.

"He's dry!" McGarvey shouted.

But Pete fired five times center mass as she walked directly toward him, not one shot missing.

He went down on his back, his eyes open, a smirk on his dead lips.

Pete stood over him. "If it wasn't so unlady-like, you bastard, I'd drop my drawers right now and piss on you."

SEVENTY-TWO

McGarvey and Pete had stayed at the Renckes' safe house in McLean for the past two days since Grand Central, mostly on Louise's insistence. They had the upstairs bedroom and en suite bathroom to themselves, and it had taken the first thirty-six hours for Pete to finally come down from what she had done.

It was eight in the morning when she got out of the shower. Mac had gone downstairs to get them coffee and he was in bed waiting for her.

"Insanity cured," she said, leaning over and kissing him.

"That's good, because Louise will be here in a couple of hours with Audie."

"Your granddaughter."

"Our granddaughter," Mac said.

Pete didn't catch it at first, but when she did she smiled for the first time in what might have been weeks. "Careful what you're saying, Kirk, because I'll hold you to it."

"I don't like to travel alone. I was thinking Paris."

"Just not Monaco."

"Lovely there this time of year. Quiet. The French haven't started their vacations yet, so everything will be open. Sailing, swimming, lying around doing nothing."

"Drive you nuts."

"The casino, maybe I could win enough to buy you a big ring."

"I don't want a ring," she said. "I never had much use for one. I just want the man."

She was sitting on the side of the bed next to him, and he pulled her down. "You have him."

. . .

They got dressed and went downstairs two hours later. Louise and Otto were in the kitchen with Audie, and when the little girl saw her grandfather and Pete, her face lit up and she came running.

"Grampyfather, grampymother," she squealed.

"By the way, the president wants you to come to the White House this afternoon," Otto said. "Page just called."

"For what?" McGarvey asked.

"He wants to thank you."

"Tell him I'm busy."

AUTHOR'S NOTE

I always like hearing from my readers, even from the occasional disgruntled soul who wants to pick a bone with me, or point out a mistake I've made.

You may contact me, McGarvey, Pete, Otto, and Louise by sending a message to kirkcolloughmcgarvey@gmail.com. But please understand that because I'm extremely busy, quite often I won't be able to get back to you as soon as I'd like. But I will make every effort to answer your queries.

For a complete list of my books and reviews please visit Barnes & Noble, Amazon, or any other fine bookseller.

If you would like me to do a book signing at your favorite store, something I have absolutely no control over, or if you would like me to attend an event as a guest speaker or panelist, please contact:

Tor/Forge Publicity
175 Fifth Avenue
New York, N.Y. 10010
Email: torpublicity@tor.com

If you wish to discuss contracts, movie or reprint rights, or e-business concerning my writing, contact my literary agent:

Susan Gleason Literary Agency
Email: sgleasonliteraryagent@gmail.com

ALSO BY SÁNDOR MÁRAI

Embers

Casanova in Bolzano

Casanova
in Bolzano

SÁNDOR MÁRAI

Translated from the Hungarian
by George Szirtes

ALFRED A. KNOPF
New York
2004

THIS IS A BORZOI BOOK
PUBLISHED BY ALFRED A. KNOPF

Originally published in Hungary as *Vendégjáték Bolzanóban* by
Révai, Budapest, 1940.

Library of Congress Cataloging-in-Publication Data

Márai, Sándor, 1900–1989
[Vendégjáték Bolzanóban. English]
Casanova in Bolzano / by Sándor Márai ; translated from the
original Hungarian by George Szirtes.
p.   cm.
ISBN 0-375-41337-5
1. Casanova, Giacomo, 1725–1798—Fiction.   I. Szirtes,
George, 1948–   II. Title.
PH3281.M35V413 2004
894'.511334—dc22   2004044208

Manufactured in the United States of America
First American Edition

AUTHOR'S NOTE

Given the appearance and behavior of my hero, the reader will no doubt identify the characteristic profile of that notorious eighteenth-century adventurer, Giacomo Casanova.

To identify, for some people, is to accuse, and it is not easy to mount a defense. My hero bears an unfortunate resemblance to that homeless, desperately roguish, and generally unhappy itinerant who, at midnight on October 31, 1756, escaped from the cells under the lead-roof ducal palace, the so-called Leads, let himself down into the lagoon by a rope ladder, and, with the help of an unfrocked friar called Balbi, fled the territory of the republic and took the road to Munich. My excuse is that it was not so much the romantic episodes in my hero's life that interested me as his romantic character.

For this reason, the only details I have taken from the infamous *Memoirs* concern the time and circumstances of his escape. Everything else the reader comes across is fable and invention.

—S.M.

Casanova in Bolzano

A Gentleman from Venice

*I*t was at Mestre he stopped thinking; the dissolute friar, Balbi, had very nearly let the police get wind of him, because he had looked for him in vain as the mail coach set off, and only found him after a diligent search, in a coffeehouse, where he was blithely sipping a cup of chocolate and flirting with the waitress. By the time they reached Treviso their money was gone; they sneaked through the gates dedicated to St. Thomas, into the fields, and, by creeping along the backs of gardens and skirting the woods, managed to reach the outskirts of Valdepiadene about dawn. Here he took out his dagger, thrust it under the nose of his disgusting companion, and told him they'd meet again in Bolzano: then they parted. Father Balbi slunk off in a bad mood through a grove of olives, brushing past their bare trunks, a shabby, slovenly figure disappearing into the distance, casting the odd sullen look behind him, like a mangy dog dismissed by his master.

Once the friar had finally gone, he made for the central part of town and with a blind, sure instinct sought accom-

modation at the residence of the captain of the local militia. The captain's wife, a mild-mannered woman, received him, gave him supper, had his wounds cleaned—congealed blood was sticking to his knees and ankles, from the scraping he had given them when he had leaped off the lead roof—and, before falling asleep, he learned that the captain happened to be away searching for an escaped prisoner. He stole out in the early dawn and made a few more miles. He slept over in Pergine, and, three days later, arrived—by coach this time, having extorted six gold pieces from an acquaintance—in Bolzano.

Balbi was there waiting for him. They took rooms at The Stag. He had neither baggage nor topcoat and was ragged on arrival, rags being all that remained of his fine-colored silk suit. A harsh November wind was already snapping at the narrow streets of Bolzano. The innkeeper nervously examined his tattered guests.

"The finest rooms?" he stuttered.

"The finest," came the quiet but firm answer. "And look to your kitchen staff. You tend to cook everything in rancid fat rather than in oil in these parts, and I haven't had a decent meal since leaving the republic! I want capon and chicken tonight, not one but three, with chestnuts. And get some Cyprus wine while you're at it. Are you staring at my clothes? Wondering why we have arrived without any luggage, empty handed? Don't you get news here? Don't you read the *Leyden Gazette*? Nincompoop!" he shouted in a cracked voice, having caught a chill on his journey, his windpipe seized by agonized coughing. "Have you not heard that a Venetian nobleman and his servants

were robbed on the frontier? Have the police not been round yet?"

"No sir," answered the frightened innkeeper.

Balbi sniggered into his sleeve. They were eventually shown to the finest rooms: a parlor with two big casement windows giving onto the main square, furniture with gilded legs and a Venetian glass above the fireplace. There was a French four-poster in the bedchamber. Balbi's room was at the end of the corridor, at the foot of steep and narrow stairs that led to the servants' quarters. The accommodation was greatly to his satisfaction.

"My secretary," he said to the innkeeper, indicating Balbi.

"The police are very strict," apologized the innkeeper. "They'll be here any moment. They register all visitors."

"Tell them," he carelessly answered, "that you have a nobleman as guest. A gentleman . . ."

"Indeed!" enthused the innkeeper, now humble and curious, bowing deeply, his tasseled cap in his hand.

"A gentleman from Venice!" he affirmed.

He pronounced this as though it were some extraordinary title or rank. Even Balbi pricked up his ears at the tone of his voice. Then he wrote his name in a precise and expert hand in the guest book. The innkeeper was red with excitement: he wiped his temples with a fat finger and couldn't make up his mind whether to run to the police station or to go down on his knees and kiss the man's hand. Being undecided he simply stood there in silence.

Eventually he lit a lantern and escorted his guests up

the stairs. The servants were busying themselves about the apartment: they brought large gilt candlesticks, warm water in a silver jug, and canvas towels manufactured in Limburg. The visitor undressed slowly, in regal fashion, like a king at his toilette. He handed his filthy garments one by one to the innkeeper and his servants, his blood-bespotted silk pantaloons having to be cut away on both sides with scissors because they were sticking to him, and then soaked his feet in a silver bowl full of water while leaning back in an armchair, matted and solemn, almost faint with exhaustion. At certain points he dropped into sleep, mumbled, and cried out. Balbi, the innkeeper, and the servants came and went about him with open mouths, making up the bed in the chamber, drawing the curtains, and snuffing out almost all the candles. They had to knock at his door for some time when it came to supper. As soon as he had eaten he fell fast asleep, and remained sleeping till noon the next day, his face smooth and untroubled, as indifferent as a day-old corpse.

"A gentleman," said the girls, giggling, whispering, and singing as they went about their tasks in the kitchen and the cellar, washing cutlery, wiping plates, chopping up firewood, serving in the bar, now talking in low voices with fingers held to their mouths, now giggling again, eventually calming down, and passing on the news offi-ciously then laughing: a gentleman, yes, a gentleman, from Venice. In the evening two men from the secret service appeared, drawn by his name, that name so notori-ous and irresistible, so dangerous and fascinating, a name redolent of adventures and flight, a name that attracted

the secret service in whatever town it appeared. And they wanted to know everything about him. Is he asleep? . . . Has he no luggage?

"A dagger," replied the innkeeper. "He arrived with a dagger. That is his sole possession."

"A dagger," they repeated, nodding vigorously, bemused. "What kind of dagger?" the secret service men inquired.

"A Venetian dagger," answered the innkeeper, in awed tones.

"Nothing else?" they insisted.

"Nothing," the innkeeper said. "Nothing but a dagger. That's all he has."

The information took the secret service men by surprise. They would not have been amazed to find that he had arrived bearing loot: precious stones, spirits, necklaces, and rings that he had slipped off the fingers of innocent women as he traveled. His reputation preceded him like a herald announcing his name. The prelate had already sent word to the police chief that morning, requesting the force to send the notorious guest on his way. That same morning, and after mass in the evening, the taverns of Tyrol and Lombardy were full of tales of his escape.

"Watch him," the secret service men said. "Watch him carefully and take note of every word he says. You have to be extremely wary of him. If he receives any mail you must find out who it is from. If he sends any, you must find out where it is addressed. Observe his every movement! It seems," they whispered into the innkeeper's ear, cupping

their hands, "that he has a protector. Not even his grace, the prelate, can touch him."

"Not for the time being," added the innkeeper, sagely.

"Not for the time being," echoed the secret service men, solemnly.

They departed on tiptoe, with gloomy expressions, oppressed by their cares. The innkeeper sat down in the tavern and sighed. He didn't like notorious guests who roused the prelate's or the police's suspicion. He thought of the guest himself, the dark fires and embers that flickered in his sleepy eyes, and he was afraid. He thought of the dagger, the Venetian dagger, his guest's sole possession, and was even more afraid. He thought of the news that dogged his guest's footsteps and he began, silently, to curse.

"Teresa!" he barked angrily.

A girl entered, already dressed for bed. She was sixteen and held a burning candle in one hand while clutching her nightshirt with the other.

"Listen to me," he whispered, and invited her to sit on his knee. "I can't trust anyone except you. We have dangerous guests, Teresa. That gentleman . . ."

"From Venice?" the girl asked in a singsong schoolgirl voice.

"Venice yes, Venice," he muttered nervously. "Straight from prison. Where the rats are. And the scaffold. Listen, Teresa. Mark his every word. Let your eyes and ears be ever at his keyhole. I love you like a daughter. Indeed, I have brought you up as I would my daughter, but if he calls you

into the room, do not hesitate. Enter. You will take his breakfast in to him. Guard your virtue and watch him."

"I will," said the girl, then got up to return to her room, delicate as a shadow. At the door she stopped and complained in a thin, childish voice.

"I am afraid."

"Me too," said the innkeeper. "Now go to sleep. But first bring me a glass of red wine."

All the same, none of them slept well that first night.

News

They slept in flurries, snoring, panting, and puffing, and, as they slept, were aware that something was happening to them. They sensed that someone was walking through the house. They sensed someone was calling them and that they should answer in ways they had never answered before. The question posed by the stranger was insolent, saucy, aggressive, and, above all, frightening and sad. But by the time they awoke in the morning they had forgotten it.

While they were sleeping the news rapidly spread: he had arrived, had escaped the Leads, had managed to row away from his birthplace in broad daylight, had thumbed his nose at their graces the terrifying lords of the Inquisition, had run rings round Lawrence the militia chief, had sprung the unfrocked friar, had more or less strolled from the doges' citadel, had been spotted in Mestre bargaining with the driver of the mail coach, been observed sipping vermouth in a coffeehouse in Treviso, and there was one peasant who swore he had seen him at the border putting

a spell on his cows. The news spread through Venetian palazzos, through suburban inns, and as it did so, cardinals, their graces the senators, hangmen, secret agents, spies, cardsharps, lovers and husbands, girls at mass and women in warm beds, laughed and exclaimed, "Hoho!" Or in full throat, with deep satisfaction, laughed out loud, "Haha!" Or giggled into their pillows or handkerchiefs, "Teehee!" Everyone was delighted he had escaped. By next evening the news had been announced to the Pope, who recalled him, remembering when he had personally presented him with some minor papal award, and he couldn't help laughing. The news spread: in Venice, gondoliers leaned on their long oars and closely analyzed all the technical details of his escape and were glad, glad because he was a Venetian, because he had outwitted the authorities, and because there was someone stronger than tyrants or stones and chains, stronger even than the Leads. They spoke quietly, spitting into the water and rubbing their palms with satisfaction. The news spread and people's hearts grew warm on hearing it. "What crime had he committed, after all?" they asked. "He gambled, and, good God, he might not have played an entirely honest hand, he certainly ran tables in low bars and wore a mask when playing with professional gamblers! But this was Venice, after all! Who didn't? . . . And yes, he roughed up a few people who betrayed him and he lured women to his rented apartment in Murano, a little way from town, but how else do you spend your youth in Venice? And of course he was impudent, had a quick tongue and talked a lot. But was anyone silent in Venice? . . ."

So they muttered and, every so often, laughed. Because there was something good about the news, something satisfying and heartwarming. Because everyone knew the Inquisition had its teeth in one or another piece of their own flesh, that one or another part of them was already living in the Leads, and now somebody had demonstrated that a man could overcome despotism, lead roofs, and the police, that he was stronger than the *messer grande,* the emissary of the hangman, and the bringer of bad news. The news spread: in police stations they were slamming files on tables, officers went round shouting, magistrates listened with reddened ears to those accused of crimes and angrily sent men to prison, into exile, to the galleys, or to the scaffold. They spoke of him in churches, preached against him after mass for having concentrated all seven deadly sins in one accursed body, which, according to the priest, would boil in its own individual cauldron, then roast in a fire especially set aside for it in hell, forever. His name was even mentioned in the confessional booth by women with heads bowed low, who beat their breasts while accepting the prescribed penance. And everyone was pleased, for something good had happened in Venice, and in every village and town of the republic he passed through.

They slept, and smiled as they dreamed. Wherever he went they took greater care than usual to close their windows and doors by night, and behind closed shutters men would spend a long time talking to their wives. It was as if every feeling that yesterday had been ashes and embers had started to smoke and spout flames. He cast no spells

on cows, but cowherds swore that calves born that year were prettier and that there were more of them. Women woke, fetched water from the well in wooden buckets, kindled fires in their kitchens, warmed pans of milk, set fruit out on glazed trays, suckled their infants, fed the men, swept out the bedrooms, changed the beds, and smiled as they worked. It was a smile that took some time to disappear from Venice, Tyrol, and Lombardy. The smile spread like a highly active and harmless infection: it even spread over the borders, so that they had heard of it in Munich, and waited for it, smiling in readiness, as they did in Paris where the tale of his escape was recounted to the king while he was hunting in the deer park, and he too smiled. And it was known in Parma, and in Turin, Vienna, and Moscow. And everywhere there was smiling. And the policemen, the magistrates, the militiamen and the spies—everyone whose business it was to keep people in the grip of fear of the authorities—went about their work suspiciously and in ill temper. Because there is nothing quite as dangerous as a man who will not yield to despotism.

They knew he had nothing but a dagger to call his own, but for several weeks they doubled the guard at border posts. They knew he had no accomplices and that he did not concern himself with politics, yet the chief executive of the Inquisition drew up a complete campaign strategy to recapture him, to entice him back into the cage, dead or alive, with gold or with violence, no matter what. They explained the details of his escape to the doge, that squat figure with piercing eyes, and he beat the table with

his ringed fingers and swore to send the militiamen to the galleys. Senators gripped the creases of their silk coats with delicate yellow hands and clutched them closer to their bosoms, sitting silently in their armchairs in the great hall, sniffing the air through noses yellowed with diabetes, their faces expressionless, occasionally glancing up to examine the ceiling paintings or the main joists of the council room through narrowed lids while voting for new draconian measures, shrugging their shoulders and remaining silent.

But the smile spread like influenza: the baker's wife, the goldsmith's sister, and the daughter of the doge all caught it. People in the privacy of their carefully locked rooms slapped their stomachs with delight and laughed fit to burst. There was something eerily consoling in the news that someone could spirit himself through walls a yard thick, past a set of vigilant guards wielding lances and pikes, and break the links of chains as fat as a child's arm. Then they went off to their places of work, stood in the marketplace or the bar, sipping a little Veronese wine, and the usurers among them weighed out gold dust on delicately adjusted scales, the pharmacists brewed laxatives, love potions, and deadly poisons that could be ground to a fine powder and secreted in signet rings, women with ample bellies garnished low market stalls of fish, fruit, and raw meat with scented herbs, merchants of fashion items arranged newly delivered stockings from Lyon and bodices crocheted in Bruges, displaying them in calfskin boxes perfumed with potpourri, and what with all the work, the chatter, the trade, and the administration, everyone found a moment to raise hand to mouth and have a good snigger.

The women felt that the escape and all that followed may, to some degree, have served their interests. They couldn't explain this feeling very precisely, but, being Venetian women, it was not for them to split hairs when it came to feelings, and they accepted the instinctive, half-whispered logic of heart and blood and passion. The women were glad that he had escaped. It was as if a long-shackled force contained by legends, proverbs, books, memories, dreams, and yearnings had found its way into the world at large, or as if the hidden, somewhat improper, yet terrifyingly true, alternative life of men and women had moved into the foreground, unmasked, without its powdered wig, as naked as a prisoner emerging from the solemn tête-à-tête of the torture chamber; and women glanced after him while raising hands or fans to cover mouths and eyes, their heads tipped a little to one side, without saying anything, though the veiled, misty eyes that peeked at the fugitive said, "Yes," and again, "Yes." That was why they smiled. And, for a few days, it seemed as though the world in which they lived over-flowed with tenderness. In the evening they stopped by their windows and balconies, the lagoon below them, the lyre-shaped veils of fine lace fixed to their hair by means of a comb, their silk scarves thrown across their shoulders, and gazed down into the oily, dirty, indifferent water that supported the boats, returned a glance that they would not have returned the day before, and dropped a handkerchief that was caught far below, above the reflections in the water, by a lithe brown hand: then they raised a flower to their lips, and smiled. Having done so, they closed the

window and the lights went out in the room. But there was something in their hearts and their movements, in the eyes of the women and in the glances of the men, that shone. It was as if someone had sent a secret signal to tell them that life was not simply a matter of rules, prohibitions, and chains, but of passions that were less rational, less directed, and freer than they had hitherto believed. And for a moment they understood the signal and smiled at each other.

The sense of complicity did not last long: the books of the law, with all their written and unwritten rules of behavior, ensured that their hearts should forget the memory of the escaped prisoner. Within a few weeks they had forgotten it in Venice. Only Signor Bragadin, his gentle and gracious supporter, still recalled it, and a few women to whom he had promised eternal fidelity, along with the odd moneylender or gambler to whom he owed money.

"A Man"

This is how he escaped, how the news preceded him, and how they remembered him, for a while at least, in Venice. But the town soon found something else to worry about and forgot its rebellious son. By the middle of the festival season everyone was talking about a certain Count B. whose body had been discovered—masked and wearing a domino cloak—hanging at dawn before the house of the French ambassador. Because, we should not forget, Venice is a cruel city.

But for now he slept, in Bolzano, in a room of The Stag Inn, behind closed shutters; and because this was the first time in sixteen months that he had slept in a properly secure, clean, and comfortable bed, he surrendered himself to the blissful underworld of dreams. He slept as if crucified, his head bathed in sweat, his legs and arms spread-eagled, lost in a passion of sleep, without a thought but with a tired and scornful smile playing on his lips, as if aware that he was being observed through the keyhole.

And indeed he was being observed, and this is how;

first by Teresa, the girl the innkeeper referred to as his own child, who played the role of servant to distant relatives in the house. The girl was well developed and, according to relatives, of an even and pleasant temper, if a little simple. They tended not to speak about this. Teresa, relative and servant, did not say very much either. She is simple, they said, and gave no reasons for their opinion, since it was not thought worthwhile, indeed not fitting, to bother about her, for the girl counted for less in The Stag than did the white mule they harnessed each morning to drive to market. Teresa, to them, was a kind of phantom relative, a figure who in some ways belonged a little to everyone and was therefore not worth bothering about or even tipping. She is simple, they said, and traveling salesmen and temporarily billeted soldiers would pinch her cheeks and arms in the dark corridors. But there was a kind of gentleness in her face and something a little severe about her mouth; her hand, too, which was always red from washing, gave off a certain nobility, and a kind of question hung about her eyes, a quiet and devout sort of question, so that one could neither address it nor forget it. Despite all that, for all her heart-shaped face and questioning eyes, she was a person of no consequence. It was a shame to waste your breath on her.

But there she was now, kneeling by the keyhole and watching the sleeping man, which might well be the reason that we ourselves are wasting breath on her. She had raised her hands to her temples so she could see better, and even her gently sloping back and strong hips were wholly given over to the task: it was as if her whole body were

glued to the keyhole. What she was seeing was, in fact, of no particular interest. Teresa had observed a good many things through keyholes: she had been serving at The Stag for four years, since she was twelve years old, had kept her mouth shut, taken breakfasts into rooms, and had regularly changed the beds in which strange men and women slept, some singly, some together. She had seen much and wondered at nothing. She understood that people were as they were: that women spent a long time before the mirror, that men—even soldiers—powdered their wigs, clipped and polished their nails, then grunted or laughed or wept or beat the wall with their fists; that sometimes they would bring forth a letter or an item of clothing and soak these indifferent objects with their tears. This is what people were like when they were alone in their rooms, observed through keyholes. But this man was different. He lay sleeping, his arms extended, as though he had been murdered. His face was serious and ugly. It was a masculine face, lacking beauty and grace, the nose large and fleshy, the lips narrow and severe, the chin sharp and forceful and the whole figure small-framed and a little tubby, for in sixteen months in jail, without air or exercise, he had put on some weight. I don't understand it at all, thought Teresa. Her thoughts were slow, hesitant, and naïve. It's beyond understanding, she thought, her ears reddening with excitement: what do women see in him? For all night in the bar and all morning in the market, everywhere in town, in shops and in taprooms, he was the sole topic of conversation: the way he arrived, in rags, without money, with that other jailbird, his secretary. Best

not even mention his name. But mention it they did, and most frequently, both women and men, for they wanted to know everything about him, how old he was, whether blond or dark, the sound of his voice. They talked about him as they would have some famous visiting singer or strongman, or a great castrato actor who played women's roles in the theater and sang. What is his secret? wondered the girl, and pushed her nose harder against the door and her eyes closer to the keyhole.

The man lying on the bed asleep, his arms and legs spread-eagled, was not handsome. Teresa compared him to Giuseppe the barber: now Giuseppe was clearly handsome, rosy cheeked, with soft lips and blue eyes like a girl. He often called at The Stag and always closed his eyes and blushed when Teresa addressed him. And the Viennese captain who spent the summers here: he was handsome too with his wavy, pomaded hair and the moustache he twisted into sharp points. He wore a fine satchel beside his broad sword, stomped about in boots, and spoke an unintelligible language that sounded utterly alien and savage to her ears. Later somebody told her that this savage tongue spoken by the captain was Hungarian or possibly Turkish. Teresa couldn't remember. And the prelate was a handsome man, too, with his white hair and yellow hands, with that scarlet sash around his waist and the lilac cap on his pale head. Teresa had, she thought, a working appreciation of male beauty. This man was most certainly not beautiful, no, rather ugly in fact, quite different from other men who normally appealed to ladies. The lines on the sleeping stranger's unshaved face looked hard and contemptuous,

confirming an impression she had formed the previous evening. The cramps and tugs of indignation had tightened the muscles around his mouth. Suddenly he grunted in his sleep, and Teresa leaped away from the door, moved to the window, opened the shutters, and gave a signal with her mop.

It was because the women wanted to see him, those women in the fruit market, just in front of The Stag, and Teresa had promised the flower girls, Lucia and Gretel, old Helena the fruit vendor, and the melancholy widow Nanette, who sold crocheted stockings, that she would, if she could, let them into the room and allow them to look through the keyhole at him. They wanted to see him at all costs. The fruit market was particularly busy this morning and the apothecary stood in the doorway of his shop opposite The Stag holding a long conversation with Balbi the secretary, plying him with spirits flambé in the hope of discovering ever more details of the escape. The mayor, the doctor, the tax collector, and the captain of the town all dropped in at the apothecary's that morning to listen to Balbi, glancing up at the shuttered windows on the first floor of The Stag, all excited and more than a little confused in their behavior, as if unable to decide whether to celebrate the advent of the stranger with torchlight processions and night music or to send him packing, the way the dogcatcher grabs and dispatches hounds suspected of mange or rabies. They could come to no conclusion on this matter, either that morning or in the following days. And so they waited at the apothecary's, chattering and listening to Balbi, who was literally swelling with pride and

passion as he gave a series of wildly different accounts of the great exploit, which hourly was being furnished with the ever-new apparatus and detail of heroic verse; and all the while they stood, their eyes darting toward The Stag with its closed shutters, or walked up and down among the fruit stalls and delicacies of the surrounding shops, acting, on the whole, in a somewhat nervous fashion, displaying as much anxiety and confusion as might be expected of respectable citizens who are responsible for the security of the town gates, for putting out fires, for the maintenance of water supplies, and for the defense of the town in case of attack by hostile forces, not knowing, all the while, whether to gag with laughter or to call the police. And so they walked and talked till noon, still lost for a plan. Then the women began to pack their stalls away and respectable citizens went off to lunch.

It was now that the stranger woke. Teresa had let the women into the darkened parlor. "Show us . . . what is he like?" the women whispered, screwing up the corners of their aprons and cramming their fists in their mouths; and so they stood in a half circle by the door that led into the bedchamber. They were pleasantly frightened, some on the point of screeching with laughter, as if someone were tickling their waists. Teresa put her finger to her lips. First she took the hand of Lucia, the hazel-eyed, plump Venus of the marketplace, and led her to the door. Lucia squatted down, her skirt billowing out like a bell on the floor, put her left eye to the keyhole, then, blushing, gave a faint scream and crossed herself. "What did you see?" they

asked her, whispering, and gathered round her with a peculiar flapping like rooks settling on a branch.

The hazel-eyed beauty thought about it.

"A man," she said in a faint and nervous voice.

It was a moment before they could take this in. There was something idiotic, strange, and fearsome in the answer. "A man, dear God!" they thought and cast their eyes to the ceiling, not knowing whether to laugh or run away. "A man, well, would you believe it!" said Gretel. The ancient Helena clapped her hands together in a faintly pious gesture and mumbled meekly through her toothless gums: "A man!" And the widow Nanette stared at the floor as if recalling something, and solemnly echoed: "A man." So they mused, then started giggling, and one by one took their turn to kneel at the keyhole and take a peek into the room, and felt unaccountably good about it all. Ideally, they would have brewed up some decent coffee and sat down round the gilt-legged table with coffee mugs in their laps, waiting in a ceremonial and gently impudent manner for the foreign gentleman to walk in. Their hearts beat fast: they felt proud of having seen the stranger and of having something to talk about in town, at the market, round the well, and at home. They were proud but a touch anxious, particularly the widow Nanette and the inquisitive Lucia, and even the proud, somewhat dim Gretel felt a little nervous, as if there were something miraculous and extraordinary about the arrival in town of "a man." They knew there was something foolish and irrational about their heightened, coltish curiosity, but, at the same time,

they sensed that this improper curiosity did not account for the whole feeling of excitement. It was as if finally, albeit only through the keyhole, they had actually seen a man, and that husbands, lovers, and all the strange men they had ever met, had, in that moment of glimpsing the sleeping figure, undergone a peculiar reappraisal. It was as if it were utterly unusual and somehow freakish to find a man that was ugly rather than handsome, whose features were unrefined, whose body was unheroic, about whom they knew nothing except that he was a rogue, a frequenter of inns and gambling dens, that he was without luggage and that there was something dubious even about his name, as if it were not really or entirely his own; a man about whom it was said, as of many a womanizer, that he was bold, impudent, and relaxed in the company of women: as if all this, despite all appearances, was in some way extraordinary. They were women: they felt something. Faced, as they were, with the mysterious stranger, it was as if the men they had known were coming out in their true colors. "A man," whispered Lucia, faint, anxious, and devout, and they felt the news taking wing across the market in Bolzano to the drawing rooms of Triente, through the greenrooms of theaters, through confessional booths, quickening heartbeats, telling all and sundry that he was on his way, that at this very moment a man was waking, stretching, and scratching in a room of The Stag Inn in Bolzano. "Can a man be such an extraordinary phenomenon?" asked the ladies of Bolzano in the depths of their hearts. They did not say as much, of course, but they felt it. And a single heartbeat, a heartbeat

impossible to misconstrue, answered: "Yes. Most extraordinary."

For men—or so, in that moment, however mysteriously, their beating hearts told them—were fathers, husbands, and lovers who enjoyed behaving in a manly fashion: they jangled their swords like gallants and paraded their titles, rank, and wealth, chasing every skirt in sight; this was the way they were in Bolzano and elsewhere, too, if stories were to be believed. But this man's reputation was different. Men liked to act in a superior manner, bragging, sometimes almost crowing with vanity: they were as ridiculous as roosters. Under their display, though, most of them were melancholy and childish, now simple, now greedy, now dull and insensitive. What Lucia had said was true, the women felt: here was a man who was genuinely, most resolutely a man, just that and no more, the way an oak tree is just an oak tree and a rock is simply a rock. They understood this and stared at each other wide-eyed, their mouths half-open, their thoughts troubled. They understood because Lucia had said it, because they had seen it with their own eyes, and because the room, the house, and the whole town were tense with an excitement that emanated from the stranger; they understood, in short, that a genuine man was as unusual a phenomenon as a genuine woman. A man who is not trying to prove anything by raising his voice or rattling his sword, who does not crow, who asks no favors except those he himself can grant, who does not look to women for either friendship or maternal comfort, who has no wish to hide in love's embrace or behind women's skirts; a

man who is only interested in buying and selling, without hustling or greed, because every atom of his being, every nerve, every spark of his spirit and every muscle of his body, is devoted to the power that is life: that kind of man is indeed the rarest of creatures. For there were mummy's boys and men with soft hands, and there were loud and boastful men whose voices had grown hoarse declaiming their feelings to women, and there were vulgar, oafish, and panting kinds of men—none of whom were as real as this. There were the handsome, who cared less for women than for their own beauty and success. And there were the merciless, who stalked women as though they were enemies, their smiles sticky as honey, who carried knives beneath cloaks wide and capacious enough to hide a pig. And then occasionally, very occasionally, there was just a man. And now they understood the reputation that preceded him and the anxiety that had spread through town: they rubbed their eyes, they sighed, their breath came in shallow gasps, and their hands flew to their breasts. Then Lucia gave a scream and they all backed away from the door. For the door had opened and behind the great white panels stood the low, tousled, unshaven, slightly stiff figure of the stranger, his eyes blinking, somewhat inflamed in the strong light, his whole body bent over as if exhausted but ready to leap.

Waking

The women backed away toward the wall and the door. The man turned his tousled head to one side, blinked—there were traces of down from the pillow in his hair, and he looked as if he had come fresh from a masked ball or some underworld carnival of dreams where he had danced like a dervish until witches had tarred and feathered him—then ran his piercing glance over the room and the furniture, turning his head this way and that at leisure as if he had all the time in the world, as if he knew that everything was of equal importance, because it is only the feelings we have about what we see that makes things seem different. At this point he noticed the women and rubbed his glazed, half-closed eyes. He stood for a moment like that, with his eyes closed. Then, his head still tilted to one side, he surveyed them in a proud, inquisitorial manner, the way a master looks at his servants, a real master, that is, who does not regard his servants as peculiarly fallible people just because he is the master and they his servants, but as people who have willingly undertaken their roles as

servants. Now he raised his head and seemed to grow a little. He drew his gown over his left shoulder with a rough movement of his short arms and bony yellow hands. It was a grand, theatrical gesture. The women sensed this and it was as if they were released from the spell that had first bound them, for, with this movement, the man showed that he was not as certain of himself as he first seemed, that he was merely strutting and miming the actions of the privileged and powerful: and so they relaxed and started coughing and clearing their throats. But no one said anything. They stood like that a long time, silent, unmoving, locking eyes with him.

But now the man laughed, as easily as he might sneeze, with no intervening change of mood. He laughed silently, more with his eyes than his mouth, his eyes opening wide and filling with light: it was like a sudden opening of windows in a dark room. This light, which was good-humored, crude, blinding, and impudent, inquisitive yet confidential, touched the women. The women themselves did not laugh: they did not cry "Aha!" or exclaim "Oho!" or giggle "Tee-hee." They listened carefully and watched him. Lucia turned her eyes away a little, looked up at the ceiling as if expecting help from there, and silently, under her breath, groaned, "Mamma mia!" Nanette wrung her hands in an attitude somewhat like prayer. The man, too, kept silent and continued laughing. Now he showed his teeth, yellowing, slightly splayed, part of a large and powerful structure like an undamaged, predatory set of tusks, and his eyes, mouth, teeth, and the whole face laughed silently, with a lazy, comfortable, self-conscious good humor, as if

there could be nothing finer or more amusing than this scene, here, in Bolzano, in a room of The Stag, around noon, facing a bunch of startled women who had sneaked in to watch him wake in order that they could gossip about him later in the town and around the local wells. The laughter shook his upper torso. He put his hands on his hips and leaned back gently so as to laugh better. It was as if a feeling that had long been trapped within his body had broken into pieces and was now coursing through him in hot currents, a feeling that was neither deep, nor high, nor tragic, but simply hot and pleasant, like the sense of being alive: so the laughter slowly began to bubble up his throat, found voice, cracked as it stumbled forth, then suddenly flooded out of him the way a crude, popular song might flow from the mouth of a singer. And within a few seconds, his hands still on his hips, he was bent backward and laughing out loud.

This laughter, a volley of uproarious, all-compassing, tear-wrenching, side-splitting power, filled the room and was audible down the corridor, even across the square. He was laughing as if something had just occurred to him, as if he had understood what had happened, as if the range and depth of human treachery, which was indeed infinite, had irritated him to laughter. He laughed like someone who, having woken from a nightmare, remembered where he was, saw things clearly, and would not be satisfied with mere shadows of whatever he found fearful and laughable. He laughed as though he were preparing for something, some enormous practical joke that would dazzle the world; he laughed like an adolescent, in full throat, with

an oddly wolfish howl, as if he were about to sprinkle itching powder on a woman's bodice, or on the nightshirts of the great, the powerful, and the grand; he laughed as if he were set to execute a marvelous, earth-shaking caper; as if, out of sheer good humor, he were to blow earth itself to smithereens. Both hands on his hips, his belly shaking, his chest protruding, his head cocked to one side, he laughed a hoarse, long, twitching laugh. The laughter choked, then turned to coughing, for he had developed a chill during his travels, and the altitude—the air of the mountains combined with the effects of the November weather—was hard on his constitution. His face grew contorted and flushed.

When the spasm was over, his sense of humor seemed to desert him and a terrible fury took hold of him. "I see I have lady visitors," he muttered through clenched teeth, his voice cracked and sibilant. He crossed his arms across his chest. "What a privilege, dear ladies!" He bowed deeply, ornately, disposing both hands and legs in a parody of courtesy, as if he were in a corridor at Versailles, greeting ladies of the French court on a fine morning, while the king, plump-bellied and purple-faced, was still fast asleep, or as if he were idling away his time with flâneurs and toadies, practicing manners with them. "What a privilege," he repeated, "for a gentleman of the road like myself! For a fugitive who has only just escaped the hell of a damp, rat-infested prison, having seen not one friendly face nor met a single expression of tenderness in over a year and a half! What honor, and what privilege!" he mocked and minced in a somewhat threatening way.

The women felt the threat in his voice, drew closer together like hens in a storm, and slowly backed away toward the door, Lucia using the lower half of her body to feel her way along the wall. The man took slow deliberate steps toward them, pausing at every stride. "To what do I owe the good fortune," he began, then continued in a cracked but louder voice. "To what do I owe the good fortune of discovering the assembled beauties of Bolzano crowded in my room as I wake? What has prevailed upon the ladies of Bolzano to visit the fugitive, the exile, the man rejected by the rest of society, who is even now pursued by police dogs and wolf packs over borders, whose trail the mercenaries of the Holy Inquisition are trying to follow through bushes and across forest floors with pikes and lances in their hands? Are the ladies not afraid that they come upon the poor fugitive in one of his less charitable moods, at this precise time, the morning after he has spent his first night in a bed fit for human occupation, not on straw that smells of incontinent dogs? Are they not afraid of him now that he has woken and begun to remember? What do the beauties of Bolzano desire of me?" he asked, by now at full volume, his voice breaking with fury. He straightened up in a single violent movement and it was as if, for a moment, he had grown more handsome. His face was bright with anger, like a bare landscape lit by lightning. "Who, after all, am I that the ladies of Bolzano should steal into my room when I have come to claim rights of hospitality in the temporary lodging of the homeless?" It was clear to see that he was enjoying the effects of his speech, the panic it wrought in the

women and the advantage it gave him in the situation. His confidence was growing: by now he was playing with them the way a swordsman plays with a lesser opponent, coming closer with every step, his every word like a swish of the blade. "Beauties of Bolzano! You, the haughty brunette, yes you! You, with your virtuous looks and the rosary beads over your cloak! You, with the ample bosom there in the corner! And you, old lady! What are you all looking at with such curiosity? A fire-eater or sword swallower might have arrived in town to demand your attention, but here you are, sneaking about, gaping at a poor feral creature like me! This is not a cage in a traveling circus, ladies. The feral creature is awake and hungry!"

He laughed again, but bitterly now and in ill humor. "Where have you come from?" he asked with quiet contempt. "From the market? From the inn? There is already talk in town that I am here: spies are sniffing round and keeping their ears open, women are gossiping in parlors and in boxes in the theater, as are you in the market, I suppose. He's here, they are saying, he's arrived, how entertaining! What honor you do me!" he repeated indifferently, with just a hint of complaint. "So, here I am. Look at me! This is what I look like! This is the way I really am, not the way I appear in the evening, wigged, lilac-coated, with a sword at my side and rings on my fingers! This is what I'm like, not a whit more handsome, not a day younger! Do you like the look of me? Do you fancy me? Do I live up to my reputation? What do you expect of me? Why don't we elope, all six of us, hop on a mailcoach and set off to see the world? Am I not Giacomo, itinerant

lover, servant to all and exploiter of all, at your ladyships' service, whenever, wherever you desire? Go away, you brood of hens, clear off!" he cried, his voice terrifying, his brilliant black eyes beginning to glimmer with a faint green light, or so Lucia said later, as she wept and trembled in the marital bed one night, confessing all to her husband. "Imprisoned for sixteen months in the name of virtue and morality! Have you any idea what that means? Sixteen months, four hundred and eighty-eight days and nights on a bed of straw with the stink of human misery in my nostrils, prey to fleas and lice, in the company of rats; sixteen months, four hundred and eighty-eight days in the dark, without sunlight or even real lantern light, living like a mole or a rat, alone with my youth, with the ambitions and desires of manhood, alone with my memories, memories of the life I lived, memories of waking to brightness and of the sweetness of retiring to bed; alone, excluded from the world, in the name of virtue and morality, of which I am the sworn enemy—or at least that is what the *messer grande* said when he had me arrested! Four hundred and eighty-eight days stolen from life, erased from it; four hundred and eighty-eight nights when others could look upon the moon and the sea in the harbor and on people's faces illuminated by lantern light, on women's faces at the moment the lantern goes out when the only light remaining is that reflected in the eyes of lovers!" His own speech had intoxicated him by now and he was talking extremely loudly, like someone who had been silent for a very long time. "Why are you backing away?" he bellowed and stretched forth his arms. "Am I

not here! I have come! You, granny, why are you cowering by the door, and you, you vain silly brown-eyed creature, why don't you come closer? See, this is the arm that has squeezed many a woman's waist, these are the hands you have longed to see! Are you not frightened of them? . . . They can twirl a sword and flick through a pack of cards, but they are capable of caressing too! You, you delicate blonde powderpuff, are you acquainted with these fingers? Even in the dark they can tell clubs from spades, but they can also tickle your fancy so you scream out at their touch, and later, when you are toothless, you can lisp to your grandchildren about the time when these fingers closed about your neck! Ladies of Bolzano! Go forth into town and declare that I am here, I have arrived, the performance is about to begin! He is here, the fop, the lady's consolation, the healer of broken hearts with his arcana of remedies for heartache, the man who knows the recipe for the meal that must be fed the lackluster lover so that he may rise again, virile and amusing in bed the next night! Tell them how you managed to break in, that you have seen me with your own eyes and can certify that I am truly here and have not wasted away in prison: that you have seen this arm, this heart, these shoulders, and all the rest, all present and correct, all in working order! Spread my fame, ladies. And tell your husbands at some appropriately intimate moment, just as you undo your belts and let your skirts drop, that Giacomo, the man who was consigned to prison, darkness, and the underworld, all in the name of virtue and morality, has arrived and is now a truly virtuous and moral creature who craves their forgiveness and sup-

port. Do beg for mercy on my behalf, dear ladies, and appeal to the mighty and virtuous, those so clearly without a fault that they dare to, and are able to, pass judgment upon sinners! For a sinner is what I am; go therefore and proclaim how Giacomo repents of his sins. I am a sinner because I know all there is to know about men and women, and because my reputation says that I respect life all the more for it! Go and spread the news that I have arrived."

He went over to the window, stretched out his arms, and opened the casement wide. The cold expansive November light flooded into the room with the force of an alpine waterfall. He held the window open, his head bent back in the light, bathing his pale face in the brightness, his eyes closed to its refreshing touch, and he smiled.

"Go now!" he said without moving, with closed eyes, still smiling, to the women cowering in the corner. "Go and say that I am here. The underworld has vanished. The sun is out."

He breathed deeply. Quietly, with a touch of wonder in his voice, as if he were informing the world of a particularly rare piece of good news, he declared: "I am awake."

And so he stood with eyes closed, not bothering to turn his head toward the door over whose threshold the inquisitive women of the Bolzano market tiptoed out into the corridor. Female feet tap-tapped with sharp quick steps down the stairs. He heard their clatter, neither moving nor opening his eyes, but with half-opened mouth gulped down the cold light like someone who could see and was aware of everything that was happening in the

room. Then he called out to Teresa, the young girl who had remained behind and whose red but not unshapely hands were even now on the door handle.

"You, you stay here."

He spoke casually yet commandingly, knowing that his orders were not to be countermanded. He was watching the square, scanning the clear outlines of the houses bathed in light. He gave a gentle sigh as if he were only just now waking and stirring, finally realizing that he had things to do and that the day had imposed certain obligations on him. "Come closer," he said in a distracted, friendly voice.

Five-finger Exercise

*H*e turned and moved swiftly across to the gilt-
legged, floral-silk-covered armchair that stood
before the fireplace and the great mirror, sat down, and
crossed his right leg, which was sinewy and powerful like
those of people who ride or walk a lot, over his left knee,
resting his arms on the chair, keeping his eyes on the girl,
solemnly inspecting her. "A little closer," he ordered her
quietly. "Come right up to me." And when the girl had
finally made her steady way over to him he took hold of
her small red hand and lifted it lightly into the air as if he
were a cavalier and she his partner at a dance, or like a tai-
lor inspecting his latest ball gown as demonstrated by a
model; he took it in an amiable, professional manner,
turning the girl in a half circle with a gentle, almost incidental adjustment of his hand.

"What is your name?" he asked, and when Teresa told
him, inquired further. "How old are you?"

Having heard the answer he nodded, humming and
hawing as he considered it.

"Why," he eventually asked, "why did you let those women into my room?" And then, as if he were not expecting an answer, he immediately continued: "People think I am a decadent fellow, Teresa, and indeed I am just what they say. I am tired of traveling. A man gets a reputation because the world is small and because transport has very much improved these last few years, so news travels fast. Thanks to gossip in the press and in the corridors of theaters, people know everything and there are no more secrets: indeed, I do believe, there is no personal life left. It was quite different when I was young. Venice today is like a glass box with people sitting in the window, cheating, lying, stuffing their bellies, and making love in public. Have you ever been to Venice? I'll take you there sometime. From a Saturday through to a Monday," he added as an afterthought. "No, dear child, you should not believe what Venetians say. Look into my eyes. Do you see how sad they are? . . . The gossips have turned me into a figure of fun, a marketplace scandal, so that everywhere I go now, spoiled youths and spies, denizens of gambling dens, and women who prosper because there are women younger and clumsier than themselves, turn their heads to watch me; poor wallflowers and others who hang about dance halls whisper my name to each other as they promenade; from balconies and from passing coaches, with beagle eyes, they follow me; women glance at me as if shortsighted. They raise their gilded lorgnettes, turn their heads away, and lisp: 'Oh! Is that he? . . . What a disgrace! . . . Why do they tolerate such people in town?

Invite him in!' That's the way women go on. Come closer, my dear. Look into my eyes. Are you afraid of me? . . ."

"I'm not afraid," said the girl.

The stranger thought this over.

"That's not good," he responded a little anxiously.

But Teresa, who was both servant and relative at The Stag, really did not fear him. Now that she is standing there, allowing her hands to be at once caressed and grasped in this peculiar manner that seems both to give and take, perhaps it is necessary to say something about her after all. For though the girl was a person of no account, an unattached young female, there was occasionally something that played about her lips that spoke volumes to men. She was sixteen, as has already been stated, acquainted with the rank secrets of the rooms and recesses of The Stag Inn; she made and stripped beds, she emptied basins after guests had used them, she had a skirt of dark-blue cloth that was given her as a memento by a trader from Turin, she had a neatly cut pale-green bodice that was left behind at the bottom of a wardrobe by a traveling actress, she had a prayer book bound in white leather that included a portrait of the Blessed Saint of Padua, and other than that she had nothing at all to call her own. Except perhaps a Venetian comb. She slept in the attic above the guest rooms, near the space occupied by Balbi, and her home was in the southern Tyrol, in a village that practically gasped for air at the foot of a great mountain, so oppressed was it by the peak, by the condition of the land, and by poverty. Her father set off one day to become

a mercenary in the service of the king of Naples and never returned. Teresa looked at the stranger and was not afraid.

The fear that had first gripped her the previous night when the innkeeper, who sometimes beat her and sometimes invited her into his widower's bed, asked her to observe the stranger; the fear that startled her when she saw the stranger half-asleep, snoring and snuffling, shortly after he had eaten his meal, had, now that the man had taken her hand, passed away. She was a little embarrassed by her hand, which was red from washing and carrying wood, and rough and scaly from the wind that eternally whistled round Bolzano, the wind she thought she would never get used to. She was therefore somewhat reluctant to yield her hand to this man whose own hand was firm yet soft, aristocratic, and smooth to the touch, like cool, finely worked leather. But touching it relaxed her. Yes, his hand, the grip of it, had about it something that would both give and take. And from his cool palm there slowly spread, across the skin and through the veins, an extraordinary warmth different from that which the stove gave out, more like when one went and sat out in the sun. This warmth radiated and extended; then, for a moment or two, it seemed to cease, as when one blows out a candle or a draft puts out a lantern—it was a sensation of approaching flames and thunder. Then it warmed again. Teresa was no longer afraid. She wasn't thinking of anything. Her favorite pastime was talking to the dog, the sharp-eared little white dog in the garden of The Stag, and to no one else; she also liked to spend an hour or two, winter or summer, in one of the chapels of the church, under the

picture of the Virgin, just beneath the pulpit. At these times she closed her eyes and thought of nothing. Occasionally she did think of love but only in the way a fisherman thinks of the sea. She was acquainted with love and was not afraid of it.

Now that the man had finally touched her—the stranger was holding her hand with two fingers as if requesting the pleasure of a dance, while resting his head on his other hand—Teresa's intuition told her that she was the stronger. The feeling surprised her. The stranger, to all appearances, was powerful and elegant despite having arrived in rags; what was more, he was older, much older than Teresa, and to cap it all he was famous, and every woman desperately wanted to see him. Teresa should have had every reason to be afraid of him. He had also promised to take her to Venice, and Teresa was afraid of promises, because people who made promises were known to lie: the only people really to have given her something were those who had not said anything about it beforehand. She didn't even know what exactly the man wanted from her. For there had been those who had pinched her or patted her buttocks or wanted to kiss her or whispered lascivious words into her ear, many of which were coarse and crude, or begged her for favors or made loathsome offers, inviting her into their rooms after midnight, when everyone else had gone to bed. No, Teresa knew men, all right. But this one did not pinch her, extended no invitation, and said nothing crude. He simply gazed with an expression of close concentration on his slightly careworn face, like someone who was thinking furiously about

something he had forgotten: a name, some memory, some important, life-enhancing idea.

"You're not afraid," the man muttered under his breath. With the gentlest, most courteous, almost solicitous, yet completely unambiguous gesture, he sat the girl on his knee. Teresa allowed herself to be seated. She sat in the stranger's lap quite decorously, as if visiting another person's house, prepared at any moment to run should someone ring a bell or call her. They were both solemn. They looked into each other's eyes attentively, the man slightly squinting so as to see her better, as, with two fingers, he turned Teresa's face to the light. The girl tolerated these movements exactly as if she were visiting the doctor: it was reasonable to grant reasonable requests. "It is sixteen months," said the stranger calmly, "since I looked into a woman's eyes. Yours have a nice color, Teresa, like the sky over Venice. I sometimes saw that sky from a window when they took me for exercise down the prison corridor. It was a blue sky, bluish gray to be precise, a slightly cold blue, as if somehow it were reflecting the sea. You have the color of eternity in your eyes," he told her politely. "But you don't understand this. Not that it matters whether you do or not. There is a sort of misunderstanding between us, an eternal misunderstanding as between all men and women, and I am always ashamed of myself when I am with a woman and babble on too long. Kiss me," he said in a friendly and natural fashion.

And when the girl made no move but continued staring at him with that gray-blue, glassy gaze of hers, her head held stiff and straight, he repeated, "Kiss me. Don't

you understand?" in a slightly puzzled voice, but still friendly. Later Teresa recalled that it was the sort of voice in which he might have asked her for a glass of water, or told her to send in Balbi because he was bored. There was simplicity and ease in his request: "Kiss me." But Teresa had never kissed a man like this, so she continued staring, her eyes still glassy, more empty than intelligent. The man took her waist with, it seemed, half a hand, and this too he succeeded in doing in an almost incidental fashion as if reaching for a book or comb, then, amiably, in a mildly inquiring manner, asked her what she felt.

"Nothing," replied the girl.

"You don't understand," he said, a little annoyed. "You don't understand my question. I am not asking you what you feel in general about life, about men or about love. Listen here, child. What I am asking is what you feel when I touch you, when I encompass that piece of your arm above your elbow with two fingers, what you feel when I touch your heart—like this—what you are feeling now, this very moment?"

"Excuse me, sir," said the girl decorously, as she stood up, bobbed to the stranger, and with two hands, as she had sometimes seen others do in the restaurant, slightly raised the edge of her skirt. "But I feel nothing."

Now the man, too, stood up. Legs apart, arms crossed, his head bowed, his voice dark and troubled.

"That's impossible," he exclaimed, spluttering in his confusion. "It is impossible that you should feel nothing, while I . . . Wait, hang on a minute!" With a swift movement he embraced the girl, bent his head over her fresh

young face, and stared deeply into the pale blue of her placid, maidenly, gently shimmering eyes.

"Not even now? Now that I have my arms around you? Can't you feel my hot breath? The pressure of my hands on your ribs? . . . Can't you feel how close I am to you? That in this mere moment we already know each other and that I am bringing you a miraculous gift, the gift of life and love? . . . You are seized by a peculiar trembling, are you not? A trembling that runs through you from your brow to the tip of your toes, a trembling you have never felt before, as if you had realized for the first time that you are alive, that this is the reason you have lived so far, the reason you came into the world?" And when he got no answer, he asked, "So what happens now?" Utterly lost, he let the girl go, allowed his hand to float to his brow, and looked about bewildered.

For the girl standing opposite him, only one step away from him, this little, slightly slatternly, raggedy, bare-footed slip of a girl, the common plaything of every innkeeper, the kind of girl he knew so well—and, if he wanted to be honest with himself, the only kind of person he ever really knew—truly did feel nothing, as he could see perfectly well. He was so confused he began groaning. The fresh young body had not shuddered pleasantly at his expert touch: not even when he had held her waist had those clear, rather glassy eyes clouded up like a mountain lake when the storm gathers above it; nor had her heart, whose pulse he had felt through her canvas blouse as he touched her warm, maidenly skin, suddenly begun to race, not even when he pressed his hot hand against her

breast more firmly. The girl continued breathing evenly and stood in front of him at arm's length. He raised his arm but it stopped in midmovement, in midair. The resistance he occasionally met with in women had always encouraged him. Was there a more beautiful game, a more exciting struggle, than the duel with a woman who resisted, who slipped from his hands, who protested, and, haughtily or in panic, fended off her amorous opponent? It was at these times that he felt the full power of his humanity, when words tumbled from his mouth with the greatest ease: only at these times could he be at once bold yet submissive, demanding yet worshipping, daunted yet daring. For resistance was already a form of contact, a game half-won; resistance was a form of surrender: she who resisted knew why she resisted and already desired that from which she was escaping. . . . But this girl here, in the guest room of a hostelry in a strange town, this slim, not particularly well nourished servant girl, the first woman to whom he had opened his arms after sixteen months of prison, loneliness, misery, and obscurity—this girl wasn't even defending herself. She was not resisting. Here she stood, perfectly calmly, as if he weren't standing right opposite her, a sweet little rag doll facing a man who had not so long ago rented a palazzo in Murano for the most beautiful nun in all Venice and who, quite recently, had been taught how to pen amorous verses by a countess in Rome, at the home of a cardinal and patron. . . . Here she stood and there was nothing he could do with her because she was neither defending herself nor yielding to orders and demands; she stood like light before a shadow

and no female instinct was telling her to flee. He took a deep breath and wiped his brow, covered in cold sweat.

What had happened? That which had never before happened. He looked wildly around the room as if searching for something and his eye fell on the dagger he had left on the mantelpiece the previous night. With a fluid movement he seized the dagger with both hands and began carelessly to flex the blade. He was no longer concerned with the girl but walked up and down the room with the dagger in his hand, talking quietly to himself: "Well then," he mumbled. Then: "It's impossible!" He felt truly awful. He felt like a great actor who had not appeared in public for years and who, when the time came for him to sing again, was confronted by an icy auditorium and silence in the stalls. He was not hissed off the stage, he hadn't failed, but this icy silence, this unechoing indifference was more terrifying than failure. He felt like a singer who notices with horror that something has happened to his voice, and that however much he bawls or attempts those well-practiced florid musical phrases, the warm resonance of his voice, the individual attractive timbre that once made his listeners shiver with delight so that women's eyes veiled and misted over and men stared solemnly at the ground in front of them, all paying close attention, as if the perfect moment for regret and judgment had finally arrived—was gone. . . . It was as if he had forgotten something, a voice, a pose, some secret faculty that had been his alone, which had been the secret of his success, of his very being, and he simply couldn't understand why people no longer applauded the performance when only yesterday

they were cheering it to the rafters, and he knew that despite his talent, despite his practice and experience, something had gone wrong: his effect on the audience was not what it used to be! . . . What could he do? Faced as he was by the icy indifference of the auditorium, he realized that he no longer possessed his old power of attraction. He found himself groaning and raising his hands to his throat in panic, wanting to emit some sound—an aaah! or aaiigh!—but failed to make any sound whatsoever. He stood there, dagger in hand, staring at the girl.

"Impossible!" he said once more, louder this time. "You feel nothing, nothing at all? No fear? No trembling? No desire to run away? . . ." He was almost begging her to say something. He was aware what a pitiful figure he must cut, with a dagger in his hand and this imploring note in his voice. "Why don't you look me in the eye?" he asked more quietly, slightly hoarsely, the voice quite melancholy now. Noticing his tone, the girl looked up and slowly turned to face the stranger, allowing her own eyes to be explored by the solemn, piercing pair of the man before her. "Ah, you see," the man sighed with relief, shifting position as if ready to fence or to leap. "My voice has touched you," he rejoiced, the voice quieter and more tender now. "I want you to feel that I am talking to you personally. Because I know you, I would know you now among a thousand women, even at a masked ball. See, you are responding, your eyes answer mine. I knew it. How could it be otherwise?" He gave a low whistle in his joy, then resumed in the warm, deep, sad voice he seemed to deploy like a conjuror his apparatus. "For that is the only

secret, my dear, that is all: there is no trick, no catch, it's always this simple. It's like touching a person. You touched me when you stepped into the room, and sometimes I think that is the most mysterious form of contact. Sometimes I think it is the cause, the very meaning, of life. Is your heart beating a little faster? . . . Are you blushing? . . . You know perfectly well that you can't go now. Come closer, return to where you were before."

And when the girl drew closer he addressed her in his calmest, most straightforward manner:

"Don't you remember? I asked you to kiss me."

Slowly, with a sure and leisurely movement, he held out his arms, gently took the girl by the shoulder, and watched tenderly as she leaned her head against his arm.

The Kiss

*A*nd now, on the third day after his escape from the notorious Leads where he had spent sixteen months, he finally kissed the maid in a room of The Stag, in Bolzano. What was it like? To begin with he simply kissed the girl's cracked lips which met the male mouth, softly, helplessly, without responding before the two mouths parted. They stayed like that a long time. He watched her eyes, catching her glance, the startled clear look of another living being, then blinked as if blinded by the strong light. Both of them shut their eyes for a moment. This was a situation both recognized, in their different ways. It was as if it were the single most natural, most sensible position in human existence, and it was impossible to understand why they had ever bothered with anything else or with any other position, having prepared themselves a long time for precisely this moment, bending every effort and every desire, awake or asleep, to this end. The girl shifted in the strange man's arms, her expression serious and relaxed. She was like someone who, after a long search and hours of

puzzling, had finally sighed and declared, "Oh, I see! So this is what it was about!" Suddenly everything fell into place. She shifted her weight in the man's arms, quite carefully, with delicate, small movements, shy yet certain, feeling that every adjustment of her body had a meaning; and so the great wordless dialogue started, one established a long time ago by man and woman, the dialogue that is continued by every pair of lovers the moment one embraces the other. It was the right position she sought. To be accurate, she was not even moving but simply allowed her body to settle on his knee into the position prepared for her by the median route between resistance and attraction. She leaned her head against his arm and her youthful body readily bent back, his strong, relaxed arms supporting her without effort, taking the alien weight, almost appearing to lift it slightly as if disobeying, if only for a few moments, the force of gravity. The girl's precise position at that point might be described as collapsing in the stranger's arms, on tiptoe, head bent back, slightly off balance, keeling over to one side. Had anybody been observing them through the keyhole, he or she might have thought that the girl had fainted or had just been dragged from some invisible stream and was languishing unconscious in the arms of the person who had saved her, soon to be deposited on the bed or the floor where she would have her arms raised and her heart massaged so she might be brought back to life. Because the girl's posture suggested someone lost and unconscious yet rescued. It is, as a matter of fact, how the girl herself felt at that moment:

she felt like a would-be suicide who had plunged into the river but who had been rescued and was just now being carried to shore. Essentially, she was adjusting herself to her new situation.

Being in the arms of a strange man was both a new and yet a painfully, joyously, and frighteningly familiar situation. It is, after all, a most desirable thing for a person to be embraced by another. Teresa vaguely recalled her mother—a woman as freckled as a turkey's egg and as short and round as a Tuscany barrel—and how she once had held her in her arms like this. Yes, this new situation was familiar, as familiar as life to a newborn baby; there was nothing particularly difficult or clever to do, no need to argue: one had only to accept and to allow events to carry one along, to resign oneself, to let the two bodies discover their own equilibrium as they engaged under the pressure of his arms but according to attractions and powers beyond such pressure. And it was right, it was absolutely in order, that this man, unknown to Teresa until yesterday, who talked a great deal, waved his dagger about, and had emerged from bed that morning with down in his tousled hair, a man who slept with his legs spread and with a furious twisted expression on his face, should now have his arms locked about Teresa, and that she should only have to make a slight adjustment in the position of her head so that it rested more comfortably, to leave her mouth softly and gently open and to close her eyes, and otherwise do nothing at all, for her to feel that everything was as it should be, as was right and proper. So

much she understood. And now that she knew and understood everything she smiled, her eyes still closed, and her breathing became lighter and faster.

They stood before the window in the fierce, cold light. The man had his back to the window and was watching the girl's powerfully lit face: he watched the woman in his arms as he moved in a peculiarly encouraging and threatening manner that suggested both rescue and assault, the movements precise and appropriate to the moment. He too found the situation reassuringly familiar. He was no longer afraid that lonely, empty months of damp and solitude had led him to lose his voice. He was aware that every word, every movement of his, found favor with the audience. He looked at the girl contentedly, being in no hurry, having plenty of time to spare. The face, that heart-shaped face, whose every feature, every subtle shade of color, was amplified by the strong light, was simply the face of a woman, that was all—which did not mean that he was lying when he said he would recognize it among a thousand women's faces, even under a mask. One woman's face was as a hundred women's faces, faces he had bent over in similar situations with just such tender and solemn solicitude, as if each were a puzzle he had to solve, an arcane script, a word written in signs taken from the cabala or some other realm of magic, each a word that added some meaning to life. He watched the face patiently, solemnly. Because these signs on a woman's face, the slightly upturned, delicately freckled nose, the mouth which was raw like the cut flesh of a plump fruit, the golden down

above the upper lip, and the chin, that childish little chin set among curves, the brilliant fine-drawn line of the closed eyes, the ample blonde swell of the eyelashes, and, next to the nose and the mouth, the two harsh lines that life had left as its legacy of fear and suspicion and which now, touched by light and by a strange pair of arms, seemed to soften and melt; all this was the rune, the secret script whose meaning he had to decipher. The two faces—the serious male face, gazing, and the girl's face with its closed eyes, its relaxation, its faint smile, and air of expectation—swam next to each other like two planets tied together by an unbreakable law of attraction.

"Why hurry?" thought the man. And so did she.

What was this? Was it love? . . . He was pretty sure that it was not. But now that he leaned over the girl's face and felt the warm breath of her young mouth on his skin, now that the attraction, which was gradual and irresistible, forced him to move closer to her lips, advancing very slowly, with an almost religious reverence, his whole body bending, like a fugitive dying of thirst and worshipping at the fount of water he leans over, he did consider the question. "Could this be the One? . . ." But he already knew that she wasn't, or, more precisely, that she was only one among many others who were also not the One, or, even more precisely, that she, too, was the One. He would have recognized the girl among a thousand other female faces—his powers of recollection worked with a remarkable, almost supernatural power when it came to remembering women's faces, employing precisely the same

instincts as a beast of prey does when he picks up traces and scents in the jungle—but he also knew that this relationship would be as inconclusive as the rest, for no relationship was ever conclusive: whatever the power of the mysterious, dumb, yet harshly insistent voice emanating from certain women, the signal never said anything more than, "Here I am: we have something in common that we could explore, you and I." There was never any other signal but this. He always heard the voice and heeded the call, like an animal in the jungle. His ears would prick up, his eyes begin to shine and he would straighten his back. And so he would set off in the direction of the sound, following the scent, sniffing, listening, constantly on the alert, his instincts always reliable. This was the way they called to him, the young, the beautiful, the ragged, the mature, and the aging, serving maids and princesses, nuns and traveling actresses, seamstresses and serving girls, women who could be paid in gold and more discriminating women who lived in palazzos (who also, eventually, had to be paid, and more plentifully, in gold). So it had been with the baker's widow, with the canny daughter of the Jewish horse trader, with M.M. the French ambassador's favorite, with C.C. the ruined child bride in the convent, and with the dirty, lecherous creature who only recently had been swept away to be deposited in his harem at Versailles by His Most Christian Highness Louis of the Bourbons. So it had also been with the young wife of the French captain, with the lady mayoress of Cologne, and with the princess d'Urfé who was as old as the hills and so skinny that a man was likely to prick his finger on one of

her bones when embracing her. . . . Each time he heard the voice and at every call he set out, never once lacking the feral excitement of sniffing the air or failing to experience the erotic trembling and the thrill of concentration when the mysterious question once again presented itself. "Could this be the One? . . ." But no sooner did he face the question than he knew that it wasn't, that not one of them was. And so he moved on.

And everywhere there were inns, and theaters with nightly performances, and every day miraculously produced someone, something, provided one wasn't afraid. No, I have never been afraid, he reflected with satisfaction, and drew the girl's unresisting body still closer to him. "But it would be good if this were finally she, the One I have been looking for," he thought. "It would be good to rest. It would be good to know that there was no more need for quick thinking and elaborate strategies, that someday the plot might be reduced to something perfectly simple, that one might live one's life with a woman who loved one back, and so desire nothing more. It would be very good," he ruefully thought. But it was as if the plot had become fatally confused at some point and had now to be straightened out, as if somewhere, at some time in the past, the fragile image of truth that he was seeking had been shattered and was lying in pieces at his feet. And now he had to bend down and recover each and every fragment of it. This girl, for example, had lovely ears, pink and childlike, a fine pair of ears with a most delicate shell-like curve, a lovely interplay between bone, cartilage, and the lobe's faintly comical, simple fleshiness: yes, her ears were

a practically edible delight. What should he whisper into such ears? Should he say, "You are wonderful, unique. . . ."? He had said it so often before. But it was as if he were afraid of losing his touch, and so, more for the sake of practice, for memory's sake, he leaned toward the girl's ear and with his hot breath whispered into it: "You are wonderful, unique."

Fine and delightful as the ear was, it blushed to hear the words. Indeed, the girl blushed along her whole face. For the first time she felt embarrassed. There was something impudent, aggressive, almost improper in the words, as there is in every lie told at important moments. But there was something familiar and encouraging in them too, something reminiscent of certain patriotic songs, the kind of songs that people had been singing for centuries, in the shadow of public monuments and other sacred places. "Unique," he had said, and the girl blushed as if she had heard something deliciously risqué. She blushed because she sensed the lie, and then the man fell silent again, flushed by success and a little amazed at the inevitability of it all, knowing it could not be otherwise, that there was no greater lie to be told. And both of them felt that this lie was in some way a secret truth. So they kept silent, the pair of them, somewhat disoriented. They sensed that, in its own mysterious way, "unique" was, like all eternal verities, a truth, that is to say as much a truth as when someone pronounces the words "Motherland!" or "So it must be!" and begins dutifully to weep. And however vulgar and shameless the sentiment may be, such a person feels that the grand mendacious cliché is, in some

deep way, as true as his patriotism or sense of destiny, or indeed the words "You are wonderful, unique." And so, because they could not think of anything else to say to each other, they set to kissing.

The two mouths engaged, and, almost immediately, some force started them rocking to and fro. This rocking had an incidental soothing effect, as when an adult takes a child into his arms, the evening drawing on and the child having exhausted itself and grown melancholy with running about. And the adult says something like, "That's enough play, you are tired, little one; go and rest awhile. Don't do anything, just close your eyes and rest. How hot you are! You are really flushed! And how your heart beats! . . . Once you've calmed down, a little later in the evening, I'll give you a nice piece of Neapolitan wafer." And then the girl, somewhat capriciously, even haughtily, will sometimes pull her lips away like a child protesting, "But I don't like Neapolitan wafers!" They kissed again. The rocking, that sad strange rocking, gradually drew them into the element of the kiss which was exactly like the sea, the rocking of which signifies relaxation and danger, adventure and fate. And like people who, in their dizziness, slip from the shores of reality and are amazed to observe that it is possible to survive and move in a new element, even in the alien element of fate, and that perhaps it is not really so awful to drift away from the shore with such slow rocking motions, they began to lose all contact with reality and slowly to advance, without intention, without any specific desire, toward annihilation, occasionally, between kisses, glancing dreamily round, as if raising

their heads from the foam before falling back into the dangerous, joy-bringing, indifferent, rocking element, to think, "Perhaps it is not so awful being annihilated! Perhaps it is the best life can offer, this rocking and forgetting, the point at which we lose our memories and everything grows vague, familiar, and misty." The arms they had opened with such gestures of begging and inviting, gripped and held each other's heads.

And so they would have continued had not Balbi stepped in at that moment. He hesitated by the door and in a fearful voice said: "Giacomo, don't do it!"

Slowly they drew away from each other, loosened their hold, and glanced about them in confusion and curiosity. Now that he had let go of the girl, the man noticed that he was still gripping the dagger in his hand, in the left hand with which he had embraced the girl's waist.

A Writer

When the girl had left the room, her head bowed, treading as silently as only those who are used to going about barefoot can tread, Balbi spoke. "I was really frightened. You were holding that dagger in your hand as if you were about to stab her."

"I'm not a murderer," he solemnly replied, a little short of breath as he put the dagger back on the mantelpiece. "I am a writer."

"A writer?" gasped Balbi. He left his mouth open for a while. "Have you written anything?" he asked incredulously.

"Written? Of course I've written," muttered the stranger. He spoke grudgingly, as if he hardly thought it worth his while to answer a companion so far below him that he was sure he wouldn't understand. "I've written a great many things. Poems, for example," he proclaimed triumphantly, confident he had the evidence to back his claim.

"For money?" Balbi inquired.

"For money, among other things," he answered. "Real writers always write for money, you blockhead. I don't suppose you're capable of understanding writers, Balbi. It's a pity I didn't stick this knife between your ribs that time on the outskirts of Valdepiadene when we were on the run and you almost got us into trouble. Then, perhaps, I might really have been the murderer you thought I was a few moments ago. There would also have been one less idiotic rogue in the world and the world would have thanked me for it! I never cease to regret the day I rescued you from that rat-infested gutter."

"You would not have escaped without me, either," the friar answered calmly. He was not easily insulted. He sat down in the armchair, spread his legs, and crossed his hands over his full belly, blinking and twiddling his thumbs.

"True enough," came the matter-of-fact answer. "When a man is in trouble he will grasp at anything, even the hangman's rope."

They were weighing each other up. "Yes, it was a pity," he repeated, and shrugged his shoulders to demonstrate how pointless it was for a man to dwell on all the things he had failed to do in life. "And you, potbelly, you don't understand, are incapable of understanding, that I am a writer. What have you ever written in your life? Love letters, two-a-penny, to sell on the market to servants with holes in their shoes, a few fake contracts to self-employed tradesmen and petty criminals, some begging letters with which you might trouble your betters, people who were

sufficiently easygoing and forgetful not to send you to the galleys."

"All the same," replied the friar in his mildest, friendliest manner, "it was writing that saved me, Giacomo. Cast your mind back. We wrote each other such letters, we might have been lovers. Long, ardent letters they were, and Lorenzo the warder, was our go-between. We made our acquaintance through those letters, told each other everything, both past and present. If I were incapable of writing I would never have started a correspondence with you, nor would I ever have escaped. You despise me and look down on me. I know you would happily kill me. You are not being fair. I know as well as you do that writing is very important, a great source of power."

"Power?" his fellow fugitive repeated, and surveyed the friar haughtily from under suspicious, half-closed eyelids, his head thrown right back. "It's far greater than that. It is not a matter of 'sources,' Balbi, but power itself. Writing is the one and only power. You are right, it is writing that freed you. I really hadn't thought of that. The scriptures, the sacred writings, are right when they tell us that even fools are not without grace. Writing is the greatest power there is: the written word is greater than king or pope, greater than the doge. We are living proofs of that. It was in writing that we plotted our escape, letters formed the teeth that cut through our chains, letters were the ladder and the rope on which we let ourselves down, it was letters that led us back from hell to earth. Some say," he continued, "that letters can lead us from earth up to heaven too. But I don't believe in their power to do that."

"What then do you believe in?" asked the friar conversationally.

"In fate," he answered without hesitation, "in the fate we create for ourselves and thenceforth accept. I believe in life, in the multifariousness of things that eventually, miraculously, chime in harmony, in the various fragments that finally combine to make one man, one life. I believe in love and in the wheel of fortune. And I believe in writing, because the power of writing is greater than that of fate or time. The things we do, the things we desire, the things we love, the things we say, all pass away. Women pass, affairs pass. Time's dust settles over all we have done, over everything that once excited us. But words remain. I tell you, I am a writer," he declared with delight and satisfaction, as if he had just discovered the fact.

He ran his fingers through his uncombed hair and threw back his head like a great musician about to raise the violin to his chin and assault the strings with his bow. It was a pose he had learned to strike in his youth when he played the instrument in a band in Venice. Agitated, he paced in a somewhat peculiar limping manner across the room, then added quietly, "Sometimes it surprises even me."

"What surprises you?" asked Balbi like a curious child.

"I am surprised to find that I am a writer," he replied without thinking. "I cannot help it, Balbi, there is nothing I can do about it, so I beg you to keep the secret to yourself since I don't like the idea of bragging and complaining in the same breath. I am telling this to you alone, because I have absolutely no respect for you. There are many ways of

writing. Some people sit in a room and do nothing but write. They are the happy ones. Their lives are sad because they are lonely, because they gaze at women the way dogs gaze at the moon, and they complain bitterly to the world, singing their woes, telling us how much suffering they undergo on account of the sun, the stars, autumn and death. They are the saddest of men but the happiest of writers because their lives are dedicated to words alone: they breakfast on proper nouns and go to sleep with a well-fleshed adjective in their arms. They smile in a faintly wounded manner when they dream. And when they wake in the morning they raise their eyes to heaven because they are under a permanent spell and live in some cockeyed rapture, believing that by grunting and stuttering their way through all those adjectives and proper nouns they will continue to succeed in articulating that which God himself has succeeded in articulating once and once only. Yes, the happy writers are those who walk about looking sad, and women deal gently with them, taking considerable care of them as they might of their simpleminded nearest and dearest, as if they were the writers' more fortunate, wiser sisters, obliged to comfort them and prepare them for death. I wouldn't want to be a writer who does nothing but write," he declared a little contemptuously. "Then there are writers who run you through with their pens as they would with a sword or dagger, writing in blood, spattering the page with bile, the kind of writers you find in the study with tasseled nightcaps on their heads, berating kings and parasites, traitors and usurers, writers who enter the service of ideas or of human causes

as either volunteers or mercenaries. . . . I've known some of them. I once spent some time in the company of that scarecrow, Voltaire. Don't interrupt me, you've never even heard of him. He had no teeth left but that did not stop him biting: kings and queens sought to earn his approval, and this toothless wretch with a single quill between his gouty knotted fingers could hold the world to account with it. Do you understand? . . . I do. Writing, for these people, was a means of changing the world, but the writers who exercised power on the basis of their strength and intellect were unhappy, both as men and writers, because they lacked silence and reverence. They could plunge daggers through constitutions and stab a king through the heart with a single sharp word but they were incapable of articulating life's deepest secret, which is the miraculous sense of being here at all, the delight of knowing that we are not alone but are cared for by the stars, by women and by our demons, not to mention the happy realization of the extraordinary fact that we must die. Those to whom the pen is just a sword or dagger can never articulate such things, however much power they wield on earth. . . . Such people may influence thrones, human institutions, and individual destinies, but they can do little to suspend our sense of time. . . . And then there are writers like myself. They are the rarest kind," he declared with satisfaction.

"Absolutely," Balbi agreed in awe. "And why are they the rarest, my lord and master?"

His deep, rasping voice bore the impress of prison, alcohol, and disease, as well as wayside hovels and the beds

of kitchen maids. Now it was a mixture of curiosity and wariness. He sat with his mouth wide open, still twiddling his thumbs, as if he had blundered into a theater where the actors were performing in some language he only imperfectly understood.

"Because what they write is what they have to lose, which is the text of their own lives," Giacomo's voice was rising. "Do you understand me, you pot-bellied flat-footed fool, you hero of hovel and brothel, do you understand? I am that rare creature, a writer with a life to write about! You asked me how much I have written? . . . Not much, I admit. A few verses . . . a few essays on the magical arts. . . . But none of these was the real thing. I have been envoy, priest, soldier, fiddler, and doctor of civil and canonical law, thanks be to Bettina, who introduced me to knowledge of the physical world when I was fourteen, and thanks, too, to her older brother, Doctor Gozzi, who was my neighbor in Padua, who knew nothing of what Bettina had taught me but introduced me to the world of the fine arts. But that's not the point, it's not the writing, it's what I have done that matters. It is me, my life, that is the important thing. The point, you fool, is that being is much more difficult than doing. Gozzi denies this. Gozzi says only bad writers want to live and good writers find that writing is enough. But I refute Gozzi because there is only one great struggle in life and that is between powerful, justified assertion on the one hand and powerful, justified denial on the other. However Gozzi may dismiss me as a writer now, my being, my life, is the important thing. I want to live. I cannot write until I know the world. And I am only

beginning to know it," he said, more quietly, almost in awe. "I am forty. I have hardly begun to live. I can't get enough of life. I have not seen as many dawns as I would wish, there are too many human feelings and sensations that I do not know, I have not yet finished laughing at the arrogance of bureaucrats, dignitaries, and all manner of respectable persons; I have not succeeded as often as I'd like in stuffing the words of fat priests down their throats, I mean those fat priests who count their indulgences in pennies. I have not yet laughed myself sick at human folly; have not rolled into enough ditches in uncontrolled amusement at the world's vanity, ambition, lust, and greed; have still not woken in the arms of a sufficient number of women to know anything worth knowing about them, to have learned some truth that is more substantial than the sad, vulgar truth of what they hide beneath their skirts, which excites the imagination only of poets and adolescents. . . . I have not lived enough, Balbi," he repeated stubbornly, with a genuine tremor in his voice. "I don't want to leave anything out, you see! I am not ambitious for worldly acclaim, I am not ambitious for wealth, for a happy domestic life: there'll be time enough later for strolling about in slippers, for inspecting my vineyard and for hearing the birds singing, for carrying a volume of *De consolatione philosophiae* by the pagan Boethius under my arm, or indeed one of the books of the sage Horace, who teaches that a just man is always accompanied by two heavenly sisters, Knowledge and Pity. . . . I don't want to give myself over to pity now. I want to live so that, eventually, I might write. This comes at a great cost.

Understand this, my unlucky companion, my fellow in the galleys, understand that I must see everything: I must see the rooms where people sleep, I must hear their whimpers as they enter old age when they can only buy a woman's favors with gold, I must get to know mothers and younger sisters, lovers and spouses who always have something true and encouraging to say about life. I must at least get to shake their hands. I am the kind of writer who needs to live. Gozzi says only bad writers want to live. But Gozzi is not a man, Gozzi is just a timid indolent bookworm who will never write anything of permanent value."

"But when will you have time to write, Giacomo? . . ." asked Balbi. "If you spend it all seeing, hearing, and getting to smell everything you've talked about you will never find enough time for writing. You are right, I don't understand such things. I do, however, know something about the chore of writing, and my experience tells me that even writing a letter takes a long time. Real writing, the work that writers do, would need even more leisure, I imagine. Perhaps a whole lifetime of it."

"I shall write when I have done as much living as I consider necessary," he replied and stared at the ceiling, his lips moving silently as if counting something. "When I have lived, I shall want to write."

Somebody was laughing in the yard beneath the window. It was a warm, youthful, broken laugh and the stranger hurried over to the window and leaned over the balcony. He waved and bowed, and grinning widely, put two fingers to his mouth and blew a kiss.

"Bellissima!" he cried. "My one and only! Tonight! . . ."

He turned around, his voice somber.

"I have to do everything now for the sake of writing later. I have to experience life and everything life offers. Writing demands serious commitment. . . . I must see everything so I may describe habits and habitations, the places where I was once happy or miserable or simply indifferent. I don't yet have time for writing. And those people," he cried with a sudden fury, so angrily that for a moment the whites of his eyes looked enormous, "had the nerve to lock me up in jail! Venice denied me. They denied a man who, even in the galleys, was as true a Venetian as any dignitary painted by Titian! They dared deprive me of my right to be an author, a real author who dedicates each day of his life to gathering material for his work! They dared stand in judgment on me, on a writer, and a Venetian writer, at that! The bigwigs of Venice took it on themselves to shut me away from life, from sunlight and moonlight; they stole an important part of my time, of my life, a life that is nothing more than a form of service undertaken for the community. . . . Yes, that, in my fashion, is the service I perform! I serve the community! . . . And they dared take sixteen months of life from me! A plague on them!" he declared lightly but firmly. "A pestilence and plague on Venice! Let the Moors come, let the pagan Turks come with their topknots and cut the senators into delicate little pieces, all except Signor Bragadin, of course, who was a father to me when I had no father and who gave me money. I'm glad I remembered him. In fact I must write to him immediately. May shame and desolation be the lot of Venice who threw me, the truest son

of Venice, into a rat-infested cell! I will make it the mission of my life to revenge myself on Venice!"

"Bravo!" cried Balbi enthusiastically, his fat face, yellow and warty as a marrow, beginning to glisten. "You are right, Giacomo, I understand you. I feel the same. I might not be a Venetian when it comes down to it, but I, too, know how to write. Well said: a plague on Venice. I'm with you there, believe me."

But he could not finish what he was saying as the stranger suddenly seized him by the neck and set about strangling him.

"How Dare You Curse Venice"

"*How* dare you curse Venice?" he gasped. "That's for me to do! Do you understand? . . . I will take care of Venice!" His voice was terrifying. He struck his breast with his left hand and his face was strangely twisted in the heat of the moment, scarcely human, like the half-comic, half-horrific masks worn by Venetians at the wildest peak of the carnival. His right hand was gripping the friar's shirt collar and lapel while his left hand hung in the air like a bird of prey, blindly seeking the dagger he had just deposited on the mantelpiece. And so they retreated together toward the fireplace, Giacomo dragging the friar, whose face slowly changed from its customary marrow color to a bright puce as the grip tightened. His hand located the dagger on the marble shelf, seized it, and raised it high in the air. "How dare you curse Venice?" he repeated, calmly this time, the point of the dagger raised, his victim pressed against the wall. "No one except me is allowed to curse Venice! No one else has the right! You understand? No one!" He spat the words out, not simply

DO NOT REMOVE SLIP FROM ITEM

SHIPPING SLIP

06-NOV-2017

Ship To:
Delivery Point:

Requesting Library:

Westlock Municipal Library - TRAC
ID: AWES
Address: Westlock Municipal Library, ILL
Dept
#1-10007-100 Ave
Westlock, AB
T7P 2H5

Phone: (780) 349-3060

Westlock Municipal Library - TRAC
ID: AWES
Address: Westlock Municipal Library, ILL
Dept
#1-10007-100 Ave
Westlock, AB
T7P 2H5

Phone: (780) 349-3060

Ship From:

Edmonton Public Library
ID: AE
Address: Edmonton Public Library, ILL Dept
10230 Jasper Avenue NW
Edmonton, AB
T5J 4P6

Phone: (780) 496-7077

Responder Req. 1670129
No.:
Item Barcode: 31221075356704
Title: Casanova in Bolzano [a novel]

"Returned"
Delius Dec14/17
DX Dec14/17

"Received"
DX Nov16/17
RBins Nov16/17
Hep
✓
Returned

1/5/17

in a figurative sense but quite physically, his lips swollen, the boiling white-hot saliva issuing from his yellow gums and spraying the friar's face as he spoke: it was as if something in the excited human cauldron within him had suddenly boiled over and the contents of his entire life were bubbling and spitting, and had started to overflow. He was pale, a grayish-yellow, all passion and fury. "I'll curse her myself!" he reiterated, whispering the words into the ears of the terrified, silent, and by now perfectly blue friar as if they were a seductive promise of pleasures to come. "I alone! Only a Venetian is allowed to do that! What do you know, how could you know?! . . . How would you know, you loafers, vagrants, wastrels, and layabouts? You might as well claim to know the courts of heaven as to know the least thing about Venice! You sit in the taverns in the alleys of the Merceria, sipping sour wine, and think you are in Venice! You stuff your guts with fish, flesh, and fowl, with pâté and long strings of pasta, with *dolce latte* and other smelly cheeses, and think you know Venice! You lurk in cheap bordellos, tickling the fancy of some Cypriot whore on a rotten mattress, and because you can hear the bells of St. Mark's in the distance you make believe you are part of Venice! You stop by the balcony of the Doge's Palace, cheering with the crowd, anticipating a handout, or looking around with an eye to a bargain, and you imagine yourselves to be Venetians! Leave Venice alone, do you hear! You are not to lay a finger on her! What can you possibly know of her, what can you see of her, what can you hear of her? Do not dare to speak of Venice, you have nothing to say about her. Worms will be feeding on your

fat belly, which is the legacy of Venetian bakeries and Venetian pots and pans, before you are ready to say anything on the subject! You will keep your mouth shut about Venice as the Jews of the Diaspora do about their God. You will keep silent if you value your life and if you ever hope to see Venice again! How could you know Venice? . . . You have seen only the paving stones, the iron feet of the casseroles, the heels of Venetian women, the thighs of Venetian servants and the indifferent sea that carried you to Venice along with all the rest: with the French and their verses, their diseases, and their fine manners; with the Germans, who wander through our squares and gaze at our statues with such anxious looks on their faces, as if it were not life that were the important thing but some lecture they sooner or later had to give; with the English, who prefer warm water to red wine and are capable of staring through their glasses for hours at one or other altarpiece, not noticing that the model for the painting is the marriageable daughter of a nearby innkeeper and that she is praying right next to them on the steps of the altar, recalling her sins, sins that are the talk of all Venice but which Venice has long since forgiven. Because Venice is not the doge or the *messer grande,* not the round bellied canons, nor the senators who, given a bag of gold, are anybody's. Venice is not only the bell ringer in the Piazza San Marco, the doves on the white stones, the wells built by Venetian masons, by the ancestors of my mother and father, and stamped with their genius; Venice is not just the rain glinting in narrow streets or the moonlight falling on the little footbridge, nor is it just the bawds, drovers,

gamblers, and fallen women whose numbers the procurators register in their musty offices: Venice is not simply what you see. Who knows Venice? . . . You have to be born there to know her. You have to taste her damp, sour, stale smell in your mother's milk, smell the noble scent of decay which is like the breath of the dying or the memory of happy times without fear of either life or death, when the spell of the moment, the dizziness of reality, the enchanted consciousness of living here and now in Venice, filled each fiber of your body and every nook and cranny of your intellect. I bless my fate and I go down on my knees in gratitude to the destiny that decreed I should be born in Venice. I thank heaven that my first earthly breath was of the rotten wisdom that lingers in the scent of the lagoon! I was born a Venetian and that means everything is mine, that everything that makes life worth living has been given to me as a gift: the sense of freedom, the sea, art, manners . . . and, having been born there, I know that to live is to struggle, and that to struggle is to be a true, noble Venetian! Venice is happiness!" he cried, letting go of the friar's purple neck and spreading his arms, staring about him with a pale face and a glazed expression like a priest announcing the miraculous news that the light of heaven was to be found here among us mortals. "It is a source of pride and delight to me that Venice exists, that over and above reality, which is flat and dull, there floats something whose stones are suspended between the sky and the water, that is supported not only on columns but on the souls of my forefathers. It delights me that the streets and squares where the nations of the world remove

their shoes and go about on bare feet, their faces purple with devotion, were simply places where I played as a child, where I took the part of policeman or criminal, of Turk or Moor, in games with the children of street sweepers and patricians! Venice is a city of miracles where everyone, even the street waif larking among pigeon droppings by the campanile, can aspire to be an aristocrat. Mark my words, Balbi: every Venetian is indeed an aristocrat, and you should address me with due reverence! The milk that a Venetian sucks with the first hungry movement of his lips from his mother's breast tastes of the sea and the lagoon: it tastes and smells of Venice, that is to say it is a touch salty, lukewarm and terrifyingly familiar. Wherever I go and smell the sea it is always Venice that comes to mind, Venice and my mother. Things were always best in Venice. I was three years old when I learned to walk on water like the Savior. We were filthy and ragged, and everything belonged to us. The marble palaces, the gateways with their stone arches that looked like fine lace, and the harbor, where, from morning to night, they were loading and unloading cargoes, ferrying gold and ivory and silver and amber and pearls and rose oil and cloth and silk and velvet and canvas, everything that could be bought in the bazaars of Constantinople or was manufactured by the studios of Crete, by the fashion houses of France or by English armament factories: everything was disgorged here, in the harbor in Venice, and everything was ours and, because I was a Venetian, it was mine too. Even when I was a child at play I was aware that I was a Venetian. And when I grew up, stood on the Rialto, and watched the

world's nations bringing their wares and throwing them at Venice's feet, I saw that the gold, frankincense, and myrrh they were bringing was in adoration of Venice. His Merciful Highness, the first secretary, that bureaucratic bloodhound of the Inquisition, accused me of the false use of a noble surname! But who in the world is more properly entitled to be aware of his nobility than I, who am Venetian born? . . . Show me the pope, the emperor, the king, or the princeling who is better fitted to bestow nobility on a man than the Queen of all the World, my birthplace, Venice? . . . My mother and father were both Venetians, I and my siblings were all born there: could there be a more genuine *grandezza* or nobility than ours? . . . Are you beginning to understand? You will not curse Venice!"

He stood pale, with circles round his eyes: he looked to be in a kind of trance. Balbi kept feeling his neck and breathed with difficulty after the fright he had suffered. He mumbled through his cracked and gritted teeth.

"I understand, Giacomo. I understand now, the devil take you. I recognize the fact that you are a Venetian. But if you lay your hands on my neck again I'll bite your nose off."

"I wasn't going to hurt you," replied Giacomo, laughing. "You can run and play now if you want. We shall spend a few days in Bolzano because I have things to do here: first, I must write a letter to Bragadin and wait for his answer, and while we are waiting we should get some new clothes because, without finery, even a Venetian nobleman looks like a beggar. Yes, there are things to do here in Bolzano, but by the end of the week we can be on the road

again. I shall take you to Munich, so you may visit the order of which you are, alas, no longer a member. My destiny as a writer calls me further afield. Revenge can wait. The thought of it is deep in my heart, though, and will never fade. You must nurture revenge as you would a captive lion, by feeding it daily with a little raw flesh, the bloody remnants of your remembered insults, so as not to blunt its taste for blood. Because I will return to Venice one day! But in the meantime, no one but me will be allowed to curse her. The fires of revenge will continue burning, but that is a matter between the two of us: between myself and the Inquisition, between myself and the first secretary, myself and the Venetians. If you value your life at all, you'll not raise a finger against Venice. I will take care of her in due course, don't you worry. And, mark my words, Balbi, by Venice I do not mean the Venetians. No one knows them better than I who was born among them, who is blood of their blood, the blood of those who humiliated me and cast me out. Who should know them better than the man who introduced the male prostitute to the cardinal? The man who obtained a state loan for the senator responsible for artistic affairs by raiding the state funds reserved for the orphans of the republic? The man who introduced the castrato singer to the gracious head of the supervisory committee? The man who saw the exalted, the high-minded, and the pious, masked and with their collars turned up, sneaking through the notorious doorways of Madame Ricci's house after sunset? The man who knows that, in Venice, the price of a man's life is five gold pieces? The man who knows the precise addresses of hired

assassins who spend their days hanging about the taverns in the side streets by the fishmarket and who are just as openly eager to place their poisons and daggers at the disposal of the exalted, the high-minded and the pious as the religious-goods vendors are their candles and icons? Who else knows what happened to Lucia, the adopted daughter and secret lover of his grace, the papal delegate? How did she vanish? Who is in a better position to know from whom, and from where, they bought the needle, the thread, and the sacking with which, on Michaelmas night, they stitched up the body of Paolo, the wild son of His Most High Excellency? . . . Who is in a position to reveal what still lies rotting in the cellars of certain Venetian houses and which head belongs to which torso as they both drift down the Grand Canal on the day after the Carnival? These are the people! . . ." he cried and grabbed the table whose great oak top shook as he touched it. "These are the people who judged me! Patricides, murderers of their own sons, usurers, gluttons, parasites, living off orphans' tears and sucking the blood of widows with their taxes—and these are the people who dared pass judgment on me! Murderers! Thieves! Exploiters! Mark my words, Balbi! One day I shall return to Venice."

"Yes," agreed the friar and crossed himself. "But I wouldn't like to be traveling with you when you do, Giacomo!"

They glared at each other. Then, still staring into each other's eyes, they started to laugh and were soon shaking with uncontrollable hilarity.

"Send for the barber," said Giacomo. "And for a cup of

chocolate. And ink, a finely-cut pen, and some paper to write on. I must write to Signor Bragadin, who was father to me when I had none. I might be able to squeeze a hundred or so gold pieces out of him. Look sharp, Balbi: don't forget you are my secretary and manservant. We might have to spend a few more brief days in Bolzano. Go carefully, keep your eyes open, don't spend all your time sniffing round the skirts of kitchen-maids because, for a plump pigeon like you, there is always a cage like the Leads, ready and waiting. And I won't pull you out through the bars again. Get a move on. There is a banker in the town, a man called Mensch, a well-known moneylender. Find out his address."

Using a gesture he had learned from the pope—the extending of the hand for a kiss on its ringed fingers—he dismissed his traveling companion. He went over to the mirror and, with careful, precise movements, began to comb his hair.

Francesca

*T*eresa brought in the chocolate and announced that Giuseppe, the pretty, rosy-cheeked, blond, blue-eyed boy, had arrived and was even now waiting for his instructions. Giacomo gave the girl money, had some white stockings brought over from the nearby fashionable haberdasher, then—on credit—ordered two pairs of lace gloves and a pair of clasped shoes as an extra. While the barber lathered him, the various servants proceeded round him on tiptoe, changing the bed, pouring hot water into basins, and ironing his clothes, for he had taken considerable pains to impress upon Teresa the importance of carefully starching the ruffles on the front of his shirt. The barber's soft hand moved over his face, rubbing the lather in, then, like a conductor, wove and teased each curl of his locks into place.

"Talk to me," said the guest, his eyes closed, stretching his limbs out in the armchair. "What news in town?"

"Town news?" the pretty barber began in a singing, slightly effeminate voice, lisping a little. "You, sir, are the

news. No other news in Bolzano since sunset last night. You alone. May I?" he asked, and with the ends of his scissors he began to snip at the hair sprouting from the guest's wide nostrils.

"What are they saying?" came the question, along with a sigh of satisfaction. "You are allowed to tell me the worst as well as the best."

"There is only the best, sir," the barber answered, snapping his scissors in the air, then taking the heated curling tongs, breathing on them, and turning them about. "This morning, as usual, I was up at the crack of dawn with His Excellency. I'm there every morning. You should know, sir, that His Excellency does us the honor of affording our company his patronage. It is my privilege to shave him and to prepare his peruke for him, since His Excellency—and I tell you this in confidence—is perfectly bald now. My boss, the renowned Barbaruccia—they say there is no one, not even in Florence, who possesses his skill in cutting veins or restoring potency with a special herbal preparation—is both doctor and barber to His Excellency. My job, as I have explained, is to shave him. And Signor Barbaruccia's wife massages him twice a week, but at other times, too, whenever he feels in need of it."

"Surely not!" he replied coldly. "His Excellency requires both massage and restoratives? . . ."

"Only since he got married, sir," answered the barber, and began to curl his thick hair with the hot tongs.

He only half heard the news, stretched out as he was in the exquisite minutes of self-indulgence afforded by the submission of one's head to the soft fingers of a barber.

Giuseppe's fingers were nimble but he was even nimbler in his talk. His voice was light and gentle, like the sound of a spring, full of lisping, eyeball-rolling scandal; he spoke in the manner peculiar to barbers, who are at once friends, experts, counselors and confidants for whom the town holds no secrets, for they know about aging bodies, about the cooling of the blood, about scalps that are losing their former glories, about the slackening of the muscles, about the delicate creaking of frail bones, about toothless gums and bad breath, about the crow's-feet gathering on smooth temples, and who listened with attention to everything that the bloodless lips of their customers had to say. "Chatter away!" thought Giacomo and stretched his body again, yielding himself to the effeminate voice, to the fine scent of the burned alcoholic tincture being rubbed into his brow and the rice powder being sprinkled on his wig. He enjoyed this half hour in this distant town, as he did in every distant town, these moments when, after rising, he would welcome the appearance of the barber, the official traitor to the municipality, who snapped his scissors and whispered the secrets of the living and the dead. He encouraged the nimble youth with the odd blink or brief aside—"Really? Completely bald?"—in mock astonishment, as though it were the most important thing in the world, as though he had his own suspicions as to the condition of the gracious gentleman who required feeding and massage now that he was married. "But surely there remain a few stray locks on his nape at least?" he asked confidentially, narrowing his eyes.

"Yes," Giuseppe brightly replied with the unselfish vol-

ubility of one prepared to divulge still darker and more melancholy information. "But how thin those locks are, exceedingly thin. His Excellency is a great patron of ours. My master, Signor Barbaruccia, is among his favorites, as am I. It does us no harm, that sort of thing. We order him roe from Grado for the increasing of his desire, and Signor Barbaruccia's wife prepares a brew of beetroot, horse-radish, and spring onions for him to ward off apoplexy should he then be assailed by particularly carnal thoughts. His Excellency has mentioned you, sir."

"What did he say?" he asked, his eyes wide with amazement.

"Only that he would like to meet you," answered the barber in his best obedient-schoolboy manner. "His Excellency, the duke of Parma, would like to meet you. That's all."

"I am very much obliged," he responded carelessly. "I will pay my respects to His excellency, if time allows."

So they chattered on. The barber completed his task and left.

"The duke of Parma!" he muttered, then washed himself, drew on the white stockings that Teresa had left at the side of the bed for him, drank his chocolate, licked his fingers and smoothed his bushy eyebrows before the mirror, trimmed his nails with a sharp blade, pulled on his shirt, and adjusted the hard-ironed pleats with the tips of his fingers while occasionally touching his neck with the index and ring fingers of his right hand, as if testing his collar size or wishing to ascertain that his head was still there. "The duke of Parma!" he grumbled. "So he wishes

to see me." The possibility hadn't occurred to him when he escaped and hired the trap to drive him to Bolzano. He whistled quietly, lit the candles in front of the mirror because the early afternoon had already filtered into the room with its brownish blue shadows, sat down at the spindle-legged table, arranged paper, ink, and sand for blotting, and with goosequill held high above his head, his upper body slightly reclined, his eyebrows suspiciously raised, he peered attentively and curiously into the mirror. It was a long time since he had seen himself like this, in circumstances so fitting for a writer. It was a long time since he had sat like this, in a room with fine furniture, before a fire, in a freshly starched shirt, in long white pearlescent stockings, with a real quill in his hand, ready for literary production in the hour most apt for solitude and meditation, for complete immersion in the task before him, which, at this precise moment, was neither more nor less than the composition of a begging letter to Signor Bragadin. "What a letter this will be!" he thought with satisfaction, the way a poet might contemplate a sonnet the first few rhymes of which are already jangling in his ears. "The duke of Parma!" he reflected once more, compelled by an association of ideas he could not dismiss. "Can he still be alive? . . ." Pursing his lips, he began to count aloud.

"Four," he counted, then stared thoughtfully at the ceiling, adding and subtracting. "No, five!" he declared, precise as any tradesman. He gazed into the candle flame, fascinated and round mouthed. "I am a poet about to write a poem," he thought, quill in hand, leaning back in

the armchair, facing the writing desk and the fireplace, his hair lightly combed, his clothes washed and starched. He was enjoying the situation. "Five," he considered again, this time a little anxiously, and raised the five fingers of his hand, as if showing or proving something to someone, like a child claiming, "It wasn't me!"

"Five," he grumbled, and bit hard on his lower lip, wagging his head. Screwing up his eyes, he gazed into the flame, then into the deep shadows of the room, then finally into the far distance, into the past, into life itself. And suddenly he gave a low whistle, as if he had found something he had been looking for. He pronounced the name, "Francesca."

He raised the quill and with a gesture of amazement wrote the name in the air, as if to say, "The devil take it! But what can I do?" He stretched his legs in the scarlet light of the fire, breathed in the scented warmth, threw away the quill, and watched the flames. "That's the one," he thought. "Francesca!" And once again: "The duke of Parma! Bolzano! What a coincidence!" But he knew there was no such thing as coincidence, and that this was no coincidence, either. Suddenly, it was as though a hundred candles had been lit in the room: he saw everything clearly. He heard a voice and was aware of the familiar scent of verbena mingling with the sane, cheerful smell of freshly ironed women's underwear. Yes, it had been five years, he thought, mildly horrified. For these last five years had swept away everything in their filthy hot torrent, everything including Francesca, nor had he once reached out to save what had vanished in it. Yes, it had been five years:

and he wondered whether they recalled the story in Pistoia, in the palazzo from which the aged countess would ride out in a black baldachin-covered coach into Florence at noon when the gilded youth and little lordlings of the city went promenading before the exquisite stores of the Via Tornabuoni? Would they still recall the midnight duel in Pistoia where the bald and elderly aristocrat waited for him, sword in hand, where they fought in the square before the palazzo, in the presence of the silent Francesca and the old count who kept rubbing his hands? They had fought silently, for a long time, their swords glittering in the moonlight, in a genuine fury that transcended the very reason for which they were fighting, so there was no more yearning for revenge or satisfaction but simply a desire to fight, because two mortal men in pursuit of one Francesca was one too many. "The old man fought well!" he acknowledged under his breath. "He didn't need Signor Barbaruccia's wife's aphrodisiacs then: he could vie for Francesca's affections without such things." He covered his eyes to see more clearly, unable, not even willing, to shut out the images that now grew clearer and assumed ever more life-size proportions behind his closed eyelids.

There stood Francesca in the dawn breeze, in front of the crumbling stone wall of the count's garden, slender, wearing a nightgown, fifteen years old, her dark hair falling across her brow, one hand clutching a white silk shawl across her breast, her eyes wide, staring at the sky. Had it been five years? No, it was only the swish of swords that had happened five years ago; the moment in which he had first seen Francesca was stored away in a deeper, more

secret crevice of time. There she stood before the garden wall in the shadows of the cypresses, and the sky above them was a clear and gentle blue, as if every human passion had dissolved and gentled in that clear, all-pervading blue. The wind is embracing Francesca, the soft folds of the nightgown are hugging her girlish body like a swimming costume. Francesca seems to have stepped from a bathing pool compounded of night and dreams, her body shimmering, dew-drenched, and in the corner of her eyes there is some sparkling liquid whose precise nature is hard to define, a teardrop, perhaps, or a drop of dew that has deserted its usual habitat in the depths of the flower cup to settle on a young girl's lashes. . . . And he stands opposite the girl and listens. Only desire can listen with such intensity, he now thinks. I tend to talk a lot, far too much, in fact, but I listened then, in Pistoia, by the crumbling castle wall, in the garden, where the olives ran riot and the cypresses stood about as somber as you could wish, as somber as the halberdiers of a king in exile. Francesca has stolen from her bed in the castle, out of the night, out of childhood and out of a sheltered life into the garden on the morning of the day that he exchanges dueling cards with the duke of Parma. He saw and felt everything now. He caught the scent of the morning, and it stirred up jealousy and other intense feelings in him, memories of moments experienced only by those who are no longer young. Because Francesca represented youth and so did those silent gardens: perhaps it was the last minute of his own youth passing in the impoverished count's garden in Pistoia; perhaps these were the somber, tattered, grandiose

theatrical props of his own decaying memory, a memory that was disintegrating under the pressure of years; maybe this scene represented his youth as it was many years ago in a garden in Tuscany when the sky was blue and Francesca stood by the garden wall, her hair and clothes fluttering in the wind, her eyes closed; when they were both listening, confused and intoxicated by a feeling, that even now sank its claws into him and tortured him. "How extraordinary she was!" he thought, and pressed his fists even tighter into his eyes. It was as if she were saturated with light, so intensely did that sweet yet disturbing energy flow from her to touch the man standing opposite her. Yes, she was filled with light. It was the rarest of all sensations, he reflected approvingly, like a connoisseur. There was light in her, and when a man looked into her eyes it was as if lamps were being lit all over the world; everything around him was brighter, more real, more substantially true. Francesca herself stood as if entranced and he did not speak as the old suitor stepped through the garden gate, offered his arm to Francesca, and led her back into the house. That was all. And a year later, in the very same place, in a corner of the yard before the castle gate, quite possibly at the same precise hour, two men fought each other.

The old man fought well, he thought again, curling his lip in homage, and smiled bitterly. Was that all? . . . Perhaps the adventure was simply about youth, the last year of real youth, that mysterious but exciting interval when even the nervous traveler lets the reins of his horse go, relaxes into the gallop, looks round, wipes his brow, and

sees that the road waiting for him ahead is steep, that far off, beyond the woods and the hills, the sun is already beginning to set. When he first met Francesca it was still bright, still high noon. They stood in a valley in the foothills of Tuscany. He had just arrived from Rome, his pockets bulging with the cardinal's gold and with letters of introduction. Travel was different then, he thought with satisfaction and a touch of envy. Few could travel the way I did, he proudly reflected. He had a shameless self-confidence born of genius, of an artist at the top of his form: "The sound I can get out of that flute! Remarkable! Can anyone compare with me? . . . Let him try!" There were indeed few who could travel like him and even fewer who could arrive in the style he did, in the good old days, five years ago! For there's a trick, a manner of carrying things off on the stage of human endeavor, and he knew all the theatrical tricks; that there's a way of choosing the horses, the equipment, the dimensions of the coach, and, yes, even the coachman's uniform; that one must master the art of arriving at the palazzo of one's host or at an inn of good reputation, as well as the art of driving through the gates of a foreign city and of leaning back in one's seat in one's lilac-edged gray traveling cloak, or of raising one's gilt-handled lorgnette in one's gloved hand and crossing one's legs in a careless, faintly interested manner, the way Phoebus himself might have traveled at dawn in his fiery chariot drawn by four prancing horses above a world that, to tell the truth, he mildly despised. These were the tricks you had to master; this was the best way to travel and to arrive! How few people knew such tricks! There were

remarkably few people who were capable of understanding that it was vital that, within half an hour of arriving at the inn or at your host's palazzo, the whole serving staff of the establishment should be buzzing around you! This was the way he arrived one day at Pistoia, at the home of the old impoverished count who was related to the cardinal who now, in turn, was sending his blessing to the family, to the fat countess and to Francesca, his godchild. He proceeded to stay a month, entertained the family, made over a gift of two hundred ducats and golden caskets to the count, returning twice the next year, and at the end of that year, one moonlit night, fought a duel with the ancient suitor, the duke of Parma. He opened his shirt and examined the wound on his chest.

He touched the scars with his fingertips, itemizing and remembering them. There was a line of three scars on his left, all three just above the heart, as if his enemies had unconsciously yet somehow deliberately, instinctively, aimed precisely at his heart. The central scar, the deepest and roughest of them, was the one he owed to His Excellency of Parma and to Francesca. He put his index finger to the now painless wound. The duel had been fought with rapiers. The Duke's blade had made a treacherous incursion above his heart, so the surgeon had had to spend weeks draining the blood and the suppuration off the deep wound; and there had also been some internal bleeding, as a result of which the victim, after fever fits, bouts of semi-conscious delirium, and stretches of screaming and groaning insensibility, finally bade farewell to adventure. He lay in Florence in the hospital of the Sisters of Mercy where he

had had himself conveyed in the duke's coach on the night of his wounding. He had not seen Francesca since that moment, and he learned of the engagement only some three years later in Venice, at a masked ball, from the French ambassador, who regretfully let fall that the cousin of the grand duke, a Parmesan kinsman of His Most Christian Majesty, forgetting his rank and high connections, had, in the idiotic thoughtlessness of his declining years, married some little village goose from Tuscany, a rural demi-countess of some kind. . . . He had smiled and held his peace. The wound no longer gave him any pain, and only when the weather was damp did he feel the slightest pang. So life went on and no one ever mentioned Francesca's name.

Why is it, he wondered, that I have remained aware of her all these years? And later, too, when I received the second wound, that long jagged one above the little carte de visite left me by the duke of Parma, that long brute across the chest, administered with a sword at dawn by the hired assassin of Orly the cardsharp as I was leaving the gambling den at Murano, my greatcoat stuffed with hard-earned gold prized from the pockets of a cheating banker and various other rogues, gold earned through the judicious use of quick wits and even quicker fingers; why was it that, in those days after the assault, as I lay in a state between life and death, this image of Francesca by the garden wall under the blue Tuscan sky kept coming to mind? And the third scar, that odd scratch where the Greek woman went at him with her sharp fingernails, and which hurt more than other cuts and thrusts received at the

hands of men, that mysterious wound through which the toxins of death seeped into his body, which was less than a pinprick yet so dangerous that Signor Bragadin and the finest doctors of the council fussed around his bed for weeks, torturing the poor patient with enemas and cuppings until one day he grew weary of dying and, asking for orange juice and hot broth, simply recovered—why was it that, in the delirium caused by this deadly female weapon, he kept seeing Francesca and calling on her? "Is it possible that I loved her? . . ." he mused with a sincere, almost childlike sense of wonder, and stared into the mirror above the fireplace. "Heaven knows, I might have! . . ." he thought, and looked about him with pious stupefaction.

But life proved more resilient, more resilient than even the memory of Francesca, and every day brought something miraculous to a man providing he was healthy and did not go in fear of anything. Who was Francesca, what was she, in the years when gold coins spilled from his fingers at gaming tables, into women's palms, into the pockets of fashionable tailors, into the fists of layabout acquaintances, into the hands of whoever happened to be about when he needed medicine to cure the terrible pox or to save him from a frightening, secret boredom? "I am a writer," he thought, "but I don't like being alone." He considered this peculiar phenomenon. This might be why life dealt him such a cruel hand in the enforced solitude of the penitentiary; perhaps the sapient and subtle masters of the Inquisition knew about his secret terror; perhaps they suspected that boredom and loneliness were as much a form of torture to him as the Spanish boot, the red-hot

pincers, or being broken on the wheel was to others? What was the point of life if one were removed from the busy commerce of the world? However one dreamed or imagined, thought and recalled, or meditated on sensations that life had burned up and reduced to ashes, it was no compensation for the loss of the most humble, most idiotic detail of a life experienced directly! Anything but solitude! he thought and shuddered. Better to be abject and poor, better to be mocked and despised yet able to slink over to the light and crouch there where lamps are burning and music is being played, where people crowd together and enjoy the greasy, foul-smelling yet cheeringly sweet, bestial sense of community that constitutes human life. Life was company for him, nothing more: he was always in company, always carelessly taking his wares to market because the market was where he wanted to be. He loved the racket, the proximity of other bodies, the sheer buccaneering adventure of it. Sometimes the bargaining was rough and crude, at other times sophisticated and sly, but most of the time it was like a game, a competition in which one took on all comers much as one did one's own destiny. The marketplace was the only place for him, for the writer in him. It was life itself. He scratched his ears and felt a cold thrill run down his spine.

And that was why his clever, superior torturers had punished him with solitude, a fate worse than death, he thought with disgust. Four hundred and eighty-eight days! And the memories! Each memory just one more condemned soul. And sometimes the image, that shining blue-and-white moment in the Tuscan garden: Francesca!

For hers was the only face, the one and only face he had not gazed at with the brazen curiosity he usually directed at women's faces. Her face persisted more obstinately and with greater force than reality itself, even in his underworld prison where living men groaned and wept. It was a banal enough occasion when their paths first crossed. The cardinal's kinsman was entertaining him in a coat with ragged elbows, in a room full of clouded mirrors and broken-legged Florentine furniture while the Apennine wind whistled through the cracked windows. As in all houses where not only plaster but discipline itself has begun to crumble, the servant had been confidential, pushy, chatty, and fat. The countess no longer wished to know about anything except occasional excursions to Florence in her threadbare coach, excursions that might take in a mass and a promenade down the corso where she might glimpse the ghost of her much-admired younger self. The count bred doves and, like the pitiful old man he was, regretfully and fearfully awaited the arrival of the messenger from Rome who on the third day of every month would bring him papal gold in a lilac-colored silk purse, this being the modest pension provided for him by the cardinal. The house was dense with dreams, spiders, and bats. Francesca's first words to him were, "What is it like in Rome? . . ." She stared at the stranger with wide eyes and an expression of terror on her face. For a long time after that she said nothing at all.

This love matured slowly, for like the best fruit it needed time, a change of seasons, the blessing of sunlight and the scent of rain, a series of dawns in which they

would walk through the dewy garden among bushes of flowering may, conversations where a single word might suddenly light up the landscape locked in her tender, cloistered heart, when it would be like looking into the past and seeing ruined castles, vanished festivals where traps with gilded wheels rolled down the paths of neat, properly tended gardens past people in brightly colored clothes with harsh, powerful, and wicked profiles. There was in Francesca something of the past. She was fifteen but it was as if she had stepped out of a different century, as if the Sun King had seen her one morning on the lawn at Versailles playing with a hoop covered in colored paper, and had summoned her to him. There was a kind of radiance in her eyes that suggested women of long ago, women who would risk their lives for love. But it was he that had risked his life, he the suitor, the soldier of misfortune, when his old, terrifyingly rich, and disturbingly aristocratic rival pierced his bare chest just above the heart. Francesca watched the duel from an upstairs window. She stood calmly, her unbound hair hanging in black tendrils over her soft youthful shoulders, wearing the nightgown that the duke of Parma had ordered for her from Lyon a few days earlier, for he had personally taken charge of his future fiancée's trousseau, stuffing heaps of lace, silk, and linen garments into individual boxes. Calmly she stood in the moonlight in a window on the second story, her arms folded across her chest, watching the two men, the old one and the younger one, who were prepared to shed their blood for her. But why? she might have wondered in that moment. Neither had received any favors, neither was tak-

ing anything away from the other, but there they were, leaping about in the silvery light, their bodies bare from the waist up, the moonlight flashing off the blades of their swords, the steel chiming like crystal goblets, and the duke's wig slightly askew in the heat of the contest so that Francesca was genuinely afraid that this noble encounter might result in His Excellency of Parma losing his artificial mane. Later she saw the younger man fall. She watched carefully to see if the loser would rise. She tightened the silk scarf above her breasts. She waited a little longer. Then she married the duke of Parma.

"He wants to see me!" muttered Giacomo. "What does he want of me?" He vaguely remembered a rumor he had once heard that His Excellency had inherited some lands near Bolzano and a house in the hills. He felt no anger thinking about the duke. The man had fought well. There was something lordly and absolute about the way he had whisked Francesca away from the house of dreams, spiders, and bats, and Giacomo could not help but admire his aristocratic hauteur, even now, when he could no longer recollect the precise color of Francesca's eyes. "The seduction was a failure," he noted and stared into the fire. "The seduction was a failure, but the failure may also have been my greatest triumph. Francesca never became my lover. It might have been stupid and oversensitive of me but I felt only pity for her. She was the first and the last of those for whom I felt such pity. It might have been a great mistake, maybe even an unforgivable mistake, there's no denying or forgetting that, but there was something exceptional about Francesca. It would have been good to

have lived with her, to drink our morning chocolate together in bed, to visit Paris and show her the king and the flea-circus in the market at St. Germain, to warm a bedpan for her when her stomach ached, to buy her skirts, stockings, jewels, and fashionable hats and to grow old with her as the light fades over cities, landscapes, adventures, and life itself. I think I felt that when she stood before me in the garden under the blue sky. That is why I fled from her!" The thought had only just occurred to him, but he took it calmly. He had to face the laws of his own life. "That's not the kind of thing I do," he said to himself, but he threw aside the pen, stood up, and felt the restless pounding of his heart.

Perhaps it pounded only because he was now reminded that the gossip had been right, that Francesca and the duke of Parma were living nearby. For all he knew they might have been his very neighbors or occupying some palazzo in the main square, since it was likely, after all, that in winter they would leave their country house and move into town. And now that he recalled his ridiculous failure and remembered the melancholy lingering sense of triumph that accompanied it, he couldn't help feeling that the morning that Francesca saw him lying wounded on the lawn of the garden of the Tuscan palazzo did not signify the end of the affair, that it hadn't actually settled anything. You cannot after all settle things with a duel and a little bloodshed. The duke, having wounded him, was courteous, generous, and noble in bearing, and had personally lifted him into the coach. Even half-conscious as he was, he was amazed at the old man's strength when he

picked him up! It was the duke in person who had driven the horses that bore the invalid to Florence, driving carefully, stopping at every crossroads, dabbing with a silk handkerchief at the blood issuing from him, and all this without saying anything, confident in the knowledge that actions spoke louder than words. It was a long ride by night from Pistoia to Florence. The journey was tiring and he was bleeding badly, the stars twinkling distantly above him with a peculiar brightness. He was half sitting, half lying in the back seat and, in his fevered condition, could see the sky in a faint and foggy fashion. All he could see in fact was the sky full of stars against the dark carpet of the firmament, and the slim straight figure of the duke keeping the horses on a short rein. "There," said the duke once they had arrived at the gates of Florence in the early dawn. "I shall take you to the best surgeon. You will have everything you need. Once you are well you will leave the region. Nor will you ever come back. Should you ever return," he added, a little more loudly, without moving, the reins still in his hand, "I will either kill you myself or have you killed, make no mistake about it." He spoke in an easy, friendly, perfectly natural manner. Then they drove into the city. The duke of Parma required no reply.

Theatrics

Finally he got down to it and wrote the letter to Signor Bragadin. It was a fine letter, the kind a writer would write, beginning "Father!" and ending "I kiss your feet," and, over six pages, he related everything in considerable detail: the escape, the journey, Bolzano, the duke of Parma, his plans, and he mentioned Mensch, too, the secretary, money changer, and usurer, to whom money might be sent. He needed more than usual, if possible, or, better still, a letter of credit he could take to Munich and Paris, because his journey would lead him far afield now and it would be a great adventure that would test him to the limit, so it was possible that this letter might be the last opportunity to say goodbye to his friend and father, for who knew when the hearts of the Venetian authorities would soften and forgive their faithless, fugitive son? The question was rhetorical, so he labored to blend bombastic phrases with hard practical content. What could I, the exiled fugitive, offer Venice, that proud, powerful, and ruthless city? he asked, and immediately answered: "I offer

my pen, my sword, my blood, and my life." Then, as if realizing that this did not amount to much, he referred to his understanding of places and human affairs and to his store of ready information on everything and everybody that the Holy Inquisition might wish to know. Being a true Venetian, he knew that the republic had no need either of his pen or of his sword, but that it could always use sharp ears, smooth tongues, and well-trained eyes; that what it required was clever, well-born agents who were capable of observing and betraying Venetians' secrets.

He had no desire to return to Venice for the time being. The insults he had borne still glowed fiercely in his heart and gave off a dense smoke that clouded every dear and charming memory that might gently have reminded him of the city. For the time being he was content to hate and to travel. Surely Signor Bragadin, that wise, good, noble, and pure soul, understood that. The senator, who to this very day believed that the half-conscious Venetian fiddle player he had laid gently in his boat in the lagoon one dawn had later saved his life with an extraordinary combination of spells and potions, snatching his rapidly cooling and decaying body from the grasp of doctors and even death; that noble member of the Venetian Council, Signor Bragadin, was perhaps the only friend he had in this world, most certainly the only friend in Venice. It was as impossible to explain this friendship as it was to explain human feelings generally. The truth was that from the very first he had cheated, gulled, and laughed at the noble gentleman. Signor Bragadin was selflessly good to him in a way no one else had been; so good, he suspected, that he

would never, in all his insecure rough patchwork of a life, meet his like again. His goodness did not fail or tire: it was silent and patient. Giacomo observed this human phenomenon for a long time, keeping a suspicious, uncomprehending eye on it; there are, after all, certain colors a color-blind man is unable to distinguish. He scrutinized goodness from under lowered lids, his eyes flicking to and fro, wondering when that goodness would exhaust itself and be revealed in its true colors, when it would be time to pay for all the fatherly tenderheartedness with which the old man overwhelmed him, when the doting old gentleman would remove his mask and show his true and terrifying visage. The time could not be delayed for long. But months and years flew by and Signor Bragadin's patience did not tire. He occasionally admonished him for the gold he squandered, refused the odd wild and impudent demand, warned him of the value of money, preached the joys of honest work, pressed on him the significance of honor in human conduct, but he did all this without any apparent ulterior motive, with a tact and patience born of good breeding, expecting no gratitude, in the knowledge that gratitude is ever the mother of revenge and hatred. For a long time Giacomo failed to understand Signor Bragadin. The old man with his silk waistcoat, aquiline nose, thin gray hair, smooth, ivory-colored brow, and calm and gentle blue eyes, might have stepped out of a Venetian altarpiece: a minor dignitary, a martyr-cum-witness in a toga, a pillar in the earthquake of life. "He must want something!" thought Giacomo impatiently. There were times he loathed this all-comprehending goodness and the

almost inhuman patience. "Who could possibly love me without desire or thought of advantage?" he wondered.

Such people were extremely rare, much rarer than friends or lovers, and this one inhabited a different world from his own, a place to which, he instinctively felt, he would never gain true access. He could only stand on the threshold and gape at Signor Bragadin's calm, patient, and upright world from there. "What does he know about me?" he puzzled every so often, at dawn, on his way back to the palazzo across the lagoon, passing the sleepy houses, his gondola swaying through the dreamy leaden water in the heartbreaking silence of first light, disturbed only by the splashing of oars which Venice alone offers by way of greeting to the nocturnal traveler as he emerges into dawn, moving down the Lethean current into the mysterious heart of the city. Signor Bragadin's household was still asleep and only the old man's window at his balcony showed the flickering of a night light. He crept up the marble stairs on tiptoe, into his room, the adopted child and prodigal son of this noble residence, opened the window to the Venetian sky, collapsed on the bed, and felt ashamed. He had spent the night at the card table as usual, living on promissory notes and on the credit of his patron, then made the rounds of the dives near the docks in the company of his drunken friends and the giggling, silk-frocked inhabitants of Venetian nightlife, and, now that it was dawn, had arrived here, in this quiet house where this lonely soul kept vigil for him and received him without reproach. . . . "Why?" he asked ever more impatiently of himself. "Why does he tolerate me? Why does he forgive

my misdemeanors? Why does he not hand me over to the authorities, knowing, as he does, all there is to be known about me, such terrible things that the merest whiff of them would be enough to set the eyes of the Venetian magistrates rolling and have me sent to the galleys? . . ." Signor Bragadin was the sort of man you don't read about in books, the sort who made sacrifices without expecting gratitude or reward, and unlikely as it was, he could look kindly and with almost superhuman forbearance on every variety of human passion and weakness. He was one of the powers behind Venice, but one that exercised his power with care, knowing that it was better to govern with intelligence and understanding than with terror.

He wrote the letter to Signor Bragadin, smiling as he did so. "Maybe it was precisely why he did forgive me," he thought and stared into the fluttering candle flame. "Maybe it was precisely because I lack everything that the tablets of the law, both human and divine, demand of me, except the laws of desire." He read over the lines with close attention, carefully struck out an epithet, and gave a sigh, his breathing shallow and light. The wisdom of Signor Bragadin was so noble, so mature, it was as if he had become a distant accomplice to all that was errant, lustful, and human in him. "He's like the Pope," he reflected with satisfaction. "And like Voltaire, and the cardinal. There are a few such people in Italy, in the domain of his Most Christian Majesty. They exist; not many of them, though. . . . For what I know by instinct, through my sense of destiny, in my bones, such people know with their hearts and minds; they know that the law under which I

was born is the law of wounds and scars, not the law of virtue. They realize that there is another law, itself a kind of virtue, one loathed by the guardians of morality but understood by the Almighty: the law of the truth to one's nature, one's fate, and one's desire." The articulation of this perception sent a shiver through him from the ends of his hair down to his toes; he trembled lightly as though feeling a sudden chill. "Perhaps that is why Signor Bragadin has stood by me," he thought. "He has sat in the council with the others, hearing secret reports, dispensing rewards and punishments, but deep in his soul he has realized that under the letter of the law there is another, unwritten, law, and that one must do justice to that, too." He felt delightfully moved. He watched the flickering candle flame with shining eyes. "You should send the money to Bolzano, care of Signor Mensch," he added with true feeling, in clear firm letters.

"I shouldn't have sold the emerald ring, though," he reflected as an afterthought. His fatherly friend had chosen the emerald ring for him from among his family treasures, lending it to him for one night only as he was setting out to some glittering occasion, on one of those dangerous but enchanting Venetian Carnival nights, dressed as an Eastern potentate. The emerald ring was a memento, an item favored by the late wife of his generous friend. "It was a mistake to pawn it that night while the banker was dealing. It couldn't be redeemed later. . . . I even passed the ticket on. Well, people make mistakes," he thought, generously excusing himself. And when he was offered it for redemption by a man introduced to the

noble gentleman after Giacomo himself had been incarcerated in the Leads, he redeemed it! Redeeming such slips of paper might have had an alienating effect on his father and friend, but he never mentioned it. "He paid the price and redeemed it," he thought, and shrugged his shoulders. He paid up without any song and dance, his one and only Signor Bragadin, he who sent him parcels at Christmas and for New Year's while he was imprisoned, his old heart full of impotent rage, for it was plain that he could not live without loving somebody, even in his old age, even if the object of love was unworthy of such noble feelings, even if that object had gambled away his most highly prized emerald ring and managed, with passable ingenuity, to forge his signature on documents commonly circulated in commercial transactions. None of this counted for much with him. There were times he almost envied Signor Bragadin this selfless impulse, whose true meaning he could comprehend only through the intellect, not through his emotions. For a while he suspected that the noble gentleman's love for him was of a perverted kind that he might not be able to admit, even to himself. But the old man's life was an open book, for never once, in all the time since he was born, had he left his birthplace: he had lived his life in the morass that was Venice, surviving it the way a pure and healthy plant continues to thrive in the fumes of a marsh. All the same, he could not bring himself to believe that a person could love somebody without an ulterior motive or a sensual impulse: the concept simply did not fit into his intellectual framework. For a long time he thought that there must be something wrong with him.

There were too many secret ties of affection and attraction, and he had encountered them all in the Venetian docks, where desires of East and West mingled. You could tell what was going on by the way people looked at each other. He hated this other, perverted love: for though he was happy to plumb the depths of depravity himself, those depths always yawned between the opposing shores of men and women; this was how it was, how it had always been, and how it would be in the future. Venice provided a market stall where castrati, Orientals, and other slaves to lust could be bought and sold like meat at a butcher's shop; and it was precisely here, in Venice, that he, of all people, never once strayed from the beaten path of desire. He trawled the sexual bazaar with a wrinkled nose and a contemptuous smile that spoke of mockery and disgust in equal proportions, observing the sick unfortunates who sought the favors of Eros on shores beyond the world of women. "Ah women," he reflected with a calm, dark rapture, as if pronouncing the words "Ah, life!"

But because he lived in Venice he regarded even Signor Bragadin with suspicion for a while. The Venetian market offered too much variety, too much clatter, too great a range of color. Yet not even the foul mouths of Venetian pimps could find a single aspersion to cast at the good name of Signor Bragadin. No one in St. Mark's Square could boast of having sold favors for cash or privilege to the honorable senator. The senator was as much a child of Venice as he was, but he was not a product of the filthy and narrow alleys of the theater: he was the scion of a prominent, aristocratic marriage bed, had always lived in

Venice, was married and widowed here, and even in great old age continued to mourn the early death of his beloved. He lived a lonely life, without relatives, with only a few wise, sophisticated friends and his old servants for company. His house, which was among the most private, most respected in the republic, would open its doors only to a handful of choice spirits, on the occasions when he organized supper for friends: to be invited to one of them was a mark of distinction that few could boast. And this fastidious, private nobleman, this pure fine being, had raised him from the shadows of his murky existence, fished him out of the muddy swirls of the lagoon, him of all people, at the very moment that every star in his firmament had more or less gone out. And why? Not because of secret lusts or passions but out of sheer compassion and a decency that never once tired.

True, not even Signor Bragadin could save him from a cell in the Leads; not from the cell, nor from exile, either, not even in his office as senator when it came to the powers of the Inquisition. The charge the Merciful Ones had brought against Giacomo was laughable. He knew that it had nothing to do with practicing the black arts, nor with orgies, nor debauchery, nor even so much with the diligence of the passion with which he turned the heads of Venetian ladies and maidens. "Not much turning required," he recalled. "People never understand this. It was never I who made the first move." Not that this was something he could discuss with the first secretary. People were apt to lie about such matters as they were about everything that really counted in life. So he was referred to

as the notorious "seducer," the officially branded "faith-less" lover, the model of inconstancy, the skirt lifter: he was a clear and present danger and labeled as such by the authorities . . . if only they knew! He was not in a position to tell them that it was not he that picked his victims but they that picked him; there was no way of putting into writing the fact that women's views on virtue and the way they actually went about things did not entirely accord with what was proclaimed in public offices or promoted from the pulpits of churches. There was no one he could tell: indeed, there were only rare moments of solitude when he himself could face the fact that when it came to the high combat of love it was he who was the exploited party, the abandoned one, the victim. . . . But this was not the point. The redeeming of pawn tickets, the episode with the emerald ring, the orgies, the days and nights of gambling, the broken promises, the strutting posture, the obstinate bearing: none of these were genuine charges. This was simply what life was like in Venice. . . . What they couldn't forgive, the reason they threw him into jail where even the mighty Signor Bragadin could not save him, was that the danger and corruption he represented for them referred to something else, something other than any crime or indiscretion he might have committed: it referred to his entire manner of being, his soul, the face he presented to the world. "That is what they couldn't for-give," he realized, and shrugged. For what the world demands is hierarchy and obedience, the painful act of self-surrender, the unconditional acceptance of mortal and divine order. Deep inside him burned the threatening

flame of resistance to such things, and that was unforgivable.

There was nothing anyone could do about this: even Signor Bragadin was helpless to change it. At Christmas he had sent a fur-lined coat, a purse full of gold, and something to read in prison. That was all he could practically do. There is no saving a man from the world; one day it will break in on him and force him to his knees. But that day, his personal day of judgment, had not yet arrived. He had escaped from prison, escaped from them, and now he had to fight like a soldier, to choose his weapons and prepare for combat. So he wrote the letter, got dressed, and set out to seek appropriate ammunition in Bolzano.

He thought he would make a quick, anonymous survey of the town, so he turned up the collar of his coat and walked as fast as he could. Night was already drawing in, flakes of snow drifted across the street. No one recognized him. He fairly swept along, examining things intensely as he went, surveying the terrain. There was nothing particularly attractive to tempt him. It was as if the place were living not only in the shadow of the mountains but of its own prejudices: the houses were pretty enough but there was a suspicious look in people's eyes. He found this uncomfortable. Like all the great artist-raconteurs, he was only truly relaxed in the company of receptive kindred spirits. "Not much of a place," he thought with fierce antipathy, crossing the grand central square and entering the back streets. Everything was precisely halfway between high and low: it was a mode of being out of his normal range. The town existed precisely in the no-man's-land

between all he loved and all he avoided in life. It was sober and well ordered, which is to say it frightened him. He hurried along the street with his handkerchief to his mouth because he feared the strange air might give him a sore throat and he pulled his hat down over his brow because he feared the gaze of the local people, though his own half-closed eyes flickered into life every time he crossed glances with a passing man or woman. He kept casting anxious looks at doorways and peering through lit windows trying to guess which of these gabled houses might be the residence of the duke of Parma. "It's a nice town," he thought bitterly when he had done his tour. "A clean town. A foreign place, too foreign." Foreign to him, was what he meant: there was no tempting familiar complicity in its air, no joie de vivre, no passion, no pomp, none of the mysterious radiance that emanates from the desire for pleasure, a radiance he could detect as readily in cities as in people. It was a solemn, virtuous town, he thought, and felt the goose pimples rising on his flesh.

He began counting the days. According to his calculations, it would be five days before he could expect an answer from Signor Bragadin. Nevertheless he entered the vaulted shops and set about shopping. He needed a great many things, indeed he did, if he meant to establish himself and stand on his own two feet again. "I must rise from my ashes like the phoenix," he thought, mockingly adopting a literary turn of phrase, and "What do phoenixes need?" he asked himself in the next breath. He stopped on a street corner below an oil lamp whose low, flickering flame was being snuffed out by the north wind. Throwing

his coat over one shoulder, half-hiding his face with it, he gazed at passersby, his eyes flickering and sputtering with light, like the windblown flame of the oil lamp. More than anything he needed some lace-embroidered shirts, say a dozen, some white Parisian stockings, lace cuffs, two frock coats, one green with gold edging and one lilac with gray epaulettes; he needed some lacquered shoes with silver buckles, crocheted gloves for evening wear, and a thin pair of kid gloves for the day; one heavy winter coat with fur collar, a white silk Venetian mask, lorgnettes—without which he felt defenseless—a three-cornered hat, and a silver-handled cane. He totted them up silently. He had to have all this by the next night. Without the right clothes, without appropriate outfits and accessories, he felt naked, positively abject. It was imperative that he be dressed as only he knew how. Seeing a lottery shop opposite he quickly stepped inside and invested in three numbers that corresponded to his birthdate, the day of his imprisonment, and the day of his escape. He also bought two sets of playing cards.

Carefully concealing the cards in his pockets, he sought out Signor Mensch. He found him behind the church, in a single-story house, in a dark room that overlooked the courtyard, surrounded with caskets and balances. At first glance it seemed that despite the literal meaning of his name, there was little that was human about him. A short, scrawny creature, he was sitting in a dressing gown at a long narrow table, the fingernails of his delicate, yellow hands grown sharp and curling, so that he appeared to grasp things the way a bird of prey seizes its

quarry, his lank gray locks hanging over his brow, and his small, bright, intelligent eyes, eyes that glowed from beneath deep, wrinkled lids, staring with burning curiosity at the stranger. He greeted Giacomo in his dirty kaftan, lisping and bowing stiffly without rising from his chair, mixing French, Italian, and German words in his speech but mumbling all the while, as if not quite taking him seriously but thinking of something else, not really listening to his guest. "Ah!" he said, once the visitor had given his name, and raised his eyebrows until they met the dirty locks above them. He blinked rapidly, like a monkey hunting for fleas. "Have these old ears heard correctly? Is an invalid to trust these poor ears of his?" He spoke of himself in the third person, with a kind of tender intimacy, as if he were his own nephew. "Mensch is a very old man," he lisped ingratiatingly. "No one visits him nowadays, old and poor as he is," he mumbled. "But here is a stranger come to call," he concluded and fell silent.

"As a matter of fact you are the first person I have called on," the stranger replied courteously.

They spoke quietly about money, the way lovers speak of their feelings. There was no preamble: they got straight to the point, passionate, full of curiosity, like two professionals meeting each other at a party, like guests who isolate themselves in some alcove so they may discuss the marvelous secrets of their common trade while the hostess is busy playing the piano or someone is reciting verses, to argue a point about masonry or the physiology of the emu. Money was the subject they talked about, their speech plain but littered with technical terms, and there

was no need for a glossary since both were entirely at home in the matter. "Security," said Mensch, and the word fizzed in his mouth like an oath. "Credit," declared the other with some heat, convincing and natural, certain that nothing could be simpler, as if the sound of the word and its firm enunciation were sure to touch the old man's heart. They discussed the two concepts readily and at some length. If anyone had been watching them from a distance he might have thought he was witnessing an abstruse argument between two scholars. Both of them were articulating deeply held beliefs, beliefs that corresponded to the essential inner truths and realities of their beings, beliefs so fervently adhered to they would have staked their lives on them. Because what "security" represented for the one represented "credit" for the other, and not just at this precise moment, at the specific dusk of this one evening, but at other times, too, in every circumstance of life. That which one could conceive of only in terms of security and guarantee, the other demanded in terms of credit from the world, his demand consistent and passionate beyond the material business of the present, itself an item of faith. One could experience the world only insofar as he could accept it as security, the other wanted all life on credit: happiness, beauty, youth, but above all, money, possession of which was the essential condition of life. It was ideas, not amounts, that they were discussing.

Signor Bragadin's name clearly impressed the moneylender. "A most honorable gentleman," he said, blinking even more rapidly than before. "A sound name. Worth its

weight in gold!" There was a certain suspicion in his voice, for he was sure that the stranger was wanting to cheat him, to sell him something of dubious value, something that didn't exist, or even that, ultimately, he wanted to sell Signor Bragadin's own person. "A ring, perhaps!" he ventured, and raised his little finger with its long, black fingernail, crooking it to indicate that almost anything was better, more valuable, more apt for commercial purposes than a human being. "A little ring," he wheedled in a singing, pleading voice, like a child asking for marzipan. "A little ring, with a precious stone," he added grinning, and winked, rubbing the thumb and forefinger of his right hand together to demonstrate what a pretty, fascinating object a little ring could be, especially one with a precious stone, a ring on which one could offer some security. His myopic eyes filled with tiny teardrops thinking of it, but he kept a careful watch on his visitor, busily blinking all the time, anxious, yet striving to give an impression of cheerfulness, like a duelist who, however unwillingly, recognizes that the man he has taken on is a genuine adversary, worthy of his attentions. He would like to have been over the contest but his fingers and toes were tingling with excitement: the feeling was hot and arousing, it resembled desire. It was the excitement of knowing that the moment had arrived, that rare moment when he found himself pitched against a real opponent, a fit adversary who knew the secret ceremonies and strategies of conduct, who was, in effect, part of the meaning of his own life, the kind of opponent for whom he had always most earnestly

yearned. He drew the sleeves of his kaftan further up his skeletal arms as if to say: "So now it is the two of us! Let battle commence!" They eyed each other in admiration.

Mensch knew that he would eventually give the man money because there was no alternative, and the visitor knew he would eventually receive money even in the unlikely event that Signor Bragadin failed to send him the gold he had pleaded for in such convincing literary manner. "Mensch will give me money," he had thought even in the Leads when he was planning the details of his escape, when the name itself had been enough to rouse his imagination, so that he could almost see him, as in a vision; and now that he stood face to face with the usurer he noted with satisfaction that the vision was pretty close to the truth, that reality did not disappoint him. It was this same mysterious instinct that had whispered to him that Mensch, whose name he had heard but once from a Dutch trader in raw cloth, would be a proper adversary and an appropriate business partner, that their fates were linked, and that, one day, he would have to appear before him, and that however Mensch might snigger and squeal, he would do him no real harm. Here's his address, people said, there you are, take it down; but what value did an address have? What did it mean? . . . A great deal, as he well knew: an address was practically a person, an event, an action, you only had to breathe on it, warm it, bring it to life with the breath of imagination and desire, and the address would tentatively assume independent existence, become a reality, and finally take a form that, however it ground its teeth, would eventually hand over the money.

He knew of such addresses in Lyon, in Paris, in Vienna, and in Manchester, too. Such addresses were passed on by oral tradition, like the legends that animate a nation's life: in Naples, for instance, there lived a moneylender to whom all you had to say was, "May Charon come knocking for you!" and he'd immediately begin to weep and agree to the deal. So he regarded Mensch calmly, marveling only that reality and fantasy could so completely agree: he was so calm that the calm was verging on tenderness. And Mensch looked at him in the same way, blinking and blinking in the frightening yet exciting consciousness that fate had brought this man to him.

So Mensch finally gave him some money—not a lot, but just enough to cut a proper figure in Bolzano, where, Giacomo felt, his audience must be waiting impatiently for him to appear. Mensch gave him thirty ducats, which he counted out in gold at the lacquered table, his hands trembling with astonishment, without ring or forfeit, as advance against nothing more than a piece of paper assuring him of the credit of Signor Bragadin, a gentleman who might have lived on the moon as far as he was concerned, or at least a considerable distance off, as did all money that did not actually lie on the table in front of him. When he had wrapped the gold in parchment and handed it over he rose from the table, and bowing with the religious reverence of a high priest, ushered his guest to the door. He watched him for some time from the threshold until his customer disappeared in the fog.

The man to whom he had so trustingly advanced the money hastened down the twilit street while Mensch con-

tinued bowing and mumbling Italian, German, and French words under his breath. By now he was racing, practically running toward the lights of the main square. He arrived near the church just in time to see a carriage with two lackeys in the backseat holding torches. Behind the glass he caught sight of a pale face he recognized.

"Francesca!" he cried.

Suddenly it began to snow. He stood alone in the square, under the snow, as the carriage drove by him. He was stricken with the pain one always feels when desire becomes reality. Then he returned to The Stag, his hands clasped behind him, his head bowed, his body weighed down by his thoughts. He felt lonelier here and now than he had in the underworld, under the Leads.

The Consultation

That evening he sat in the restaurant of The Stag drinking mulled wine, waiting for the card party to arrive. They appeared cautiously: the chemist whom Balbi brought along, the dean who had visited Naples, a veteran actor, and an army officer who had deserted the day before at Bologna. They played for low stakes, going through the motions, getting to know one another. The chemist was caught cheating and was asked to leave. The soldier pursued the fat, foolish-looking man to the door and threw him out into the street where the snow was still falling. By midnight Giacomo was bored. He and Balbi went upstairs to his room where they lit candles and, with elbows propped on the table, set about marking the pack of cards he had bought that afternoon and which the engraver and printer had decorated with the legend STAMPATORI DE NAIBI immediately below an image of Death and The Hanged Man. The friar was surprisingly skilled at the work: they labored in silence, waxing the corners of

the most important cards and using their nails to carve identifying symbols into the wax.

"Are you not worried this might get us into trouble?" asked the friar in passing, absorbed in his task.

"No," he replied, holding an ace of diamonds up to the light and examining it through half-closed eyes before winking and painstakingly marking it. "What is there to be worried about? A gentleman is never worried."

"A gentleman?" queried Balbi, sticking his tongue through his pursed lips, as he tended to do when expressing astonishment. "And which gentleman might that be?"

"I," he said and touched the marked card gently with his fingertip. "Who else could I mean?" he stiffly remarked. "There are only two of us in the room, and it is certainly not you."

"Do gentlemen cheat?" asked the friar and yawned.

"Of course," he replied, throwing the cards away and stretching his limbs so his bones cracked. "It is very difficult to win otherwise. It is the nature of cards to be fickle. There are very few people who can win without the aid of some device. In any case," he went on in a matter-of-fact voice, "everyone cheats. At Versailles the most respectable people cheat: even generals and priests."

"Does the king cheat too?" asked Balbi, somewhat awestruck.

"No," he answered solemnly. "He simply gets cross when he loses."

They considered the nature of the king's anger. Soon enough Giacomo was alone, and eventually he, too, sighed, yawned, and went to bed. For three days he con-

tinued in this deeply solitary fashion with only Balbi, Giuseppe, and little Teresa for company. He played faro with messenger boys and oil salesmen in the bar of The Stag, frequently winning, thanks to the waxed cards which certainly helped, though he occasionally lost because everyone else cheated at the time, especially in the taverns of London, Rome, Vienna, and Paris, where professional itinerant gamblers offered *banque ouverte* to all and sundry. He remembered one occasion when he had fought a Greek whose remarkable dexterity enabled him to produce ace after ace from his sleeve, but he felt no anger at the time, it was only to keep in practice.

He didn't see Francesca nor did he make any special effort to look for her just yet.

It was as if life itself were slumbering in thin air below mountain peaks.

Then there came three days of raging winds when the windows of The Stag were plastered over in snow. The sky was thick with gray woolly clouds as dirty as the cotton in Mensch's ears. The suits, the shirts, the coats, the shoes, the white silk Venetian mask, the walking stick, and the lorgnette were delivered, and he had a coat for Balbi too, if only for the sake of cleanliness and respectability, because the friar was running round town in a robe that might have been worn by a corpse freshly cut down at a public hanging. But most of the time he just sat in his room alone in front of the fire, in the apathetic, melancholy frame of mind that, despite a lively curiosity and an acquaintance with music, action, lights, and the thrill of the chase, he, of all people, had been ever more frequently

afflicted by these last few years. It was as if everything he had planned and dreamed about in jail—life, pleasure, and entertainment—now that he was back in the world and had only to stretch out his hand to grab it, had lost something of its attraction. He was seriously considering returning to Rome, going down on his knees to his generous friend, the cardinal, and asking for forgiveness: he would beg to join the priesthood or plead for a position as a librarian in the papal offices. He thought of towns where nothing awaited him but inns, cold beds, women's arms from which he would sleepily have to disentangle himself, the corridors of theaters where he'd hang about and tell lies, and salons and bars where his carefully prepared cards might provide him with a modest haul of gold: he thought of all this and yawned. He was acquainted with this mood of his and was afraid of it. "It'll end in flight and a bloody nose," he thought and drew together the nightgown covering his chest because he was shivering. This condition had begun in childhood and it was accompanied by a fear and disgust that, without warning, would suddenly come over him and end in nosebleeds that only Nonna, his strong, virtuous grandmother, could cure with herbs and lint. He thought of Nonna a lot these days, never of his mother or his siblings, but of this strong woman who had brought up three generations in Venice and had been particularly fond of Giacomo; she kept appearing in his sad and somewhat disturbing dreams. Nonna used to place an icy piece of lint on his neck and cook him beetroots because she believed that beetroots were effective against all sorts of bleeding, and eventually both the bleeding and

the sadness would pass away. "Nonna!" he thought now, with an intense yearning that was keener than anything he had felt for other women.

Francesca lived nearby: by now he knew which house, knew the Swiss guard with his silver-tipped stick and bearskin cloak, had seen the lackeys, the hunters, and the postilions who escorted the duke of Parma on his journeys into town, and, in the evening, he would walk past the palazzo whose upper windows glimmered overhead—the duke enjoyed a busy social life, receiving guests, giving parties—and in the light that streamed from the window across the street he would imagine the magnificence of the reception halls. Balbi, who had talked to the servants, told him that every evening they replenished the golden branches of the chandeliers with three dozen candles, candles of the finest sort, made of goat fat, which the chandlers of Salzburg provided specially for the duke. "Francesca lives in the light," he acknowledged with a shrug of his shoulder, but he didn't talk about her to Balbi. Yes, Francesca lived in the light, in a palace, attended by lackeys, and on one or two evenings he could even hear the stamping and neighing of the bishop's horses as he drew up at the coach entrance and imagined the horses glittering in silver and dressed with a variety of official insignia. For the duke of Parma kept a busy house in the winter months, as befitted his rank, and perhaps the dignity of his young wife, too. And yet there would have been nothing easier than to enter the house and pay his respects to Francesca; the duke would no longer complain of his attentions, and had, in any case, intimated that he wanted

to see him—or that, at least, was what Giuseppe had said. It was true that he mentioned it only once, on his very first visit and not since then, for he came every day to run his delicate pink fingers along Giacomo's jowls, to rub his temples and reset his curls, and, every morning, he would recount in considerable detail the events of the previous night: the manner of the reception, the nature of the party games, the gaiety of the dancing at midnight, and the ins and outs of the card sessions conducted into the early hours of dawn. Giacomo noted them all. Every evening there was dancing, cards, reciting of verses, and playing of party games; every evening there was feasting and drinking at the duke of Parma's. "Does the duke not get tired?" he occasionally asked in his most arch manner. "What I mean is, does he not tire of so many parties, every night? He stays up late each time; don't you think this might be tiring for a man of his age? . . ." Giuseppe shrugged but refused to say any more.

The barber had mentioned the invitation only once, on the first day, and having mentioned it once remained eloquently silent on the subject, skirting the guest's ingenuous questions. "Is the duke tired? . . ." he echoed and, lisping fastidiously, chose his words with care. "He would have every reason to be tired, I suppose. His Excellency always rises early and goes to hunt at dawn, however late he retired the previous night, then he takes his breakfast in his wife's bedroom, where they receive guests at the morning levee. Is the duke tired?" he repeated the question and shrugged. The tiredness of the privileged was quite different from the exhaustion of the poor. The wellborn eat a lot

of meat and that is what makes them tired. He, Giuseppe, would only say that, as far as he personally was concerned, he was never tired of dancing, flirtation, or of cards, but thinking, fine manners, and the general standards of behavior required by high society had often exhausted him. "The duke is given to thinking!" he whispered confidentially. And he winked and fluttered his eyelashes as if he were betraying some secret passion of the duke's, a major vice or a tendency to a peculiar form of depravity; he winked as if to suggest that he could say more if he chose, but would not, because he was a careful man and knew the ways of the world. The stranger heard the news and bowed. "Given to thinking, eh!" he asked in a low voice indicating intimacy. They understood each other perfectly. The language they spoke was their mother tongue in the full meaning of the word, the language of people who, without knowing it, share certain tastes, certain traits of character: it was an underworld language that the inhabitants of a superior world can never quite understand. However, Giuseppe made no further mention of the duke's invitation to the visitor: it was something he passed on, that first day as a matter of minor courtesy, then kept his peace, a peace that, in its own way, said as much as his loquaciousness.

"Is the duchess beautiful?" asked the visitor one day, in a disinterested, airy sort of way, as if the question were of no importance. The barber composed himself to answer. He put the tongs, the scissors, and the comb down on the mantelpiece, raised his epicene, long-fingered hand like a priest bestowing a blessing during mass, cleared his throat,

then quietly embarked on a singsong, pleasantly lilting speech. "The duchess has dark eyes. On the left side of her face, near her downy pitted jaw, there is a tiny little wart which the chemist once treated with vitriol, but it has grown back again. The duchess artfully covers up this wart." He recited all this, and a wealth of other minor detail, as though he were a priest delivering a sermon or an apprentice painter discussing the graces and shortcomings of a masterpiece. The coolness of his judgment signified an appreciation far surpassing mere enthusiasm. For Giuseppe was every day in the presence of the duchess, before the lesser and the greater levee, when the maids were depilating Francesca's shins with red-hot walnut shells, polishing her toenails with syrup, smearing her splendid body with oils, and scenting her hair with the steam of ambergris before combing it. "The duchess is beautiful!" he sternly declared, the solemn expression ludicrous on a face as childish and effeminate as his, a face so chubby it was not quite human, the kind of face some highly respectable artist might have painted on the walls of an aristocratic woman's bedchamber at Versailles as the face of a shepherd in a naïve, sentimental, wholly unselfconscious, and charmingly corrupt pastoral. The visitor waited while the long, delicate fingers finished with his face and hair and, having learned that the duke was given to thinking and that the duchess was beautiful despite the fact that a tiny wart had grown on her face again, he listened to various other interesting items of news. He remained silent while the other talked. They might have shared a common language but now they were speaking of

different things. The fact remained that the duke had not repeated his desire to see the visitor.

So he stayed in town, that foreign, somewhat alien town, even after Signor Bragadin had sent the requested gold, along with a wise and virtuous letter full of noble, practical advice that was perfectly impossible to follow. Mensch was delighted that Signor Bragadin had obliged, and enthusiastically counted out the money with trembling, assured fingers, using a blend of German, French, and Italian expressions, separating interest and capital, with much mention of the terms "credit" and "security." Signor Bragadin had in fact sent more money than his adopted son had asked for, not a lot more, just a little extra to show that an official loan was being topped up by the affections of the heart. "A noble heart," thought the moved fugitive, and Mensch nodded: "A sound name! Fine gold!" As to Signor Bragadin's letter, it contained all that a lonely, aged man could or might say while exploring such unconventional feelings, for all feeling is a form of exploration, and Signor Bragadin knew that this relationship would do nothing to enhance his whiter-than-white reputation and spotless respectability. No gossip or suspicion dared attach itself to the senator's name but, when it came down to it, how far would Venice understand the deep morality underlying his affection? An ordinary Venetian would wonder whether this feeling, even in such irreproachable form, were all it seemed to be, and would not understand why a nobleman, a senator of Venice no less, should squander the affections of his old and none too healthy heart on a notorious playboy. "Why should

he?" asked the Venetian public, and the more vulgar of them put their hands to their mouth, gave a wink, and whispered, "What's in it for him?" But Signor Bragadin's knowledge was deeper than theirs: he knew humanity's most painful obligation is not to be ashamed of true feeling even when it is wasted on unworthy subjects. And so he sent money, more than his fugitive friend had requested, and wrote his long, wise letter. *"You have made a new start in life, dear son,"* he wrote in firm, angular characters, *"and you will not be returning to your birthplace for some time. Think of your home with affection."* He wrote a great deal on the subject of his homeland, a page and a half. He advised Giacomo to forgive his birthplace because, in some mysterious way, one's birthplace was always right. And a fugitive, more than anyone, especially he, who was now to be swept to the four corners of the world, should continually reflect on the fact that his birthplace remained his birthplace in perpetuity, even when it was in error. He wrote gracefully, with the certainty that only very old people with highly refined feelings can write, people who are fully aware of the meaning of every word they use, who know that it is impossible to escape our memories and that it is pointless hoping that we might pass our experiences on to others; who realize that we live alone, make mistakes alone, and die alone, and that whatever advice or wisdom we get from others is of little use. He wrote about his birthplace as he might of a relative who was part tyrant and part fairy godmother, stressing that, whatever the strains, we should never break off relations with our family. Then he wrote about money and,

much more briefly and practically, about a friend in Munich who was prepared to help a traveler at certain times, up to certain amounts; he wrote of the Inquisition which was greater than the great ones of the world, or as he put it, how the *"powers of Church and State were fully united in the hands of the leaders of this incomparable institution."* But he had to write this, for as the addressee recognized, a sentence to this effect could not be omitted from any Venetian letter, for even the letters of Signor Bragadin were open to the inspection of the *messer grande.* Then he gave his blessing for the journey, and for life itself, which he said was an adventure. Giacomo read the letter twice then tore it up and threw it on the fire. He took Mensch's gold pieces and could have set out for Munich or elsewhere immediately. But he didn't. It was his fifth day in Bolzano and he had got to know everyone, including the captain of police, who called on him to ask most courteously how long he intended remaining in town. He avoided answering and cursed the place after the official left. He paid off debts and gambled away the rest in the bar of The Stag and in the private apartments of the chemist whom they had earlier ejected from The Stag but who was now hosting sessions of faro at home. Without money, and with the address of Signor Bragadin's acquaintance in Munich in his pocket, he had every reason for moving on. But now that he had paid the innkeeper and the shops, had bought a present for Teresa, and offered a handsome tip to Giuseppe; now that the gold had allowed him a few moments of Venetian brilliance, he could afford to stay. He enjoyed credit, not only with Mensch, whom

he had sought out again in the last few days, not just with the shops who had been paid off once, but with a more problematic company, the gamblers. An English gentleman—who, when he wasn't gambling, was studying the geology of the surrounding mountains—accepted his IOU address in Paris. Given such losses and gains achieved by dint of experience and light fingers, having paid off old debts and piled up new ones, the natural ties of his new situation, based on interest and a general relaxation in his circumstances, slowly established themselves. Everyone was happy to extend credit to the stranger now because they knew him, because they recognized that the odds on him winning or losing were impossible to calculate: they accepted him because the town quickly got used to him and tolerated his presence behind its walls the way any man tolerates a degree of danger.

And is that why he stayed? No, it was because of Francesca, of course, and because the duke had said he'd like to see him. He waited for the call the way a peasant youth waits at the bar of his native village when someone challenges him. He stands there with his hands on his hips, as if to say: "Here I am, come and get me!" Giacomo struck the same attitude: he waited silently. What did he want of Francesca? Her very name was disturbing, full of the regret of unfinished business. He could of course have decamped, penniless, to Munich, where the elector of Saxony had just arrived and the weeks ahead promised splendor and amusement with pageantry, first-rate theater, Europe's most brilliant gamblers, and mounds of snow. He could have left at any time, not sneaking off at night or

when it was foggy, but in broad daylight, in a fancy carriage, his head held high, because he had paid his debts to innkeeper and shopkeeper at least once and because Mensch was still sufficiently under the spell of Signor Bragadin's credit to service him. But instead of going, he stayed because he was waiting for a message from the duke. He knew the message would come eventually, that the palazzo guarded by the solemn Swiss guard with his silver-tipped staff would send for him. He understood that the lack of communication was itself part of a secret dialogue, that there was a purpose in his arrival in Bolzano, that he had things to do. So every day had a meaning: he was waiting for something to happen. Because to live is, in some respects, to wait.

One afternoon, when the main square was full of blue-gray shadows and the wind was hooting and screeching like an owl through the flues of the fireplaces in The Stag, he was sitting idly in the fireside chair, his skin covered in goose pimples, leafing through a volume of Boethius in his lap, when the door opened and Balbi stumbled in, waving his arms.

"They're here! . . ." he declared triumphantly.

Giacomo turned pale. He leaped from his chair, smoothed his rice-powdered hair with all ten fingers, and whispered hoarsely, his voice a faint squeak.

"Get me my lilac coat!"

"Don't bother," said Balbi, tottering closer. "You can greet this lot in shirtsleeves if you like. Only don't undersell yourself!" And when he saw the look of fear and incomprehension on his fellow fugitive's face, he stopped,

leaned back against the wall, and clasped his hands across his belly. His speech was a little slurred and he giggled with embarrassment, his full stomach shaking. He was enjoying the secret delight of knowing that he was the begetter and abetter of a wonderfully clever piece of mischief.

"There are only three of them this time," he said, "but all three are rich. One of them, the baker, is quite old; he is first in line. He is old and deaf, so you must be careful to address his more intimate problems in sign language or the whole of Bolzano will hear of his shame. He will be followed by one Petruccio, a captain who considers himself a gallant. He is not quite the gallant now. He is waiting quietly with his arms folded, leaning on the banisters and gazing into the deep. He looks so miserable that he might be contemplating murder or suicide. He's a stupid man: easy game. The third client, the priest's secretary, arrived precisely at the hour I told him to. He's young and looks as if he might burst into tears. And there'll be more of them coming. Allow me to inform you, dear master, that your reputation both frightens and attracts people. Ever since you arrived they have been bombarding me with questions in private, in bars, in doorways, and later in shops and warehouses, but also in the street, anywhere they could confidentially take me aside, press a few pieces of silver into my palm, and invite me for a drink or a roast goose. They are begging to be introduced to you. Whether your name attracts or frightens them it seems they can't forget it."

"What do they want?" he asked mournfully.

"Advice!" said Balbi. He put two fingers to his lips then raised them into the air, rolling his eyes, his belly shaking with silent laughter.

"I see," said Giacomo and gave a sour smile.

"Now be careful," Balbi warned him. "Mind you don't set too low a price on your services. How long do you want to stay here? A day? A week? I'll make sure you have visitors and clients every afternoon: I'll have them lining up on the stairs as they do for famous doctors when someone's dying or coming down with the plague. But remember not to set your price too low: demand at least two gold pieces for each item of advice, and if it's potions they want, ask for even more. I learned a lot in Venice, you know. During the period of my retreat"—this was how Balbi delicately referred to his time in prison—"I came to the conclusion that a thought can be as sharp as a file and worth its weight in gold. You are a clever man, Giacomo. There are purses out there overflowing with gold. Let them weigh your wisdom by the pound. What do you say? . . . Shall I send in the baker?"

And so they began to arrive in patient, sheeplike manner, Balbi herding them in each afternoon, from noon to dusk. His new profession amused Giacomo. He had never played this game before. People came to him with wasted bodies and troubled souls and stood in a line at his door exactly as Balbi had said they would, much as they did outside surgeons' apartments in big cities, but instead of arms in slings and broken ankles they brought broken hearts and wounded self-respect for treatment. What did they want? Miracles. Everywhere people wanted miracles:

they wanted love that would cater to their vanities, power without effort, self-sacrifice that wouldn't cost more than a gold piece or two, tenderness and understanding providing they wouldn't have to work too hard to earn them. . . . People wanted love, and wanted it free, without obligations, if possible. They stood in line at his door, in the corridor of The Stag, the crippled and the humiliated, the weak and the cowardly, those who thirsted for revenge and those who wanted to learn forgiveness. The range of their desires was diverting enough. And there was an art to the handling of the private consultation that offered a glimpse into the mysteries of love, a mystery he himself had never had to learn. Venetians were born knowing the ways of love, they knew them down to their fingertips and their traditional wisdom coursed like an electric current through his every nerve. The art he inherited was ancient too, and once he got over his initial surprise and recognized the ailments the sick brought to him, once he had learned to explore the hidden places and the secret scars, he gave himself willingly and passionately to the project of quackery. His fame soon spread and it quickly became known that he was holding surgeries every afternoon until dusk. Balbi dealt efficiently with the business side of things and kept a strict eye on the waiting patients.

Everyone came to see him, not only from the town but from outlying districts, too. The first to arrive was the deaf baker, who in his seventieth year had become a victim of passion. He hobbled in, a bent figure leaning on his stick, his stomach so fat it hung over his knees, and his brown felt cloak hardly covered it. "Let me tell you what hap-

pened," the baker began, panting, and stopped still in the middle of the room to draw a ring in the air with his short rough stick. Then he went on to describe what had happened, as they all did eventually, though only after an initial period of stubborn silence or a sulky shrug of the shoulders. Then they blushed and the first few words came stumbling out, a stuttering confession or two, after which their entire manner changed: they no longer felt ashamed and told him everything. The baker was angry and spoke very loudly the way a deaf man does when he is furious and full of suspicion; he had to be calmed with tactful, fluttering gestures. In a voice that was as deep as it was loud, he informed Giacomo that he could not cope with Lucia, and the only question was whether he should hand her over to the Inquisition or strangle her with his own bare hands then cremate her in his large oven where the lads would bake their long, crumbly loaves each morning. It was a straightforward choice, and it was in such simple terms that Grilli the baker, the seventy-year-old president of the master bakers' guild, saw matters relating to Lucia. The person to whom these questions were addressed, whose advice and professional opinion was being sought, sat and listened. He stroked his chin with two fingers, as scientists were supposed to do, crossed his arms, and from under knitted brows darted sharp, quizzical glances at the angry old man, hearing his complaints with some amazement. "It is a tricky problem!" he exclaimed in a loud stage whisper so that the baker should hear him. "Damned tricky!" Suddenly he grabbed the old man by the arm, dragged the scared, resisting body to the window, took the

warty wrinkled face in the palms of his hands, turned it to the light, and spent a long time peering into his rheumy eyes. The consultation took some time. The baker wept. His weeping and snuffling was a little theatrical, not altogether sincere, perhaps, but it was involuntary, if only because he didn't know what else to do. Some terrible intimate disaster had occurred and he could not reconcile himself to the disgrace that would now follow him to the grave. "I have a recommendation," the stranger ventured after careful consideration. "You should buy her rings. I saw a few over at Mensch's, quite attractive ones, with sapphires and rubies." The baker grunted. He had already bought rings and a gold chain and a little cross with diamonds and a silver figurine of the saint of Padua, with enamel inlay. But none of it helped. "Buy her enough silk for three skirts," he advised. "It will be Carnival soon." But the baker waved the advice away and wiped a few tears from his face. The cupboards at home were full of silk, cotton, felt, and brocade. They thought a while in silence.

"Send her to me," said Giacomo generously, with a new firmness.

The baker hummed and hawed, then slowly began to back away towards the door.

"That will be two gold pieces," said the stranger, accepting the fee, flinging the finely minted coins on his desk, and courteously escorting his guest out. "Send her tomorrow morning!" he added as an afterthought, as if doing him a considerable favor. "After mass. I shall have more time then. I'll speak to her. Please don't kill her just yet." He opened the door and waited while the old man,

careworn and somewhat terrified by both the advice and his own helplessness, crossed the threshold. "Next please!" he cried to the dark staircase and pretended not to see the shadows huddled in the half-light. "Ah yes, the captain! This way, my valiant fellow!" he warbled cheerily, ushering the grim figure through the door.

And so he conducted his surgery. The varieties of sickness did not surprise him; he knew them and understood that it was the same old disease, only under various guises. What was the disease? He thought about it, and once he was alone in the room, he pronounced its name: selfishness. It was the grinning mask of selfishness that lay behind every problem, stinting what it could and demanding everything one person could demand of another, ideally without having to give anything in return, nothing real or substantial in any case. It was selfishness that bought its darling a palazzo, a coach-and-four, and jewels, and believed that by presenting her with such gifts it had parted with something secret and more precious without the exchange of which there can be no true attraction or peace in one's heart. It was selfishness that wanted everything and believed it had given everything when it devoted time, money, passion, and tenderness to the male or female object of its affections, while withholding the final sacrifice consisting of a simple, almost incidental, readiness to leave everything and devote its life and soul to the other without expecting anything in return. For this is what lovers, those peculiar tyrants, actually wanted. They were happy enough to give money, time, rings, ornaments, even their names and hands, but in all this welter

of gift giving, there was one thing they were all determined to keep back, and that something was themselves, whether that self was Lucia or Giuseppe or the gallant captain, Petruccio, now standing in the middle of the room, grasping his sword with both hands and looking as grim as he might at his own execution.

"What is the problem, dear captain?" he asked in his friendliest, most charming manner. But the captain was warily turning his head about, like a wild animal examining his cage. Then he bent to the stranger's ear and whispered the secret. He stood there with burning eyes, gripping his sword, his warrior heart wildly beating, and whispered it. No, this was not a matter he could advise him on. He shook his head in complete understanding and tutted indignantly. "Perhaps," he said in a low voice, "you should leave her. You are a man. A soldier." But the captain did not answer. He was like the dead who realize that nothing will ever change again, that they are stuck in this uncomfortable position in the grave, under the earth, under the stars. He was not a man who took readily to advice, preferring to treat his injuries as lower ranks: a senior officer does not consort with lower ranks. "Leave her!" Giacomo repeated, warmly, with genuine sympathy. "Even if you can't bear it, it's better than your current suffering." The captain groaned. His understanding was that there was no advice, no consolation, no remedy for his grief. That groan, that wounded, hopeless grunt of his, was a declaration. "Even this suffering is better than not seeing her; it is better to live like this than to leave her," it said. Some people just can't be helped.

Many more people came, usually arriving near dusk. The priest's secretary, a spotty-faced boy who read Petrarch and could not bring himself to write a letter to the lady of his heart's desire, received his advice at the cost of one gold piece. The stranger wrote the letter for him, solemnly escorted him out, then shut the door and laughed till his sides split, throwing the gold into the air, before passing it over to Balbi, who took his hands as they shook each other in delight. "Doctor Mirabilis!" cried Balbi, his cracked voice whinnying with laughter. "They're even coming in from the countryside now!" Snow was falling thickly, but they kept arriving despite the drifts and showers, not only men, but women, too, with veils over their faces, promising cash in hand, tearing the jeweled brooches from their bosoms, casting their veils aside. "Work your wonders, Giacomo, talk to him, brew me a magic potion, tell me your opinion, is there any hope for me? . . ." they begged.

One day there arrived a woman, no longer young, a solid, respectable figure, her dark fiery eyes ablaze with passion and hurt. "I came in the snow," she told him, her voice raw with feeling, as she stood by the fire, opened her fur stole, shook her head, and waited for the sparkling snowdrops caught on her veil and scarf to melt. "One horse died. We almost froze as the evening closed in. But here I am because they say that you give advice, understand magic, and know people's hearts and souls. So get on with it." She spoke indignantly, as though smarting from an insult. He offered the lady a chair and paid close attention to her. He had known women in every state and con-

dition of life, and having found reason enough to be wary of them, kept his eyes open for changes of mood. She ignored his offer. She was past forty, tall, red-faced, and healthily plump, the kind of woman happy enough to stand in the kitchen and watch the pork roast, who washes her face in rainwater and whose linen cupboard smells pleasant without the use of scents, the kind of woman who would happily administer even an enema to the man she loved. He regarded her with respect. There was enough passion smoldering under the furs and in those flashing eyes to set a forest on fire. She was used to giving orders and probably kept her household on a tight rein. Servants, guests, relatives, and admirers would all listen devotedly to whatever she had to say and would be sent scattering by her fury. Even her tenderness would smolder with a sharp aroma, like the brushwood fire in a forest when herdsmen forget to put it out after preparing game. She was a woman strong in anger through whom the tide of feelings ran most powerfully, and she stood now in commanding fashion, ready to deal the world several sharp blows, after which, with a single passionate movement of her firm arms, she would sweep some chosen loved one to her breasts in a deathly embrace. The snow, the cold fields of Lombardy, and the smell of the River Adige all emanated from her presence. "Here I am," said the woman, puffing slightly, her even voice barely under control. "I have come to you. I have come, though the laundry has piled up at home, though they are smoking salami, and though they say that in November, in the hills

round here, a traveler is likely to be eaten by wolves. I am a Tuscan," she said quietly but firmly.

The stranger bowed. "And I am Venetian, madam," he said, and, for the first time, gazed more deeply into his guest's eyes.

"I know," the woman replied and took a gulp. "That's why I am here. Listen, Giacomo. You have escaped from prison and know the secrets of love, so they say. Look at me. Am I the sort of woman who should humbly beseech a man to love her? Who is it who looks after the house? Who works in the fields in July at harvest time? Who shops for new furniture in Florence when we have to present an imposing face to the world? Who takes care of the horses and their equipment? Who mends the socks and underwear of her fastidious master? Who makes sure that there are flowers on the table at noon and that musicians with flageolets are playing in the next room when it is somebody's birthday? Who keeps all the drawers in order? Who washes in cold water every morning and every night? Who has linen brought over from Rumburg so that the bed in which the man of the house embraces her should smell as fresh as the fields of Tuscany in April? Who keeps an eye on the kitchen so that every requirement of his delicate stomach and demanding palate should be satisfied? Who tests the flesh of the young cockerel before it is slaughtered so it should be as plump and tender as he likes it? Who checks the smell of the calf's leg brought over from the butcher in town? Who goes down to the cellar, down those dangerous steep stairs, to sulphur the wine

casks they have rolled in barrels from the vineyard? Who makes sure that the glass of water they have left on the small table by his bed at night should contain a spoonful of sugar because after his carousings and lecheries, his weak heart needs a drop of sugar before he can sleep? Who stops him eating too much ginger and pepper? Who turns a blind eye to his lustful moods when ropes and chains can't keep him at home? Who keeps her peace when she can smell the rotten perfume of other women on his coat and linen? . . . Who puts up with it all? Who works and says nothing? Look at me, Giacomo. They say you are wise in the ways of women, a brilliant doctor of love. Look at me. I have borne two children and lost three, no matter that I groveled on my knees before the image of the Virgin, begging her to keep them alive. Look at me. I know time has had its way with me, that there are those who are younger, who smile more obligingly, and are better at wiggling their hips; nevertheless, here I am. Am I the kind of woman whose kisses are to be rejected? Just look at me!" she cried in a hoarse, powerful voice, and opened her fur coat. She was wearing a dress of lilac-colored silk, her dark brown hair covered by a headscarf of Venetian lace, a golden clasp holding together the shawl across her mature, pleasantly full bosom, her build tall and muscular without a trace of excess fat, firm of flesh and sound of blood, a solid forty-year-old woman with white arms, her head thrown proudly back. She stood before him and he bowed to her with a natural male courtesy, in genuine admiration. "There's no need to bow," she said, lowering her voice, a little embarrassed. "I haven't left the estate in a

snowstorm and traveled all the way to Bolzano just so that I should be bowed to by a stranger. It's not consolation I am seeking. I know what I know. I am a woman. I can sense when a man is looking at me. I can recognize genuine desire in an impudent, unrespectful stare but can also feel the circumspect passion in a mere glance. I know I have a few years left in which to make the man who loves me completely happy."

She drew the fur across her chest once more, as if cold or embarrassed, hesitated, then continued in a fainter, more tremulous voice. "Why can't I have what I want? . . ." she asked. Her voice was perfectly quiet now, and she was taking deep gulps in an attempt to hold back her tears, speaking humbly, without a trace of Tuscan pride. "What should I have done? . . . I gave him everything a woman can give a man, passion and patience, children, excitement, peace, security, tenderness, freedom from care . . . everything. People tell me that you understand love the way a goldsmith understands gold and silver: question me then, stranger, examine my heart, make your judgment, and give me your advice! What should I have done? I have humbled myself. I was my husband's lover and accomplice. I understood that there had to be other women in his life, because such was his nature. I know he desired in secret and that he came running back to me to escape the pressures of the world, to escape his own passions and adventures, and that he still escapes because he is frightened, because he is no longer young, because death is breathing down his neck. Sometimes I have willed him to grow old and to be plagued by gout, so

that he should be mine again, so I could bathe his aching feet. . . . Yes, I have longed for old age and for sickness, may Our Lady forgive me and may God pardon my sins. I gave everything. Tell me what else I should have given. . . ."

She was abjectly begging for an answer, her voice faint, her eyes full of tears. The man thought about it. He stood before her, his arms crossed over his chest, and his verdict was courteous but final.

"You should have given happiness, signora."

The woman bent her head and raised her handkerchief to her eyes. She stood dumbly weeping. Then she gave a great sigh and answered subserviently in a cracked voice.

"Yes, you are right. It was only happiness I couldn't give him."

She stood, head bowed, fondling the gold brooch with her delicate fingers, as if distracted. Still staring at the floor, she added, "Don't you think, stranger, that there are certain men to whom you cannot give happiness? There is a kind of man whose whole attraction, every virtue, every charm, emanates from his incapacity for happiness. The entire faculty for happiness is absent; he is stone deaf to happiness, and, just as the deaf cannot hear the sweet sound of music, so he is insensible to the sweet sound of happiness. . . . Because you are right, he never was happy. But, you see, this is the man that heaven and earth have chosen for me, and it was not as if he found happiness anywhere else, either, however he looked for it, in over fifty years. He is like the man who buries his treasure in a field then forgets where he has buried it. He digs up every-

thing in sight, he turns his whole life over. . . . I sold my rings and pendants so that he could travel further afield to seek it, because, believe me, there was nothing I wanted more than to see him happy. Let him seek happiness on voyages across seas, in strange cities, in the arms of black women and yellow women, if that is his fate. . . . But he always came back to me, sat down beside me, called for wine or read his books, then spent a week with some slut with dyed hair, usually an actress. That's the kind of man he is. What should I do? Throw him out? Kill him? Should I go away myself? Should I kill myself? . . . Every morning after mass I have knelt before the Savior in our small church, and, believe me, I searched my heart carefully before coming to you with my grief and wounded pride. Now I will go home and my pride will no longer be wounded. You are right: I did not give him happiness. From now on I shall only want to serve him. But please tell me, for I am desperate to know: seeing that there are men incapable of happiness, do you think the fault is entirely mine? He is restless and melancholy and seeks happiness at every turn: in the arms of women, in ambition, in worldly affairs, in murderous affrays, in the clinking of gold coins; he seeks it everywhere, all the while knowing that life can give him everything but happiness. Is there anyone else like this? . . ."

She spoke the last words challengingly, as if she were demanding something or accusing him. Now it was he who bowed his head.

"Yes," he said. "Take comfort. I do know such a man. He stands before you."

He spread his arms and bowed deeply, as if to signal that the consultation was over. The woman gazed at him for some time. Her fingers trembling, she clasped her fur coat together and the two of them moved toward the door. Then as if talking to herself, by way of good-bye, she said:

"Yes, I felt that. . . . I felt as soon as I stepped into the room, that you too were that kind of man. Perhaps I felt it even before I set off in the snow. But he is so terribly lonely and sad. . . . There is a kind of sadness that may not be consoled: it is as if someone had missed some divine appointment, and had found nothing to interest him since. You have more self-knowledge than he does, I can tell that from your voice, see it in your eyes, feel it in your very being. What is the trouble with these people? Is it because God has punished them with too much intelligence, so they experience every feeling, every human passion, with the mind rather than the heart? . . . The thought had occurred to me. I am a simple woman, Giacomo, and there is no need for you to shake your head or to be polite. I know why I say these things. I make no apology for my simplicity. I know there are forms of intelligence beyond those admired by the vainly intellectual, that the heart has its own knowledge, and that it too is important, very important. . . . You see, I came to you for advice, but now that it is time to go it is I who am feeling sorry for you. How much do I owe you?"

She drew a silver-crocheted purse from the lining of the coat and extended it nervously toward him.

"From you, signora," said the man, bowing once more

as at the end of a dance, his knee slightly bent, his arms spread wide, "I will not accept any money."

He declared this in a spirit of generosity, humbly enough but with just enough hauteur in his voice for the woman to turn around at the threshold.

"Why?" she asked over her shoulder. "It is what you live on, after all."

He shrugged.

"You, dear lady, have already paid a great price. I would like you to be able to say that you met with a man who gave you something for nothing."

He escorted her as far as the stairs, where they looked at each other once more in the gloom with serious and somewhat suspicious expressions on their faces. He raised the candle high to light his guest's way, for it was already dark and the bats were beginning to flitter through the stairwell of The Stag.

The Contract

*I*t was dark. They were ringing the bells of Santa Maria, and down in the shadows the bar and restaurant of The Stag were tinkling with silver and glass as they spread the tables, when he heard sleigh bells. He stood still a moment, leaning over the banisters, listening. He, too, was a bat, suspended upside down over the world, the kind of creature who comes to life only when the dull lights and sounds of evening awaken him. The sleigh stopped by the doors of The Stag, someone shouted, servants came running with lanterns and fixed them to the ends of long pointed poles, settling silence on the intimate noises of restaurant and bar, the kind of noises he loved to hear down the corridors of inns in foreign towns, when he would emerge from his room on tiptoe, his black gold-buckled half soles on his feet, his white cotton stockings stretched tight over his full legs, wearing a violet-colored frock coat and a narrow, gilt-handled sword strapped to his waist under the black silk cloak that came down to his ankles, his hair carefully sprinkled with rice powder, his

fingers bright with rings, a purse made of fish bladder containing gold coins hanging at his side, and a packet of marked cards in his pocket; and, thus prepared for the evening, he would be ready to face the world, impatient for adventure, his heart expectant and melancholy, expectancy and melancholia being much the same thing, then patter down the stairs, eyes darting here and there, knowing that in various rooms in the same town there would be women sitting next to candles from which the smoke gently billowed while they looked into the mirror, quickly tying a bow in a bodice, pinning flowers in their hair, anointing themselves with rice powder and perfume, adjusting the beauty patch on their faces, knowing that musicians would already be tuning up in the theaters, the stage and auditorium rich with the sour-bitter smoke of oil lamps, and that everyone was preparing for life, for the evening, which would be festive, secretive, and intimate: it was the time at which he loved to stop on the stairs of strange inns and listen to the faint brushing noises of waiters and servants and the clinking and chinking of the cutlery, the glass, the silver, and the china. There was nothing finer in life for him, anywhere in the world, than observing preparations for festivities: the prelude, the fuss, every detail infused with the sense of anticipation of all that was unpredictable and surprising. What delight it was to dress at about eight o'clock, when the church bells had stopped ringing, and when pale hands, their movements sensitive and mysterious, reached from windows to fasten the shutters, thereby closing out the world and safeguarding the house which always represents some mutuality, some

turning away from worldly affairs; to put on one's clothes and prepare for the evening with the pleasant quickening of the heart that tells us we are capable of anything, of both happiness and of despair; to stride with sure, light steps past houses, toward the dim shores of the darkening evening. It was this part of the day he loved best: his walk changed, his hearing grew keener, his eyes glittered and he could see in the dark. At such times he felt wholly human, but also, in the complex but not at all shameful sense of the word, like a creature of the wild that, after sunset, when tamer beasts have retired to shallows and watering holes, stands like a great predator, still and silent in the brush, listening to the sounds of twilight, his head raised in rapt attention. So it was now when they were laying tables that he heard the shuffling, tinkling noises rising from the restaurant, and in that instant the whole world seemed festive. Was there any feeling to compare with it, he wondered, a feeling that so quickened the heart and made it pound with apprehension as that of waiting for festivities to begin?

The clatter had stopped now. The shuffling of feet was followed by the sounds of a lighter, younger pattering movement, then he heard the knocking of shoes with wooden soles breaking into a run. "An important guest!" he thought as he stuck his tongue out and licked his dry lower lip in quick, thirsty anticipation. The agitation of the house coursed through him. To his highly developed ear, the word "guest" was one of the most magical sounds in the world, along with other words like "prize," "prey," "suddenly," and "luck": it was, in short, among the finest

sounds a man could wish to hear. "A substantial guest!" he thought in approval, with a pleasant excitement. The light of the torches moved about the upper floor. The voices below were barking short, hard words: the guest must have been at the very door, the host of The Stag bowing before him, issuing stern orders and promising who-knows-what earthly and divine delights. "A difficult guest!" he thought, like a fellow professional, for he himself was just such a "difficult" guest who liked to make his host squirm with a long series of testing questions, to visit the kitchen and examine the size of the salmon, capon, or saddle of venison for himself, to try its quality, to have a much-praised vintage brought up from the cellar then take his time sniffing the cork after the bottle was opened, to wave away the offered wine with contempt and ask for a new bottle and, when it arrived, solemnly and with utmost concentration, to taste the thick, oily, blood-red drops of the French or South Italian grape, then, graciously, with a slightly sour expression, finally agree on the potential of some specific wine, and to turn round at the top of the cellar stairs, or at the door of the kitchen, with a finger half-raised to remind his host in harsh, admonitory tones that he should take care that the chestnuts, with which they were to stuff the breast of the turkey, be boiled in milk and vanilla first, and that the Burgundy be warmed in its straw carafe precisely forty minutes before serving; and it was only after all this that he would take his place at the table and haughtily survey the hall, rubbing his eyes to signify a slight weariness and satisfaction, taking in the furniture and the paintings, whose arrangement and whose local or

international character did not truly interest the "difficult" guest, since the most difficult part was over, and one only had to watch that the serving staff always stood at a distance of two paces, far enough not to hear any whispered conversation, but close enough to leap to the table at the lowering of an eyelid and attend to any business immediately. "They are negotiating something!" he thought, for the hard voice of the guest and the humble, fawning voice of the host were still engaged in conversation. "A guest from out of town!" he thought. He remembered that there was a ball tonight at Francesca's, a masked ball, to which the local nobility had been invited. There had been a lot of talk in town about the ball in the last few days, and all the tailors, cobblers, haberdashers, ribbon makers, seamstresses, and hairdressers were proudly complaining that they couldn't keep up with demand, as a result of which he himself had spent three useless days vainly demanding his two frilly evening shirts from the washerwoman, who was too busy starching, washing, and ironing the finest linen for Francesca's ball, and the whole town was filling up with guests preparing for wonderful games and high festivities, all caught up in the kind of exciting, intense, and, to all purposes, good-natured activity that in its own twisted and mysterious manner touches even those who are not directly involved in the affair. . . . I expect a lot of people will be spending the night after the ball at The Stag, he thought. The weather is dreadful, the Tuscan woman was almost eaten by wolves, and the local gentry and their ladies are hardly likely to set straight off after the event across snow-covered roads, at dawn, in their sleighs and

foot muffs. And this "difficult" guest, he too must be bound for the ball, he thought, and felt a sharp stab of envy, as people do when they suddenly discover that they are barred from attending a desirable occasion. The feeling surprised him. It reminded him of his childhood when he learned that adults were planning something strange and wonderful without him. He shrugged, listened a moment longer to the discussion between guest and host, then turned back to his room.

"In other words, nobody!" the harsh commanding voice declared at the foot of the stairs, down in the depths. The answer must have been silent: he could imagine the obliging landlord, his hand crossed over his heart, his upper body bowed, and his eyes cast heavenward to indicate that everything would be as the guest demanded. But something about the voice stopped him as he was about to enter his room. It was a familiar voice, an intimately and frighteningly familiar voice, the kind a man recognizes because there has already been unavoidable and close contact between it and him. This instinctive recognition was an important force in his life: he had set his compass by it. He raised his head, listening intently, like an animal on the scent. The voice was unmistakable! He stood at the door with a serious, almost respectful look on his face, his fingers on the handle, his whole body tense, some instinct telling him that he was on the verge of a fateful encounter. He knew by now that the footsteps slowly, laboriously ascending the stairs with such even tread were a vital component of his own life, that the anonymous voice rising from the depths was bringing him a personal message. The

"difficult" guest was looking for him. The astrological chart of his life was, in a few moments, once again, and not for the last time, about to undergo a dramatic readjustment. He took a deep breath and straightened up. A nervous shudder ran through him, and as always in such situations, his instinct momentarily overcame his reason, and he felt the urge to run into his room, climb through the window, shimmy down the storm drain of The Stag, and disappear in the accustomed manner, into the evening and the blizzard. It was, after all, the only voice he was afraid of, this "resonant" voice already drawing closer in the half-light on the stairs. He recognized the same unavoidable "resonance" when it radiated from women or from men who belonged to women. He had been happy enough to fight a duel in Tuscany, bare-chested in the moonlight, with only a narrow sword in his hand, against an old man maddened by jealousy who was skillful and dangerous with swords; he had been quite prepared to leap from rooftops and to tangle with vagrant scoundrels on the floor of a dive in a pub brawl; he was, in short, afraid of nothing but this "resonance," which he associated with a specific feeling, for he sensed that every feeling, but this one above all, was woven to bind him. It was this that really frightened him. That was why he thought he should shut the door now, seize his dagger, and leave by the window. At the same time he knew that, in the end, there was no escape from this particular kind of resonance, that it was a trap from which one could not escape unscathed. So he waited at the threshold, his hair standing on end, with fear and anticipation, gripping the handle of the door,

staring over his shoulder, scanning the dim space with sharp, suspicious eyes, seeking the man who would shortly address him in that familiar voice. It was past eight o'clock. The steps hesitated, apparently tired, resting at a turn of the stair. There was no more clattering of cutlery in the bar and the silence was such that you could hear the snow fall; it was as if the mountains, the snow-covered street, the river, and the stars, the whole of Bolzano, were holding its breath. "There is always this moment of silence at a vital turn in a man's life," he found himself reflecting, and smiled with satisfaction at the phrase, because he was, after all, a writer.

Then they came into view, the landlord first, stooping and turning as he ascended, muttering, explaining, assuring, a smoking taper in his hand and a soft satchel-shaped hat of red material on his head, the kind of hat that used to be worn by Phrygian shepherds and more recently by publicans and freethinkers in the cellars of Paris and out in the provinces. The innkeeper's ballooning stomach was covered with a leather apron that he must have been wearing in the cellar where he was probably tampering with the sugar content and temperature of the wine, a foul habit he could not bring himself to abandon, and over the apron, a blue jerkin whose splendor exceeded that of the ceremonial vestments of guilds and connoisseurs and suggested a long-standing religious ritual such as might be conducted by a lower grade priest of an ancient, pagan cult whose devotees were crowned with rings of onions. It was he who came first. He looked over his shoulder, muttering and assuring with a great show of humility and concern, like

any hotelier with an important client, for it is the duty of the hotelier to be solicitous in his attentions, to see his guest rise and set off in the morning, leaving behind a messy room, the bed his noble body had vacated, the basin with its dirty water, the vessel containing human effluent, and things even the most exquisitely refined of human beings leaves as evidence of his presence in the room of a hotel. And so the innkeeper bowed and scraped with remarkable zeal, his every gesture speaking of five decades of experience as landlord and jack-of-all-trades to all and sundry. He kept three steps ahead of his guest, much as a postilion does at night when the king, the prince de Condé, or, as it may be, the duke of Parma, happens to be passing through. And in his wake there followed the procession of four men ranged about a fifth, two in front, two behind, each member of the escort equipped with a five-branched silver candelabrum raised high above his head, each clad in his lackey's uniform of black silk jerkin, knee breeches, and white wig, with silver chains about his neck and a flat-cocked hat on his head; the heavy calfskin pelisses around their shoulders billowed like enormous wings as they walked stiffly on, looking neither behind nor ahead, their pace as mechanical and jerky as those of marionettes at an open-air performance in the market-place. The guest proceeded slowly in the cage of light they made for him. He gauged each step of the stair with caution before moving on, his body shrouded in a plain, violet-colored traveling cloak that flapped about his ankles, a cloak brightened only at the neck and narrow shoulders by a wide, beaver-skin collar; and so, leaning on

a silver-handled stick, he made his way gradually upstairs, carefully fixing the point of the stick on the edge of the next step, as if each tread required careful consideration, not just as an intellectual proposition but as a physical problem occasioned by the condition of his heart, for his heart was finding the burden of stairs ever more difficult. The procession therefore wound on extremely slowly with the ornate and rigorous ritual of a man who has all but lost his freedom of movement but remains enslaved by his own rank, the trappings and obligations imposed on him by his station in life. "It's not hard to see," thought Giacomo, wide-mouthed, his contempt tempered by a grudging respect as he stood at the half-open door of his room, "that he is related to Louis Le Gros!" And so thinking, he took a step back into the shadows of the room, on the far side of the threshold, and waited there with both hands on the door frame, carefully flattening himself against the wall in the darkness while the duke of Parma made his way upstairs.

By now the procession had reached the landing, and had arrived just where the corridor curved away, so he could see a complete line of faces where the attendants formed a double guard with their raised candles, waiting for their master to get his breath. Of course he had recognized the duke of Parma before he got to the top of the stairs, even before hearing his voice; he recognized him because the duke was intensely resonant, a man of whose presence he would immediately be aware, a man with a pivotal role in his life. He knew he was nearby long before he even saw him: he was aware of it when the Tuscan

woman left his room to return to her shadowy, joyless servitude, to life with her melancholy, much-traveled husband; he felt his presence when the sleigh stopped by the door and the landlord began his wheedling and assuring. Few people knew how to arrive like this, and he contemplated the arrival with a certain professional satisfaction, as if he himself were a landlord, porter, or waiter or, better still, the perennial guest accustomed to grand entrances; he studied the duke's manner of entering, from the point of view of a fellow craftsman, with a peculiar mixture of mild contempt and involuntary respect, for the manner was formal, meticulous, and appropriate to the company that automatically accommodated itself to the rituals of the duke's person and role, even now, even here, in this bat-infested provincial inn of somewhat dubious reputation, as if he had drawn up outside at his palace in Bologna, his sleigh dripping with dead foxes, wolves, and wild boars bagged along the way, or had marched into Monsieur Voisin's or the Silver Tower Restaurant in Paris, or alighted from his carriage at Versailles, at the entrance of the Trianon, where His Celestial Host was entertaining a bevy of beauties at the royal court with a game of pin the tail on the donkey. . . . The duke of Parma did not simply "turn up" at The Stag but "made an entrance"; he didn't simply go upstairs but was escorted there as part of a procession; he didn't just stop when he reached the upper floor but made a ceremonial appearance. The entire progress was dreamlike: it was like a vision of the final judgment.

Now the guest drew himself up and ran his eye severely

down the length of the shadowy corridor, across deep pools of tremulous darkness, while the servants raised their elaborately embroidered arms to light his way with their blazing scarlet candelabras.

The duke of Parma, the kinsman of Louis, was this year completing his seventy-second year. "Seventy-two," calculated the stranger quite calmly as he caught his first glimpse of the visitor. He did not move from the doorway but stood clutching the doorpost, nonchalant yet watchful, exuding the indifference of someone accidentally coming upon an ordinary guest of no particular importance in a dark and none too salubrious inn, a silent, disinterested witness to a rather overelaborate procession. "It's the only way he knows how to conduct himself," he thought, and shrugged, but then another thought occurred to him. "He wants to intimidate me!" The idea struck him with irresistible force, flattering his self-esteem. "No one takes a room at The Stag in such a manner!" His hunches were correct as far as they went, though they did not go far enough, he suspected, and even as he watched the duke of Parma surveying the corridor, his head thrown back and his eyes screwed up until he discovered the man he had been seeking in the doorway, the tingling in his toes and stomach confirmed the suspicion. One casual glance assured him that the duke's escort was unarmed, and, as far as he could see, the duke himself carried no weapon. His appearance, movement, and progress seemed dignified rather than threatening. At this hour of the late afternoon—or was it early evening? a stranger could not go by what usually happened at such hours in more metropoli-

tan, glittering places—when the palazzo would have been getting ready for the ball, an especially brilliant ball, a champagne occasion that the whole district had been talking about for days, the host would not have sallied forth without good cause, not with such a splendid escort, certainly not so that he could take up rooms in a dubious inn just two steps from his own home. "It is I he has come to see, of course!" thought the stranger, and was deeply flattered, above all by the ceremonial manner of the visit. At the same time, however, he knew that this procession was only the most general of homages to him; that he was merely an itinerant, someone with whom the duke of Parma had exchanged a few valedictory words some years ago on a misty sea-colored morning at the gates of Florence; that the ceremoniousness had to be interpreted as a permanent and natural feature of the guest's mode of existence, the pomp an organic part of his being; that the procession was the equivalent of the brilliantly colored tail the male peacock permanently drags behind him, something the peacock, when he becomes aware of being watched, opens as casually as one might a fan. This was the way the duke of Parma had traveled everywhere for a good long time now. Now he waved the lackeys aside. He recognized the straight figure standing in the doorway, carelessly raised to his eyes with a well practiced movement the lorgnette that had been dangling on a golden chain at his breast, and, slightly blinking, as if unsure that he had found what he had been looking for, gazed steadily at the stranger.

"It is him," he pronounced at last, terse and satisfied.

"Yes, Your Excellency," the innkeeper enthusiastically agreed.

They were talking about him in his presence as if he were an object. He was amused by the neutrality of their tone. He remained where he was, making no haste to welcome his visitor, nor did he go down on his knees, for why should he? . . . He felt a deep indifference, a blend of contempt and impassivity in the face of every worldly danger and even more so now. "What's the point?" he thought and shrugged. "The old man has come to warn me off, perhaps to threaten me; he'll try a little blackmail then call on me to leave town or else have me transported back to Venice. And what's it all for? . . . For Francesca? He does have a point, of course. Why haven't I already left this rotten town to which nothing ties me? I have sucked Mensch dry, can expect no further assistance here from papa Bragadin, there's nobody in town with whom I could discuss the finer points of literature, I am fully acquainted with the enticing, walnut-flavored kisses of little Teresa, Balbi is pursued every night by jealous butcher's boys wielding cudgels and machetes, and playing cards with the locals is like taking on a pack of wild boars. Why am I still here after six, or is it eight, days now? I could have been in Munich days ago. The elector of Saxony has already arrived there and will be blowing a fortune at faro. Why am I still here?" And so he pondered in stillness and silence while the duke, the innkeeper, and the lackeys carefully examined him like an object that someone had temporarily mislaid but had eventually found after a not particularly thorough, half-hearted search, an object not

especially desirable or even clean, about which the only remaining question was how to handle it, whether to grasp it or hold it at arm's length with one's fingertips, and whether to dust it down with a rag before throwing it out of the window. . . . He considered the various possibilities. Then, perfectly naturally, his mind turned to Francesca. "Of course!" he thought. And in that instant he understood how all this was the result of a logical and necessary chain of events that had not begun yesterday nor would be certain to end this coming night; how once, in the dim and distant past, a process had begun whereby his own fate and the fates of Francesca and the duke of Parma were tied together. The present situation was merely the continuation of a conversation begun a long time ago, and this was why he had not moved on, why he was standing here, facing the duke of Parma, who even now was staring at him, lightly puffing and somewhat out of breath, standing at the head of his lackeys like a general preparing to charge: yes, he thought, a general with his troops. "Hello!" Giacomo exclaimed in a very loud voice and took a step toward the ornately costumed group. "Anyone there?"

The tone was sharp and it rang like a sword. There was undoubtedly a "someone" out there in the corridor, a person large as life and plain as a mountain, a river, or a fortress: you couldn't miss him. That "someone" stood leaning on a silver-handled cane, his gray head, cocked to one side, boldly and gracefully balanced on the broad shoulders surmounting the slender figure like a miraculously carved ivory globe at the tip of a fashionable ebony walking stick. It was as if the balding, perfectly rounded

skull, fringed at temple and nape by a sheen of thin, silky, metallic hair, had been turned on a lathe. Granted this, Giacomo's voice sounded arrogant, almost insolent, for even a blind man could feel, if not see, that the person of the "someone" who had arrived at The Stag was not a person to be snubbed or taken in with a sidelong glance, that a man making a call like this, with his complete retinue, was not to be ignored, shouted at, or addressed in terms such as "Hello! Anyone there?" Aware of the potential outrage, the lackeys shrank back in terror and the innkeeper covered his mouth and crossed himself. Only the duke himself remained unruffled. He took a step forward in the direction of the voice, and the light of the candles illuminated the bloodless, ruthless, narrow mouth that appeared to be smiling in surprise at both question and tone. The question must have pleased him. "Yes, it is I," he replied, his voice faint and dry, yet refined. He spoke quietly in the knowledge that every word of his, even the quietest, had weight and power behind it. "I have something to say to you, Giacomo."

He advanced once more, ahead of the innkeeper and the lackeys who formed an effective guard of honor and, with a wave of his hand, instructed them to leave. "Tell the sleigh to wait," he said and stared stonily ahead of him without catching the eyes of those he commanded. "You people wait in the stairwell. No one is to move. You," he gestured, without so much as a flicker of his eyelids, though everyone knew he meant the innkeeper, "you will see to it that no one interrupts us. I'll let you know when we have finished." The lackeys set off silently according to

command, disappearing along with the light to the bottom of the stairs: it was as if dusk had settled in. The innkeeper followed them with nervous stumbling steps. "May I impose on you?" asked the duke with the utmost courtesy once everyone had gone, bowing slightly, as if he were addressing a close confidant or a member of the family. "Would you be kind enough to receive me for a short while in your room? I will not take up too much of your time." The request was made in the most elegant and aristocratic manner but there was something in the tone that sounded less like a request than a strict order. Hearing that tone, his host immediately regretted using terms like "Hello" and "anyone." Like any host, assured that his visitor was a man of some importance and that conversation was by no means to be avoided, he bowed silently and indicated the way with a motion of his outstretched arm, allowing his guest to precede him into the room, then closed the door behind them.

"I am most grateful," said the guest once he had taken his position by the fireplace in the armchair his host silently offered him. He stretched his two thin, pale hands—the anemic but commendably muscular hands of an old man—toward the flickering fire and for a while bathed himself in its gentle glow. "Those stairs, you know," he confided. "I find stairs hard nowadays. Seventy-two is a substantial age and little by little one learns to count both years and stairs. I am relieved that I did not climb them in vain. I am glad to find you at home." He gently folded his hands in front of him. "A stroke of luck," muttered his host. "It is not luck," he answered politely

but with some finality. "I have had you watched these past eight days, and have been aware of your every movement. I even know that you were at home this afternoon, receiving visitors, halfwits who come to you for advice. Though it is not for advice that I come to you, my boy."

He said this tenderly, like an old and trusted friend who understands human frailty and is anxious to help. Only the expression "my boy" rang a little ominously in the dimly lit room: it hung there like a highly delicate, hidden threat. Giacomo scented danger and drew himself up, casting an instinctive and well-practiced glance at his dagger and at the window.

He leaned against the fireplace and crossed his arms across his chest. "And what gives the duke of Parma the right to have me observed?" he asked.

"The right of self-defense," came the simple, almost gracious answer. "You know perfectly well, Giacomo, you above all people, who are well versed in such matters, that there is a power in the world beyond that of ordinary authorities. Both the age in which I live and my own decrepitude, which has turned my hair white as snow and robbed me of my strength, justify me in defending myself. This is the age of travel. People pass through towns, handing keys to one another, and the police can't keep up: Paris informs Munich of the setting forth of some personage who intends to try his luck there. Venice informs Bolzano that one of her most talented sons intends to room there on his travels. I cannot trust authorities alone. My position, age, and rank compel me to be careful in the face of every danger. My people are observant and reliable: the

best informers of the region answer to me not the chief of police. It was they who told me earlier that you had arrived. I would have found out anyway, since your reputation precedes you and makes people uneasy. Did you know that since you arrived, life beneath these snow-covered roofs has become more fraught? . . . It seems you carry the world's passions about with you in your baggage, much as traveling salesmen carry their samples of canvas and silk. One house has burned down, one vineyard owner has killed his wife in a fit of jealousy, one woman has run away from her husband—all in the last few days. These things are nothing directly to do with you. But you carry this restlessness with you, the way a cloud carries its load of lightning. Wherever you go you stir tempers and passions. As I said, your reputation precedes you. You have become a famous man, my boy," he sincerely acknowledged.

"Your Excellency exaggerates," Giacomo replied without moving.

"Nonsense!" answered his guest with some force. "I will accept no false modesty, you have no right to assume it. You are a famous man, your arrival has touched people's souls, and they announced your arrival to me the way they would have announced a guest performance of the Paris opera: you are here and people find an ironic delight in the fact. You arrived eight days ago, strapped for cash. News of your escape caught people's imagination and set it alight. Even I was filled with curiosity to see you, and thought of contacting you the day you arrived, of giving you some sign. But then I hesitated. Why has he come here? I asked

myself. Our agreement was final and binding, the agreement we made at the gates of Florence just before I gave your wounded body up to the surgeons, to the world. After all, I thought, he knows very well who I am, and that my orders are never revoked. I don't have much faith in human oaths and promises: promises flow from human mouths more easily than spittle from a cow in season. But I do believe in actions, and, I argued, he knows that my words are as good as my deeds, and that I have promised to kill him if he once so much as looks at Francesca ever again. That's what I said to myself in my heart, for the less time we have left to live the more we have to remember and recall. And now here he is! He knows he is risking his life. Why is he here? With what purpose? I asked myself. Is he still in love with the duchess? Did he ever love her? . . . It is not an easy question, not one he can answer, I told myself, because he knows nothing of love: he knows a great deal about other realms of experience, about feelings that resemble love; he knows the anxious, agonizing temptations of passion and desire, but about love he is perfectly ignorant. Francesca was never his. He knows it, I know it. There have been times down the years when I was extremely lonely, when I almost regretted the fact. Are you surprised? . . . I am surprised that you should be. There is a time of life, and I, through the ineffable wisdom of time and fate, have now arrived at that time, a time when everything—vanity, selfishness, false ambition, and false fear—drops away from us, and we want nothing but the truth, and would give anything for it. That is why I sometimes thought it was a pity she had never been yours. Because if

Francesca had ever at any time been his, I reasoned, my vanity and selfishness would have suffered, and perhaps Francesca might have suffered, too, but he would have been miles away by now, nor would he ever have returned to Bolzano as his first stop from prison, and I could be certain that something that had begun a long time ago had come full circle in human terms and ended. Because what man learns in his dotage, the total sum of all he understands and learns, is that human affairs need to run their full course and cannot be terminated before they do so: the course cannot be left unfinished, because there is a kind of order in human affairs that people obey as they would a law, one from which there is no escape. Yes, my boy, it is far harder to escape from unfinished business than it is from a lead-roofed prison, even at night, even by rope! You cannot know this yet: your soul, your nervous system, and your mind are all different from mine. I don't even care whether you believe me or not. All you need to know is that I promised that I would kill you if you ever returned and tried to gain access to us or if you so much as glanced at the duchess. Do you believe me when I say I am pleased to see you? Do you understand, wise counselor, who for the tinkle of a few gold coins dispenses advice all day long to the simpleminded and vulnerable, how, in view of all that has happened between us or, more precisely, not happened, given the news of your impending arrival, I was confirmed in my own belief that you have been drawn into the vicinity of our premises and lives involuntarily, without design or subterfuge, by a fateful attraction, in simple obedience to a law as fixed as the law that dictates

the course of the moon about the earth, and that I am therefore delighted to find that your first instinct has brought you to Bolzano. Do you believe me when I say I am delighted? . . . Yes, Giacomo, it is a delight and relief to me that you are here. Can you understand that?"

"I don't understand," he replied, intrigued.

"I will do everything in my power to explain," came the ready, courteous, slightly sinister response. "I was not being quite precise enough when I referred to my feeling as delight. This miraculous language of ours that the great lover, Dante, made potent with his kisses is occasionally clumsy when articulating ideas. Delight is a common word, with a commonplace ring: it suggests a man rubbing his hands and grinning. I did not in fact rub my hands on hearing of your arrival, and I certainly did not grin: my heart simply beat a little faster and I felt the blood accelerate through my veins in a way that distantly reminded me of delight, to which the feeling I am seeking to name is undoubtedly related, for the same deep well feeds all human emotions, whether these appear as stormy seas or gentle ripples on the surface. *J'étais touché*, might be the best way of putting it, to adapt a precise expression from fencing terminology, a terminology imbued with human feelings, for fencing is an analogous language that you will be as familiar with as I am. The fact is that something touched me and the expression struck me as an accurate one, one that you as a writer—for that is what I hear you are, according to the rumors spread round town by your accomplice and familiar—would certainly understand and approve. I should say that the notion of your

being a writer—Bolzano is a small town where no human frailty can be hidden for long—pleasantly surprised me; I have never doubted you had some special vocation, and indeed believed that you had been entrusted with a kind of mission among your fellow human beings, but I must confess I had never, until now, associated you with this particular vocation or role; somehow I always imagined that you were the sort of person whose fate and character was part of life's raw material, the sort of man who wrote in blood not ink. Because your true medium is indeed blood rather than ink, Giacomo; I trust you know that? . . ."

"Your Excellency is quick to judgment," he haughtily replied. "Artists take time and pains to discover the material with which they most prefer to work."

"Of course," the duke answered with surprising readiness and almost too much enthusiasm. "Pardon me! What am I thinking! You see how age afflicts me! I had forgotten that the artist is merely the personal embodiment of the creative genius that drives him, that he cannot choose, for his genius will press a pen, a chisel, a brush, or even, occasionally, a sword into his hand, whether he will or no. You will be thinking that the great Buonarroti and the versatile Leonardo—products of our cities, like you—wielded pen, chisel, and brush in turn; and yes, Leonardo, with his remarkable and frightening sense of adventure, even employed a scalpel, so that under the cover of night he might edge a little closer to the hidden secrets of the human body, as well as designing brothels and fortresses; just as Buonarroti, that tetchy and monstrous demigod,

scribbled sonnets and plastered domes, and, my dear Giacomo, what plastering, what domes! And he designed arches, funerary monuments, and in the meanwhile, because he had time to spare, he painted *The Last Judgment*! There's an artist for you! The human spirit swells, the heart throbs, when it contemplates the enormous scope of such geniuses; ordinary people grow faint when faced with such far horizons. Is that what you mean, when you say you are a writer? I understand, I really do. I am delighted to recognize the fact, my boy, for it explains a great deal to me. We have a very high regard for writers where I come from, and you, in your fashion, are a fine example of the species, as indeed you told your secretary, who faithfully repeats and disseminates all you say; you are a writer who dips his pen, now in blood, now in ink, though for the time being, to judge by your completed works, the uninitiated observer would be inclined to the opinion that so far you have written them entirely in blood, at the point of a dagger! Don't deny it! Who is in a better position to understand this than I, who have written several bloody masterpieces with my ancestral sword? The last time, when we faced each other with swords in our hands, we must have been engaged in an as yet unwritten but perfect dialogue, a dialogue that, at that particular moonlit moment, we considered finished, with its own full stop or period to mark the end. But now I understand that you truly are a writer," he declared with the same ambiguous air of satisfaction, "a writer who travels the world collecting material for his books!" He nodded vigorously in enthusiastic approval, his eyes shining

with rapture. He was like an old man in his second child-hood finally comprehending a complex web of relation-ships: it was as if he fully believed that the person he had sought out was indeed a writer and that the belief filled him with astonishment and delight. "So now you are coming to an end of your years of wandering! Vital years they are, too, ah yes . . . there was a time when I myself . . . but of course I have no right to compare myself to you, because I have composed no great work, no, not even in my own fashion: my work was my life and nothing more, a life that I had to live according to rules, customs, and laws, and in that enterprise, alas, I fear I have almost succeeded. Almost, I said, dear boy, and I beg you not to split hairs in your desire for exactitude, for I too have learned enough to know that we should be as precise in our use of words as possible if we want them to be of any value or help in life. Almost, I said, for you see, I, who am not a writer, find every expression difficult and am simul-taneously aware of both my difficulty and of my inability to solve it. Indeed, there is nothing more difficult than expressing oneself without ambiguity, especially when the speaker knows that his words are absolute, that behind each sentence stands the specter of death. And I really do mean death, you know, yours or mine," he added, his voice quiet and calm.

Receiving no answer, he stared at the scarlet and black embers in the fire, his head tipped to one side, gently wag-ging, as if he were dreaming and remembering at once.

"I am not threatening you, Giacomo," he started again in a slightly deeper voice, but still very friendly in manner.

"We are no longer at the stage when threats are appropriate. It's just that I would like you to understand me. That is why I used the word, 'almost.' It was death I was talking about, pure and simple, nor was it my aim merely to admire the formal beauty of a frequently discussed philosophical concept while exploring its darker significance. The death I am talking about is direct and personal, a death that is timely and fully to be expected should we be unable to come to some agreement in an ingenious, wholly human way. For, you see, I no longer feel like fighting, if only for the simple reason that fighting never solves anything. We discover everything too late. Assaulting someone is not a conclusive way of ending any business, and defending oneself only settles things if our defense is just and reasonable: in other words, we must employ not just arms and fury, however delightful the exercise of both may be, but the wiser, leveling power of the active intellect. How old are you now? Forty next birthday . . . ? It's a good age for a writer. Yes, Giacomo, it's the time of one's life, and I can remember that time without envy, for it is not true to say that the more quickly life vanishes the more we thirst for what is gone—though the time is indeed gone, isn't it? Do help me out if I express myself inadequately: you are after all a writer! Have we in fact lost what we had before? Are we in danger of suffering what those people who are prey to easy and false sentiments label, wholly imprecisely, 'loss,' meaning loss of youth, youth that bounds away from us into the distance like a hare in the meadow, and loss of manhood, manhood over which one day the sun begins to set, in other words the loss of the

time we have enjoyed, the time in which we acted, that we once owned as we own objects, as a form of personal property? No, the time that is gone is a self-contained reality and there's no reason to bewail its passing; it is only the future that I view with anxiety, with a certain intensity that may be appropriate to regret; yes, the future, however strange and comical it may seem at my time of life. As to lost time, I have no wish to recover it: that time is well-stocked and complete in itself. I do not mourn for my youth, which was full of false perceptions and fancy words, with all those touching, tender, lofty, confused, patchy, and immature errors of heart and mind. I view with equal satisfaction the vanished gilded landscape of my adult self. I have no desire to reclaim anything of the past. There is nothing as dangerous as false, unconscious self-pity, the wellspring of all man's misery, sickness, and ignorance: self-pity is the common well of all human distress. What has happened has happened, nor is it lost, preserved as it is by the miraculous rituals of life itself, which are more complex than those dreamed up by the early priests and more mysterious than the activities of contemporary entomologists who preserve the organs of the dead for posterity. As far as I am concerned the past has its own life and it stinks of power and plenty. I am interested in the future, my boy," he repeated very loudly, almost shouting. "Being a writer, you should understand that."

He clearly required no answer. And there was no mockery in his voice when he stubbornly repeated the word "writer." With great sympathy he described the exiled writer who must now be reaching the end of his

wanderings, having gathered material—such as his adventures here in Bolzano, where the duke of Parma lived with his duchess for example—material that he would, one day, use for his books; he spoke as if he fully and enthusiastically approved the writer's calling and the manner of behavior it entailed, as if he were addressing a fellow reveler at a masked ball with a courteous wink, as if to say: "I have recognized you, but I won't tell. Keep talking." But his host remained silent: it was only the visitor that spoke. After a short silence, he continued:

"The future concerns me, because my life isn't quite over yet. It is not just writers like yourself who like a story to be properly finished, the world, too, likes it that way: it is only human nature that both writer and reader should demand that a tale should reach a genuine conclusion and end appropriately, according to the rules of the craft and in line with the soul's inner imperatives. We want the well-placed period, the full stop, all *t*'s crossed and all *i*'s dotted. That's how it has to be. That is why I repeat the word 'almost' once more, thinking it might be of some help in bringing our mutual history to a conclusion. Something remains to say, something to settle, before the story can end, though it is only one story among many hundreds of millions of such human stories, a story so common that, should you ever get to write your book, having collected enough material for it, you might even leave it out. But for the two, or should I say three, of us, it is of overwhelming importance, more important than any previous story composed either with pen or sword; to us it is more important than the visit the great poet of heaven once

made to hell. And we must conclude it here on earth, because for us it is more interesting than either heaven or hell. Whatever may yet happen to round off the sentence and allow us to dot our *i*'s and cross our *t*'s; whatever arranging and winding-up of our affairs is required to conclude the history of the two, or rather, the three, of us, and whether that arrangement turns out to be somber and funereal or cheerful and sensible, depends on you alone, you the writer. You can see that I am visiting you at a bad time of life, when I am plagued by gout, when, by the time evening comes round, I prefer to remain in my room with my old habits and a warm fire to console me. Nor would I have come now if I did not have to, for believe me, as we enter our dotage, our bones creaking with age, our spirits exhausted by wicked words and harsh experience, our sense of time grows keener and we develop an intelligent, economical orderliness of manner, a kind of perceptiveness or sensitivity that tells us how long to wait and when, alas, to act. I have come because the time is right. I have come at the hour when everyone in the house is preparing for festivities, when the servants are setting the tables, the orchestra is tuning up, the guests are trying on their masks, and everything is being done properly, according to the rules of the game that brings a certain delight to living, and it certainly delights me, for there is nothing I like more than observing the idiotic and chaotic rout from my corner, wearing my mask. I shall have to start home to get changed soon. Would you like to see my mask, Giacomo? . . . If you come along tonight—as I hope you will, please take these words as a belated invita-

tion—you will certainly know me by my mask, which will be the only one of its sort there, though the idea itself is admittedly unoriginal, something I borrowed from a book, a verse play written not in our sweet familiar tongue but in the language used by our ruder, more powerful northern cousins, the English. I discovered the book a year ago when visiting the library of my royal cousin in Marly, and I must admit the story fascinated me, though I have forgotten the author's name; all I know is that he was a comedian and buffoon a while ago in London, in the land of our distant, provincial cousin, that ugly, half-man, half-witch, Elizabeth. The long and short of it is that I shall be wearing an ass's head tonight and you will recognize me by it if you come and keep your eyes peeled. You probably know that in the play it is one of the main characters who wears the ass's head, he whom the heroine clutches to her bosom, she being a certain Titania, the queen of youth, and that she does so with the blind unseeing passion that is the very essence of love. That is why I shall wear the donkey's head tonight—and perhaps for another reason, too, because I want to be anonymous in my mask and hear the world laugh at me; I want to hear, for the first time in my life, through donkey's ears, the laughter of the world in its fancy dress, in my own palazzo, at the climax of my life, before we finish the sentence and dot the *i*. There will be quite a noise don't you think?" He was talking loudly now, politely, but with razor-sharp edge to his voice: it was like the clashing of swords after the first few strokes in a duel. "I really do want to hear them laughing at me, at the man with the ass's head, in my own palace. Why? because the

time is ripe: the hour, Giacomo, has finally arrived, not a moment too soon, at its own pace and in its own good time, at the point when I could bring myself to knock at your door, at the point when I am ready to put on the ass's head that befits a lover like me, the ass's head I shall wear tonight because, in my situation, if I must go as an animal, this is the most congenial and the least ridiculous such creature, bearing in mind that it is entirely possible that come the morning I might be wearing something else, the horns of the stag for example, in accordance with a humorously mocking popular expression I have never entirely understood. Really, why is it that cheated, unloved husbands are thought to be horned? . . . Do you think you, as a linguist and writer, might be able to explain that to me?"

He waited patiently, his hands clasped, blinking, slightly tipped forward in the armchair, as if it were a very important matter, as if the etymology of a humorous and mocking popular expression really interested him. The host shrugged.

"I don't know," he answered indifferently. "It's just a saying. I will ask Monsieur Voltaire should I happen to be passing his house in Ferney, and, if he lets me, I shall send you his answer."

"Voltaire!" cried the rapt visitor. "What a marvelous idea! Yes, do ask him why language presents the cuckold with ornamental horns. Do let me know! But do you think that Voltaire, who is so well versed in language, has direct experience of the phenomenon, there in Ferney? . . . He is a cold man and his intellectual fire is like a carbuncle that glows but cannot warm. To tell you the truth, I would

prefer your opinion, since I feel reasonably hopeful that your explanation might comprehend some of its power to burn. . . ."

"Your Excellency is joking," the host replied. "It is a joke that honors me and appeals to me. At the same time I feel I should answer a different question which has not yet been asked."

"Really, Giacomo? Is there a question I have failed to ask?" the visitor exclaimed in astonishment. "Could I be so far wrong? . . . Do you really not understand why I am here, and what I want to ask you? Not after all that has and has not happened between us—for as you see, the deed is not everything, indeed it is so far from being all that I would not be sitting here at this late hour, which is in any case bad for me as well as inconvenient, if you had acted rather than spoken? Now, having said that, I have all but asked the question that you can no longer answer in words. I repeat, Giacomo, I had to come now, not a moment too soon: the time for my visit is absolutely right, for the affair I need to settle with you can no longer be postponed. It urgently requires your attention. I have brought you a letter—its author may not have thought to have it delivered by my hand, and, I must confess, it is not a particularly rewarding role I find myself playing nor a fitting one, since only once in my life have I delivered a billet-doux, and that was written by a queen to a king. I am not an official *postillon d'amour,* I despise the go-between's skill and low cunning, all those qualities learned by servicing the underworld of human feeling. Nevertheless I have brought you the letter, the letter of the duchess,

naturally, the one she wrote at noon, shortly after the levee when I left her to study my books. It's not a long letter: as you must know, women in love, like great writers, write brief notes using only the most necessary words. No, the duchess could not have imagined that I would be her messenger, and even now probably thinks that the letter that she—like all lovers who share an extraordinary, blind belief in the power of the will to hurry time—was so impatient to have answered, has been lost. Lovers sometimes think they have dominion over eternal things, over life and death! There may, in fact, be reasons for believing this, because now, as I turn my eyes from the time that has vanished and concentrate entirely on the time that still remains to me, a time that, as the hourglass reminds me, is shorter than the time that preceded it, I see that the time to come may offer more than it has ever offered me before, for time is the strangest thing: you cannot measure it in its own terms, and your fellow writers, the ancients, have long been telling us that one perfect moment may contain more, infinitely more, than the years and decades that preceded it and were not perfect! Now, when I ask my question, which is also a request, the firmest and clearest of requests, I can no longer shake my head in amazement at lovers' blind confidence in the power of sheer emotion to bring down mountains, to stop time and all the rest. Every lover is a little like Joshua who could stop the sun in its orbit in the sky above the battle, intervene in the world order and await the victory, a victory that, in my case, is also a defeat. Now when I am forced to look ahead, and I don't need to look too far ahead, because even with my

poor eyesight I can see how trifling the remaining distance is, trifling, that is, only in earthly terms, for it is timeless and impenetrable to the eyes of love, I find that I do, after all, understand the extraordinary power of a lover's will, and believe that a tiny letter, a pleasantly scented letter, not entirely regular in its orthography—you are a writer so I beg you to excuse its imperfections when you come to glance over it—but intense in its feeling, a feeling that is vague and hilariously childish in some respects, yet is as a coiled spring in the sharpness of its desire, can really suspend the laws of nature, and, for a while, that is to say for a mere second from the perspective of eternity, assert its authority over life and death. Now, when I am constrained to face one of life's great riddles—and both of us are in the position of having to ask and answer questions at once, Giacomo, as in some strange examination where we are both master and pupil!—now, when I should take the rusty flintlock of my life, load it with the live ammunition of the will and take certain aim as I have often done before, with hands that did not shake and eyes that did not easily mist over, when I was not as likely as I am now to miss my mark, I do begin to believe that there is a power, a single omnipotent power, that can transcend not only human laws but time and gravity, too. That power is love. Not lust, Giacomo—forgive me for attempting to correct the essential laws of your existence and to contradict your considerable experience. Not lust, you unhappy hunter, angler, writer, and explorer, you who nightly drag the still-steaming, still-bleeding, excited body of your prize into bed, now here, now there, in every corner of the

world; not the grinding hunger that conceals itself and is always seeking its prey wherever lonely and hidden desires are to be found, staring wide-eyed, awaiting liberation; not the gambler's eye for the main chance nor the military strategy that carries a rope ladder and watches the windows of sleeping virtue, preparing to assail it with a few bold words; not the yearning born of sadness and terrible loneliness: it is not these things that prepare one for action. I am talking about love, Giacomo, the love that haunts us all at one time or another, and might have haunted even your melancholy, sharp-toothed, predatory life, for there were reasons for your arrival in Pistoia some years ago and reasons for your escape. You are neither a wholly innocent man nor a wholly guilty one: there was a time when love possessed you too.

"I chased you away at the point of a sword then, the fool that I was! You would have been perfectly entitled to call me an old fool that day. Doting old fool! you might have cried. Do you think that blades sharpened in Venetian ice and fire or scimitars forged and flexed in Damascus can destroy love? . . . They would have been fair questions—a little rhetorical, a little poetic perhaps—but as concerns the practicalities, they would have been fair. That is why this time I have come without sharp swords or hidden daggers. I have another weapon now, Giacomo."

"What kind of weapon?"

"The weapon of reason."

"It is a useless, untrustworthy weapon to use in emotional conflicts, sir."

"Not always. I am surprised at you. It is not the answer

I would have expected from you, Giacomo. Besides, it's the only weapon I have. I speak of true reason, which has no wish to argue, to haggle, or even to convince. I haven't come to beg nor, I repeat, to threaten. I have come to establish facts and to put questions, and in my sorry and precarious situation I am obliged to believe that the cold bright blade of reason is stronger than the wild bluster and bragging of the emotions. You and the duchess are bound together by the power of love, my boy. I state this as a fact that requires no explanation. You know very well that we do not love people for their virtues, indeed, there was a time when I believed that, in love, we prefer the oppressed, the problematic, the quarrelsome to the virtuous, but as I grew older I finally learned that it is neither people's sins and faults nor their beauty, decency, or virtue that make us love them. It may be that a man understands this only at the end of his life, when he realizes that wisdom and experience are worth less than he thought. It is a hard lesson, alas, and offers nothing by way of consolation. We simply have to accept the fact that we do not love people for their qualities; not because they are beautiful and, however strange it seems, not even because they are ugly, hunchbacked, or poor: we love them simply because there is in the world a kind of purpose whose true working lies beyond our wit, which desires to articulate itself much as an idea does, so that though the world has been going around a long time it should appear ever new and, according to certain mystics, touch our souls and nervous systems with terrifying power, set glands working, and even cloud the judgment of brilliant minds. You and the

duchess are in love, and though you make an extraordinary and baffling enough pair, only a novice in love would be amazed at the fact, because, where people are concerned, nothing is impossible. Animals keep to their kind and there is no instance, as far as I am aware, of an affair between a giraffe and a puma or any other beast: animals remain within the strict precincts of their species. I trust you will forgive me, for I do not mean to insult you by the comparison! If anyone should be insulted by it, it is I! No, animals are straightforward creatures, whereas we human beings are complex and remarkable even at our lowest ebb, because we try to understand the nature of love's secret power even when we remain ignorant of its purposes, so that eventually we have to accept facts that cannot be explained. The duchess loves you, and, to me, this seems as extraordinary a liaison as an affair between the sun at dawn and a storm at night. Forgive me if I abandon the animal images that seem to be haunting me with a peculiar force tonight, probably because we are preparing for the ball where I shall be wearing an ass's head. But however extraordinary the love of the duchess for you, it is still more extraordinary that you should love the duchess: it is as if you were breaking the very laws of your existence. You will be aware that the feeling of any deep emotion whatsoever represents a revolt against those laws. There is nothing that frightens you so much, that sends you scuttling away so fast, as a confrontation with emotion. You were hungry and thirsty in jail, you beat at the iron door with your fists, you shook the bars of your window, and threw yourself on the rotten straw of your bed, helpless with bit-

terness, you cursed the world that deprived you of your fascinating life, while knowing that behind your solitude, behind the filthy straw, behind bars and iron gates, behind your memories, there was another prison, worse than the cells of the Holy Inquisition, that jail was, in its way, a form of escape, because it was only the fires of lust that burned you there, because you were not condemned to the terrifying inferno of love. Jail was a shelter from the only feeling that might trip you up and destroy you, for feeling is a kind of death for people like you: it stifles you with responsibility, as it does all insubstantial, so-called free spirits. . . . But love touched you briefly when you met the duchess, who at that time was plain Francesca, and it is love that has brought you close to her again, not the memory of an affair that never quite got started. What is this love of yours like, really? I have long pondered that. I had time enough . . . from the encounter in Pistoia, through the period in Venice, and after that, when you were in jail, by which time Francesca had become the duchess of Parma, long after we fought for her. In all that time you continued, amusingly enough, to believe that she was just another brief fling like all the rest, a conquest which did not quite succeed, an adventure in which you were not fully your ruthless self. But charity is a problematic virtue. You are not naturally one of the merciful, Giacomo: you are perfectly capable of sleeping peacefully while, at your door, the woman you deserted is busily knotting the sheets you shared into the noose she is to hang herself with. 'What a shame!' you would sigh, and shake your head. That's the kind of person you are. Your

love—the way you follow a woman, the way you note her hand, her shoulder, and her breast at a glance—is a trifle inhuman. I saw you once, many years ago, in the theater in Bologna: we hadn't yet met, nor had you met Francesca, who would have been fourteen at the time, and of whom few had yet heard, though I had heard of her, as a man might hear of some rare plant in a greenhouse, one that grows in an artificial climate, in secret, to flower and become the wonder of the world eventually. . . . You knew nothing of Francesca, nor of me, and you entered the playhouse at Bologna where people were whispering your name, and your entrance was splendid, like an actor's soliloquy. You stopped in the front row with your back to the stage, raised your lorgnette, and looked around. I studied you closely. Your reputation preceded you, your name was on everyone's lips, the boxes were buzzing with you. I want you to take what I am about to say as a compliment. You are not a handsome man. You are not one of those loathsome beaux who flounces around looking ingratiating: your face is unusual and unrefined, rather masculine, I suppose, though not in the normal sense of the word. Please don't be offended, but your face is not quite human. It might, on the other hand, be man's real face, the way the Creator imagined it, true to the original pattern which years, dynasties, fashions, and ideals have modified. You have a big nose, your mouth is severe, your figure is stocky, your hands are square and stubby, the whole angle of your jaw is wrong. It is certainly not what is required for a beau. I tell you, Giacomo, out of sheer courtesy that there is something inhuman about your face, but

I had to understand your face before I could begin to understand the love between you and Francesca. Please don't misunderstand me: when I say your face is somehow inhuman, or not quite human, I do not mean that it is animal; it is more as if you were some transitional creature, something between man and beast, a being that is neither one thing nor the other. I am sure the angels must have had something in mind when they were blending the elements that made you what you are: a hybrid, a cross between man and beast. I hope you can tell from the tone of my voice that I intend this as a compliment. There you stood in the playhouse, leaning against the walls of the orchestra pit, and you yawned. You looked at the women through your glasses and the women looked back at you with undisguised curiosity. The men, for their part, watched your movements, keeping a wary eye now on you, now on the eyes of the women, and in all this tension, suspense, and excitement, you yawned, showing those thirty-two yellow tusks of yours. You gave a great terrifying yawn. Once, in the orangerie of my Florentine palazzo, I kept some young lions and an aging leopard; your yawn was like that of the old leopard after he finally ate the Arabian keeper. Without a second thought, this noble creature proceeded to demonstrate his indifference to the world that held him captive with a yawn that spoke of infinite boredom and astonishing contempt. I remember thinking that I would have to throw a net over your head and impale you on a spear if I ever found you in the vicinity of a woman whom I too found attractive. And I was not at all surprised when, a year later, you turned up

in Pistoia, by the crumbling wall in the garden, together with Francesca, throwing colored hoops with a gilt-tipped wooden stick for her nimble arms to catch. What was it I thought then? Nothing more than: 'Yes, it is natural, how could it be otherwise.' And now I have brought you Francesca's letter."

He drew the narrow, much-folded letter from the inner pocket of his fur-lined cape with a slow, leisurely movement and held it high in the air:

"Please overlook any errors you may find. Have I said that before? It is only recently that she learned to write, from an itinerant poet in Parma, a man who had been castrated by the Moors and whom I had ransomed, his father having been our gardener. I have a fondness for poets. Her hand seems to have shaken a little with excitement and there is something terribly touching about that, for her capital letters have never been good, poor dear; I can see her now, her fevered brow and her chill, trembling fingers as she scratches her message on the blotted parchment—and where in heaven's name did she get that from?—with whatever writing implements she could find, implements probably obtained for her by her companion and accomplice, the aged Veronica, whom we brought with us from Pistoia and whom, it has just occurred to me, we might have been wiser to leave back in Pistoia. But here she is, willing to be of service, and when the moment came, she found some writing paper, a pen, some ink, and some powder, as she was perfectly right to do, for every creature, even one such as Veronica, has some inescapable, traditional part to play. It is not only onstage that nurses have

acted as bawds! It is a short letter, so please allow me to read it to you. You can afford to allow it because it is not the first time I have read it; I read it first at about four this afternoon when it was passed to the groom to deliver to you, and again this evening before I set out on my post-masterly, messenger's errand: a man shouldn't leave such tasks to strangers, after all. Are you frowning? . . . Do you think it impertinent of me to read a lady's letter? . . . You wish to remain silent in your disapproval of my curiosity? Well, you are right," he calmly continued, "I don't approve either. I have lived by the rules all my life, as an officer and gentleman, born and bred. Never in all that time did I imagine that I would meet such a woman and find myself in a situation that would lead me to behave in a manner unbefitting my upbringing, abandoning the responsibilities of my rank: never before have I opened a woman's letter, partly on principle, and partly because I did not think it would be of such overwhelming interest as to tempt me to act against my principles. But this one did interest me," he continued in a matter-of-fact manner, "since Francesca has never written me a letter, indeed could not have written me a letter even if she had wanted to, because, until a year ago, she didn't know how to write. Then, a year ago, shortly after the castrated poet came to us, she began to show an interest in writing—which, now I come to think of it, was at roughly the same time as the news of your incarceration by the Holy Inquisition arrived from Venice. She learned to write in order to write to you, because as a woman, she likes to undertake truly heroic tasks in the name of love. She learned to use those terrible cryptic

cyphers of your profession—the modest, meek, and chubby *e,* the corpulent *s, t* with its lance, *f* with its funny hat—all so that she might offer you comfort by writing down the words that were burning a hole in her heart. She wanted to console you in prison and, for a long time, I thought you corresponded. I believed in the correspondence and looked out for it; I had ears and eyes, dozens of them, at my command, the best ears and sharpest eyes in Lombardy and Tuscany, and those are places where they know about such things. . . . She learned to write because she wanted to send you messages; yet, after all that, she didn't write: I know for certain that she did not write because, to a pure and modest heart like hers, the act of writing is the ultimate immodesty, and I could sooner imagine Francesca as a tightrope dancer, or as a whore cavorting in a brothel with lecherous foreign dandies, than with a pen in her hand describing her feelings to a lover. Because Francesca is, in her way, a modest woman, just as you, in your way, are a writer, and I, in my way, am old and jealous. And that is how we lived, all of us, each in his or her own way, you under the lead roofs of Venice, she and I in Pistoia and Marly, waiting and preparing for something. Of course you are right," he waved his hand dismissively as if his host were about to interrupt, "I quite admit that we lived more comfortably in Pistoia, Bolzano, Marly, and other places, near Naples up in the mountains, in our various castles, than you on your louse-ridden straw bed, under the lead roof. But comfort, too, was a prison, albeit in its own twisted, rather improper way, so please do not judge us too harshly. . . . As I was saying, the castrato

taught Francesca to write, and I watched her, thinking 'Aha!' Quite rightly. There are times when Voltaire himself thinks no more than that, particularly when Voltaire is thinking about virtue or power. Each of us is wise at those unexpected moments of illumination when we suddenly notice the changing, surprising aspects of life. That is why I thought 'Aha!' and began to pay close attention, employing the sharpest ears and eyes that Lombardy and Tuscany could offer. But I heard and saw nothing suspicious: Francesca was too shy to write to a writer like you, too embarrassed by the prospect of putting her feelings into words—and isn't it a fact that you writers are a shameless lot, putting the most shameful human thoughts down on paper, without hesitation, sometimes even without thinking? A kiss is always virtuous but a word about a kiss is always shameful. That might be what Francesca, with that delicacy of perception so characteristic of her and of most women in love, actually felt. But she might simply have been shy about her handwriting and about corresponding in general, for, though her heart was troubled by love, it remained pure. And so, when she finally got down to writing to you, I can imagine her agitated, overwrought condition and the shudder of fear that ran through her from top to toe as she sat with fevered brow and trembling fingers, with paper, ink, and sand, to undertake the first shameless act of her life in writing to you. It was a love letter that she was writing, and in giving her all and trusting herself entirely to pen and paper, and thereby to the world and to eternity, which is always the last word in shamelessness, she was venturing into dangerous territory, but she ven-

tured further than that, into yet more dangerous territory, for the point at which someone reveals their true feelings to the world is like making love in a city marketplace in perpetual view of the idiots and gawpers of the future; it is like wrapping one's finest, most secret feelings in a ragged parcel of words; in fact it is like having the dogcatcher tie one's most vital organs up in old sheets of paper! Yes, writing is a terrible thing. The consciousness of this must have permeated her entire being as she wrote, poor darling, for love and pain had driven her to literacy, to the symbolic world of words, to the mastery of letters. But when she did write, she wrote briefly, in a surprisingly correct style, in the most concise fashion, like a blend of Ovid and Dante. Having said that, I shall now read you Francesca's letter." He unfolded the parchment with steady fingers, raised one hand in the air, and, being shortsighted, used the other to adjust the spectacles on his nose, straightening his back and leaning forward a little to peer at the script. "I can't see properly," he sighed. "Would you bring me a light, my boy?" And when his silent and formal host politely picked up a candle from the mantelpiece and stood beside him, he thanked him: "That's better. Now I see perfectly well. Listen carefully. This is what my wife, Francesca, the duchess of Parma, wrote to Giacomo, eight days after hearing that her lover had escaped from the prison where his character and behavior had landed him, and that he had arrived in Bolzano: *'I must see you.'* To this she has appended the first letter of her name, a large F, with a slight ceremonial flourish, as the castrato had taught her."

He held the letter at arm's length, perhaps in order that he might be able to see the tiny letters more clearly.

"This, then, is the letter," he declared with a peculiar satisfaction, dropping the parchment together with his spectacles into his lap and leaning back in the chair. "What do you think of the style? I am absolutely bowled over by it. Whatever Francesca does is done perfectly: that's how she is, she can do no other. I am bowled over by the letter, and I hope it has had an equally powerful impact on you, that it has shaken you to the core and made its mark on your soul and character the way all true literature marks a complete human being. After years of reading it is only now, this afternoon, when I first read Francesca's letter, that I fully realized the absolute power of words. Like emperors, popes, and everyone else, I discovered in them a power sharper and more ruthless than swords or spears. And now, more than anything I want your opinion, a writer's opinion, of the style, of the expressive talent of this beginner. I should tell you that I felt the same on a second reading—and now, having glanced over Francesca's letter for a third time, my opinion has not changed at all. The style is perfect! Please excuse my shortcomings as a critic, do not dismiss the enthusiasm of a mere family member from your lofty professional height—but I know you will admit that this is not the work of a dilettante. There are four words and one initial only, but consider the conditions that forced these four words onto paper, consider that their author, even a year ago, had no acquaintance with the written word: turn the order of the words over in your mind, see how each

follows the other, like links in a chain hammered out on a blacksmith's anvil. Talent must be self-generating. Francesca has not read the works of either Dante or Virgil, she has no concept of subject or predicate, and yet, all by herself, without even thinking about it, she has discovered the essentials of a correct, graceful style. Surely it is impossible to express oneself more concisely, more precisely, than this letter. Shall we analyze it? . . . *'I must see you.'* In the first place I admire the concentrated power of the utterance. This line, which might be carved in stone, contains no superfluous element. Note the prominence of the verb, as is usual in the higher reaches of rhetoric, especially in drama and verse-play, with action to the fore. 'See,' she writes, almost sensuously, for the word does refer to the senses. It is an ancient word, coeval with humanity, the source of every human experience, since recognition begins in seeing, as does desire, and man himself, who before the moment of seeing is merely a blind, mewling, bundle of flesh: the world begins with sight and so, most certainly, does love. It is a spellbinding verb, infinite in its contents, suggesting hankering, secret fires, the hidden meaning of life, for the world only exists insofar as we see it, and you too only exist insofar as Francesca is capable of seeing you—it is, in the terms of this letter at least, through her eyes that you re-enter the world, her world, emerging from the world of the blind that you had inhabited, but only as a shadow, a shade, like a memory or the dead. Above all, she wants to see you. Because the other senses—touch, taste, scent, and hearing—are all as blind gods without the arcana of vision. Nor is Cupid a blind

god, Giacomo. Cupid is inquisitive, light-desiring, truth-demanding: yes, above all he wants to see. That's why the word 'see' is so prominent in her discourse. What else might she have said? She might have written 'talk with,' or 'be with,' but both of these are merely consequences of seeing, and her use of that verb confirms the intensity of the desire that drives her to take up the pen; the verb practically screams at us, because a heart smitten by love feels it can no longer stand the dark of blindness, it must see the beloved's face; it must see, it must light a torch in this incomprehensible and blind universe, otherwise nothing makes sense. That's why she chose a word as precise, as deeply expressive as 'see.' I hope my exposition does not bore you? . . . I must admit it is of supreme interest to me, and it is only now, for the first time, that I understand the endeavors of lonely philologists who, with endless patience and anxious care, pore over dusty books and ancient undecipherable texts, spending decades disputing the significance of some obscure verb in a forgotten language. Somehow, through the energy of their looking and the vitality of their breath they succeed in coaxing a long-dead word back to life. I am like them in that I think I can interpret this text, that is to say the text of Francesca's letter. Seeing, as we have said, is the most important aspect of it. Next comes *'must.'* Not 'I would like to,' not 'I desire to,' not 'I want to.' Immediately, in the second word of the text, she declares something with the unalterable force of holy writ—and doesn't it occur to you, Giacomo, that our young author was, in her way, producing a kind of holy writ by writing her first words of love? Don't you think

that the writ of love somehow resembles sacred hiero-
glyphs on a pagan tomb, directly invoking the presence of
the Immortal, even when it speaks of no more than
arrangements for a rendezvous, or of a rope ladder to be
employed in the course of an escape? . . . Naturally, there's
nothing irrelevant in Francesca's discourse: she is far too
fine a poet for that as we may see at a glance. Poet, I said,
and I don't believe that my feelings or my admiration lead
me to exaggerate in the use of the word, which I realize
signifies status, the very highest human status: in China,
as in Versailles, it is poets like Racine, Bossuet, and
Corneille, that follow the king in a procession, sometimes
even those who in life were a little dirty or disreputable
looking, such as La Fontaine: they all take precedence over
Colbert, over even Madame Montespan and Monsieur
Vendôme when the king grants an audience. I know very
well that to be a poet is to belong to an elite, an elite
accorded intimate luster and invisible medals. That may
be why I feel that Francesca is a poet, and in saying that, I
feel the same awe as I would if I were reading the first work
of any true poet, an awe that sends shudders through me
and fills my soul with dizzy admiration, with an extraordinary flood of feelings that unerringly signify the most ele-
vated thoughts about the solemnity of life. That, then, is
why she wrote *must*. What refined power radiates from the
word, my boy! Its tone is commanding, regal: it is more
than a command because it is both explanation and significance at once. If she had written 'want' it would still have
been regal but a little peremptory. No, she chose precisely
the right word, the perfectly calibrated word, the word

that, while it commands some humility: *must,* she says, and thereby confesses that when she commands, she herself is obeying a secret commandment; *must* suggests that the person requesting the meeting stands in need of something, that she can do no other, can no longer wait, that when she addresses you severely and gives you to understand her meaning she is throwing herself on your mercy. There is something touchingly helpless and human about the word. It is as if her desire to meet you were involuntary, Giacomo. Yes, it's true! I cannot tell whether my eyes are capable of reading clearly anymore, whether I can trust these old ears of mine, but there is something in the whole sentence, which might be the first line of a poem, that is helpless and abject, as when a man confronts his destiny under the stars and tells the sad, brilliant truth. And what is that truth? Both more and less than the fact that Francesca *must* see you. The voice is anxious, in need of help; she commands but, at the same time, admits that she is both the issuer and the helpless executor of the command. I *must see:* there is something dangerous about the association of these words; only people who are themselves in danger issue commands like these. Yes, they would prefer to withdraw and defend themselves but there's no alternative, and so they do what they must: they command. The words are perfect. And there follows, naturally enough, a word that is like the lin-lan-lone of bells in the distance: the word *you. You* is a mighty word, Giacomo. I don't know whether anyone can say something that means more to another, or is of greater importance to them. It is a fulfilling word whose reverberation fills the entire human

universe, a painful word that forms and names, that enlivens identity and gives it a voice. It is the word God used when He first addressed man at the Creation, at the point that He realized that flesh was not enough, that man needed a name, too, and therefore He named him and addressed him with the familiar *You.* Do you fully understand the word? There are millions upon millions of people in the world but it is *you* she wants to see. There are others nobler, handsomer, younger, wiser, more virtuous, more chivalrous than you, oh indeed there are, and without wishing to offend you, I do think it incumbent on you to consider, however unpleasant it may be, however it may hurt your self-esteem, that there may also exist people more villainous, more artful, more deceitful, more heartless, and more desperate than you are; and yet it is *you* she desires to see. The word elevates you above your fellow mortals, distinguishes you from those whom in part you resemble; it hoists you up and slaps you on the back, it crowns you a king and dubs you a knight. It is a fearsome word. *You,* writes Francesca, my wife, the duchess of Parma, and the instant she writes the word you are ennobled; despite your notoriety as an adventurer, despite hitherto having assumed a false aristocratic name, you are ennobled. *You,* she writes, and with what a certain hand, the letters leaning with full momentum, like arms raised for action, pumping blood and flexing powerful muscles: by now the author knows what she wants to say and is no longer seeking alternatives. She places on paper the only word that can hold the sentence, the syntax, together as though she had addressed the subject of it by its proper

name. *You* . . . A mysterious word. Just consider how many people there are in the world, people who are interesting to Francesca, too, people worth seeing even if there is no *must* about it, people who would offer her something more substantial, more true, more of everything than you can, notwithstanding the fact that you are a writer and traveler. For there are men out there who have voyaged to the Indies and the New World, scientists who have explored the secrets of nature and discovered new laws for humanity to wonder at: there are so many other remarkable men alive, and yet it is *you* she wants to see . . . and in so naming you it is as if she were engaged in an act of creation, re-creating you. Because, for example, it is possible that she might want to see me, but there would be nothing out of the ordinary in that, I am her husband after all: but it is *you* that she must see, only *you!* . . .

"Well, there is the text and we have explored its meaning. And now, let us behold it once more with amazement, having examined its parts, seeing the compact, solid whole, admiring the logic of the thought, the momentum of the execution, the terse perfection of the style that, without a hint of superfluity, tells you everything. And finally, let us consider the signature, which is so modest, a mere initial—for true letters and true works of art require nothing more: the work itself identifies the author, is one with her. No one imagines that the *Divine Comedy* required the name of the author below the title . . . not that I wish to invite comparisons, of course. But what need for names when the whole text speaks so clearly, the words, the syntax, the individual letters; when everything

is infused with the same character, the same soul, a soul driven by necessity and inspiration to creation, in the recognition that its fate is to see you, nothing more. And having said that," he added carelessly, holding the letter between two fingers and passing it over, "we have done. Here's the letter." And when the host and addressee did not move, he lightly placed the letter on the mantelpiece beside the candlestick.

"You will read it later?" he asked. "Yes, I understand. I think you will often read and reread that letter in the years to come, but later, when you are older. You will understand it then." And he fell silent, breathing heavily, as if he had overexcited himself with all that talking, his heart worn out, his lungs exhausted.

"We have done," he repeated, old and tired now, and leaned against his stick, holding it with both hands. But he continued speaking, still seated, leaning on his stick, not glancing at his host but staring into the fire, frequently blinking and screwing up his eyes, watching the embers.

"I have accomplished one of my missions by giving you the letter. I hope you will look after it properly. I wouldn't like the love letter of the duchess of Parma to be left on the wine-stained table of some inn, nor would I want you to read it out while in bed with a whore, in that boasting and bragging way men have when under the influence of cheap wine and cheap passion. I would not be in a position to prevent that, of course, but it would cause me great pain, and therefore I hope it will not happen. Yet we may be sure that this kind of letter will not remain a secret, and I would not be at all surprised if at some later

time, in another, more refined and more generous age, such brief masterpieces were taught in schools as a model of concision. Nor do I doubt that the letter will be imitated, as is every masterpiece, that through the fine capillaries of memory it will enter the general consciousness of our descendants: lovers will copy it and make irreverent use of it without knowing the least thing about the author and its provenance. They will copy it, and not just once, as if they themselves had composed it, committing it to paper, declaring *I must see you,* and signing it with their own names or initials, and by some mysterious process the text will actually have become theirs—like all true texts it will be diffused into the world and be blended with life itself, for that is its nature. All the same, I would prefer it if this process were to follow literary precedent at an appropriate pace, not through your bragging and boasting, or declaiming the text aloud in taverns or in a whore's bed. I would be extremely sorry if that were to happen. But now that I have given you the letter whose true meaning we have, I hope, solved and understood, we must be careful lest our enthusiasm as literary critics, the peculiar and obstinate delight we take in studying it, should divert us from our true obligation: for letters can be as passionate and terrifying as kissing or murder; there is something real and living in them, and we two critics—you the writer and I the reader and connoisseur—have almost forgotten the person behind the letters, she who has committed these perfect lines to paper. It is, after all, she whom we are discussing, and Francesca is inclined to the belief that she must see you. That is the reality to which we must return

now that we have finished admiring the beauties of the letter. And here we must be businesslike, since time is passing and the evening is upon us—isn't it the case that time never flies so fast as when we lose ourselves in admiration of the hidden graces of a first-class text?—but our business is to proceed beyond the eternal literary merits of the text and to explore the meaning in its practical sense, that meaning being neither more nor, alas, less than that the duchess of Parma has fallen in love and must see you. That is an obligation you cannot avoid, even should you wish to. I have already said that I have not come to threaten you, Giacomo: I have simply brought you a letter and all I want is to understand, articulate, and settle something. I have not come to threaten: there is no need for you to stand so rigidly or to twitch like that, there is no question of us engaging in another armed encounter for the sake of Francesca, as we once did in such a laughable and yet admirably masculine manner in Tuscany, our chests bare in the moonlight! The time for that is gone: and I don't mean just the time of year, however awful in its effects that may be, for the cold cuts through me to the bone even when I am wearing my furs, and heaven knows what it would do if I presented myself half-naked, no, I mean another kind of time, the time that has passed. I have thrown away my sword. I could, of course, buy other swords, better and finer than the old one, for once upon a time, as you will recall, I was not altogether hopeless in a duel. I could buy a sword, one that glittered as I wielded it, a rapier of ice-cold steel to twist wickedly between your ribs: I do, after all, hold your life in my hands. But this is

not a threat either, Giacomo: it is a statement, no more. Please don't protest. There is no need to get excited. Your life is in my hands, that's all: in vain did you escape from the republic, in vain did the world look on and chuckle in approval, in vain do local laws protect you with their guarantees of personal and institutional freedom, in vain does tradition underwrite the international rights of refugees. According to laws and customs you are invulnerable here, untouchable. But people are aware, and you in particular have good reason to know, that there exists another law, a more subtle, unwritten law, whose custom and practice underlie the visible, practical, and constitutionally approved sort, a law that is more real and more effective everywhere. It is my kind of law: I dispense it, I and a few others in the world, those who are sufficiently intelligent and powerful to live by such unwritten laws without exploiting them. Believe me, Giacomo, when I say that it really was in vain that you escaped, clever monkey that you are, from the Leads on the roof of the Doge's Palace; in vain that you scuttled like some fugitive water-rat down the filthy and noble waters of the lagoon and reached the far shore in Mestre and later, Valdepiadene; it is in vain that you reside here beyond the perilous border, in a room of The Stag, strutting with confidence, as if you had escaped every danger, for if I wished it you'd be back on the other side of the border in the clutches of the *messer grande* by this time tomorrow, after sunset, you can bet your life on it. And why? . . . Because power does not work precisely as these local boobies believe it works, and you, who are better traveled and more nimble-witted than

they are, will be perfectly aware of the fact. You therefore know that there is no nook or cranny in the world where these calloused, exhausted hands, that are no longer up to dueling, would not reach you if I so wished. That is why I am not threatening you. And it's not out of the kindness of my heart, nor out of any false if noble sense of compassion that I allow you to keep running—because run you must, Giacomo, on fleet horses, in covered coaches, or on sleighs with polished runners before the night is through. As soon as you have finished your business in Bolzano and met the duchess, who, as she has commanded both you and me, *must* see you, we will draw a line under the affair and place a full stop at the end of the last sentence. That is why I have no thought of threatening you in revealing to you the vague outline of what might happen behind the scenes, and exposing the real, effective relations of power. I am merely explaining and cautioning. And there is no trace of bitterness in my heart when I say that, no sense of injury, no false male pride, not any more. For you, like me, are merely a cat's-paw, an actor, the tool of the fate that is toying with us both, a fate whose purposes sometimes appear unfathomable. Sometimes it seems the hand it is playing is not entirely above board, that it is playing for its own amusement; a manner of playing that you, who understand not only written slips of paper but those prinked out with spots and numbers too, are in the best position to comprehend. That is why I have come to you. What I want is that you should stay till morning and accommodate yourself to the duchess's desire, which is more command than desire, something neither of us can

refuse to obey, for behind it lies the *must* to which the duchess of Parma gives such perfect literary expression. You are, therefore, to remain in Bolzano until the morning. Should I threaten you? Should I reason with you? Should I beg you? Explain things to you? What should I do with you? . . . I could kill you, but then you would be more deadly than before. You would retain your current stocky, fleshy, full-blooded reality, a reality I would have turned into a shade, a memory, a rival impervious to blows, the rotten corpse of a once vigorous presence, an amorous shadow forever lurking in the folds of the curtains of my wife's four-poster bed, taking my place on her pillow after midnight, your voice haunting other men's voices, your eyes looking at her through unknown men's eyes. That is why I will not kill you. Should I send you away? Order you now, this very night, to take to the sledge waiting at the gate, shrouded in the wings of your cloak, so that, under the stewardship and protection of my servants, you should rush over mountain passes, through moonlit forests restless with the shadows of wolves, into a foreign country where you might disappear from the best years of the duchess's life? . . . I could insist on that, too, and you'd have no choice but to obey, because, after all, you want to save your skin, and it is that fact which allows me to exercise a degree of control over you, for you are still careful of your life, solicitous of your esteemed person, your flesh and bones and are not desperately anxious to risk them, while I, on the other hand, no longer fear for my life and am interested only in one thing which, to me, is finer and more valuable. That is why you must obey me.

For this and other reasons of your own. For now I am willing to put my power and strength at the disposal of your own interests and intentions, providing we can come to a friendly, sensible agreement. That is the reason I have come to you tonight. I want to make you an offer. I have thought a great deal about you. I saw before me your face in the theater at Bologna, the way you yawned, and I remembered how, in that moment, without knowing anything much about you, I instinctively understood the nature of your being. And now I know you properly, or as well as anyone can know you, I am sure it would be a mistake to kill you. A man who is loved is a dangerous rival in death: you'd sit with us at table, lie beside the duchess in her bed, precede us into rooms, your light, ghostly footsteps would tread close behind us as we walked through the garden: you would, in short, be omnipresent. You would become funereal, your outlines blurred by ceremony, hidden among the silver and black hangings of feeling and memory. But a fierce scarlet cloud of revenge would trail behind you, its silently smoking fire lighting up the corridors. And I would have become the selfish, cowardly, stupid nonentity who had killed the unique, the miraculous person that Francesca had to see! No, my boy, I will not kill you. I could, of course, simply hand you over into the clutches of the *messer grande* and he wouldn't make the same mistake twice. I could do it because I have influence and influence has long arms and moves in mysterious ways. Do you remember that morning some sixteen months ago when Venetian agents forced their way into your room and you railed at them, spitting with

indignation, demanding that you be informed of your crimes? You will certainly recall the next sixteen months, buried away, sprawling on a rotten straw bed, still wondering what it was you were accused of. Do you think it might have been a word in the right ear, a little flexing of muscles that landed you there? It might easily have been my doing. Not that I am saying it was, I only mention it because I think you should consider it as a possibility among others, something you should give some thought to once this night is through. Because, although I am not a writer and am not preparing to embark on any kind of career, and though I am losing my hair and suffer shooting pains in my arms, and though time is certainly not on my side, I am nevertheless possessed of effective means. And, if I wanted to, I could still stretch out my arm and touch a life that considers itself secure in Venice, under the protection of Papa Bragadin. How pale you look! You have taken a step back. Are you looking for your dagger? Is it revenge you want? . . . Control yourself, my boy. I have come unarmed, as you see, and there is nothing to stop you running me through in an act of revenge and then taking to your heels to escape the police of half the world, until you are caught and find yourself on the scaffold. But how pointless that would be! You would lose everything and even your revenge would be tinged with doubt about my part in your imprisonment. Calm down. I haven't said I was responsible for that. I have merely thrown a little light on the faint possibility that I might have been. I have fought too many battles and have lived too full a life to feel any compassion for you. My compassion is not easily

earned. Only weak and frightened people shed crocodile tears and hug their enemies to their bosoms with false enthusiasm. I will not take you to my bosom, Giacomo. I will neither kill you nor exile you before your time is due. What course, if any, is there left to me, then? . . . Well, I believe I have found the only acceptable solution. I will strike a bargain with you. I realize that in proposing this bargain, which will be not a whit more crooked or honest than such bargains usually are, I am addressing both your feelings and your intelligence. So let me put it plainly: I want to buy you, my boy. You can name your price, and in case false modesty, false ambition, or any other false feeling prevent you, I will tell you the price, the price I am willing to pay to prevent the reality from becoming a ghostly rival, to ensure that you finally vanish from my life, having completed your business and played your part by allowing the duchess to see you, as she must, as she wishes. . . . I am buying you: these are ugly words, not the words an author or a duchess are likely to use, but they are my words, and they, too, are precise. I have weighed them and chosen them carefully. I know your services will not be cheap, but I am rich and powerful and I shall pay you in gold and clemency, in advice and connections, in documents and cash. Whatever it costs it will be a bargain. Please don't protest. I shall buy you as people buy a donkey for carrying water on the market in Toulon, as they buy a slave on the market at Smyrna: I shall buy you as if I were buying a curio from one of the silversmiths on the Ponte Vecchio. Are you still protesting? Are you staring at the floor and biting your lips? . . . Are you planning some

terrible act of revenge, a revenge that might at once wipe out this insult as well as the disgrace of your imprisonment in Venice? . . . Please control yourself. Naturally, I must pay you for those injuries, too, and will offer you the full pleasures of the world, for one has to buy the whole man, with the full complement of his moods and passions, or the bargain is meaningless. I am buying you because you are a mere mortal. Think it over carefully: it is almost a compliment. I used the word 'almost' at the beginning of our conversation and I repeat it now because words bind and their binding power extends to both the past and the future. It is almost a compliment, believe me, for what is man in the daily traffic of the world? . . . A chance combination of character and fate, no more. I know your character and have researched your history, so I know, with absolute certainty, that however pale you grow, however you gasp and stare, you will kill neither me nor yourself. Not because you are a coward!—not at all!—but because it is simply not in your character to do so, because, in your heart of hearts, you are already calculating how much you dare demand of me, because the bargain fundamentally appeals to you, and because there are certain things that you can do nothing about for, after all, how could you? . . . It's how you are. The fact that you are not averse to a bargain might be the one and only fully human feature of your character. Don't worry about how much you can demand of me, Giacomo: I will give you what you ask for. And more on top of that! I may be acting against my business principles in telling you this, but let that be, for I confess that whatever figure you dream up is of no interest

to me. Let me offer you a thousand ducats in gold this very evening. Is that too little? Fine. Let us say two thousand, in cash, to see you through Munich and Paris. Not enough? That's all right, my boy, carry on by all means, I understand. Let us therefore say ten thousand ducats, together with a letter of credit for use in Paris. Still not enough? . . . I understand, I really do understand, my boy. Let me throw in a letter of safe passage for use on the road, so you may travel like the prince de Condé, and, in addition, a personal introduction to the elector, who will be happy to hear the story of your escape from your own lips. Is that still not enough? . . . Well, why not? I'm not a petty man. All right, I will trump it all with a letter of introduction to my cousin, Louis himself."

He extended the wasted, aristocratic hand that had until now been held to the fire and turned it over, palm upward, as if he were offering him the world.

"See this?" he asked, almost moved by his own generosity. "Nobody has received as much from me. It is true that the situation is unique in that I have never before played postman, lawyer, and go-between in persuading a man and woman to come together for a common purpose. . . . This evening is indeed unique, since for the first time in my life I shall be wearing in public the mask that befits every aging lover. The ass's head. So it's settled. You will receive that letter, too. Have you any idea of its value? And you will have money on top of that, money in gold and money in the form of credit to be redeemed at the most exquisite address, at any town from any conveyor of your choosing, to the full amount I have promised. I

am paying a high price for you, Giacomo, as one must for a gift purchased at the close of one's life, for something one wants to offer a woman by way of farewell, the only woman one loves. That is why I want to strike a bargain with you. I am buying you in a proper, aboveboard fashion, and the letter I shall write to my cousin, Louis, which a trusted servant will give you at dawn, providing everything happens as we have agreed, will be the first and last begging letter I address to His Most Christian Majesty, who will not deny my request. Louis will receive you at Versailles: the letter guarantees that! It is no more than I owe—not to you, nor even to myself—but to the woman on whose behalf I have played postman, the woman I love. It is your price tag. And now that I have settled that price I don't think you can demand more of me. The other letter will open frontiers for you, and you will sleep as comfortably in the inns of foreign towns as your mother once did in the lap of the beautiful diva. The police will no longer bother you, and should clouds of strife or entanglement gather around you and enemies pursue you, it will be enough for you to show that letter and your pursuer will immediately be transformed into an admiring friend. I do this so you may safely find your way through this ugly world. It is the price of our contract. What do I demand in exchange? A great deal, naturally. I demand that you accommodate yourself to the wishes of the duchess of Parma. I demand you spend this night with the duchess of Parma."

He raised the silver-handled stick high in the air with an easy movement, and at the end of the sentence he

knocked twice, lightly, on the marble floor with it, as if knocking might put the seal on his words.

"Your Excellency seriously wishes this?" his host asked.

"Do I wish it? . . . No," his guest answered with grave calm. "I command it, my boy."

"I have said," he continued more quietly, more confidentially, "that my contract is intended to appeal both to your feelings and your reason. Listen then. Lean closer. Are we alone? . . . I trust that we are. I have contracted you for one night, Giacomo. I made that decision without deluding myself, without ambition, fear, or confusion. I made the decision because my life is almost over, and that which remains of it I want to freight with the only possible cargo. That cargo is my wife, Francesca. I want to keep this woman for the time that remains, which is not long now, but is not entirely negligible, either: in fact it is precisely as long as fate has ordained for me. I want to keep her: I want not only her physical presence, but her feelings and desires, too, feelings and desires that are currently confused by the fierce intensity of the love she feels for you. I regard this love as a kind of rebellion. It may be a justified rebellion but it runs counter to my interests and I will put it down as I have put down all others. I am not a delicate, oversensitive person. I respect tradition and I respect order, which is far more substantial, far more logical, than the average ninny believes. I believe in order as a source of virtue, though not necessarily the kind of virtue mentioned in the catechism. When the bakers of Parma raised the price of bread I hanged them in their own shop doorways though the law gave me no such right, because I

had power and reason enough, and because it kept the order in a manner of speaking, though not in the manner understood by nervous lawyers and august judges. I broke my top general on a wheel outside the gates of Verona because he was insolent and vile to a common soldier, and many found fault with me for this, but real soldiers and real officers understood, because real soldiers and real officers know that to command is to be responsible, and only those who are ruthless in their logic while remaining courteous and responsive are capable of keeping order. I have put down rebellions because I believe in order. There is no happiness, no true feeling, without order, and that is why, throughout my life, I have made use of the sword and the rope to eliminate every kind of sentimental rebellion, whose importunate aim it is to destroy the inner order of things, for without true order there can be no harmony, no growth, nor true revolution, either. This love between you and the duchess, Giacomo, is a form of rebellion, and because I can't break it on the wheel, hang it by the legs at the entrance of the city, or pursue it naked and barefoot at night through the snow, I am buying it instead. I have named the price. It is a good price. Few people have the means to pay such a high price for you. I am buying you as I would a well-known singer, conjuror, or strongman, the way we pay a visiting entertainer who is passing through the city, appears on stage for the lords of the place, and amuses them as best he can for one night. I want you to perform for me in the same way, Giacomo, to make a guest appearance in Bolzano for one night only. I am hiring you to show the customers what you know, and we

shall see whether you are applauded or jeered off the stage at the end. Are you still quiet? Do you think it is not enough? Or maybe it's too much? Are you undergoing some significant inner struggle? Enjoy yourself, my boy! Have a good laugh! Let us both laugh, since we are alone, shut away from the world, face-to-face with the facts: let us laugh, for we are intimates after all, parties to a mutual agreement. Is your self-respect troubling you, Giacomo? Ah, Giacomo! I see now I shall have to improve my offer. There must be something else I can offer you, the gallant and gambler, who wants everything and nothing . . . are you shaking your head? Do you mean you have grown up and are no longer an adolescent? So now you know that 'everything' and 'nothing' don't exist in real life: that there are always only gray areas of 'something' between the extremes of 'nothing' and 'everything,' for 'nothing' and 'everything' usually turn out to be rather a lot? Why are you hesitating? Tell me your price, there's nobody else here. Name the sum. Money is of no value to me anymore, so go ahead, you can be as crude as you like, bellow the price that fits with your conscience or whisper it into my ear, tell me how much it will take to persuade you to spend the night with the duchess of Parma. How expensive or how cheap do you estimate your art to be? . . . Speak, my boy," he said and cleared his grating throat. "Speak, because my time is up."

His host stood before him with folded arms. They couldn't see each other's faces in the half light.

"Neither expensive nor cheap, Your Excellency," he

courteously replied. "This night has no price. There's only one way you can buy this night."

"Name the price."

"I will do it for nothing."

The guest stared into the fire again. He did not move, didn't even raise his head, but his bloodless, narrow lips hissed in irritation.

"That is more than I can pay. I fear you have misunderstood me, Giacomo. I cannot pay that much." Giacomo maintained an obstinate silence. "What I mean," continued the duke, "is that the contract is meaningless at that price. It is an impossible sum for me to pay for a service, an art that you foolishly overvalue. You are singing a high tenor, Giacomo, if I may say so. It is not an aria I wanted to hear but the voice of clear calm reason ready to make a good bargain. I thought I was talking to a man, not a singing clown."

"And I thought I was answering a man," replied the other, unruffled, "not Maecenas, the patron of the arts."

"Maecenas is good," replied the duke, shrugging. "A fine answer. Eloquent words. It is an eloquent answer with a precise and respectable literary allusion: but it has nothing to do with reality. It is true that you need eloquence to bargain—a few fine words and some beating of the breast may be necessary—it may in fact be the only way for us to bargain. But we have done with eloquence. Let us descend from the empyrean. I fear you have failed to understand me. You believe this bargain is immoral. By the cowardly standards and timid morals of the world, it may be so. But

my time is short and I cannot afford to wait on the morals and judgments of the world. The woman I love loves you, but you cannot truly love a woman, because you are doomed never to be satisfied: you are the sort of man who may drink as much as he likes from a fine crystal goblet or a stone trough but can never quench his thirst and is therefore beyond redemption. Love is a form of addiction for you. It took me a long time to understand that, and I have been trying to understand it from the moment I saw you yawning in the theater at Bologna, to the moment here in Bolzano, when I gave you the duchess's letter. And now that I know your nature, and who you are, I cannot say to Francesca: 'Go! Go with the man you love!' . . . I might be able to say it, Giacomo, if you were not who you are, if I did not wish to protect Francesca from the sad fire that burns within you. And if I pity you for anything, it is for the incapacity, the deafness, that your character and fate have bestowed on you; I pity you because you don't know love, have never heard the voice of love, because you are deaf. Perhaps you, too, if only out of sheer boredom, occasionally give up a woman, or let one go her own way into the flames of her own choosing, because you like the gesture, are playing a game, or because you want to be gallant or generous. But what you cannot know is that love can make a man immoral; you cannot know that a man who loves can let a woman go for one night, indeed for eternity if it comes to that—not for selfish reasons, but because he feels obliged to serve her by sacrificing himself. Because to love is, and always has been, simply to serve. Now, for the first time in my life, I, too, wish to serve.

Even the mighty and the privileged must bow to fate. If you were not who I believe you are, I might even let Francesca with all her youth and her inexperience go with you. But I cannot allow it because all you can give her is a few days and nights while she is with you, a few moments of almost impersonal tenderness, a flame that burns but cannot warm. What can you give her? . . . Only the thrill of seduction. That is your own peculiar art form. It is a high art with a long tradition, and you are certainly a master in your field. But it is the nature of a thrill to be of short duration: that is the kind of art it is and those are its rules and proportions. Now go, and perform miracles, Giacomo!" he said, his voice a little hoarse now, and turned to him, his eyes wide open. They stared at each other a while. "Make this thrill exquisite for her. I insulted you before by offering you cash, freedom, and worldly pleasure in exchange for your art, and you got on your high horse and made a grand speech, with words like 'nothing' and 'Maecenas.' These are only words. The art of which you are a master, the art you understand as truly as a goldsmith understands rings and brooches, the field in which you are a true creative spirit, is that of seduction. So go and create your seductive masterpiece. I know who I am talking to, you see, and I trust you to do a good job. What are the requirements of a seduction? Everything you might need is at your disposal: night, secrecy, a mask, a vow, fine words, sighs, a billet-doux, a covert message, a tryst in the snowdrifts, a tender abduction, the great moment when your captive lies panting in your arms, when she gives herself and cries out, and then the slow

descent and conclusion, vows like 'you alone' and 'forever' though by that time you will be keeping half an eye on dawn as it begins to blush through the window, awaiting the moment you may leave in a manner appropriate to your vocation, having completed your work satisfactorily, in private, an artist contemplating his next appearance in some other place. You will not be bought, you said. A laudable sentiment. But I don't believe you because I know that there is nothing in this world that cannot be bought. Perhaps even the fire of love may be purchased. I am striving now to buy what may remain of Francesca's love, the tenderness that is left to comfort my remaining days, because I am weak and must die soon, and I want my last few months and days to be suffused with the wonderful light that radiates from this one body, this one soul. I realize it is a sign of weakness. I want her to get over you as she might get over an illness. It isn't some salacious fantasy that has driven me to this point, now when the musicians are already tuning up in my own palazzo and the ass's head is ready and waiting; no, these are not the pleadings of an ancient lover who can no longer yield his darling amusement and delight. No, Giacomo, you are an illness, the yellow fever, the plague, and the pox combined and we have to get over you. If there is nothing else we can do let us at least survive. That is why I come to you, asking you to spend the night with my wife—an odd enough request on first hearing, but when we take everything into consideration, if we examine our emotions in their true context and use our brains, a most natural one. I see the dangers of the pox, the plague, and the yellow fever and realize that it

is vital that we pull through. That is why I need you to work a miracle! There is nothing else you can give her, the poor invalid, but the thrill of seduction—so let us concoct this adventure for her, in the best and most proper manner, with dignity and skill, with the mutual understanding of true accomplices, conjoined in the melancholy complicity that is the unavoidable lot of all men who are in attendance on the same woman. Consult your art and devise one brilliant act of seduction, for it is my wish that in the morning Francesca should return to the palazzo, like a patient recovered from an illness, her heart free, her head held high, not sneaking home down shady alleys, but as proud as I would have her be, for she too has a rank and I am unwilling to see her lose anything of her dignity. This is the way I have contrived in order to keep her with me for the short time that remains to me, now that I understand so much more than I did before, now that my life is almost over. That is why I am addressing my offer not to the man, the ordinary mortal in you, who takes it as an insult, but to the immortal artist and craftsman. All I want is for you to remain true to your art and to create a masterpiece. Ah, now you are looking at me! I think we are beginning to understand each other. . . . Look into my eyes. Good, my boy. We should face each other in the cold light of day, as accomplices. How wonderful it is to have awakened the interest of an artist. The Pope must have felt like this when he persuaded the mighty Michelangelo to raise and complete his dome. Very well, let us construct our dome, in our own fashion, and finish the business properly," he said and gave a sad, twisted smile. "You value

your art highly and I am prepared to pay a high price for it, so there's no point in us bandying words, for by dawn tomorrow you will have need of ten thousand golden pieces and of my rare, invaluable letter. Let us not waste any more breath on the subject, nothing could be more natural. I merely mention the details in passing. What is more important is that I finally see the light of understanding in your eyes. Only a few moments have passed but now I know I have touched the artist in you: I can see the idea interests and excites you. You have a preoccupied look and are probably turning the campaign over in your mind even now, anticipating the problems of execution, wondering how to build momentum at the beginning . . . am I right? I suspect I am. You see, I have calculated carefully, Giacomo: I know that an artist cannot escape the siren call of his art. I am quite confident that you won't disappoint me and that you will do something wonderful, if only because there is no alternative: you stand or fall by your success. The kind of masterpiece I want you to produce is what they call a miniature: a concentrated form of the art in which that which normally takes a month or a year happens in a few hours. I want the beginning and end to be miraculously apposite and to follow close on each other's heels, and who in all Europe is in a better position to accomplish that than you, you above all people, and precisely at this moment when you are fresh from the prison where time and enforced meditation will have matured your talent and skill? . . . I know your performance will be perfect, Giacomo! It has to be: that is why I am reasonably, justifiably, paying a high price for you, in

words, in gold, in the letter and in blood-curdling threats, all of which you deserve, all of which are in keeping with your person, with my person, and with the person of the woman for whose sake all this is being arranged! I want you to compress and concentrate your art. I realize it is the most difficult thing to do, but I want you for a few hours to suspend the laws of time and to produce a conjuring trick, like the Eastern magi who, in a mere few seconds, can make a bud blossom into a flower that is perfect in scent, color, and form, but dies immediately. The death of the flower is a more melancholy event, but just as spellbinding and mysterious as its blossoming. The miracle of decay, completion, and destruction and the miracle of birth are equally remarkable. How wonderful, how terrifying the relationship between awakening, climax, and conclusion. But I want this to be more than just a conjuring trick, all gold leaf and hollow words: you must give her everything, the true thrill of seduction, a whirlwind affair complete with night, fog, flight, true vows, and real passion, otherwise it is all for nothing. And everything must happen quickly, very quickly, Giacomo, because time presses. I cannot wait long, I don't have weeks to spare for you, not a day or night more than this present one. That is why I have hired you, only you, the one giant among a crowd of fashionable fops who might perform the same service. Because I appreciate and almost—how that word keeps coming back to haunt me!—almost admire your artistry. I know the task requires an impossible blend of intelligence, craft, finesse, and ice-cold strategy on the one hand and fury, passion, tears, ecstasy, madness, the fever-

ish beating of the heart, and even a degree of suicidal torpor on the other, and that what you will do in miniature and in accelerated form in one night would take the average bourgeois lover a long time, perhaps even an entire lifetime to achieve. That is what makes you as much an artist as the man who can engrave an entire battle scene on a tiny piece of stone or paint a crowded city full of people, dogs, and spires on a slip of ivory. Because an artist, and only an artist, can shatter the laws of space and time! And you must shatter them tonight! Tonight you will visit us because Francesca feels that she must see you! You will come in costume, wearing a mask like everyone else. Once you have recognized her, you must call her away, bring her here, and perform the miracle! I can see by the expression in your eyes that you are willing, and I, in my turn am willing to pay the price. What I want, Giacomo, what I demand, is that the duchess be back in the palazzo by dawn. In the meantime I promise you that not a word will ever again pass between us about the events of this night, however it turns out, whatever life brings us in the future. Tonight the duchess will see you, as in her sickness she desires to do, and she will know you, in the precise biblical sense of the word, for love, that contagious fever, is nothing if not a matter of getting to know. Your business as an artist, as a healer, is to ensure that by the time dawn comes round she is free of infection. I am not interested in the secrets of your craft. I want her to recover from you but in such a way that at dawn she returns to me, not surreptitiously but without her mask, as befits a woman of rank, a

rank bestowed by me on her, the woman I love. In other words she will not be reliant on the silent, conspiratorial mercies of paid lackeys and procurers but will go about with her head held high. Life is an accident. I don't want the duchess of Parma to break her neck as a result of that accident. I still have need of her. Let her return to me, to her home, at dawn, not creeping but striding, with head held high in the full light of morning, even if all Bolzano happens to be looking on. Do you fully understand me now? I want her to come home completely cured. She is yours to know, Giacomo, but you must make her realize that there is no other life for her but the one I designed for her; let her know that you are an adventure, a fling; that there is no prospect of life with you, not for her; that you are night, the storm, the plague, something that rumbles over the landscape but disappears when the sun rises in the morning and people go about their domestic chores, smoking, plastering, and scouring. That is why I am ordering you to perform a miracle. Within a few hours I want you to reveal your true self to the duchess, and by morning I want that secret self to have become a painless unintrusive memory. Be good to her, but be ruthless and malicious too, as is your way: be tender with her and hurt her, as you always do, as you would if you had a longer time to do it; squeeze everything that can happen between two people into a single night; finish all that can be finished by two people and let it be over by daybreak. Then send her back to me, because I love her and because you have nothing more to do with her."

Having said that he stood up.

"Do we have an agreement, Giacomo?" he asked, leaning on his stick.

His host strode over to the door, his hands behind his back. He opened it, gazed meditatively at the threshold, and asked, "But what happens, Your Excellency, if the performance is unsuccessful? . . . I mean, if I am unable to condense and accelerate everything in such a fortunate manner as Your Excellency requires? What will happen if, come the morning after the night before, the duchess of Parma feels that the night is merely the beginning of something. . . ."

He was unable to finish the sentence. With surprisingly quick and youthful steps the guest hurried past him, hesitated on the threshold, looked him in the eye, and answered in his most cutting manner:

"That would be a big mistake, Giacomo."

They regarded each other for a few long minutes.

"Your Excellency's wish is my command," the other replied and shrugged his shoulder. "I shall serve Your Excellency to the best of my ability, as he wishes and as only I can." He made a deep bow.

The duke turned to him with a last parting shot.

"I told you to be tender with her and to hurt her. Please don't hurt her too much, if that is at all possible."

He went out without closing the door behind him, slowly, slightly bent. Tapping his stick on the stairs he brought his servants hastening to meet him with their torches. Then he began to descend.

In Costume

So what are you waiting for? Get dressed, you aging mountebank, you trembling old quack! Your room is full of shadows: the shadows of your youth. Youth is gone, isn't it? . . . but you can still hear its voices, like the tinkling of bells on your decrepit guest's sleigh. Off he goes, as if bowing and blowing kisses to an invisible audience, together with his servants, his magnificent horses, and his tinkling sled. He is passing under your window right now. They've swaddled him in pelts so you can't even see the tip of his nose, a gaunt and graceless figure in the depths of the carriage, wrapped in fur, protected by his rank, old and in pain, and despite what he says, however he preaches and pontificates, on the point of death. It is he who is wounded now, not as I once was, bleeding in the garden in Pistoia and at the gates of Florence: his wound is fatal. And what about you? Are you happy now, Giacomo? Are you dead? Have they already crossed your arms across your chest? If you had your way you yourself would be making bows and blowing kisses to your invisible audi-

ence, receiving their applause. Are you lost for words? Is there a sour taste in your mouth as though you had overeaten and drunk too much? Is it penance and herrings you need? It is a mad world! Now you must kill everything in you: strangle your memories, strangle every tender feeling with your bare hands as if it were an unwanted kitten, strangle everything that smacks of human contact and compassion! Is the time of your youth over? . . . No, not quite. Yes, you are missing two front teeth. You find the cold harder to bear and like to snuggle up to the fire, muttering, in fur gloves, watching what you eat and carefully rinsing your mouth before kissing anyone because neither your digestion nor your teeth are exactly perfect any more! But this does not constitute a terminal condition. Your stomach, your heart, and your kidneys are faithful servants; your hair is only just beginning to go, a little thin on your crown and your temples: you will have to be careful where your lover plants her hands when she takes hold of your hair! You are not old yet, but you have to be a little careful . . . particularly of the pox that seems to be ravaging the world, so people say. But all is not lost. That great energy, that spontaneous overflow, that all-or-nothing the old fool spoke about with such contempt, may serve you awhile yet! The virtues of caution, wisdom, forethought, and reason are nothing without the instinctive passions of youth to heat them. What kind of life is it without the desire to take everything the world has to offer and to blow all your resources at the same time, to grab and discard at once? . . . Enough of this. You are not at the carnival now. You have a different kind of appoint-

ment, a different deadline! A deadline that marks the end of youth. You are an adult now, in one of your mature moments of wisdom, the kind you get at four in the afternoon in mid-October. A fine time. Your sun is still shining. . . . Look around, take a deep sweet breath, feel the rays of the sun, slow down, pay more attention, there's nothing else you can do in any case. Your youth is leaving you . . . elsewhere people are laughing, glasses are clinking, a woman is singing, there's the scent of falling rain, you are standing in a garden, your face wet with tears and rain, the flowers are dead but your heart is wild and happy, you yearn for completeness and annihilation, all the trodden flowers lie around you . . . that's what it was like, something like that. Later perhaps, when you are an old man, you will remember it. Now get dressed, because time is passing, there are people already waiting in the ballroom and one inexpressibly tender and alert pair of eyes is looking for you because she must see you. . . . Where's the note? Yes, it's there where he left it. Let's have a look. Large writing, careful, careworn letters . . . she's not the first woman to have written to me, nor will she be the last, I suppose. And with what trembling fingers and glittering eyes that wounded old crow, her husband, explained the meaning of the letter! It really was most amusing! Sometimes it is worth being alive! I must see, yes. . . . Well, poor thing, what more could she have written when she has been literate for barely a year? He says that no one could mean more or write more beautifully, and perhaps he is right; it is an elegant note, and it might be that other women, like the marquesa, the cardinal's niece, and

M.M., who knew a great deal about both love and literature, wrote more wittily and at greater length, complete
with verses, classical references, high vulgarity, and passionate bombast, but, I must admit, they wrote nothing
more true. The jealous old fool is right to admire it. . . .
Well, my dove, you shall see me as you desire! You shall see
me, though I am not the youngest or handsomest of men,
nor, as His Excellency remarked, the greatest of villains,
either. . . . You, my dove, will see me, as you wanted and
as he, too, wanted, the ruffled old crow! What a speech he
made! What convoluted strategies he devised! All that
threatening and prodding! Could he have been the man
who betrayed me to the authorities some sixteen months
ago in Venice? . . . The council is glad to do little favors
for influential outsiders; the *messer grande* is a courteous
man and he would not deny a minor service to the cousin
of the French king. Well, my duke of Parma, you shall
have what you asked for! You made a fine job of dressing
your proposition as a gift, you spoke with feeling like a
philosopher, you wanted to be producer and patron, master and accomplice, in this curious business, and you shall
have what you want. . . . Might it have been really those
two old arthritic hands of yours that deposited me on my
straw bed in Venice? . . . he didn't say so, not in so many
words. Like a retired hangman he consulted his secret list
and simply hinted at the possibility before tucking the slip
of paper back in his waistcoat pocket and going off with it!
Chew on that! he thought. Beware, in case I do it again!
He has a point there: it was no fun in the cells. He was
right, too, in speaking of other laws and other forms of

order, though I could tell him a story or two myself, albeit brief ones, with neat punchlines. Father Bragadin is no angel, of course, when it comes to the public good or when one can gain one man's favor by selling another man's life. It is simply the way of the world. We are slow to learn its lessons but maybe it's better that way. We prepare ourselves to face the world, we find out how it works, and soon enough we discover that there is business more dirty and dangerous than a game of cards, that affairs conducted under a veil of respectability are just as dirty. Take care, Giacomo! Take care tonight! And take care tomorrow morning, too, at cockcrow, when you take your leave in the snow. This is too carefully planned to be harmless: beware the aging grandee, the ancient, august lover who prefers not to strangle his rival, but to use those hands of his rival to strangle love itself and the memory of love . . . take care! Lights are still burning in the stable, you still have a few gold coins left over from yesterday jangling in your pocket; how would it be if you quickly packed, grabbed that hot sixteen-year-old spring chicken, Teresa, whose kisses have ensured a good night's sleep these last eight days, and, true to the laws of your own being, following your impeccable logic, forgot the ball, the agreement, and the grand performance, and made off with her tonight? . . . It might be better than waiting for dawn. Perhaps you should let them get on with it, let the duke of Parma wear his ass's head and ever after fret over his precious Francesca, her memories of her literary lover, and about what he might yet get up to with her? . . . Concentrate, Giacomo, little brother! Are you in two minds? Are

you thinking of staying now? Do you think your agreement obliges you to carry out your role? Can you not escape a performance that is bound to be false and sad as well as dangerous and unnatural, a performance that may end in real tears and real blood trickling across the boards of the stage, with a real corpse for the stagehands to remove? . . . But you can already feel the excitement, the involuntary shudder: everything else is beginning to lose focus, desire is stoking the fire in you. Is that desire no longer subject to reason? Do you feel you have no choice but to play the part? Could it be that the jealous old coxcomb calculated right when he appealed to the artist in you, when he drew attention to your art, so you were certain to accept even if it meant that not just the memory of the artist but the artist himself came to a sticky end, stitched up by His Excellency of Parma? But no, you must not rebel, you must not protest: accept the fact that you must stay and finish your business. You can't escape the responsibilities of your art: your entire life has been fraught with danger, so why stop now? You need the danger, you need to feel that at any moment the curtains of your bed might open and someone stick a knife between your ribs: you need to be aware of the possibility of annihilation; you need the impossible thing that the respectable citizen so desperately and helplessly craves and dreams about as he snores in his nightcap at his wife's side, while you are creeping through somebody's cellar or scrambling about on a rooftop, fighting hired assassins, living the reality that they, the virtuous, the shuffling, dare only dream about. You represent change and transforma-

tion: you are the flesh-and-blood version of what they call adventure or art. What else can you do? You will assume the part allotted to you, you will use your talent. So it is settled and you are staying! To work then! Clap three times and get them to bring water in the silver jug, let Balbi shift his horny feet and find you an appropriate outfit in town, let Giuseppe be called for to steam and pamper your face, and have a word with little Teresa, tell her to wrap her things in a bundle and to meet you at the edge of town at dawn. I will take her to Munich and sell her as wife to the elector's chief secretary. I will do things properly. Cheer up, there's nothing else you can do. The duke of Parma has thought of everything. He understands me completely and has calculated correctly; he knew I would stay and make my one-night-only guest appearance, however demanding it may be, even if it cost me my neck in the end, even if the lovely ladies of Bolzano finish up singing mournful three-part harmonies over my corpse. Yes, you greedy, clever, puzzled old man, you have calculated correctly. You firmly believe that wealth, power, cunning, and a little circumspection are enough to see the thing through. But let me send you a message, now, before I put on my costume, start painting my face, and summon every time-honored feature of my art for the performance: beware! For you, too, should take care! What do you think I am? Do you really think I am some kind of conjuror who can produce a masterpiece at a moment's notice: what an idea! You should be careful, for I am only human, and so is she. You demand, in your desperation, that we should collaborate on a single work of instantaneous genius. How

could I be sure of doing that? I have never known what the morning light would bring. Not that I regret it. Half my life is over and I have never regretted anything, nor was ever bored for an instant: I have been stabbed, I have been offered drinks laced with poison, I have slept under the stars without a penny in my pocket, I have no one I could call a friend: all I have is my notoriety, but I have not regretted any of it. The best part of life is gone: I have neither house nor apartment, not a stick of furniture to my name, not a watch, not even a ring that I could truly call mine. I order new clothes in every town I visit and feel no obligation to stay in any of them, yet you, the duke of Parma, are jealous of me. You who are tied to everything and are nothing but the things you are tied to—palaces, birth, name, title, lands, possessions, sentiments, and jealousies—you, who now, when life is "almost" over, as you never tire of saying—indeed you keep repeating the word in the vain hope that by flirting with it, by saying it often enough, you might actually delay your fate and avoid your final appointment with reality—find yourself in a tangle of contradictions between what you want and what there is; are you not secretly, somewhere deep in your soul, jealous of my ability to wrap myself in clouds and travel on moonbeams, to ride the wind across borders where nobody waits or takes leave of me; of me, the man without a room, without furniture, without a single possession anywhere in the world that he can truly call his own? . . . Enough, my boy, wake up, prepare yourself. Give a nice loud whoop, the way you used to. There's an icy wind hooting and tugging at the skirts of the ladies of Bolzano:

you, too, should be like the wind, hooting with laughter! Life isn't over yet, there's no question of "almost" for you. You need not rely on conjuring tricks because you are the real thing! So beware, Duke, I am no longer afraid of the morning. Let the storm whose gusts are already blowing about my heart and through my mind carry me forward, let there be tears and vows, kisses and death, let everything be condensed or slowed down, as life will have it, let it all happen despite the morning. I shall serve you well tonight, dear Duke! You have purchased me in all my miraculous, wonder-working reality. I shall be like those ancient wrestlers who knew they would have to pay for their performance with their lives: I will not be churning out a dutifully composed text to whisper in her ear, no, I shall do better and improvise a true text! Are you not afraid, you old schemer, that the performance might turn out to be all too successful? . . . Her letter is rather imperious and the spell she casts may be more effective than the ingenious strategy you have devised for your remaining days. Do you think you will save the tenderness and affection you imagined she might offer you when you married her? Are you not afraid that human passions might not be subject to nice calculation, that the greatest of artists might make a mistake, that the game might turn into a reality, a kiss become a true bond, that a trickle of blood might spread and become a tide in which life itself ran away from you? . . . Yes, we have an agreement. So both of us should now see that it is carried out: you with your ass's head, in your palazzo, with your painstaking schemes and your squint, and I in costume, the perfect costume in

which no one will recognize me except the woman for whom I wear it! Are Balbi and Teresa ready for departure? . . . Balbi! . . . Hey, Balbi! . . .

Now listen carefully! What time is it? . . . Near midnight? A good time, the time when day completes its magic round and witches reach for their broomsticks. Are you drunk? Your breath stinks of garlic, your lips are shiny with grease, you look positively cross-eyed. It must be that Verona wine. Stop staggering about for an instant and listen to me! We have a great opportunity, Balbi! There has been a wonderful turn of events! You may well rub your hands because your prayers are answered: our time in Bolzano is over and we shall set out at dawn. Tell the innkeeper to prepare the bill and hitch up some horses! You will pack and bid farewell to the kitchen maids and to all the people you gulled, you old skirt-lifter, you horse thief. . . . No, on the other hand, wait, it may be better not to say anything to them just yet. You can write your fond and amorous farewells from Munich in the morning. I want you to pack, if there is anything to pack, then to go to your room and wait for daybreak. Make sure it is the best horses they are hitching up, and have a word with the coach keeper too: it's a closed carriage I want, with fur blankets and hot water bottles! Make sure everyone is ready and everything in its place! Tell them that it's either a shower of gold or a sound beating for them in the morning, it depends on them which! No questions! Clap both hands over your mouth and listen very carefully. When I call you I want you to grab your things and to dash to the carriage. You will seat yourself next to the driver! I am not

asking you to do this, Balbi, but ordering you! Take utmost care until we are beyond the reach of Venice for the palm of the *messer grande* is as itchy as your neck. I want no complaints from you! Have I had bad news? . . . You will find out about a hundred miles from here, if I judge the time to be right. Now go into town and find me a costume! What kind? One for a ball, numbskull, a marvelous, perfectly unique costume, the kind that will turn everyone's head when I step into the ballroom, but under which no one will recognize me. . . . What's that? All the costumes in Bolzano have been sold for tonight? Idiot! The kind of mask and costume I am looking for is not the traditional carnival outfit, not Pierrot or Harlequin, not Prince of Persia with Vizier, not Head Cook and Scullery Boy, not Oriental Knight, not Pasha in Turban with Scimitar, not Court Fool in pretend rags, with cap-and-bells and mock scepter. That stuff is old hat: it is boring and conventional. No, Balbi, let's find something new and original for tonight. What if I dressed simply as a knight appropriate to my name and rank, a chevalier of France fresh from the court of King Louis . . . ? No, perhaps not. Hush, don't disturb me when I'm thinking. Wait! What if I went as an author, a scholar, a philosopher, with black-rimmed pince-nez perched on my nose, a mortarboard on my head, wearing a white collar and a black cloak? Not such a bad idea, an author . . . it takes one author to know another. What do you think? Are there other writers in Bolzano? Think about it carefully, Balbi. The brotherhood of authors is a secret society, with invisible insignia: you, being uncultured, think that Monsieur Vendôme or

Madame Montespan might have precedence over authors in an audience with the king, but it's not like that. Messieurs La Fontaine and Corneille and even Bossuet are at the front of the line, though Corneille is a little unkempt . . . you, of course, understand nothing of this, how could you? No, the author costume is wrong. We must find something else. What if I went as a hunter, with horn, dagger and bow, Nimrod at the Chase, Nimrod and Diana in the Primeval Forest? No, the symbolism is too transparent. Have you no ideas of your own? Don't the kitchen maids like you to entertain them with your wit and garlic breath? . . . That's it, Balbi! I have it! Kitchen maids! It's perfect! Quick, call for little Teresa! And let them bring a skirt, a blouse, white stockings, a beauty spot, some Viennese cloth for a shawl, a bonnet, and a white silk mask . . . what are you staring at? . . . yes, tonight I shall dress as a woman! Take that stupid grin off your face! It's the perfect disguise. I shall want a fan and something to stuff my bodice with, Neapolitan fashion: feathers from a pillow will do. Now hurry! Wake the servants! And let's get this room tidy, open some windows, build up the fire, let's have some sweet dessert wine on the table, a little cold chicken, some dressed salad, and ham and cheese, too, with white bread, silverware, and porcelain, the best of everything. Innkeeper! . . . Where are you hiding, you old pimp, you murderer of tourists and traveling salesmen? . . . Come here and do as I say! I want that fire blazing in the grate, fresh sheets on the bed, the best and finest pillowslips, a counterpane with your best lace cover, some ambergris sprinkled on the embers, two arm-

chairs placed by the fire, a small ebony table with flowers over there, I don't care what it costs, do you hear, red roses, yes, now, in November, in the snow! Where from? That's up to you. From the duke's greenhouse, for all I care, but now, tonight! The chicken should be accompanied by pickled eggs. I want the ham and cheese on a glass tray in one piece. . . . Wait! The bread should be toasted in thin slices, and the butter should be served on freshly fallen snow! Now let's get busy. The coachman should begin to warm the coach with hot water bottles, let the horses be given some fodder, have him polish the brasses until they glitter, and let everyone stand by at dawn, in a heated kitchen, with some hot and cold food for the journey and a cask of wine, the best of everything! During the night, though, the place should be as silent as the grave, the grave where you yourselves will be resting, I assure you, if you do not carry out my orders immediately and to the letter! No, my friend, you don't yet know me: I am terrifying when in a temper! Please be aware that my connections and influence exceed the merely mortal . . . there's no need for me to spell them out to you, since you yourself have seen the kind of people who have been waiting outside my door tonight and every night! You, you murderer of traveling salesmen, you shall have a hundred gold pieces if all is done as I demand: inform your staff that however overcast the sky of Bolzano may be at daybreak it will shower them with gold, providing everyone remains at his or her station through the night, on constant call! And let all this happen without any noise whatsoever, you understand, silently and invisibly! Are you still here? . . . Close

the window now, that's enough fresh air. Sprinkle some attar of roses on the bed and draw the curtains round it. Have the flowers arrived? . . . Where did you get them? You found them in the reception room of the lady from Bergamo? . . . Tomorrow we shall send her better ones, a finer-scented selection, a whole basketful of them, a hundred, no, ninety-nine as a mark of delicacy, don't forget! Yes, you may spread the table and bring the food! The wine. . . . Show me, let's have a sniff! I am not going to taste it but you will answer with your head if I can smell the slightest trace of cask on it! I won't taste it now because I have just rinsed my mouth. . . . Giuseppe, good, I am glad you have arrived, throw the towel over my shoulders: I want some blush on my cheeks, yes, both cheeks, a little something for the lips, a beauty patch just under my right cheekbone, some rice powder on my wig, and now we shall tie it up in the little bonnet we have borrowed from Teresa. Is it past midnight? . . . Now you can go. Be off with you all. I don't want to see any of you till dawn. Not you, Teresa, my little one, you stay with me. Tie the skirt around my waist, adjust the garter on my knees, lend me the silk shawl I bought you yesterday, and arrange it across my shoulders. . . . That's right, thank you. Am I sitting properly with my legs crossed, the way a woman sits, fan in hand, when she is being attended by a gentleman? . . . I find I am not at all sure of the way women move. Is this how you hold a fan? . . . Thank you, my dear. Do you find me pretty like this? . . . My nose is too big? The mask will cover it, Teresa. Now come here, little one, sit on my knees, and don't worry if you crease the folds of your skirt.

I'll buy you a finer one in Munich, a velvet and silk outfit, as many outfits, of whatever kind you want . . . are you surprised? But that was the idea, right from the start. You don't want to fade and droop here, my little snowdrop, in the bar, in the arms of drunken travelers. Tomorrow, at dawn, I shall take you with me. We shall take Balbi, too, but we will take care to lose him on the way. It is no more than he deserves. Yes, we are going to Munich at dawn, as soon as day breaks. Why are you crying? Give me a kiss, as you have so often done before, with closed eyes, open mouth, nice and easy. Why are you trembling like that? Hush, child, prepare for the journey, for your new life which will be wonderful: there'll be gold, a fine apartment, you shall have your own pony and trap in Munich, and a servant to pull off your shoes and stockings and help you into your silk nightdress. Don't you want that? . . . Are you sure? Are you shaking your head? Have you nothing to say? You want to stay here? You want me to leave you here? . . . Still quiet? I am leaving in the morning, child. Tonight I shall celebrate, in a costume, as is right and proper, but once light breaks we will take to the road, and you will be my companion and chambermaid, but later you will be a lady, too, at least for a while. . . . Are you smiling yet? Go to your room, pray, sleep, and prepare for the journey. Wait for me at dawn at the edge of town, where the road branches north and west, by the stone cross. You can trust me . . . you know very well you can trust me. But there is something in your smile that I have seen only once before, in Verona, I think, something unself-conscious and decadent, something gentle yet dan-

gerous at the same time. . . . I will explain that later. Scrub your hands. Wash your hair tonight, apply camomile tea to your hair and your face, then spread this cream over it . . . wait, you shall have a rose as a memento of this night. Now go and think over what I have said. . . . Go, because I myself have to go. Sweet dreams, my child. Tomorrow you will wake to a new life by the stone cross, in the carriage, in my arms, under the protection of my cloak. . . . *Addio, cara fanciulla! Addio, mia diletta! Arrivederci domani! Iniziamo una vita nuova! . . . Una vita felice!* . . . Phew! Is everyone gone? . . . Let's get going. Just the mask, quickly. It's a nice mask, familiar, Venetian style, white silk: let it cover my face as it has so often done at difficult and dangerous moments in my life. One more glance in the mirror . . . the beauty patch has slipped a little, a touch more red needed for the lips, smooth the eyebrows, and just a pinch of candle soot, the merest dab under the eyes. . . . Yes, perfect! The greatcoat will cover me as I make my way across the street. How the snow is falling! Mind your voice, Giacomo, speak with your fan and your eyes only if at all possible! Everything is in place, yes, the cold chicken, the butter on fresh snow, the wine in the engraved decanter, the roses in the marble basket, there's attar of roses on the pillow, the curtains of the bed are closed. . . . I think that should be all, yes. Perhaps one more log on the fire . . . something is missing? I can't think what it is. What was it, something important I mustn't forget . . . something more important than roses, wine, ambergris, or the roast ham. . . . Oh, I know. The dagger! Into my bosom with you, faithful companion.

Into my bosom, under the bodice, down among the feathers: an excellent costume. Only a woman could hide a dagger in such a place, and it certainly gives you confidence knowing there is a dagger just above your heart. It's much the best way of setting forth on an engagement! . . . I don't think I have forgotten anything. So get going. Wait . . . what is it now? Why aren't you on your way? You are alone. Check the mirror. The costume is excellent, everybody and everything is in place, a few more moments and the performance can begin according to the agreement, according to the rules you discussed with the duke of Parma. Why are you hanging back? Why is your heart beating so loudly? What is this feeling that has taken possession of you, grips your heart, and makes you indecisive, so you hesitate here with a dagger in your bosom, a mask on your face, and a fan in your hand. . . . What is happening to you, Giacomo? Acrobats suffer the same sense of dizziness when they look down on the crowd from the top of a human pyramid, seeking a familiar pair of eyes in the audience. . . . What unsettles you, what is it you are trying to remember? Hush, restless heart, stop this drumming. It is love you are afraid of, yes it is . . . you fear the emotion that binds, as the duke of Parma realized in his agony, in his increasing need, he who knows you all too well: it is this feeling that you fear, that casts its shadow across your path, it is the feeling you have fled ever since childhood. Don't be afraid, poor fool. You can overcome it. Don't be afraid. There is no feeling that can take complete control of you: you may suffer a few days of grief, but after a week or so of discomfort, you will find your way to the card

table, or set to entertaining people the way they have always liked being entertained, playing your part in the human comedy, laughing or being laughed at, swindling or being swindled . . . and so the memory will fade. It won't kill you, no fear of that. Come the morning, you will abscond with the kitchen maid as you have done before, and will again, no doubt, in the future. There is nothing you can do about it. Let us do it without sentimentality or fear. The teardrop you are shedding will smudge the makeup on your face and your beauty patch will come unstuck . . . but I am not afraid of a teardrop or two. *I must see you.* . . . It is a beautiful letter. I don't think I have ever received lovelier. Yes, this woman and I are fated to be linked in some fashion, in a different sort of way, by a different power, a different desire. She herself cannot prevent that. So set about your task, comedian. Stand up straight, throw the cloak across your shoulder, put on your mask. . . . How silent it is. There's only the moaning of the wind. Off to the ball with you, attend to your worldly business, follow your fate, be firm, be levelheaded. Who is there? . . .

The Guest Performance

The door opened, the candles flickered in the draft. A masked young man in a party cloak stood on the threshold. He was wearing short silk pantaloons, buckled shoes, a three-cornered hat, and carrying a slender gold-handled sword at his side. He bowed and spoke in a clear, sharp, almost childlike voice as if he had brought the coolness and good temper of the snow in with him.

"It's I, Giacomo."

He closed the door carefully and stepped forward fastidiously, a little awkwardly, as if not quite accustomed to wearing boy's clothes. He bowed in masculine fashion and baldly declared, "I waited for you in vain. So I have come to you."

"Why have you come?" the man asked, a little hoarse behind the mask, taking a step and getting tangled in his skirt.

"Why? But I explained in my letter. Because I must see you."

She said this pleasantly, without any particular stress,

as if it were the only reasonable explanation, the most natural answer a woman could give a man. The man did not respond.

"Did you not get my letter?" she asked anxiously.

"I certainly did," the man answered. "Your husband, the duke of Parma, brought it to me this evening."

"Oh!" said the woman and fell silent.

The "oh" was a quiet and simple acknowledgment, like a bird call. She leaned her slender boyish figure against the mantelpiece and fiddled with her sword. The mask she was wearing stared at the floor, solemn and empty. Then, even more quietly, she continued.

"I knew it. I was waiting for the answer and knew somehow that there had been some problem with the letter. You know it is very unusual for me to write letters. To tell you the truth it was the first letter I had written in my life."

She turned her head aside gracefully, a little embarrassed, as if she had confessed her most intimate secret. Then she started laughing behind the mask, but it was a nervous laugh.

"Oh!" she said again. "I really am sorry the letter fell into his hands. I should have expected it. Do you think the groom who volunteered to bring my letter to you is still alive? . . . I should be sorry if anything happened to him, as he is still young and has a very sad and languishing way of looking at me when we are riding, and besides, he has a large family to support all by himself. Was it the duke himself delivered the letter? . . . Poor man. It can't have been easy for him. He is so proud and so lonely, I can

imagine what he felt when he set out to bring you the letter in which I said I must see you. Did he threaten you? Offer you money? . . . Tell me what happened, my love."

She pronounced the last word loudly, confidently, enunciating clearly, as if she had articulated an important formal concept or subject with it. The mask was staring fixedly at the fire now, pale as death.

"He both threatened me and offered me money. Though that wasn't the main reason he came," the man replied. "He came primarily to give me the letter whose contents he analyzed in great detail. Then we came to an agreement."

"Of course," she said, with a brief sigh. "What agreement did you come to, my love?"

"He instructed me to dedicate my art to you alone, tonight. He asked me to make this night a masterpiece of seduction. He offered me money, freedom, and a letter of introduction that would protect me on the road and see me over frontiers. He told me you were ill, Francesca, diseased with love, and asked me to cure you. He told me that he was making us a present of this night, which should be as brief and as long as life, long enough for me to perform the impossible, so that we may experience in a single night all the ecstasies and disappointments of love, and that in the morning I should leave you to travel the world, go as far away as it is possible to go, wherever fate takes me, and that you should return to the palazzo with your head held high, where you may brighten and warm the remaining days of the duke of Parma. That is what he said. And he explained the meaning of your letter. I do

believe he understood it, Francesca, every word of it. He did not raise his voice, but spoke calmly and quietly. And he also requested that I should be tender with you but hurt you enough to guarantee that everything should be over between us by morning, so that we could put a full stop to our sentence. . . . Those were his instructions."

"He told you to hurt me? . . ."

"Yes. But he asked me, in parting, not to hurt you too much."

"Yes," said Francesca. "He loves me."

"I think so, too," the man replied. "He loves you, but it's easy for him, Francesca. Love, as he loves, is easy, especially now that his time is running out . . . or rather, has 'almost' run out, and he kept repeating the word 'almost,' which seemed to be very important to him for some reason, if I understand him properly. It is easy to love when life is almost over."

"My dear," said the woman very gently and compassionately, like an adult addressing a child, and at the moment her unseen lips pronounced the words it was almost as if the mask itself were smiling. "It is never easy to love."

"No," the man obstinately insisted. "But it's easier for him."

"And so," the other mask inquired, "did you come to an agreement?"

"Yes."

"What were the terms of the agreement, Giacomo? . . ."

"I agreed to the terms he demanded and which you

yourself declared in your letter. That we would meet tonight. That we would embrace each other, because there is a secret bond between us, Francesca, because love has touched us both. It is a great gift and a great sadness. It is a great gift because I do in fact love you, in my fashion, and because I regard love as an art; but it is also a great sadness because my love will never be easy or happy, can never grow wings and soar like a dove . . . because ours is a different kind of love from his. So we agreed that we would 'know' each other, in the biblical sense, and that you would then finish with me, cured and disillusioned, and after the morning we would never see each other again. That I would not be the shadow across your bed and would not haunt you when the duke of Parma leaned over you as you lay on your pillows; that I would be a memory for a while, but later not even that: that for you, I would be nothing and no one. That is what I agreed. It is what I must do tonight, in words, with kisses, with tears, and with vows, using all the tricks of my trade, according to the rules of my art."

He stopped and tactfully, curiously, waited for an answer.

"Then go ahead, Giacomo," said the woman quietly and calmly. And she tipped her head on one side so the mask stared indifferently into the air. "Go ahead," she repeated. "What are you waiting for, my friend? Now is the moment. Begin. See, I have come to you, so you needn't go out into the storm, for as you may have noticed a storm sprung up at midnight, an icy northern blast screaming and sweeping towers of snow along the street.

But it is quiet here, warm, and scented. I see they have prepared the bed. Attar of roses and ambergris. And the table is set for two, carefully, in the best of taste, as custom dictates. But it is past midnight, and it is time for supper. So let us begin, Giacomo."

She sat down at the neatly spread table, pulled off her gloves, breathed on her fingertips, and rubbed her bare hands together, her posture suggesting anticipation, good manners, and propriety as she looked over the foodstuffs, very much as if she were expecting the waiter to arrive so that she might start to eat.

"How will you begin?" she asked, he having made no move, then continued, now intimate and curious. "How does one seduce and then disabuse someone who has come of her own free will because she is in love? . . . I am very curious, Giacomo! What will you do? . . . Will you use force, guile, or courtesy? It is, after all, a masterpiece you have undertaken, and that is bound to be difficult. Because, you see, we are not entirely alone, for we are here with his conscious blessing, so it is a little as if there were and will continue to be three of us in the room. Naturally, he knows that you will immediately tell me everything, or almost everything: he doesn't think you capable of crude workmanship, of lying to me, and hiding the secret of his visit, of not revealing the terms of your agreement. He couldn't have imagined, not for a moment, that events would proceed otherwise than they have already done; he knew very well that you would begin with a confession, and how we should go on from there, the two, or is it

three, of us? But I myself don't yet know. After everything you have told me I am merely curious. So do begin."

Both masks remained quiet awhile. Then the male mask began talking, at first in a little boy's voice, then, slowly, as it warmed to its subject, modulating into something more feminine, as if every trace of roughness and strangeness had fallen away.

"Then perhaps I could begin . . . since I, too, am here, if not entirely according to his will nor entirely according to yours, either: I am here of my own free will, albeit masked and in male costume, in other words dressed for fun and games . . . and for all we know, the disguises help us. Do begin and perform a miracle. It should be fascinating. So this is what you said to each other, you two, the man I love and the man who loves me? . . . And by that token I must be merely obeying his instructions by being here. So, however this night turns out, it will all be according to his instructions, just as it is according to his instructions that we two, you and I, should 'know' and hurt each other? How marvelous," the voice continued indifferently. "And this is all that he could think of: this is all that you have agreed to? Could you not have devised something more ambitious, more ingenious? Two such intelligent and remarkable men as you? . . . He brought you my letter, he explained and interpreted it? But Giacomo, my love, his interpretation may not be complete. Because when I committed those words to paper, the first sensible, properly related words I have ever written in my life, and I did so all by myself, I was suddenly frightened by how

much words can say when one chooses them responsibly and carefully joins the letters up. . . . Only four words, you see, and he is on his way from the palazzo, acting as postman, ascending these steep stairs, and there you stand, dressed in female costume. . . . Four words, a few drops of ink on paper, and how much has already happened as a result! All those events set in motion on account of a few words I had written! Yes I, too, wondered and shuddered. And yet I think he may not have understood the letter as completely as he thinks. He interpreted it, you say? . . . No, let me do that, Giacomo! Let me do it, even if I do it with less literary skill than you two have done. Do you think I am the kind of woman who on a whim, a desire, leaves her home at midnight to seek out a man who is only just out of jail, whose reputation is so bad that mothers and older women cross themselves at mention of his name? . . . Do you know me so little? And the duke of Parma, with whom I share a bed, is his knowledge of me so shallow? . . . Did you imagine I learned to write because I was bored and wanted to amuse myself by sending a naughty letter inviting myself to a midnight rendezvous with you? . . . Did you bind yourself to a contract that would see me come to you for a night of romance as you had planned, you two wise men, for a fling, for a single night, between two turns on the dance floor? Did you imagine that I would hurry over from my home, masked, enter a strange man's room, and then, before the dancing is quite over in the ballroom, hasten back to the palazzo to join the other couples? . . . Do you imagine that in writing to you I am seeking some childish night to remember; and

that when I come to you, when I think of you, when I warm your memory with my breath, when I count the days you spend in jail, I mean to steal over to you for a night, for a secret rendezvous, just because you happen to be here, passing through the town where I live with my husband, or because once in my girlhood I knew you and there was some romantic feeling between us? . . . Is this the much-vaunted wisdom of the mighty duke of Parma and the omniscient Giacomo, who knows women's hearts? . . . Do you imagine that I am like a simple child, chasing shadows of the past, when I finally write the words that inform you, and yes, the duke and the whole world, that I must see you? It may be that I am not quite so simple and childlike, Giacomo, my love. Perhaps it was I that directed the groom's footsteps so that he should walk into the trap set for him by the duke? . . . Perhaps I, too, have struck a bargain tonight, with myself and my own fate if no one else, and this bargain may be as binding as the coffin, even if it bears no seal and contains no vows? Perhaps I know better than the duke of Parma why I should have climbed these stairs. What do you think, my love? Why did I write the letter? Why did I send the groom on a secret mission? Why did I wait for you? Why did I dress in a man's clothes? Why did I sneak from my palazzo? Why am I standing in this room? Having made the agreement, you should answer."

The other mask responded obediently, his voice flat.

"Why, Francesca?"

"Because I am not an object of seduction, my love, not material for a masterpiece, not the subject of a sage agree-

ment. I am not the sweetheart who hastens to her lover's side at midnight. I am not some silly goose waiting vainly for a man, chasing shadows and illusions of happiness. I am not the young woman with the elderly husband, dreaming of hotter lips and more powerful arms, setting out in the snow in search of opportunity and recompense. I am not a bored lady of leisure who cannot resist your reputation and throws herself at you, nor the sentimental provincial bride who is unable to pass over the appearance of her dazzling childhood suitor. I am neither whore nor goose, Giacomo."

"What are you, Francesca?" asked the man.

The voice sounded strange through the mask, as if it were addressing the other at a great distance. The woman replied in the silence across an enormous distance.

"I am life, my love."

The man stepped toward the fire, careful that his skirts should not catch fire, and threw two fresh logs onto the flames. He turned round with the remaining logs still in his arms, as he was bending over.

"And what is life, Francesca?"

"It is certainly not running away in the snow," the woman answered without raising her voice. "Nor is it all fever and fret nor big words nor even the situation in which we find ourselves now, you dressed as a woman, I as a man, both masked, in the room of an inn, like a pair of characters in an opera. None of this is life. I will tell you what life is. I have given it a great deal of thought. Because it was not only you who was locked in a prison where powerful, jealous hands deposited you, Giacomo; I have

been in prison as long as you have, even if my bed was not made of straw. Life, my dear, is a whole. Life is when a man and woman meet because they suit each other, because what they have in common is what the rain has in common with the sea, the one always rising from and falling back into the other, each creating each, one as a condition of the other. Out of this wholeness something emerges, some harmony, and that harmony is life. It is very rare among people. You flee from people because you believe you have other business in the world. I seek wholeness because I know I have no other business in the world. That's why I came. As I said, it took some time for me to be certain of that. Now I know. I also know that there is nothing perfect you can do in this world without me, that you cannot even practice your art, as you call it, for, without me, true and perfect seduction lies beyond you: the experience, the excitement, the thrill of the chase requires me; even the charm you exert over other women is imperfect without me. Why are you standing so stiffly there, Giacomo, with the poker and bellows in your hand, as if someone had hit you and you had tried to stand up too quickly? . . . Have you realized something? I am life, my love, the only woman offering you a whole life: you are incomplete without me, incomplete as a man, incomplete as an artist, as a gambler, and as a traveler, just as, without you, I am an incomplete woman, no more than a shadow among shadows. Do you understand now? . . . Because I do. If I were complete I would not have left the duke of Parma, who loves me and offers me everything the world has to offer: power, pomp, ambition, and meaning, and I

am not betraying a confidence or stating something improper, believe me, when I say that it was he who introduced me to the sad, solemn faces of love and desire, because love has a thousand faces and the duke of Parma wears one of them. He is in his palazzo at this very moment, wearing an ass's head because our love has hurt him and he is mortally sick with sadness. But he knows he has no choice, which is why he tolerates me being here with you at such an hour and why he wears the ass's head so proudly. But the knowledge doesn't help him nor does the fancy dress nor the agreement: nothing helps him. He has lived by violence and he will die in vanity. There is nothing I can do for him. But for you, I would never have left him, because I, too, had an agreement with him, and I was brought up to honor my agreements. I am a Tuscan, Giacomo," said the mask, and the figure wearing it straightened a little.

"I know, my dear," said the man, the poker in his hand, and it was as if his voice were smiling. "You are the second person to say that to me in this room today."

"Really?" asked Francesca, drawing out the vowel in an almost musical manner, like an amazed, well-behaved schoolgirl. "Well yes, you have had a lot of visitors recently. But that's how it was and always will be with you, you will always be surrounded by people, both men and women. I shall get used to it, my dear. . . . It won't be easy but I shall get used to it."

"When, Francesca?" the man asked. "When do you want to get used to it? Tonight? . . . I won't be receiving any more visitors tonight."

"Tonight?" the woman asked in the same calm, child-like voice as before. "No, later, during the rest of my life."

"In the life that we shall spend together?"

"Perhaps, my love. Is that not the way you pictured it?"

"I don't know, Francesca," said the man and sat down opposite her, leaning back in the armchair, crossing his legs under his skirt, and crossing his arms under his false bosom. "That goes against the agreement."

"That agreement was verbal," the woman calmly replied, "but the other agreement, the one between us, is wordless and implicit. You will always have people around you, both men and women and that, you will not be surprised to know, will be neither particularly desirable nor pleasant from my point of view, nevertheless I shall bear it," she said a little wearily and gave a short sigh.

"And when," asked the man in a most respectful, matter-of-fact and reassuring manner, as though he were speaking to a child or some mad person it was unsafe to contradict, "when do you think, Francesca, that we will embark on this life? . . ."

"But we have already embarked on it, my love," the woman answered brightly. "We embarked on it the moment I wrote the letter and when the duke of Parma passed my message to you, at which point I put on these man's clothes. Now you are talking to me as people tend to talk to children or to lunatics. But I am neither of those, my love. I am a woman, albeit in man's clothes and in a mask, a woman who is absolutely certain she knows something and therefore acts. You are silent? . . . Your silence indicates that you wish to know what it is I know with

such certainty, with such ridiculous, lunatic, deathly certainty? . . . Only that however many people surround you—men, women, probably more women—and however that is likely to hurt me, we belong to each other. My life is linked to yours, Giacomo, as yours is linked to mine. That is what I know and what the duke of Parma knows as well as I do. That is why he brought the letter, and that is why he is in his palace now with his ass's head, tolerating my presence here. That is why he hurried to make an agreement with you, and that is why you, too, Giacomo, hurried to make an agreement with him, because the agreement saves you from me, because you fear me as a man fears life, a whole life, the life that lies in wait for him . . . and everyone is a little frightened of that. I am no longer frightened," she pronounced aloud.

"And what sort of life will we have? . . ." asked the man.

"It will be neither happy nor solemn. It will not be a lucky life. There are people with perfect pitch, who can hear intervals and harmonies and recognize wholeness. You are not such a man. I know I shall be alone a good deal, and that I will seem lonely to the rest of the world, because you will often leave me. I will not be happy in the billing-and-cooing sense of the word, which is what other people mean and desire, but my life will have meaning and content, perhaps all too heavy and painful a content. I know everything, Giacomo, because I love you. I have the strength of a wrestler because I love you. I shall be as wise as the Pope because I love you. I shall be a literary scholar and an expert gambler for your sake; I am learning even

now how to mark the king and the ace without others observing me. I have had packs of cards and wax brought over from Naples. We shall prepare the cards together, you and I, before you go out to take on the rabble and scum of the world, and I shall wait for you at home while you cheat them and return in the morning or maybe only on the third day. And we shall spend this money, we shall let the world take it back, because we don't need a fortune, because you never hold on to money, because that is your nature. I shall be the most beautiful woman in Paris, Giacomo, and you will see what a conquest I shall make of the chief of police when I dine alone with him: and no harm will come to you, for I shall guarantee you greater safety than the duke of Parma's commendatory letter: every glint of my eye, every breath I take will be there to protect you, to see that no harm comes to you. Should some evil woman give you the pox, I will nurse you, rubbing your limbs with lotions, making you soup out of herbs for your convalescence. I shall be as devious as the spies of the Inquisition; I shall sleep with the doge and intercede on your behalf so he allows you to return home, so that you may see Nonna and Signor Bragadin again, or, if you like, the pretty nun for whom you rented a palazzo in Murano. I will learn to cook sensibly, my love, indeed have learned that already, and I know that you should not eat spicy food because it makes your nose bleed; I can make soups that will cure your headache, and I will go to the women that wink at you and flirt with you and act as your bawd so you should enjoy a free night with the famous Julia for whom the duke of Norfolk paid one hundred thousand

gold pieces, and who was so cruel to you at the last Carnival in Venice. I have learned to knit, to wash, and to iron, because there will be times in our lives when we will have no money, when moneylenders' agents will scamper after us and we will have to stay at worse inns than The Stag. But I will take care that you will always have clean, ironed shirts with decent frills to wear in public, my love, even if we haven't eaten anything but dry fish cooked in oil for four days. I shall be so beautiful, Giacomo, that sometimes, when we have money, and you shower me with velvet and silk and jewels, and you take a box at the opera in London, everyone will look at me rather than the performance, and you will sit beside me, cold and indifferent, as we gaze over the audience, because I won't have eyes for anyone but you on such occasions, and everyone will know that the most beautiful of women is yours, only yours. And this will suit you, because you are vain, inordinately vain, and everyone will know that your victory is complete, that I am the duchess of Parma who has left her husband with all his stately homes, to live with you; that I have thrown away my jewels and lands so that I may share a bed with you; that I accompany you as you flee across the highways of the world and sleep with you in damp and filthy hovels and never cast a longing look on another man, except only when you ask me to. Because you can do anything with me, Giacomo. You could sell me to our cousin Louis and his harem at Versailles, you could sell me by the pound and know that when strange men melt in my arms like lead in the fire, I remain yours alone. You could forbid me to even glance at another man, you could

disfigure me, you could cut off my hair, brand my breast with a hot poker, infect me with the pox, and ruin my skin, but those would be the least of my worries, for you would soon see that I will still be beautiful for you, because I would find medication, brew potions, grow new skin and new hair, just in case you should sometime later desire me and want me to be attractive for you. I want you to know that all this is possible because I love you. I will be the most modest of women, my love, if that is what you want. I will live alone in our apartment: you can brick up the windows if you like. I would even go to mass only if you permitted it, accompanied by your servants. I would spend the whole day indoors in the rooms you marked out as my prison, caring for myself, getting dressed, and waiting for you. And I would be waited on only by women of your choosing, blind and dumb women, if you want. But if you wanted other men's desires to spice up your own I would be flirtatious and depraved. If you wanted to humiliate me, Giacomo, you should know that there would be no humiliation I would not undergo for you, because I love you. If you felt you had to torture me you could strap me to a table and beat me with barbed whips, and I would scream and see my blood flow, all the while thinking of fresh means of torture to bring you greater and truer joy. If you wanted me to rule you, I would be ruthless and unfeeling, as I read some women are, in the books that the duke of Parma brought back from Amsterdam. I know such extraordinary secrets, Giacomo, that there is not a woman in the brothels of Venice who knows more than I do about tenderness, torture, the yearnings of the

body and the spirit, love potions, small clothes, lighting, scents, caresses, and abstinence. If you wanted me to be vulgar I know such words in Italian, French, German, and English as make me blush sometimes when I am alone and think of them: I learned these words for you, and would whisper them only to you, if you wished. There is not a slave in the harems of the east, my love, who knows more about the pleasures of the flesh than I do. I have studied the body and know all its desires, even the most secret ones about which men think only on their death beds, when everything is all the same to them, and the scent of sulphur hovers about them. I have learned all this because I love you. Is that enough? . . ."

"It's not enough," the man replied.

"Not enough," the woman repeated. "Well, naturally it's not enough. I just wanted to tell you so you knew. . . . But do not believe that I for an instant hoped that it would be enough, that this would be all. These are just means, my love, I know too well, melancholy means. I have simply catalogued and enumerated them because I want you to know that there is nothing you could want from me that I would not give or hesitate to grant. You are right: it is not enough. Because love has two arenas, two theaters of war, where the great two-hander is played out, and both are infinite: the bed and the world. And we must live in the world, too. It is not enough to accommodate myself to everything you desire, everything your whims might demand of me, no, I have to discover what makes you happy and provide it. I have to find out what it is that you desire but cannot confess, even to yourself, not even

on your deathbed when everything is all the same to you: I have to find out and tell you so that you know, that you should see what the good is, so that you can be happy at last. And because you are the unhappiest of men, my love, and I can't bear your unhappiness, I have to name the thing you desire . . . though that is not enough, either, that is too little, too crude, and it would show poor skill on my part, because, should you doubt it, I, too, have my art, even if it is not quite as highly esteemed and complex as yours. What is my art? . . . Nothing more than my love of you. That is why I shall be strong and wise, modest and lewd, patient and lonely, wild and disciplined. It is because I love you. I have to find out why it is you run from deep feeling and from true happiness, and once I know why I must pass that sad knowledge on to you, but not in words, not by telling you, because such knowledge is terrifying and would not save you . . . words, however precise, can only name and catalogue the discoveries of mankind, but they solve nothing, as you, being a writer, will most certainly know. No, I must be tender, watching and waiting for ways in which to tell you the secret without words, to let you know what hurts you and what you desire, what you are not bold enough to admit: because it is cowardice and ignorance that are behind all unhappiness, as you must certainly know, being a writer. And so I must find out why you are afraid of happiness, which is not merely the touch of two hands, which is neither cradle nor coffin, but wholeness, a wholeness requiring something solemn, almost severe in our composition, the wholeness which is life and truth. I have to find out what

it is you desire so badly you dare not admit it to yourself and then I have to keep that secret from you, because my words would only hurt you, and you, in your vanity, would protest and run away, cursing and denying: that is why I must stay silent, keeping the secret in my heart. And I must live so that, even without words, you should know and understand why everything is as it is, why you suffer loneliness, boredom, restlessness, yearning; why the gambling, why the orgies, why you have no home, why your art developed as it did, why all those women, why you are a seducer: and once you know all this through me, without my telling you, you will see that suddenly everything will be easier and better. You alone will be entitled to pronounce the secret. I can do nothing but wait, watch, learn, and then, silently, with my whole being, my life, my body, my silence, my kisses, and my actions pass the secret knowledge on to you. That is what I must do, because I love you. And that is why you are afraid of life and of wholeness, because there is nothing we fear so much, not the rack, not the gallows, as ourselves and the secrets we dare not face. And will all be well after that, my love? . . . I don't know. But everything will be simpler then, much simpler. We will move across our two stages, the bed and the world, as accomplices, people who know everything about each other and everything about our audience, too. There will be no more stage fright, Giacomo. Because love is togetherness and harmony, not fever and fret, nor tears and screams: it is a most solemn harmony, the firmest of unions. And I undertake that union, even unto death. What will happen? . . . I have no plans, Giacomo. I am

not saying, 'Here I am, I am yours, take me with you,' because those are only meaningless words. But you should know that even if you do not take me with you, I shall wait for you forever, secretly, until you think of me one day and your heart melts and you turn to me. I don't need to make vows or promises, because I know reality, and that reality is that you are truly mine. You can leave me, as you did once before, taking to your heels like a coward, though it wasn't the duke of Parma you fled from but the terrifying power of true feeling, the recognition that I was truly yours. You did not know as much in words, nor in your thoughts, but you knew it in your heart and in your body and that is why you fled. And escape was pointless because here we are again, face-to-face with each other waiting for the moment when we can remove our masks and see each other as we really are. Because we are still only masked figures, my love, and there are many more masks between us, each of which must, one by one, be discarded, before we can finally know each other's true, naked faces. Don't hurry, there is no rush, no need to grope for the mask you are wearing or to throw it away. It is no accident that we are wearing masks, meeting, as we do, after a long time, when both of us have escaped our prisons to face each other: we needn't hurry to throw away our masks, because we will only find other masks beneath them, masks made of flesh and bone and yet as much a mask as these, made of silk. There are so many masks we have to discard before I can get to see and recognize your face. But I know that somewhere, far, far away, the other face exists and that one day I must see it, because I love you. Once, many years

ago, you gave me a mirror, Giacomo, a present from Venice. A mirror was, of course, the only possible gift, a Venetian mirror, which is reputed to show people their true faces. You brought me a mirror in a silver frame, and a comb, a silver-handled comb. That is what you gave me. It was the best of presents, my dear. Years have passed, and every day I hold the mirror and comb in my hand, adjusting my hair, looking at my face as you imagined and wanted me to, when you gave me a mirror as a present. Because mirrors are enchantments—did you know that, you, a citizen of Venice, where the finest mirrors are produced? We have to look into mirrors for a long time, regularly, for a very long time, before we can see our true faces. A mirror is not just a smooth silver surface, no, a mirror is deep, too, like tarns on mountains, and if you look carefully into a Venetian mirror you will catch a glimpse of that depth, and will go on to detect ever deeper and deeper depths, the face glimmering ever farther off, and every day a mask falls away, one more of the masks that is examining itself in the mirror that was a gift your lover bought you from Venice. You should never give a woman you love a mirror as a present, because women eventually come to know themselves in mirrors, seeing ever more clearly, growing ever more melancholy. It was in a mirror, at some time, in some place, that the first act of recognition occurred, the point when man stared into the ocean, saw his face in its infinity, grew anxious, and began to ask, 'Who is that? . . .' The mirror you brought for me from Venice, a mirror no bigger than my palm, showed me my real face, and one day I saw that this face, my face, the face

I thought was familiar and was mine, was only a mask, far finer than silk, and behind it lay another face that looked like yours. I am grateful to the mirror for that. . . . And that is why I am not making promises, vowing no vows, not demanding anything, however madly my heart is beating at this very moment, because I recognized my face and I know that it resembles yours, and that you are truly mine. Is that enough? . . ."

"It's not enough," replied the man.

"Not enough?" the woman asked in the same singsong voice. "No, Giacomo, this time you have not been entirely sincere. You yourself know that this is not to be dismissed, that it adds up to something, maybe even more than something. It is not a little thing, not in the least, when two people know they are meant for each other. It took me a long time before I understood it. Because there was a time when I did not know myself, and that is the way I grew up in Pistoia, behind thick walls, a little neglected and unkept, like wild nettles—and you courted me then on a whim, with mock gallantry, but both of us knew that whatever we said, something true was passing between us! You found me various pet names adapted from plants, animals, and stars, as lovers often do when they are still playing with each other and trying out words, in the early days of love when they lack the courage to call each other by their true names, such as 'my love' or 'Giacomo' or 'Francesca.' By that time all other words are superfluous. But at that stage I was 'wild flower' and even, somewhat discourteously, 'wild nettle,' because I was wild and I stung and you said that your hands burned and came out

in a rash when they touched mine. That's how you courted me. I think back to those times and feel dizzy or find myself blushing, because I am sure that I knew you the very first time I saw you, in the large hall on the ground floor of the house in Pistoia among those scrappy bits of furniture with their broken legs—I remember you were just showing the cardinal's letter to my father and exchanging a few pleasantries with him, lying about something with considerable fluency. And I knew more about you at that moment than I did later, when conversation and social games hid your real nature from me. I knew everything about you at that first instant, and if there is anything I am ashamed of, or hide from myself in embarrassment, it's the consequent period of our love, when you flirted with me using those names of animals and plants and stars, when you acted gallantly, when you were false and alien to me—it is that period that fills me with shame. You were a coward then, Giacomo, too much a coward to do as your heart commanded that first moment you saw me, before we had spoken a word to each other, before you started addressing me as 'wild nettle' or anything else. It is a great sin to be a coward. I can forgive you all those things the world will not forgive: your character, your weaknesses, your maliciousness, your boundless selfishness; I understand and wholly absolve you of all those, but I cannot forgive your cowardice. Why did you allow the duke of Parma to take possession of me, to buy me as you might a calf at the cattle market in Florence? . . . Why did you let me take up residence in strange palaces and foreign towns when you knew you were truly mine? . . . I woke at dawn

on my wedding night and stretched out my hand looking for you. I was in Paris in a coach under the plane trees, on the stony road to Versailles, with the king on my right, and I didn't answer when our cousin Louis addressed a question to me, because I imagined it was you sitting beside me and I wanted to show you something. And I asked myself continually: why is he such a coward when he knows we belong to each other? He is not afraid of knives or jails or poison or humiliation, so why should he fear me, his true love, his happiness? . . . I kept asking myself that. Then I understood. And now I know what I have to do, Giacomo—it is the reason I learned to write, and to do so much else that has nothing to do with pen and ink and paper. I learned everything because I love you. And now you should truly understand, my love, that when I say the words *I love you,* I do not say them in a languishing or misty-eyed sort of way, but speak them aloud; that I shout them in your face like a command, like an accusation. Do you hear, Giacomo? I love you. I am not trifling with these words. I am addressing you like a judge, do you hear? I love you, therefore I have authority over you. I love you and therefore I demand that you take courage. I love you so I am starting again from the beginning. Even if I have to drag you from your orbit as if you were a star in the firmament I shall take you with me, I shall tear you from your natural place in the universe, remove you from the laws of your being and from the demands of your art because I love you. I am not asking you, Giacomo, I am accusing you: yes, I am accusing you of a capital crime. I am not inviting you to join a game, I

am in no mood to dally or flirt with you, I am not making sheep's eyes at you or melting with tender sighs. I am staring at you with anger, with fury: I look upon you as one looks at an enemy. I shall kidnap you for love, if not now, then later, nor will I let you off the leash for a single second, whatever borders you cross, however you try to flee me with the little serving maid at your side, the one that opened the doors for me, who started back into the shadows like a fawn that scents danger, sensing that under the man's clothes I was a woman and a rival, for I sensed that she had something to do with you, too, that she was plotting with you against me, like all the other women. That is how life is and how it will continue to be. But I am stronger for my love. I tell you this directly, and I say it aloud, like a slap across your face, do you understand? . . . Do you hear? . . . I love you. I cannot help it. It is my fate to love you. I have loved you for five years, Giacomo, from the moment I saw you in the old garden in Pistoia, when you were telling that thumping lie, after which you called me 'wild nettle' and fought over me, stripped to the waist in the moonlight, at which point you fled and I despised you and loved you. I know you are afraid, are still afraid of me. Don't try shutting your eyes under the mask, because I can see through the holes: yes, now at last I can see you beneath the mask, and your eyes, which were bright before, like a wild animal's contemplating its prey, have clouded over, as if some veil or fog had descended on them. Your eyes are almost human now. Don't shut your eyes or turn away, because I want you to know that I shall not let you go, however complicated an agreement you

have come to with the duke of Parma, because despite the agreement you remain the man that is meant for me, and I am the woman that is meant for you; we belong together like murderer and victim, like sinner and sin, like the artist and his art, as does everyone with the mission he would most like to escape. Don't be afraid, Giacomo! It won't hurt much! I must make you a gift of courage; I must teach you to be brave in facing yourself, facing us, the fact of us, a fact that may be sinful and scandalous, as is every true and naked fact in the world. Don't be afraid, because I love you. Is that enough? . . ."

"It's too much," said the man.

"Too much," said the woman and gave a short sigh. She fell silent, her hands against her mask, and stared into the fire.

The fire spluttered and carried on with its monotonous singing. They listened to its song, full of life, full of reason. Then the woman moved warily, as if afraid of tripping over her sword, and knelt before the man; raising her two long, slender arms and very gently and carefully laying her fingertips on the man's mask, she took his hidden face in her hands and whispered, "Forgive me if my love is too much, Giacomo, I know such love is a great sin. You must forgive me. Very few people can bear the burden of absolute love that is also an inescapable duty and responsibility. It is the only sin I have committed against you. Forgive me. I will never ask anything more of you. I will do everything to reduce the suffering it causes you. Are you afraid that boredom might one day grip you with its damp palm and strangle you as you wake beside me? . . . Don't

be afraid, my love, because this boredom will be as satisfying and good humored as when you stretch and yawn, and the meaning of the boredom will be that I love you. You don't know, you cannot yet know, what it is like when someone loves you. I must explain love to you because you know nothing about it. You fear your desire and curiosity, you fear all the women who will smile at you from windows, from carriages, in every inn and in every foreign marketplace, because you fear that you will not be able to pursue them, tied as you are to me, by love. . . . It is not certain that you will want to pursue them, Giacomo, knowing I love you. But if you were to leave me one day, out of curiosity and boredom, I would carry on living and waiting for you somewhere. And one day you will grow tired of the world, having known and tasted everything, and you will wake with a sense of disgust, your limbs racked with some awful disease, your bones riddled with woodworm, and you will look around you and remember that somewhere I am waiting for you. Where should I wait, my love? . . . Wherever you wish. In the country house I may retire to after the death of the duke, in the big city where you first abandoned me, perhaps here in Bolzano, in my palazzo, to which I would have had to return and wait for you once the night was over? You must realize that I will wait for you forever. And wherever I make my bed, be certain one pillow will be reserved for you. Every dish I cook or is placed before me by a servant will be your dish too. When the sun shines and the sky is blue, you must be aware that I will be staring at the sky, thinking, 'Giacomo will be enjoying the same sky.' Should

the rain come down, I will be thinking, 'Now he is standing at a window in Paris or in London, fractious and in a foul mood, and someone should really be lighting a fire in the room to keep his feet warm.' When I see a beautiful woman I will think, 'Perhaps she may afford him an hour of pleasure so he may be less unhappy.' Whenever I break a loaf, half of it will be yours. I know it is too much, this love, and I beg you to forgive me. I want to live a long time so I can wait for you to come home."

"Home? Where is that, Francesca?" asked the mask. "I have no home, not a stick of furniture, anywhere in the world."

"Home is with me, Giacomo," the woman answered. "Wherever I sleep, that is your home."

Her two palms curved very gently, as though she were holding a delicate piece of glass, and stroked the man's mask.

"You see," said the woman, her voice now faintly singing, her mask a living, smiling radiance, "I am kneeling before you, in fancy dress, like a courtly suitor attempting to charm a lady. And you are sitting before me, in a female costume, masked, because fate has playfully ordained that, for one night only, we should exchange roles. I am the gallant suitor, and you are the lady I am courting. What do you think? Is this not more than coincidence? . . . I had no idea this afternoon that I would be wearing a male costume tonight, nor did you know this afternoon that the duke of Parma would seek you out, bring you my letter, invite you to the ball, and that you would be dressing up as a woman . . . do you think this is

all just coincidence? I don't understand human affairs, Giacomo, I only have my imagination, and I begin to suspect that no vital, no unique situation is coincidental, that deep down, at bottom, everybody, men and women alike, is a similar blend of feelings and desires, that our characters and roles are not wholly distinct, that there are moments when life toys with us and shifts about those elements within us that we had believed to be unique and fixed. That is why I am not astonished to be kneeling before you, rather than you before me, as the duke of Parma had ordained in his agreement, and it is I who am endeavoring to woo you. So, you see, everything is proceeding according to the agreement, even though the actors are not precisely in the parts the duke of Parma had designed for them. I am begging you, my dear, to accept my love. I want to console you because I love you and cannot bear your unhappiness. I am the suitor, the besieging force, not you. I have come to you because I must see you. And here we are now, and you are silent. It is a powerful silence, a proper, tight-lipped silence, as it has to be, considering your role, and I echo the last words of your speeches precisely as the agreement demands. But you are still restrained, Giacomo, still acting: you are too true to your part. Are you not afraid that our time will run out, that night will pass, and you will have nothing of interest or satisfaction to report to the man who commissioned you? . . . Don't you want me, my love? How terrifying you are when you keep quiet like this, so utterly in character. Not enough and too much, you said, when I offered you everything a woman could offer the man she loved. Look

at the fire, Giacomo, see, it has flared up as if it, too, wanted to say something. Perhaps what it wants to say is that it is necessary to be destroyed by the fury of passion and be born anew in feeling, because that is life and wholeness. Everything that has happened might catch light and burn in our hearts if you so desired, if you took me with you or if you let me take you—it is all the same, Giacomo, who goes with whom—but we will have to start everything again, from the beginning, because that is how love works. I will have to give birth to you, to be both your mother and your daughter; my love will cleanse you and I, too, shall be clean in your arms. It will be as if no man had ever touched me. Are you still quiet? . . . Don't you want me? . . . Can I not console you? . . . How terrible, Giacomo. In vain do I offer you delight and peace, cleanliness and renewal, I cannot drag you into feeling, cannot prize you from your art, cannot change you or see your true face, the last face, without its mask, as I wanted in my letter. . . . Is it possible that you are stronger than I am, my love? Will the strength of my love break against your cold art and impregnable character? . . . I promise you peace and wholeness, and you tell me it is too much and not enough. Why don't you say just once that it is enough, perfect, just right? . . . Can't I offer you anything that will draw you out of your orbit? Can't I say anything to make you finally step out of character and cry, yes, it is enough! . . . Look, here I kneel, I am twenty years old. You know perfectly well that I am beautiful. I know it, too. I am not the most beautiful woman in the world, because the most beautiful woman does not exist anywhere, but I

am still beautiful, my body is perfect, my face is alive and full of curiosity, repose, delight, understanding, cheer, and solemnity all blended together. It is the blend that gives it its beauty. Because that blended animation is what beauty is. All else is merely a malleable combination of skin and flesh and bone. You still believe in the kind of women who ostentatiously draw attention to their beauty, Giacomo, who strut about proudly, not knowing that beauty is what dissolves in the crucible of love, that a month or a year after the successful wedding, no one notices beauty anymore—face, legs, arms, a fine bosom, all melt away and disappear in the flames of love, and there remains a woman who may still be able to soothe, to hold, to help you, to offer something, even when you can no longer see the beauty of her face and figure. . . . My beauty is like that, Giacomo: I am true metal, gold through and through. Even if I were worn on someone's finger, or buried deep beneath the earth, I would be true because I am beautiful. The Creator has blessed me with beauty and he has given me the odd beating, too: I am beautiful and therefore have a purpose in life, which is to please your eyes, though it is not only your eyes I must please, Giacomo. For I cannot pass through life with such beauty without being punished for it, because wherever I go I rouse passions: I am like a water diviner who discovers underground streams, who can feel them bubbling beneath her. I have to suffer a great deal on account of my beauty. I offer you the beauty and harmony with which the Creator has blessed and cursed me and you are still uncertain, saying now too much, now not enough. Are

you not afraid, Giacomo? . . . You made my acquaintance when I was still in bud, calling me your 'wild nettle,' but you permitted the duke of Parma to buy me, and fled because you feared and still do fear me, even though I represent truth and wholeness. Are you not afraid that human ties might not be enough, that maybe I am just a woman who may tire of waiting, of agreements, deals, and promises? Are you not afraid that I might be tired already and that I visit you only to confirm the fact and tell you so? . . . Because the desire and devotion that burns in my heart for you is itself a terrifying and self-consuming passion! Are you not afraid, Giacomo, that I have secrets of my own? Are you not afraid that I may be able to stir feelings in you that are not entirely tender or calm, that I might, if I very much desired, entertain you with stories that will make you cry out and finally demand, 'Enough!' I am truly yours, Giacomo, nor is there anything I desire more than to save you and to save myself, and having done that, to live with you as people do, through whatever hells we may have to face. But if your attachment to your art, to the duke of Parma's contract, and to yourself demands something more, it may be time for me to weaken and to confess that, while this flame has continued to burn within me ever since I first met you and that it is indeed unquenchable, I was unable to resign myself to your running away, to your cowardice, but allowed other men to kiss me before I gave myself to the duke of Parma. I could regale you with stories about the consolations required by a rejected fifteen-year-old girl. Shall I tell you what it was like after your flight in Pistoia, when I threw myself at the

gardener—you know the man? Are you not afraid of hearing about that night, Giacomo? I remember it very well, in every detail, just as you, in your turn, will remember the gardener who gave me flowers on your behalf: a tall, powerful, violent man, a man of few words. Shall I tell you the story of the night after your duel and your escape? . . . Would you really like to hear it in all its detail? And what about the other things that followed as the months and years passed, when I had no news from you, and this flame, that is worse than the flames and fumes of hell, worse than the flames suffered by poor victims of the Inquisition, burned me through and through? Shall I tell you the story of the house in Florence? About the palazzo on the bank of the Arno by the Ponte San Trínita, where you will find my nightgown, my slippers, my comb, and the Venetian mirror you gave me? Should I tell you about the house I frequented that I, too, might have used as a casino, Giacomo, the secret palazzo in Murano that, like you, I once enjoyed? Should I tell you all this? Should I tell you what it is like when a woman who wants to give everything that a young body and soul has to give to the man she loves is disappointed in love and begins to burn with fury, like a torch made of flesh, hair, and blood, a torch that burns in secret, like a flame in the half-light, scorching and blackening everything she touches, so that despite all the power, strength, and wariness of the duke of Parma, he is helpless to put the fire out? Should I tell you what it is like when a woman is obliged to seek the tenderness she desires from one man alone, a man who has run away, in the embraces of ten, twenty, or a hundred men? Would

274

you like names, Giacomo? Would you like proof? . . . Would you like to know the names of those noble lords, gardeners, courtiers, comedians, gamblers, and musicians, together with their addresses, every one of them kinder and more tender to me than you have ever been? . . . Do you want to know what it is like when a woman begins to move through the world like one possessed, touched, and branded by fate, without a scrap of peace in her heart because she loves somebody and has been rejected? Because I could tell you about that too."

"I don't believe you," the man said, his voice cracking.

"You don't believe me?" echoed the woman in her sweetest, most childlike, most astonished manner. "And if I had proof, Giacomo? . . . If you had the list of names and addresses that would act as proof, would you believe me then? Because I could give you the names and addresses. Is that enough? . . ."

"It is enough," said the man. He stood up and with a quick movement seized the dagger hidden in his breast.

The woman, however, did not move. Still kneeling, she turned the stiff gaze of the mask on the man, and spoke quietly and modestly.

"Oh, the dagger! Always the dagger, my love. It is the only answer you have for the world that inflicts itself on you! Put the dagger away, my dear; it is a one-word answer that explains nothing, it is a stupid, needless answer. And why answer me with a dagger when you are simply a coward afraid of loving me, when I can offer you neither true delight nor true pain, when all this is just a game, the pièce de résistance of a hired conjuror, a guest performance by a

remarkable artist who is only passing through? The dagger is not part of the agreement, my dear. I say it again, put the dagger away, and don't bother reaching for the mask with those trembling fingers. Why should you take off the mask? What could the face beneath the mask tell me? I wrote to say that I must see you, and now I have seen you. It wasn't so much a face I wanted to see, Giacomo, but a man, the man I truly loved, who was a coward, who sold me and ran away from me. But it was all in vain. It was in vain that I knew who and what kind of man you were; in vain that, for five years, the fires of Gehenna have been blazing inside me; in vain that I made futile attempts to extinguish the glowing embers of that fire and to heal the wound with the kisses of other men while never ceasing to love you; in vain that I have carried this wound about with me like a bloody sword wherever I have gone, challenging everyone who crossed my path with it; in vain that I cursed it in secret, in the depths of my soul, a hundred times or more, for I was still hoping that one day I would have enough strength to tear the mask from your face and see you, as my note demanded, to see you and forgive you. That is why I asked the castrato to teach me writing. That is why I wrote and sent you the letter. That is why I waited for you, and that is why, when you did not come to me because, true to your art as ever, you were drawing up a contract with the duke of Parma, I came to you, in men's clothes, masked, just once more, so I could see you. I told you everything, that you are truly mine and that I am the woman to whom you are eternally bound, and you knew it was true. I offered you everything I had. And your only

reply was, 'too little,' or 'too much.' But finally I have got you to say, 'enough.' That was the word I wanted to hear. Good. Now listen carefully, my love. Everything I told you is true. And now that I have seen you like this, I have no wish to see you any other way. I will go back to my house and to my guests. And you will go out into the world to live and to lie, to loot and to steal, to snatch at every skirt you come across and to roll in every bed you find. You will continue, faithful to your art. But all the while you will know, whether you are awake or asleep, even as you are kissing another woman, that I was the truth, that I meant everything in life to you, and that you hurt me and sold me. You will know that you could have had all that life has to offer but preferred slyness and cowardice: that you chose to work to a contract and that henceforth life will offer you nothing but contracts. You will know that my body, which is partly your body, will never now be yours but will belong to anybody who asks for it. You will know that I am living somewhere, in the arms of other men, but that you will never again hold me in your arms. I too am faithful in my fashion, Giacomo. I wanted to live with you like Adam and Eve in the Garden before there was sin in the world. I wanted to save you from your fate. There is no passion, no misery, no sickness, no shame that I would not have shared with you. You know what I say is true, you knew my letter was sacred. You knew but kept silent, true to your agreement with the duke of Parma. And you should know that, now that I have seen you, I have sentenced you to unhappiness, you will never again have a happy moment in your life, and

whatever sweetness you taste you will think of me. You may have seen me but you do not know me in the biblical sense, and yet you do know something, if not everything, about me now. Our time is running out. Do not forget that my sex and the name I bear demand a certain modesty and tact. You know something about me and the rest I leave you to imagine at every hour of leisure between one task and another, one contract and another, one masterpiece and another. Because you will think of me, Giacomo. I am confident in the knowledge that you will think of me. That is why I came to see you, why I promised you all a woman can promise a man, and why I tell you now that there is nothing a corrupt imagination can invent that I will not turn into reality in the future, at the very moment you think of me. That is why I came to you masked, at midnight, wearing a man's clothes, with a sword at my side. And now I can go home to my palazzo and to the rest of my life, which I know for certain will be only half a life without you. Now go: live and create masterpieces, my friend. Perhaps one day your own life will become a masterpiece, a masterpiece glowing with cold, corrupt light. The laws of your being may be what most concern you: my concern, however, was for you yourself, my love, and now, this night being over, I know that your heart is condemned to eternal pain. Because it is not a matter of having seen you as I wished to: you have seen me, too, and having seen me, you will never forget my face, the face under the masks I show the world. Because revenge can console us, Giacomo. You may not understand that at this very moment, but you will as soon as I

have left this room and vanished forever from your life, then you will suddenly understand and your whole life will be filled with that understanding. I am nobody in particular, Giacomo, not a great artist, not a man, just a woman, Francesca from Tuscany, unfit to occupy a leading place among your great works of art. But from now on I shall have some kind of place there, I have made sure of that. I have infused my being into yours, I have infused you with the knowledge that I was the truth you threw away, that you brought shame to someone who loved you and will always love you in whatever situation she chooses for herself in exacting the revenge she has vowed to take. I wanted to take other vows with you, Giacomo, vows for life. You rejected them. Life will go on, however, even like this. . . . But your life will not be what it was before, my love: you will be like the man who has been fed some exquisite slow-working poison and feels the pain at every moment. I have taken care of that. Because I, too, have my weapons, subtler than daggers. Put the dagger away, my love. I may not have been strong enough to overcome you through love, but I shall be stronger in revenge and your dagger will be useless. Put the dagger away. Or, if you want, you could give it to me as a memento of this night. I would look after it well, in Florence, keeping it together with your other gifts, the mirror and the comb. Would you like to exchange mementos? Look, I will draw this slender gold-handled sword that I strapped to my side this evening, and I will give it to you in exchange, the way enemies used to exchange hearts and arms when they had finished fighting each other. Give me the dagger as a

memento. Thank you. . . . And receive in exchange this sharp, highly refined weapon, and take it with you wherever you go. You see, we have exchanged arms, if not hearts, Giacomo. And now we should both return to our respective places in the world and live on as we must, if only because you were too weak to step out of character and reject your art. I thank you for the dagger, my love," the woman said and stood up, "and thank you for this night. Now I, too, can live on, more settled than I have been these last five years. Shall I hear anything of you? . . . I don't know. Should I wait for you? . . . But I have already said, Giacomo, that I will wait forever. Because what we share will not pass with time. It is not only love that is eternal, Giacomo: all true feelings are, including revenge."

She drew the sword and handed it over, attaching the Venetian dagger the man had wordlessly handed over to her to a link of the golden belt she was wearing. "It's almost dawn," she said in a voice as clear as glass. "I must go. Don't see me out, Giacomo. If I could find my way here by myself I can find my way back, too, to life, to my home. How quiet it is. . . . The wind has died down. And the fire, too, has gone out, you see, as if speaking its own language, which tells us that every passion, all that passes, must eventually turn to ashes. But that is not something I want to believe. Because this night has, after all, provided us with an encounter and a chance of deepening our acquaintance, even if not quite as the duke of Parma imagined or the Bible describes. Now you have a seal on your agreement, Giacomo, that seal being your consciousness of all I have told you. It is the seal of revenge, a powerful

seal, as strong as love or life or death. You can tell the duke of Parma that you were true to your agreement, that you did not cheat him, my love, nor did you fail, but have earned your fee and merit your reward. By the end of the night everything had happened as you had agreed, and now that I have got to know you I am returning to the man who loves me and is waiting for me to ease his departure from life. Travel well, Giacomo, trip through the world on light steps. Your art remains infallible and the task you took on is accomplished, not quite as you imagined, you two clever men between you, but it's the result that matters, and the result is that I know you, that I know I have no real hold on your heart, and can therefore only resign myself to my fate, the only power remaining to me being revenge. Take this confession, this promise with you as you go, for your road will be long and certain to be fascinating and full of variety. But I want something from you, too, by way of farewell. Rather unusually for me, I wrote a letter: if ever you feel that you have understood my letter and wish to answer, don't be lazy or cowardly: answer as is fit, with pen and ink, like the well-versed literary man you are. Do you promise? . . ."

And when the man did not answer, she continued, "Why will you not answer? Can the answer be so terrifying, Giacomo?"

"You know very well," the man replied, slowly and somewhat hoarsely, "that if I were ever to answer you in this life, the answer would not be given in pen and ink."

The woman shrugged and responded calmly, almost indifferently, with the trace of a smile in her voice. "Yes, I

know. But what can I do? . . . I will live and wait for you to answer my letter, my love."

And she set out toward the door. But halfway there she turned to him in a gentle, friendly manner.

"The game and the performance are over, Giacomo. Let us return to our lives, taking off our masks and costumes. Everything has turned out as you wanted. I am sure that everything that has happened has happened according to some unwritten law. But you should know that it has happened as I, too, wanted it: I saw you, I was tender to you, and I hurt you."

She stood on tiptoe, looked briefly into the mirror, and with an easy movement placed the three-cornered hat over her wig. Having adjusted it, she added solicitously: "I hope I did not hurt you too much."

But she did not wait for an answer. She left the room without looking back, her feet swift and firm, and silently closed the door behind her.

The Answer

The room had chilled down and the candles had gut-
tered but were still smoking with a bitter stench. The
man stepped out of the skirt, released himself from the
bodice, tore off his mask, and threw away the wig. He
entered the bedchamber, stepped over to the washbasin,
poured icy water from the jug over his palm, and with
slow deliberate movements began to wash.

He washed the paint and rice powder off his face,
rubbed the scarlet from his lips, peeled the beauty patch
from his cheek, and wiped the soot from his eyebrows. He
splashed the water on, its icy touch burning and scratching his face: it stung him like a blow. He ran his fingers
through his hair and rubbed his face raw with the towel,
then lit fresh candles, and in the light they gave, leaned
toward the mirror to check that he had removed every
trace of paint from his face. His brow was furrowed and
pale, his chin needed a shave, and there were dark shadows
under his eyes as if he had just returned from an orgy that

had gone on all night. Then he threw away everything associated with the mask, and with quick, certain movements, began to dress.

Somewhere, bells were ringing. He put on traveling clothes, a warm shirt and stockings, and drew his cloak about his shoulders before looking around the room. The food and drink lay untouched on the damask tablecloth with its silver cutlery, only the snow in the dish had melted and futile little islands of butter were swimming about in the remaining pool like peculiarly swollen Oriental flowers on a tiny, ornamental pond. He picked up the chicken, tore it into two, and with fierce greedy movements nervously began to gnaw it. Having finished it he threw the bones into a corner, wiped his greasy fingers on the tablecloth, raised the crystal wineglass full of viscous golden fluid, and filled his mouth with it. He held his head back and watched as it went down in slow gulps, his enormous Adam's apple bobbing up and down in the mirror. He wiped his mouth with the back of his hand and threw away the glass, which struck the ground with a light chink and broke into pieces. His voice hoarse with wine, he called for Balbi.

The friar was immediately there, as if he had been ready and waiting for some time. He stood in the doorway, ready for the journey in his thick brown broadcloth coat, in his square-toed shoes, and a flask under his arm that he was nursing as tenderly and carefully as a mother might her child. Teresa followed him in and silently, without a second glance, hurried over to the shards of broken glass and assiduously gathered up the pieces in her apron.

"Is everything ready?" he asked the friar.

"They're preparing the horses," Balbi replied.

"Have you packed?" he asked the girl.

"No, sir," the girl replied, humbly and modestly. "I will not be going with you."

She stood by the fire, her head to one side, the broken glass in her apron, gazing calmly at him with wide and empty blue eyes.

"And why will you not come with me?" he asked, throwing his head back and looking down his nose. "I guarantee your future."

"Because you don't love me," the girl dreamily replied like a dutiful schoolgirl repeating a lesson.

"Do you think I love somebody else?" he asked.

"Yes."

"Whom do you think I love?" he asked curiously, as if addressing a child who was hiding a secret and was now about to reveal it.

"The woman in men's clothes, who left a little while ago," answered the girl.

"Are you sure," he asked, astonished.

"Quite sure."

"How do you know?"

"I can feel it. There is no one else. Nor will there ever be. That is why I won't go with you. Forgive me, sir."

She stood still. Balbi waited silently in the doorway, his hands folded over his stomach, and peered at him with a mildly inquisitive expression, twiddling his thumbs and blinking. Giacomo stepped over to the maid and stroked her hair and brow with great tenderness.

"Wait," he said. "Don't go yet. An angel may be speaking through you."

He opened his cloak, sat down in the armchair, drew the girl carefully to him, and sat her down on his knee, gazing deeply into those empty, watchful blue eyes.

"Sit down, Balbi," he said eventually. "There, by the table. Take pen, powder, and paper. You will write a letter for me."

The friar sat down silently, shifting and panting with his great weight. He lit a candle and examined the pen before staring up at the ceiling in anticipation.

"Address it *Your Excellency,*" he said. "And watch your hand now. I want this to be beautifully written. I will speak slowly so you have time to form the letters. Are you ready? We may begin. *I am leaving town in the early hours of this morning. I am leaving without payment or reward, and all I ask is a single favor. Your Excellency has already volunteered his services as a postman once: I beg him now, by way of farewell, to undertake the task once more, and to inform the duchess of Parma that I call for help on whatever powers may be, and pray to God that He preserve us, she and I, now and in the future, from ever meeting again. I would that Your Excellency beg her, as she cares for her life and fears God, to avoid me henceforth, and to make sure that we never again look upon each other's faces, whether masked or unmasked. That is all I ask. For by most human expectations—and I say this with due courtesy, without any intent to offend—I am likely to outlive Your Excellency. I shall outlive him as nature and human destiny decree, and Your Excel-*

lency's noble corpse will soon be dust in his ancestors' tomb while Francesca and I continue to exist in the world: and, once Your Excellency is dead there will be no one to protect her, the woman we have both loved, each in his own fashion, according to our agreement and our fate. That is why I ask Your Excellency to tell the duchess, she whom I shall never again address in writing, to avoid me like the plague or the deluge; she should avoid me as she might sin and calumny; she must avoid me so that she might save that which is more important than life, meaning her soul. Only Your Excellency can tell her this. My carriage is prepared; in an hour I shall have left town and by evening I shall be beyond the frontiers of the state. The duchess of Parma will inform Your Excellency at some opportune hour, at a moment of tenderness perhaps or at some other proper confidential time, that I have carried out my obligations according to the terms of our agreement; not quite as we imagined, not quite as I usually do or imagined I would, but it is the outcome alone that matters, and the outcome is that I have kept my word and that the duchess of Parma has returned home by first light of dawn, known and cured, recovered from one who is as the plague and the yellow fever to her, and that she will henceforth dwell at the side of Your Excellency, without me, as is to be expected, with only the fading memory of my dangerous and wicked person in her heart. For that which was desire and passion between us has vanished in the performance, and now it is I who carry with me all that was feverish and resembled infection in that love, and the duchess of Parma is now free to dedicate her life to Your Excellency, gilding his declining years in

a calmer frame of mind.' Have you written it all down? . . .
Wait, perhaps we should say his declining months . . .
instead. It is more considerate in its honesty and, note
this, Balbi, and you too my child, that it is incumbent on
us to fight the great duels of life, even at moments of the
most desperate crisis, with consideration, for it is befitting
that we should be courteous while being true to the facts
and to ourselves. Now where were we? . . . *'Declining
months. For if I do not perish along the path, at the hand of
some assassin, or by way of accident—Your Excellency having
informed me that my entire life is an accident, albeit an accident that I am determined, tooth and nail, to survive—I will
live on, and every day I live will present a danger to the soul
of Francesca. That is my message to her. Everything else I
report speaks for itself. I am leaving the town, as agreed, and
the duchess of Parma is back at home after her adventure, as
pure as the driven snow or the fleecy clouds of spring. It may,
of course, be true that, according to the new knowledge, the
color white is an aggregation of all other colors, from the
crimson of blood through to the black of mourning: it is what
I read in the philosopher's book and I merely pass the knowledge on, adding only that the adventure was itself as pure as
most people imagine snow to be. Your Excellency desired peace
and recovery: he desired that the spell of love be broken and
that Francesca should live on at her husband's side without
pining, without memory. This has come to pass and I can go
my way. I do not say that I go with a light heart. Nor do I say
that I go proudly, shrugging my shoulders, rubbing my hands
with satisfaction, like an artist who has finished a commis-*

sion, stowed away his reward, and can hardly wait to cross the border and embark on new projects, with new techniques, ready to hammer out new agreements. I have looked into my heart and all I can say is that the tie we sought to sever with words and daggers is stronger now than it was the day before, or indeed ever before: the tie meaning that which binds me to the duchess of Parma. Knots tied by the gods are, it seems, not to be untied by human hands, however clever, tender, or violent. And that is why Your Excellency should look to the duchess's soul and ensure that we never meet again. Fire dies, said the duchess, and sooner or later all passion turns to ashes, but let me say, by way of farewell, that there is a kind of fire that is not lit by the spark of the moment, nor by the kindling of the senses; nor is it fanned by greed or ambition, no: there is something that continues to flicker in human life, a flame that neither custom nor boredom succeeds in putting out; nor do satisfaction or lechery succeed where they fail; it is a flame the world cannot extinguish, indeed, we ourselves cannot extinguish it. It is part of the fire that human hands once stole from heaven, and ever since then those responsible for its theft have faced the wrath of the gods. This is the flame that will continue to burn in my heart, nor do I have any wish to extinguish it: and wherever life leads me, wherever I present my character and exercise my art, I will know that the flame does not go out and that its heat and light fill my life. I could not say this to the duchess, since I did not want to break the agreement, and I will adhere to the letter of that agreement as to the rules of my art. I did not say to her, "I am yours alone, forever," as lovers generally do: I kept my word, and it is only

Your Excellency who can tell the duchess of Parma that some-times the artist can be a hero by obeying the conventions and obligations of performance, by not pronouncing the words that burn in his heart and on his lips, whose meaning is in the end, after all, "I am yours alone, forever." I did not pro-nounce the words, and the words I did not say will now echo forever in our two souls; that is why I report, by way of farewell, that I have kept our agreement faithfully, to the let-ter. The performance was a success, Your Excellency, and the show is over. But there is something that remains and will never be over, something upon which Your Excellency has expended all his strength, his secret influence, his terrifying omniscience and literary acuity, and yet is impossible to undo or destroy, which is the knowledge that whatever flame heaven has ignited in the human heart is not to be extin-guished by human hands or human intelligence. And there is something else I could not say for fear of breaking our agree-ment: that there is a kind of sacrifice or service in love which is more than declarations or abductions, more than "I am yours alone, forever"—you should write those words within quotation marks, I think—*'There is a kind of love which does not wish to remove or to hurt but to protect, per-haps even to save, and that this may in fact be the truest love of all, and however surprised I am to feel it, it is the feeling that the memory of the duchess of Parma prompts in me and always will. Because there is nothing easier than to remove the loved one from the world. There is nothing easier, for an expe-rienced performer like me, than to produce tears and vows, to carry out the accomplished seduction, to undertake the great somersault, to join the circle dance of nymph and faun, com-*

plete with pipes and rustic viols. I think I can say, without boasting, that I know my art, that I have performed often enough in my life, and will, no doubt, perform again should the nymphs and gods of pleasure so command. Nothing would have been easier for me—and only Your Excellency is free to repeat these words to the duchess, for I could not speak them in case the words became a reality and the reality resulted in action!—than to yield to my desires; to answer neither "too much" nor "too little" to all that a woman in love could offer me out of the depths of her pain and not to worry about her revenge, either, but to act upon desire, action, after all, having been the working principle of my life, for there has never been very much distance between my desires and my deeds, thank heaven'—I would like a semicolon there, please—*'and I say this without boasting, with a clear conscience. But I knew something that the sickly child of love, the duchess of Parma, could not yet know: I knew who I was, I was aware of my earthly task, my role, and my fate, and I also knew that the flame that keeps me alive and gives me strength is death to those who carelessly touch it. There would have been nothing easier for me than to accept her gift, to exchange body for body, and soul for soul, and thereby to take possession of One'*—write that with a capital *O*—*'One who was truly mine. And there was yet something else I knew that the duchess of Parma could not yet know: that the truth can only survive as long as the hidden veils of desire and longing draw a curtain before her and cover her. That is why I did not lift the veil and bathe truth's mysterious face in the light of reality. And now I must return to my own reality, which is many-colored. I know its taste and scents so well that sometimes they*

seem bitter to me, and I no longer expect miracles or salvation. Let us go in peace, Your Excellency! We are mortals, and that high station imposes obligations on us: we are obliged to know our hearts and our fates. That is not an easy task. There are only two divine medicaments to help us bear the poison of reality and prevent it from killing us prematurely, and these are intelligence and indifference. We are men, the both of us: we know this secret; we have encountered reality and met our truth; we understand this. But it is not the business of a young, fiercely beating, and grievously wounded heart to understand it: that is why we must silently bear her accusations and her revenge, too, the revenge that will follow us everywhere we go. And I beg her once more, as I go, before I vanish into the mist that will now be covering the mountain paths, vanish away into cities, into time, into otherness, as my fate, which I truly regard as my fate, consumes me, to avoid me at all costs. She should avoid me if she wishes to save her soul. Because goodness, experience, skill, and compassion are only means whereby we may discipline the heart from time to time, but something underlies our intentions, directing our steps, some vast imperative whose magical power we may not transgress without being punished for it. I wish you months of happiness, Your Excellency! I hope we are not disappointed in each other. And if, a little later, when passions have died down somewhat and the miraculous balm of forgetting has eased the young heart so dear to both of us, should my name crop up in the course of some tender conversation, tell her that I have carried the rapier she exchanged for my dagger into the world, and am handling it well. That I will not bring disgrace on it. Tell her this so she may be assured. It is possible

that I might have to twist the blade she has given me in a heart or two, but tell her that she need not fear, for my hand will be cold and certain at those moments. Because this hand, that she now holds in such contempt, has trembled only once in all these years, the only time that goodness, clear sight, and compassion prevented it, and that was when I did not reach out for her, who was my truth. And when you are searching for famous last words on your death bed, Your Excellency, simply pronounce the words that mark your own farewell, the words that now remain my unspoken message: "I am yours alone, forever."'"

He spoke the last words quietly and calmly into the girl's ear, clearly enough for Balbi to hear them, too.

Then he stood up and raised both arms high into the air before putting the girl down as indifferently as he might an inanimate object. He looked about him absent-mindedly, took the rapier from the table, and stuck it in his belt.

"Now make a clean copy!" he ordered Balbi.

He went over to the window, opened the blinds, and bellowed into the faint glimmering light, his voice hard and commanding: "Bring the horses!"

He wrapped the wings of his cloak about his shoulders and strode through the door. His steps echoed in the stairwell. The yard was stirring below: horses neighed, bottles clinked, and the wheels of the coach were creaking. The girl, still carrying the shards of glass in her gathered apron, took one or two slow steps and then scuttled out of the room, down the stairs, after the departing figure, as if she had understood something, as if something had occurred

to her. Now only the friar remained in the room. He wrote slowly and with great care, frowning and pursing his lips, and spelling out the end of the message letter by letter: *"I am y-o-u-r-s a-l-o-n-e, for e-v-e-r!"* . . . Then he threw the quill away, leaned back in the armchair, admired his workmanship, and, stomach shaking, fell to loud, full-bellied laughter.